AN ISLAND PROMISE

KATE FROST

GW00570036

B

First published in Great Britain in 2024 by Boldwood Books Ltd.

Copyright © Kate Frost, 2024

Cover Design by Alexandra Allden

Cover Illustration: Shutterstock

A CIP catalogue record for this book is available from the British Library.

Paperback ISBN 978-1-80280-491-1

Large Print ISBN 978-1-80280-492-8

Hardback ISBN 978-1-80280-490-4

Ebook ISBN 978-1-80280-494-2

Kindle ISBN 978-1-80280-493-5

Audio CD ISBN 978-1-80280-485-0

MP3 CD ISBN 978-1-80280-486-7

Digital audio download ISBN 978-1-80280-488-1

Boldwood Books Ltd
23 Bowerdean Street
London SW6 3TN
www.boldwoodbooks.com

For Caroline Ridding
The last three years with Boldwood have been incredible, thank you.
Amanda Ridout, Nia Beynon, Jenna Houston, Claire Fenby and every
single person in Team Boldwood, you are the absolute best.
Thank you for everything x

1

JULY 2013, TEN YEARS AGO

10 p.m. – Belle

'To friendship, fun, success and good times!' Belle shouted over the thumping electronic beat from Café Mambo's DJ booth. She slapped her hand palm down on the table that was sticky with spilt gin and grinned at her friends. Laurie pressed her hand on top then Gem did the same, her numerous rings glinting in the neon pink light. They threw their hands in the air with a whoop, picked up their drinks and downed them.

'And to returning in ten years' time!' Laurie slammed her glass on the table.

Gem grimaced. 'Bloody hell, we're going to be flipping ancient by then!'

Laurie playfully whacked her arm. 'Thirty-one is not ancient.'

'Nope, but I want to be twenty-one forever.' Gem sighed. 'This week has been the best.'

Belle reached across the table and grasped her friends' hands. 'And it's only going to get better, I promise. Ibiza is just the beginning.'

It really did feel like the start of the rest of their lives, with so much possibility in their futures. Best friends since they'd met at secondary school when they were eleven, this was their long-promised holiday together celebrating the end of an era, with each of them having recently graduated: Belle with Business Management and Marketing from Sheffield Hallam, Laurie with English Literature from Loughborough, and Gem with Art and Design from Bath Spa University.

At the end of a memorable week which had included an unforgettable booze cruise from San Antonio and an epic pool party at Ocean Beach, it had been Gem's idea to treat themselves to an evening at the iconic Café Mambo where they could watch the famous west coast sunset while celebrating their last night in Ibiza. Gem's idea to book a table had been a good one, made even better when their waiter brought over their food and replenished their drinks, his bulging biceps as appealing as the plates of croquettes, calamari, patatas bravas and the loaded nachos he placed in front of them.

'Maybe after we've eaten we should go somewhere a little less busy?' Laurie gestured across the packed terrace to where the path in front of the DJ booth heaved with people.

'Are you fucking kidding me?' Gem practically recoiled. 'It's our last night and Eric Prydz is playing. We have lucked out big time.'

'Gem's right,' Belle agreed, 'although I do still want to go to the club later.'

'Ha yes,' Gem snorted. 'As long as you get to see a certain someone of the tall, ripped, epically handsome Spanish variety...'

All Belle really cared about was getting to see Diego one last time. She considered Laurie to be the prettiest with her long sleek black hair and beautiful doll-like half-Italian, half-Japanese features, while Gem was the most outgoing and eye-catching, but Belle had been the one to pull the ridiculously sexy club promoter.

Although to be fair, Laurie and Gem both had boyfriends back home; not that it had stopped Gem getting up close and personal with a handful of guys. But Diego... Belle's insides somersaulted at the memory of the two toe-curlingly good nights she'd spent with him.

To Belle's left was a sea of tanned faces, people eating, drinking and fanning themselves in the oppressive heat, while beyond them others danced to the music's strong beat, the familiar Balearic tunes capturing Belle's attention. To the right, people spilled onto the narrow stretch of rocky beach, and San Antonio's curving seafront lit up the night with its multitude of bars, hotels and cafés. Now the blood-red sun had set, the sea was violet-black, calm and placid. Half a dozen boats were anchored out in the bay silhouetted against the silvery night sky with beacons of light topping their masts.

Laurie picked up one of the chicken and jalapeño croquettes. 'Talking about coming back here, what do you think you'll be doing in ten years' time?'

Gem wrinkled her nose. 'It's boring predicting where I'll be because I know what I want. What would be more interesting is to predict where we see each other a decade on. Belle will definitely still be pulling hot Spanish guys,' she said with a cheeky grin, 'if the last week is anything to go by!'

'I can absolutely live with that.' Belle sipped her vodka, pomegranate and lime cocktail. She knew her words were full of bluster because she couldn't imagine being with anyone who could match Diego. He was constantly in her thoughts, and the intense all-consuming feeling when she'd been with him was more than just about sex, she was sure. Over the last few days the thought of not leaving had flashed through her head. Like that could be a possibility. The strength of her feelings scared her, coming out of nowhere and crashing into her heart.

'What about me?' Laurie asked as she bit into the croquette.

'You' – Gem waved a finger in her direction – 'are so going to be married with at least three kids in ten years.'

Belle shrugged in agreement as the beat of the music switched up a notch and a cry went up from the crowd gathered round the DJ booth. 'You've already got the man – I mean, you're halfway there.'

Laurie pursed her lips, momentarily looking put-out before grinning. 'I thought I wanted to focus on my career after uni but all I can think about is starting a life with Ade. Like a proper life, not crashing at each other's or putting up with his housemates smoking weed in the living room.'

'Sounds all right to me.' Gem raised her eyebrows.

Belle cupped her hands round her glass and leaned closer. 'You're going to move in together?'

There was an excited gleam in Laurie's eyes. Talking about the guy she'd fallen in love with during her first year at university was obviously filling her with joy. 'We just need to decide where.'

'You do realise you can have both,' Gem said forcefully. 'A career and a family. You don't have to choose one over the other. We're the generation that can totally have it all. Establish your career for a few years, have the wedding of your dreams then start a family. You can have everything you want – *if* it's what you want?'

'Since meeting Ade, absolutely. I was always so focused on what I wanted to do career-wise and I still am, it's just he's changed my whole outlook. I can't imagine my life without him. And oh my God I never understood anyone who said they were broody, but since being with Ade I get it!'

'Ah, true love.' Gem pretended to stick her fingers down her throat, dramatically gagged then laughed. 'Go on then, what about me? What will I be doing in ten years?'

'Running your own business,' Belle said without hesitation as she scooped up a nacho topped with cheese and guacamole.

Laurie raised her glass of gin and tonic. 'Exactly what I was going to say.'

Belle wiped the guacamole from her lip and nodded. 'You'll have shitloads of money, a seafront apartment somewhere swanky and will travel all the time.'

'So I'm definitely escaping our shit-boring town where bugger-all happens?'

'Absolutely!' Belle said with passion. 'You could always move to London with me.'

'Maybe, after I've been travelling. I fancy living in Paris or Barcelona. God, anywhere but bloody Norfolk. I need to get out.'

'You'll have a string of guys after you in the process,' Laurie chipped in.

Gem frowned. 'You don't see me with Dan?'

Belle choked back a snort and censored her reply. 'You're going travelling without him, so really the question is do *you* realistically see yourself with him?'

A sly smile snuck across Gem's face. 'Nah, course not. At least not long term. I just like to keep my options open.'

Neither Belle nor Laurie commented further. Belle knew Gem's relationship with Dan was doomed, if the last week in Ibiza was anything to go by. She may not have fully sampled the local totty, but she'd kissed enough of them. Nope, Dan certainly hadn't been on her mind and Belle was hard-pressed to see how they could possibly have a future, not when she was taking six months out to go travelling with a friend from university who also loved to party. Belle knew exactly what she'd be getting up to without them to keep an eye on her.

'Seriously though,' Belle said as she gazed across the terrace to where people were dancing with their hands in the air in front of the electric-blue Café Mambo sign. 'Apart from continuing to pull hot Spanish guys, where do you really see me?'

'Well, you already have a dream job lined up in London,' Laurie said. 'So that's a fabulous start. I see you meeting someone, falling in love and getting married. You'll have a dream man, dream house, dream kids and dream life. You're going to have it all just like Gem suggested for me.' She raised her glass and clinked it against Belle's. 'And Gem will have it all too, with or without Dan!'

'Ditto to that.' Gem's glass joined theirs in a drunken clunk. 'And we make a promise now to have a reunion holiday here in ten years to celebrate living our best lives!'

Belle downed the remainder of her vodka cocktail. Yes, she had a job lined up, the move to London sorted and a clear path to the career and life she wanted, yet she felt certain she'd be leaving her heart behind. Unless of course her infatuation with Diego was just that and once she was home starting her new job all thoughts and feelings for him would drift away. *Of course they will*, she reasoned. Diego was a holiday fling, nothing more. It couldn't possibly be true love. Could it?

* * *

2 a.m. – Laurie

Laurie retched. Oh God oh God oh God oh God did she feel crap. It was as if she was floating in a weird kind of distorted fishbowl, other people's movement large and in slow motion.

She was definitely sitting on a stool, her legs dangling, her arms sprawled on the cold metal of the polished bar. She remembered leaving Café Mambo and she'd felt okay, happy drunk rather than whatever the hell this was. They'd stopped at some Irish bar on the way to the club, but after that... She lifted her head again and her stomach muscles constricted as a wave of nausea gripped her.

Where were Belle and Gem? She wanted to search for them but the slightest movement sent her head spinning and sick racing up her throat. The lights behind the bar were too bright yet fuzzy around the edges, the barman a sickening blur as he busied about. People jostled her, elbows jabbing into her arms, her sides.

Her throat was sore from having had a conversation with someone where they'd had to shout to be heard over the intensity of the music. He'd seemed a nice guy who hadn't been intent on trying to snog her or anything like that. He'd bought her a drink, said he was on holiday with friends. She'd said something about Ade. They'd definitely had another shot or two and that was where her memory failed.

An arm slid across her shoulders. Laurie tensed. She was out of it but not enough to realise how easily she could be taken advantage of.

'You okay?'

A voice, warm and familiar in her ear, instantly calmed her racing heart. Belle.

'I feel sick.'

'I'm not surprised.' Laughter wrapped around Belle's words. 'Do you think you can stand?'

Laurie groaned. 'Not sure. Was talking to some guy. You think he spiked my drink?'

'Nope.' Belle picked up an empty shot glass and sniffed it. 'Pretty certain you snorting vodka did this. I've been keeping an eye on you.'

Laurie retched again. 'Gonna be sick.'

'Oh shit.' Belle's hold on her shoulders loosened momentarily, then her grip tightened as she helped her off the stool.

Laurie's legs felt like a combination of shaky jelly and heavy concrete as Belle supported her. Everything spun, a sickening swirl of flashing lights, heaving bodies and laughing Joker-like faces. She might as well have been staggering across the deck of a ship in a storm, her stomach was lurching that much. It took a huge effort to stop herself from vomiting in the middle of the club as the waft of sweat and sickly perfume assaulted her. Belle's fingers dug into her skin as she shoved open a door. Laurie's relief when they entered the relative quiet of the toilets was immense as Belle manoeuvred her into an empty cubicle.

Laurie dropped to her knees, slamming hard onto the tiled floor, the fall dulled by the excess alcohol. Belle swept her hair away from her face and into a ponytail. Crouching over the toilet, she emptied the contents of her stomach until all she brought up was bitter bile. Never had she felt this bad, this sick, this drunk, this out of control. She didn't like it one bit.

* * *

2.30 a.m. – Gem

'Hey, you here on your own?' a deep voice shouted close to her ear. 'Can I buy you a drink?'

Gem looked up from her phone into a smiling but drunken face. A Brit abroad. Probably a bit younger than her if the angry spots on his face were anything to go by. He had a nice-shaped face otherwise and he'd probably grow into his good looks, a guy who'd definitely improve with age.

'I'm good thanks. Waiting for my friends.'

The guy smirked, leaned his arms on the table next to her then waved to someone. Three more guys joined them, looming as they crowded round, forcing Gem to press close against spotty guy.

'Hey, this table's taken.'

'We'll wait with you,' the spotty guy said smoothly. 'Just till your friends return.'

Gem's drunken fuzziness switched to acute clarity and the realisation that she was on her own and surrounded by drunk strangers. Drunk, unpredictable and unwelcome.

Bloody Belle and Laurie. Where the hell were they? Belle had gone to get Laurie from the bar, said she wouldn't be long; she'd even left her phone on the table. Gem had lost sight of them when a different guy had tried to chat her up. She'd played along for a bit then sent him on his way. Since then she'd lost track of time, but they'd been gone flipping ages.

These guys were more insistent. Whether they were interested in her or having somewhere to put their drinks she wasn't sure, but despite her drunkenness every part of her was on high alert. Spotty guy's body was pressed tight against hers and his friends were loud and crude joking together. She absolutely didn't want to stay hemmed in like this one second longer.

She scooped up Belle's phone and her own. 'Going to find my friends.' She squeezed past spotty guy, her heart hammering as he grabbed her bum, his laughter making her want to punch him. She pushed him away and made a beeline for the bar, but neither Belle nor Laurie were there. Silver lights cut across the dancefloor. It was packed with people and it would be next to impossible to find her friends if they were dancing. Catching sight of spotty guy heading her way, she set off in a panic towards the exit.

As she stumbled outside, the slightly fresher hit of air after the bone-shaking music inside the club snatched her breath away. She swayed, steadying herself on the wall of the car park as she tried to get her bearings. Even though Belle didn't have her phone, why the hell couldn't they have rung on Laurie's? Gem clicked her name and called, her heart sinking when it went straight to answerphone.

Then she saw them, the group of guys from the club, heading towards her, big and intimidating. Pushy pissed-up Brits. Without thinking, she staggered in the opposite direction, realising too late that she needed to head back towards the club to notify security, not away from other people.

'Hey, darling,' drawled a thickset man with tight trousers and oversized shoulders that made him look like he was on steroids. 'Can't find your friends? We'll look after you, won't we, lads?'

They sniggered. Gem's heart pounded. Her confidence in the way she looked showing off her curves in a tight, lowcut dress was usually a strength; right now it was a potentially catastrophic weakness. She was drunk and even in her sparkly sneakers she had zero chance of outrunning them.

Spotty guy hooked his arm around her waist, pulling her tight against him, wafting beer breath and an overpowering aftershave in her direction.

'Gem?'

Her head whipped round. She didn't remember telling them her name. Her heart thudded even more as 'Gem' was repeated in a deep, unfamiliar voice. With a Spanish accent. Beyond the circle of pissed-up Brits, she locked eyes with Diego. He glanced between her and the group of guys then strode over.

'Are you okay?' The concern filtering through his words matched the worry on his face. Spotty guy's arm tightened on her waist as his fingers dug into her hip. She was trembling so much her ability to speak deserted her. Sizing up to spotty guy, Diego shouldered into him. 'She's with me.'

Diego took Gem's hand and swept her away. She'd never felt more grateful to anyone for being there right when she needed them. Diego only stopped when they reached the road that ran alongside the main beach in San Antonio. Still holding his hand, Gem looked up at her Spanish saviour.

'Thank you,' she managed to utter. She understood the danger she'd been in, the recklessness of too much to drink, of losing the others and ending up on her own.

'Where's Belle?' Diego frowned down at her as he let go of her hand. 'And your other friend?'

'Belle went to check on Laurie.' Gem waved her hand in the direction of the club. 'I lost sight of them. Got freaked out by those guys. Stupidly thought it'd be a good idea to leave. They followed me.'

'It's okay now,' Diego said, his voice suddenly softer. It was only when he wiped away a tear from her cheek that she realised she was crying. 'We call Belle, yes, and find them?'

Gem held up Belle's phone. 'She left it and Laurie's is going straight to answerphone.'

Diego frowned. 'You think they come outside?'

'I don't know where they've gone.' Gem shrugged. 'I know Belle wanted to see you...' She took a deep breath. 'We can go back in and find them.'

Diego shook his head. 'They won't let you back in, not without buying another ticket.'

'Shit.' Gem cursed her stupidity, although the thought that spotty guy and his friends' night had been ruined as well was rather satisfying. 'Maybe we should walk a little. Could do with clearing my head.' She needed to breathe and calm herself down.

Diego momentarily hesitated before leading the way across the road and onto the path next to the palm tree-lined beach.

Gem hadn't really talked to Diego. She was pretty certain Belle hadn't done much talking with him either beyond the evening they'd first met. Gem and Laurie had put a 'next round of drinks on you' bet on how quickly Belle would end up kissing him. Gem had won. She'd also predicted that Belle would go home with him. She'd been right about that too. Not that she blamed her; up close, she could see how attractive he was, combined with a hell of a sexy accent. He smelled damn good too.

Even away from the lights, heat and pulsing beat of the club, her head still spun. Being outside had helped despite her drunkenness. Only Diego was the constant as they walked together, their arms occasionally brushing each other's as people passed by too close. Was he doing all the talking or was she? She felt not quite herself, not fully present, floating on a cloud of alcohol. It was their last night on Ibiza. Even with a late flight the next day, drinking to excess probably hadn't been the smartest move, but hey, she was only young once. Real life was calling: travelling for a few months before making career decisions and deciding where to live, the start of her grown-up life. She was determined to no longer be a poor student; she had dreams and an ambition to turn her Art and Design degree into a career in interior design. She wanted exactly what Belle and Laurie had predicted: to be her own boss, to smash at work and life, to snag her dream man. To have it all.

They made it all the way to the end of the tree-lined promenade next to the marina when Diego stopped.

'I can walk you back to your hotel?' he suggested. 'Maybe they've gone there?'

Gem gazed at the lines of white boats glowing bright against the inky water and the entrancing lights pooling from the hotels and bars across the road. Belle hadn't come back; Gem assumed she and Laurie were together, either still at the club or back at their hotel oblivious to her trying to call. Belle was missing her chance of one last night with Diego, while Gem didn't want to sleep. She didn't want to say goodbye to the freedom and hedonism of Ibiza.

'I'm not ready for my last night to end. I want to keep partying.' She didn't quite know where this idea had come from. Was it because she'd had a fright and Diego had been her knight in shining armour? Or was it because she was annoyed with herself for leaving the club, and a little miffed at Belle and Laurie for disappearing, whether intentional or not? 'Take me somewhere.'

8.20 a.m. – Gem

Gem had been awake for close to twenty-four hours, had drunk enough alcohol to open her own bar and would probably be over the limit for the next three days, and yet her ability to sleep was non-existent. She rolled onto her back. The whole night was a blur, fragmented moments with blank bits in between: Laurie looking sheet-white at the bar; Belle going to check on her, then losing them both; how vulnerable she'd felt with spotty guy and his friends before Diego had saved her.

Diego.

The dark room swirled as Gem fought back bile. She hadn't been ready for the night to end and Diego had outdone himself, taking her to Pacha, the iconic super club that would have been out of her price range if Diego's mate hadn't worked there and got them in. Swept up in the euphoria of the night, she hadn't cared where the others were while she partied into the early hours surrounded by beautiful people, Diego by her side. They'd danced together in the main club and talked about their hopes, dreams and ambitions on the rooftop terrace. Hands down it was the best night of the holiday, probably her whole fucking life, and yet the enjoyment had been tainted by the realisation that her friends had missed out.

She hadn't remembered leaving and had no idea of the time, just a vague recollection of being in a taxi zooming through dark streets before they'd been dropped off at an apartment block she thought was back in San Antonio. After that, there were only wisps of memories. Giggling with Diego as they'd stumbled into a room, the lamplight making her squint and head pound. Diego pouring drinks while she'd escaped to the bathroom. She'd stared at herself in the mirror, sleepy and drunken, her blonde hair tangled, a smudge of mascara beneath her eyes, her lipstick kissed off, but by who was anyone's guess. Then she'd noticed the missed calls, a voicemail plus a message from Laurie. No, from Belle on Laurie's phone because Gem still had hers. She hadn't listened to the voicemail, read the message properly or bothered to reply.

She'd stumbled back into Diego's compact room. The brief thought that drinking more was a bad idea was immediately dispersed as he'd handed her a tequila and she'd downed it.

Then the thank-yous had tumbled from her, for him giving her the best night of her life, for him saving her. He poured a second shot and her heart raced as they downed them too. Dawn had already broken, their Ibiza holiday would soon be over and in just a few hours she'd be heading home. Only temporarily, she'd told herself. She had plans, and by the end of August she'd be travelling again.

Gem had locked eyes with Diego; his were deep brown, framed by long lashes. Hot breath on her neck. A tingle as his hands settled on her hips. The brush of his lips against hers. Or was it her lips against his? Was it their first kiss or had that already happened?

He'd manoeuvred her onto his bed, and she'd wanted it. Wanted him. She'd lost herself to his kisses and caresses. Pushing all thoughts that sleeping with him was wrong to the back of her mind, she'd said yes to everything...

Gem turned her head and tried to focus on Diego, the rise and fall of his chest with only the white sheet in the dim light covering his nakedness. She wanted to sleep, desperate to be rid of the nausea. A headache forewarned of the intensity of the hangover that was brewing. Although that was the least of her worries.

Gem tucked her arms around the pillow. It smelt of perfume and smoke. Bile climbed her throat. She shut her eyes tightly, banishing the image of Diego naked next to her. The darkness made her head feel as if it was revolving round and round, and wouldn't stop.

She should have thanked him for saving her from the unwanted attention of those pissed-up guys and left it at that. When he'd suggested he walk her back to the hotel to see if Belle and Laurie were there, she should have agreed. Her eyes fluttered open again and the swirling eased a touch. Diego's handsome face was outlined by the sunlight slipping through the gap in the blinds. Gem breathed deeply as she swiped away a tear. She shouldn't be the one lying next to him flushed from the best sex of her entire life. She gulped back a sob.

Belle could never find out.

2

MAY 2023, PRESENT DAY

Belle's hands were slick with sweat and her heart raced as she adjusted her notebook and pen and glanced at her laptop screen. Still in the Zoom-call wait room. She drummed her fingers on the kitchen table. Not one for being nervous about a job interview, she felt unusually jittery about this one because she wanted it so much. She wasn't sure she'd be able to take the rejection and disappointment if she did not get it. On paper, the role of events manager at Spirit, a luxury boutique hotel on Ibiza, was perfect, the opportunity arising at exactly the right time. She'd become comfortable in her current job and had been mulling over a new challenge for a while, although her true reason for handing her notice in had moved his stuff out of her flat just weeks before. Mixing business and pleasure, or in her case having a relationship with a colleague, had been doomed from the start.

Never again.

The call started bang on time and she found herself sharing the screen with Caleb Levine, the owner of Spirit.

'Belle, hi there.' Caleb's voice was deep and warm as he looked at her intently. 'It's good to finally meet you, not quite in person, but the next best thing.'

Belle hadn't known what to expect. Most of what she'd found online was at least a decade old and only a few images of a clean-shaven young man. The man on screen sported thick stubble, had dark hair peppered with grey, a healthy tan and looked somewhere in his early forties. One of those men who had managed to get more handsome with age. She shuffled upright and focused her thoughts onto selling herself and not how attractive Caleb Levine happened to be. She'd chosen to sit at the kitchen table because the background was her attractive courtyard garden with the pink crab-apple blossom, but Caleb was sitting in his hotel bar, the background a pool, palm trees and the glittering sea. There was no comparison.

Her nerves began to settle as they talked. Caleb was business-like, efficient and quietly friendly as he asked about her career in marketing and events to date. He'd already sent her the details about the salary and accommodation, and she'd done her home-work on Spirit too but had discovered little about him apart from that he was British and a successful entrepreneur who had lived and worked on Ibiza since his late teens.

After discussing her own experience and current position as events manager at Tockbeth Hall, a large and historic venue on the banks of the Thames, he moved the conversation on to his plans for the year.

'We've recently opened our sister restaurant Serenity down the coast, plus we've teamed up with a couple of iconic venues so we can offer our guests different Ibiza experiences while keeping the chilled-out vibe of Spirit intact. This is all happening two months into the season and just as my events manager has had to urgently take time off. It's only a role for the summer season, which I'm aware might not suit someone as qualified as yourself. What I'd really like to know is how you feel about the temporary nature of the position?'

'It's actually perfect.' Belle took a breath, unsure how much she should divulge about her personal circumstances. 'I've wanted a change for a while and have been slowly setting up my own virtual event management business alongside my day job. Long term, I'd like to be my own boss. This job could be a good stepping stone.'

'And you'd be available to start asap? My events manager will be leaving in a week and you'd have to hit the ground running.'

'I actually handed my notice in before I even knew about this opportunity. Whether I get this job or not, I'm moving on.'

'Well, that's good to know.' If he seemed surprised or impressed he didn't show it, apart from a slightly raised eyebrow.

'There's no problem starting soon. The only commitment I have is a friend's wedding next weekend. Apart from that I have no ties.' That was the story of her life, but at least being single allowed her to drop everything.

Caleb picked up a coffee cup and took a sip. 'Your experience speaks for itself, but can I ask why Ibiza? Particularly when you've been managing a large team of people and I'm pretty sure you'd have the pick of jobs back home. We're a small team and the work will be hands-on, managing events and building links with new partners.'

'Which is exactly what I'm looking for,' Belle stressed, well aware that she was walking a fine line between sounding desperate rather than enthusiastic. 'Ibiza is a place I fell in love with when I first visited with friends ten years ago – actually, it's the only time I've been, but the plan was to return a decade on, which we still hope to do. A friend forwarded me your job advert and it seemed fortuitous, particularly when I've been wanting to find a way to bridge the gap between being employed full-time to running my own business.' Her image on the laptop screen was beginning to look fuzzy around the edges as if the connection was slow. She remembered reading something about broadband work being done in the area but hadn't taken much notice of the date. Typical that it was playing up now. 'A job in Ibiza for a few months before I concentrate on my own events business full-time would be perfect.'

Her image was lagging behind her words. Suddenly it froze. Open mouthed and eyes half closed, she somehow managed to look unattractive and utterly stupid with an expression like she'd been out partying and was the worse for wear. Caleb looked cool, calm and ridiculously sophisticated in the bar of his White Isle hotel, the image of him perfectly crisp.

At least he remained serious and wasn't laughing, although inside he was probably thinking there was no way in hell he'd be giving her the job.

He leaned forward, his blue eyes intensely vivid as he looked directly at her. 'As you seem to be having connection problems, we'll leave it there for the time being. I have more than enough information to go on, thank you. I'll be in touch in the next couple of days.'

He gave a slight nod and just a hint of a smile as he disappeared from the screen.

Belle sighed and logged off. She lived in central London, but badly timed internet connection issues had potentially messed up her chances. The thought of spending the summer in Ibiza was massively appealing, but she couldn't get her hopes up. Sometimes things were just too good to be true and in her experience something good was usually followed by something bad. She'd learned that the hard way – more than once. The thought of staying put in London was just too depressing to dwell on though and, regardless of the job, Ibiza would be on the cards this year. She needed to talk about it with Gem and Laurie soon, although she'd wait until she found out about the job. They'd all be seeing each other at their friend's wedding next weekend and could plan things then.

Belle made a coffee and stood by the patio door looking out at her garden. The pink blossom was a splash of colour in an otherwise overcast May day. Thinking about Ibiza brought back all kinds of memories and emotions. Ten years felt like a lifetime ago. It was crazy how such a short yet intense time could have made such an impact, and yet somehow it had, the feelings, memories and lost chances still filtering through her life nearly a decade on. That whole year had been a pivotal one with graduating, the holiday, her move to London, the accident...

Belle's stomach lurched and she returned her thoughts to the job. She didn't like waiting for things, not when it was something that would massively change the direction of her life, and yet she knew she'd be unlikely to hear back from Caleb until Monday. At least she had a distraction. Although it was Saturday, that evening she would be at a glitzy award ceremony and after party that she'd been working on for months. Her life revolved around work, which often included socialising, so it wasn't all bad. The downside was that working with her ex on a daily basis wasn't much fun. In that respect she'd forced herself out of a job she used to love. A change could only be a good thing as long as things fell neatly into place.

Handing her notice in without having anything else lined up had been a leap of faith, but she'd needed to do something drastic. She was successful, had the career she'd longed for and a flat of her own, but she'd become stuck in a rut, going through the motions of life, her relationship stagnant. When Isaac had pushed for more commitment, she'd backed off. She didn't want to be with someone just for the sake of it. He was a nice enough guy, but nice wasn't doing anything for her. It was her fault for letting their relationship become as serious as it had. Forget about the seven-year itch. She was lucky if she made it to seven months with anyone before getting cold feet.

* * *

The award ceremony would be Belle's last big event at Tockbeth Hall and, after working her way up to head of events management, her nerves were the fluttery kind rather than gut wrenching ones that used to leave her feeling queasy. Since moving to London she'd grafted even when life had thrown her curveballs. She'd said yes to everything, had taken chances and done things out of her comfort zone, but the payoff had been progressing rapidly in her career. The only thing she was uneasy about that evening was Isaac being there.

With Belle in events and Isaac in marketing, neither reported directly to each other but their work was closely connected. Since she'd broken up with him at the beginning of the year, he'd gone from upset to anger and was now avoiding her as much as possible. Apart from being honest with him, she'd done nothing wrong. There wasn't anyone else, and in her mind not leading him on gave him the freedom to find someone who was right for him. Isaac was the wrong guy for her, much like all the others who'd preceded him...

Laurie had thought she was mad, commenting, 'I really thought you'd found "the one",' the last time they'd spoken. Belle hadn't admitted that she'd known from the beginning she didn't feel that way about him, but then she hadn't felt that way about anyone. Actually, that wasn't technically true; she had felt that way once but she didn't say that to Laurie. She hadn't admitted that to anyone; she didn't even like admitting it to herself because it made her wonder what her life would have been like if she'd made different choices ten years ago.

Belle put on her game face as she entered the ballroom. The tables were all laid out, the wine glasses glinting in the light from the sparkling chandeliers. The stage was set and the sound check in full swing. This point of an event used to feel like the calm before the storm, but Belle knew everything was in place, and even if there was a crisis, she had enough experience to tackle it with calm confidence. The only uncertainty she felt was when she clocked Isaac looking dapper in a suit, a dream man in so many ways that made her seriously question what on earth she was after. Someone who made her heart sing. Despite his many good qualities, Isaac never had.

His cool glare landed on her and she looked away. She just needed to get through tonight, be civil and professional, and hope to goodness she'd get good news on Monday.

3

Caleb had known from just her resumé that Belle Madden was hands down *the* person for the job, the same way his events manager Cara had too, telling him in no uncertain terms that offering it to her was a no-brainer, but he wanted to do things properly, so had Zoom interviewed three other possibilities just to be sure.

By the time the connection had started playing up and Belle's screen had frozen, he knew she would be the best replacement, but that knowledge still didn't ease his disappointment and worry about Cara leaving, even if it was only temporary.

Caleb leaned forward and focused on Belle frozen on the screen. Wavy, honey-blonde hair cascaded over her shoulder, while her semi-closed eyes were framed by long dark lashes. 'As you seem to be having connection problems, we'll leave it there for the time being. I have more than enough information to go on, thank you. I'll be in touch in the next couple of days.' He nodded, took one more look at her face still frozen on the screen and ended the call.

He rested his hands on the edge of the padded bench, leaned back and sighed.

Clutching her tablet, Cara scooted round from the other side of the table to join him. 'So, what do you think?'

'I think you should have interviewed her with me.'

'I've been listening carefully.' She ran her hand through her cropped blonde hair. 'You're the one who has to work with her; it needs to be your choice, not mine.'

'Mmm. No one's going to be able to replace you.'

'Of course not, but someone has to.' Cara flashed him a 'you know I'm right' kind of look. 'And she sounded—'

'Nice.'

'Perfect. I was going to say perfect.' She placed a hand on his shoulder. 'But you already know that. *And* you like her.'

Caleb shut his MacBook. 'I like her because she's immensely qualified and I'm sure she could do the job with her eyes closed, but that still doesn't change a thing. She's not you.'

'Nope, she's not, but I think she'll make an excellent replacement *and* she can start soon.'

'The others were enthusiastic...' He wasn't sure why he was feigning the possibility that he was even considering anyone other than Belle.

'Yes, young, enthusiastic and keen on a summer in Ibiza. They'll probably put having a good time over a decent work ethic whereas I get the feeling Belle Madden will work hard. And to find someone with her experience who's available at short notice.' She raised her eyebrows. 'You'll only have to manage one week without an events manager.'

'You understand you're way more than just my events manager, right?' He gazed past her to the fronds of greenery and banana plants that divided the bar into private spaces. The sound of breakfast being served in the restaurant floated across the pool. The day at Spirit was getting off to a leisurely start, the sun already blazing across his pocket of Ibiza. 'I'm going to miss you.'

Cara took his hand. 'I'm going to miss you too. And you know there's no way I'd be going back unless I had to. Mum and Dad need me.'

'I know.' Caleb squeezed her hand tight. He brushed away the tear rolling down Cara's cheek. 'It'll be okay, I promise. Once you're there, things will feel less stressful. It's hard being so far away—'

'I feel utterly useless and helpless.'

'Which is why it'll be different when you're back. You'll be able to see them, be there for them. Say goodbye when the time comes.'

The sob that erupted from Cara jabbed at Caleb like a knife twisting into his heart. Of course he understood the loss she'd be facing, because his own grief consumed him as he pulled her into a tight hug. His grief was always rumbling beneath the surface, forever toying with him. He never knew quite when it would hit but he should have expected that talking about Cara's dad's terminal illness would make him relive his own loss.

Cara pulled away. 'Fuck it. This was going to happen at some point.' She gestured to her damp face and puffy eyes.

'Don't bottle it all up, Cara.' Caleb drained his coffee and put the cup back on the bleached wood table. 'Yes, you need to be strong to support your folks, but trust me, not letting your emotions out isn't helpful in the long run.'

Cara nodded and bit her lip. 'I'm more emotional about going back to Australia and having to confront the reason I left in the first place.'

'All that other stuff, try not to worry about it. Focus on your parents and what's important. Your psychotic arsehole of an ex is not in your life any longer so you won't have to deal with any more shit. You've got friends back home who will protect and support you, plus you can call me anytime.'

'Hmm, not quite so easy with the time difference.'

'Anytime, Cara, I mean it.' Caleb looked at her firmly. 'I don't care if it's the middle of the night if you need to talk.'

'The same goes for you – talk to me whenever you want to.'

'See, I told you no one can ever replace you.'

'No, no one can replace me, the same way no one will ever replace Paloma, but you'll learn to move on and embrace someone new. I'm not opposed to you having another friend, Caleb, and at the very least Belle will make an excellent addition to the Spirit and Serenity team and will ease my stress that you'll have help and someone who knows what the hell they're doing while I'm gone.'

4

It was early on Monday morning and because Belle had been rushing about grabbing breakfast and a coffee, she hadn't had time to feel nervous as she answered Caleb's video call. While his face appeared on her phone screen, his warm voice filled the kitchen.

'I was hoping I'd catch you before you left for work to give you the good news,' he said. 'I'd be delighted to welcome you to Spirit. The job is yours if you're happy to take it?'

Holding the phone in one hand and clutching a half-eaten piece of toast in the other, Belle stared at the screen, his words taking a moment to sink in.

'Belle?' Caleb frowned. 'You've not frozen again, have you?'

'Yes. I mean no.' She dropped her toast onto the plate and grinned. 'I'm here, but my goodness yes, I'd absolutely love the position. Thank you.'

All her anxiety over her recent decisions, from breaking up with Isaac to handing in her notice, was replaced by a fizz of possibility.

She thanked Caleb profusely and he promised to be in touch with more details. Belle headed to work with renewed energy, her foreseeable future in motion. With only a week and a half left, she'd have very little to do with Isaac which was a huge relief. Now she needed to sort out what she was going to do about her house while she was away. And pack and plan. There was lots to do but she hadn't felt this light, this free or excited for a long time.

* * *

On the Tube she messaged Hannah, her best friend in London, and arranged to meet for dinner at a pizza place not far from where they both worked. The job offer was as thrilling as it was terrifying and Hannah was the first person she wanted to tell.

'So, how did the award ceremony go?' Hannah asked the moment their drinks had been brought over.

'Like a dream.' Belle raised her glass of lemonade. They were sitting opposite each other at the end of a long communal table with flattering overhead lighting that highlighted Hannah's trademark red lips. 'The ceremony itself went without a hitch and Bill Nighy hosting was such a hit—'

'Oh God, I'd love to meet him.'

'He was utterly charming; you'd have loved him even more than you already do. And the dinner and party afterwards, honestly, I couldn't have asked for more. It was the perfect way for me to bow out.'

Hannah suddenly leaned forward, her eyes wide. 'Oh my God, the job interview! I totally forgot. How did it go?'

'It's actually the reason I suggested meeting this evening. I was offered the job.'

Hannah's squeal was cut short by the waiter bringing over their pizzas. Grinning, she shook her head and sat back in her chair.

'I am made up for you, I really am, but it's Ibiza,' she said once the waiter had left. 'You're going to be so far away.'

Belle picked up a slice of her chargrilled aubergine and smoked mozzarella pizza. 'That's the point, to get away. It's been difficult and so awkward since I ended things with Isaac. I've always loved going to work but recently I've been dreading it.'

'I know it's been challenging, but you breaking up with someone shouldn't have to impact *your* career.'

'But the job in Ibiza is actually a great opportunity. It's different, but I think it'll do me good.'

Hannah took a bite of her creamy spinach and parmesan pizza. 'I'm just selfishly wishing nothing was changing and you could carry on living in London and working harmoniously with Isaac.'

Belle studied Hannah. 'How's still living with your ex-husband going?'

Hannah pursed her lips and raised her glass of lemonade. 'Touché.'

'I'm sorry,' Belle said. 'I know my situation is completely different because Isaac and I didn't even live together – at least not properly. We were never serious. Although judging by his reaction, he obviously felt differently. We weren't going anywhere. I refuse to settle just to be with someone.'

'It's good you know your own mind but breaking up with some-one, quitting your job *and* moving to another country in a short space of time is a lot. Not many people would be able to do what you've done.'

'I just need to get away. You've been understanding about me and Isaac but most people including my parents and some other friends don't get it because they thought he was perfect. On paper maybe.' Belle tapped the left side of her chest. 'In here, not so much.'

'Well,' Hannah said, swallowing a mouthful of pizza, 'if anyone understands that, it's me.'

Belle nodded, hesitant to ask the question because she could so easily have found herself in Hannah's position if she'd made different choices. 'Do you regret marrying Jake?'

'No, because I loved him and we got married for the right reasons. It just didn't work out. Like you and Isaac, our feelings for each other weren't strong enough to weather the ups and downs. Although him cheating ended it. The problem is having a mortgage together. Working in London and trying to find somewhere affordable separately is a nightmare. Living together while not being together like you just pointed out is shit. How the hell we're supposed to move on mentally, emotionally and physically is beyond me. I mean, what happens if I meet someone else and want to bring them home?'

'I guess you don't at the moment. Not ideal, I know, but it won't be forever.' Belle paused. 'But I do have a suggestion for a short-term fix if you're interested.' Belle finished a mouthful of smoky pizza and explained how she didn't want to leave her house empty for months. 'So if you can come to some agreement with Jake, and you're okay paying me just enough to cover the bills, then you're welcome to stay at mine until I'm back.'

'Oh my God! Are you serious?' Hannah practically launched herself out of the chair. 'That would be amazing; I'm sure Jake will jump at the chance. Not that I should care what he thinks.'

'As long as you don't mind being the one to move out temporarily?'

'Into your place? Are you kidding me? It's closer to work, I'll have a garden throughout the summer and no grumpy ex to try and avoid day in, day out.' She practically squealed. 'Sounds perfect. Rather like you avoiding working with your ex and escaping to Ibiza for the summer...'

'I really am, aren't I? You're the first person I've told because I knew you'd be happy for me.'

'I am, and not just because I get to stay in your lovely flat and you're saving me from more awkwardness and stress. Why haven't you told Gem and Laurie though? I thought they'd be the first to know.'

Belle shrugged and watched the guy working behind the marbled counter flip some pizza dough. 'I'll tell them when I see them on the weekend.'

'You've not talked to them recently?'

'I don't tend to talk to Gem properly unless we actually see each other, just the odd text every so often. I've given up really, because if I tell her about an exciting event I'm working on she's quick to change the subject; and if I tell her about something that's gone wrong or I'm upset about she rolls her eyes like I have no right to moan.'

'Do you think she's jealous?'

'Maybe. She works part time to fit in with her kids but I know she's desperate to work full time. She doesn't mind her job, but being a PA at a solicitors isn't what she wants to do.'

'She's still trying to set up an interior design business?'

'Which she'll never do unless she takes the plunge.'

'Difficult when she's got young kids.' Hannah dabbed away a spot of tomato sauce from her lips with a napkin.

'She's got a huge following on Instagram and stages her house beautifully; there's so much potential.' Belle sighed and scooped up another slice of pizza. 'It's hard to know what's really going on without talking to her properly. There's a distance that was never there before and I feel like we're less and less a part of each other's lives as the years go by.'

'It'll be different when you see her. I have friends like that who I don't speak to for ages, then we meet up and slip back into our friendship like no time has passed at all.' Hannah shuffled her chair sideways as the guy next to her made to leave. 'And things are okay with Laurie?'

'Sort of. I talk to her often but I get the feeling she's holding something back. We skirt around personal stuff. To be fair, I've been doing the same, not really talking about my feelings over Isaac, mainly because I'm aware everyone thinks I'm mad for letting him go.'

'But if you weren't happy, it was the right thing to do.'

'Gem thought I was nuts; she just didn't get it.' Belle gazed across the restaurant, clocking the loved-up couples among the tables of colleagues grabbing a bite to eat post-work. 'I wasn't happy, but I wasn't sad either, just discontented which sounds pretty pathetic.'

'No, it sounds realistic. I get it.' Hannah shrugged. 'It's what we all do, spend years chasing a dream job and perfect relationship and when they don't live up to our expectations, it's disappointing.'

Belle knew it was her personal life rather than her professional one that had been the problem, which was why mixing the two by having a relationship with a colleague had been a mistake, although perhaps it had been the push she'd needed to make a positive change. She couldn't continue to feel lost and uncertain, or shoulder the constant feeling of failure for never being satisfied despite everything she'd achieved.

Hannah sipped her lemonade. 'But the job in Ibiza, you're sure about it?'

'It's a risk and an unknown but I feel so hemmed in and troubled here without really understanding why. I'm not sure what I want apart from doing something different.'

'I think what you're doing is brave, but then you've been brave and focused and determined from the moment I met you.' Hannah looked at her with a mixture of awe and pity. 'Do you think all these drastic changes have something to do with the ten-year anniversary of the accident coming up?'

Belle's chest tightened and her palms felt sweaty as she put down her half-eaten pizza slice. 'I think being somewhere completely different for a while can only be a good thing.'

Hannah nodded but didn't comment further. She raised her glass. 'Well, I'm happy for you. Congrats, Belle. You're going to smash it; new job, new country, all that partying...'

'Mmm, I'm not sure clubbing will be my top priority this time. But a summer of sunshine by the sea, organising exclusive events, forgetting about my string of disastrous relationships, getting away from London and being able to focus on myself for a while is much needed.'

5

The good thing about the move to Ibiza happening so quickly was the lack of time to dwell on her decision with the next few days flying by in a whirl of planning, packing and organisation. Working her notice was hectic because of the amount of things she needed to handover, culminating in a leaving do where Isaac's absence was conspicuous but expected. As the days ticked by, Belle's anxiety increased. A bead of doubt buried deep inside made her question if she was really doing the right thing.

The drive to Norfolk for a school friend's wedding gave her time to think as she put the bustle of London behind her for the slower pace of a country life she'd so eagerly left behind. Although she'd grown up in a small north Norfolk town, returning never felt like coming home even on the rare occasions she visited her parents. Perhaps a decade on was the perfect time to make another move. Yet fear needled her because her move to London hadn't been without incident. Her first few months had been full of unexpected challenges that continued to fuel her worry that as soon as something positive happened, something catastrophic would follow. And was returning to Ibiza really the smartest idea when she could have gone anywhere? She may have only spent one week there but it had made an impact. Meeting Diego, being consumed by him, loving him, wanting him, needing him, missing him... The one who had got away. There were so many what-ifs, but none were helpful. She couldn't change the past, although it was crazy how often Diego would slip into her thoughts, even now.

Belle didn't mind rocking up to a wedding on her own. In many ways she felt more comfortable going solo, happy to spend time with her friends without worrying about Isaac. Of course he'd been her plus-one when the invitation had arrived the year before. Her main concern, beyond having messed up the seating plan, was that some other poor single sod had been added to their table in a pathetic attempt to matchmake.

On the lawn in front of the grand Tudor house, Belle caught sight of Gem looking effortlessly chic in a blue and orange flowery maxi dress, her ash-blonde hair styled into a loose updo. Nerves batted her chest, a ridiculous reaction to the thought of talking to one of her oldest friends, but she often felt like this. There was a distance with Gem that never used to be there, more than just a physical distance because she'd remained in Norfolk while Belle had gone to London, something she'd never felt with Laurie even after her move to Manchester with Ade.

'You look fabulous.' Not allowing her anxiety to get the better of her, Belle swept Gem into a hug.

'So do you.' Gem pulled away and held her at arm's length. 'As always.'

Belle had splashed out on a new dress, an A-line strappy one that she'd take to Ibiza, and had thrown a pashmina stole around her shoulders to ward off the chill of the clear but sunny late May day.

'Dan's not with you?' Belle asked as a waiter paused with a tray of Pimm's.

Gem took a glass and rolled her eyes. 'Dan's not like Ade, happy to chat to everyone and anyone.' She shrugged. 'It was much easier for him to stay home with the kids.'

'And you're okay being on your own?'

'As fine as you are, I'm sure.' Gem looked at her pointedly from beneath fake lashes.

'Indeed.' Belle raised her glass of Pimm's. 'To my car crash of a love life.'

Hannah had been right that once they started to talk they'd slip back into the comfortable friendship they used to have. The glimmer of a younger Gem was hidden behind a toughened exterior. Belle's nerves hadn't completely dispersed but they had eased by having her breakup with Isaac to talk about. Her own failings made her feel less like she was rubbing her London life in Gem's face.

After chatting for a good twenty minutes, Belle was relieved to see Laurie strolling towards them, her arm hooked in Ade's, her long dark hair sleek, her powder-blue trouser suit hugging her slender frame, the floral blouse feminine and very Laurie.

'Traffic!' Laurie said with a shake of her head as she pulled them into a group hug. She was the one who united them, the easy-going non-confrontational friend who eased any tension and helped the conversation flow. 'I knew we should have booked two nights and travelled down yesterday. Never mind, we're here now.'

Ade greeted them too with a kiss to their cheeks.

'You're not staying with your mum and dad then?' Belle asked.

'No, we wanted to treat ourselves but we'll see them before heading home.'

Laurie's parents had always been warm and welcoming, happiest when their house was filled with kids, and Belle and Gem had spent plenty of time there. As a teenager Belle had been jealous of the attention Laurie received from her parents when her own were always working. Laurie had the company of two younger sisters as well, which only accentuated Belle's loneliness as an only child. More often than not she'd get home from secondary school to an empty house and heat up a microwave meal, while Laurie's Italian dad would welcome his girls with homemade pasta or the tastiest pizza. Gem had managed to have a healthy relationship with her parents too, although she hadn't always got on with her older brother, but their house was homely and lived-in. Belle had understood why Gem had wanted to escape their small town, but she'd have done anything for the close and loving relationship Gem had with her parents, although that had changed once Gem had become pregnant, her parents' disappointment obvious even if they'd unconditionally supported her. With absent parents for most of her childhood, starting afresh in London had been a no-brainer for Belle.

Gem had been right about Ade being happy to chat to everyone. He introduced himself to people he didn't know and reconnected with partners he'd met at other social gatherings. Gem's partner Dan had never been like that, which meant with Ade content to do his own thing, the three friends were able to spend time together.

After drinks on the lawn and photographs by the lake, everyone was ushered inside the converted barn for the speeches and sit-down meal. The circular tables looked fresh and springlike with vases of pink and purple flowers and fronds of greenery, and the high ceiling was crisscrossed by oak beams and lines of fairy lights.

Belle and Gem were seated together next to Laurie and Ade with another two couples who they knew in passing, and it was a jolly couple of hours feasting on slow roasted pork with glazed shallots and braised red cabbage with a Sicilian lemon tart and raspberry sorbet for dessert, before champagne was poured ahead of the speeches.

After the father-of-the-bride and the best man had finished speaking, Belle turned to Laurie. 'This reminds me of your wedding.'

'Just not as fancy.' Laurie raised an eyebrow and lowered her voice. 'Or anywhere near as expensive.'

'But in a place just as beautiful,' Belle stressed. 'It's not always necessary to throw a tonne of money at something to make it special.'

'Says the person who organises mind-boggingly expensive events all the bloody time,' Gem cut in.

'It's different when it's my job compared to someone's hard-earned cash.'

'True.' Gem leaned forward and looked pointedly at Laurie. 'The other difference with your wedding is you drank like a fish, whereas today I've noticed you're not drinking at all.' She tilted her head. 'Anything you'd care to share?'

Laurie's sharp intake of breath, rapid blinking and clenched jaw immediately suggested that Gem's question was way off the mark. 'No, I'm not drinking but not for the reason you're assuming.' She flashed a worried glance in Ade's direction but he was deep in conversation with the husband of another friend.

Belle had also noticed during the toasts that Laurie had raised her glass of champagne but hadn't taken a sip, switching instead to sparkling elderflower. She'd figured if Laurie wanted to tell them something then she would.

'Oh come on, Laurie.' Gem folded her arms and lowered her voice. 'Even if you're before twelve weeks you can tell us. That bad luck stuff is bullshit.'

Laurie's chair screeched on the polished wood floor as she

pushed it back. She stood up, her eyes damp as she glared at Gem. 'You really can be bloody insensitive at times.'

Belle's insides constricted as Laurie paced away, weaving past the other tables, her slight frame looking incredibly vulnerable as she retreated.

Belle turned to Gem. 'Seriously, why the hell would you say that?'

All the recent conversations Belle had had with Laurie when they hadn't really talked about anything in particular slotted into place. Following Laurie and Ade's wedding four years ago, every conversation had been filled with the excitement for the future, of trying for a baby, of Laurie looking forward to having a family and taking time out from the data-entry job she hated. It was only now that Belle realised all that kind of talk had petered out as if was too hard for her to discuss any longer.

Belle shook her head at Gem. 'There can be many reasons for someone choosing not to drink – for their health or simply personal choice. I've also got a colleague who's gone teetotal while going through fertility treatment.'

'Oh shit.' Gem sighed. 'I'll go after her.'

'No,' Belle said, standing up. 'We'll go together.'

6

Belle shivered as they stepped from the warmth of the barn with its music and twinkling lights into the fresh May evening. She wrapped her pashmina tighter round her shoulders as she tried to keep up with Gem, watching her footing as she crossed the gravelled terrace in her heels.

They caught up with Laurie in the shadows next to the box hedge. Her black hair was outlined by the purple-pink hues of the dusky sky.

She turned to them with tears streaking her face. 'I didn't mean to snap at you back then, it's just...' She rounded on Gem. '*You* speak without thinking. You always do.'

'Oh, well, sorry if I'm not bloody perfect like you.'

Laurie gaped at her like she'd been slapped in the face. 'There you go again, proving my point.'

'Hey, you two.' Belle held out her hands and glanced behind them at the courtyard terrace filled with wedding guests. 'That's enough. Remember where we are.'

Gem folded her arms and took a deep breath. 'I'm sorry, that was uncalled for. And inside before, I spoke without thinking. I just assumed.' She gestured clumsily towards Laurie's stomach and Belle winced again. 'You've talked so much about wanting children... What's going on, Laurie? You can tell us.'

'I've wanted to, it's just difficult because I'm not pregnant.' Her jaw tightened as she cast a glance between Gem and Belle. 'And it's highly unlikely I'll get pregnant naturally as I've been diagnosed with a low ovarian reserve. The more time that passes and the further away the chance of me getting pregnant gets, the harder I'm finding it to talk about, because it upsets me so much.' She shook her hand in front of herself. 'Leaves me an emotional mess particularly at times like this when I remember our hopes and dreams on our own wedding day.'

'Oh Laurie, that's hard when I know how much you want a baby.' Belle delved into her clutch and handed her a tissue. She'd known something was wrong, so why hadn't she asked the difficult question before Laurie was forced into this situation? Actually, there was nothing hard about asking 'how are you really?' She'd held back because she hadn't wanted to deal with someone else's disappointment and stress when she'd been dealing with her own worries. Some friend she'd been. 'What about fertility treatment? Is that an option?'

'We did our first cycle of IVF at the end of last year.' Laurie dabbed her damp cheeks with the tissue. 'Obviously it wasn't successful.'

Belle tried not to show her shock that Laurie had been through something like that without telling them, but Gem's reaction was less subtle.

Her eyes widened. 'Bloody hell, Laurie. How on earth have you not said anything?'

'It wasn't intentional. Honestly, after more than three years of trying I felt like a failure. And there was so much to deal with juggling appointments and injections around work and everything. I was hoping for a good outcome and then I'd have been able to let you know the happy news. I didn't want to have to share our disappointment.'

'It didn't work at all?' Belle asked softly. 'As in, you didn't get pregnant?'

Laurie shook her head. 'Four eggs were fertilised and two were transferred, but neither stuck.'

'I'm so sorry.' Belle hugged her.

'Me too.' Gem wrapped her arms around them both. 'And you're *not* a failure. You're going to try again, right?'

'I actually started the stimulation injections a couple of days ago, so yes, we're trying again.'

Belle squeezed her tighter. 'Oh Laurie, that's great, so there's hope.'

'That's all I've got,' Laurie said sadly as they let go of each other.

A waiter with a tray of drinks paused next to them, a sufficient distraction as Gem grabbed a glass of Prosecco and Laurie and Belle opted for elderflower. They left the shadows by the hedge and found a free table next to the stone fountain at the centre of the courtyard.

'Please keep it to yourselves,' Laurie said quietly once they'd sat down. 'The only other people who know are our parents and I wish I'd never told mine. Mum's doing my head in offering advice like I haven't already tried everything and phoning every day asking how it's going, how I'm feeling. I know she's only trying to help, but it's a lot.'

'So that's the reason you didn't stay with them last night,' Belle said.

'They don't seem to understand that I want to talk about anything else, rather than focus on something that's out of my hands and down to a combination of science and luck.'

Belle completely understood Laurie's reluctance to talk about the thing in her life that was upsetting her the most, so she took the hint and led the conversation in a different direction.

It was a beautiful early summer evening, the clear sky speckled with stars. Light spilled from the barn and dance music filtered out through the large open doors, a reminder of happy times. Not that Belle was desperately unhappy, just lonely even while sitting with her best friends. Discontented was the perfect word to describe how she was feeling, exactly as she'd admitted to Hannah, but it wasn't something she wanted to talk about with Laurie and Gem.

The music switched to Calvin Harris's 'I Need Your Love' featuring Ellie Goulding, which immediately transported Belle back to Ibiza. It was funny how music did that; certain smells would too, vividly whisk her to an earlier time in her life.

'Oh God, this song always reminds me of Ibiza.' Gem's look of longing was hard to miss.

'That's exactly what I was thinking.' Belle looked between them both. 'And it's something I've been meaning to talk to you about for ages. This summer will mark ten years. We've got to have another holiday there together.'

'Do we though?' Gem picked up her Prosecco and took a gulp. 'Maybe we should go somewhere completely different.'

Belle sat forward. 'Oh come on, Gem. You *loved* Ibiza. You were the one who made us promise to have a ten-year reunion holiday, so I'm going to hold you to it.'

'If you hadn't noticed, my life is very different to what it was back then, because I have responsibilities and bloody...' Gem trailed off and tried to hide her annoyance and sadness with another gulp of Prosecco.

Belle looked at Laurie. 'I know you've just started IVF again, but what do you think?'

Laurie remained quiet for a moment, nursing her elderflower. 'It depends on when and how things work out...'

Inside, Belle was screaming with frustration at their lack of enthusiasm, but she held her tongue. 'I just think it will be good for us to all spend some proper time together because we so rarely do. Perhaps we could tentatively plan something for July.'

'Yes, well, by then I'll either be pregnant or disappointed.'

'Oh God, I'm so sorry. And I didn't want to upset you either, Gem.' She felt as if she was walking a tightrope with them both. The music switched from the Ibiza dance tune to cheesy S Club 7 pop, but it was certainly less emotive. 'I just thought you'd both jump at the chance and would be excited about a holiday together.'

'Having a holiday without the kids would be amazing.' Gem paused as if checking herself and Belle cringed on Laurie's behalf. Her friends were polar opposites; one who was desperate for children, while the other couldn't wait to get away from her nine- and four-year-old. Gem cleared her throat and continued. 'But maybe we should go somewhere else. Is it really a good idea to return to the same place, to what? Try and recapture that time in our lives? We're not twenty-one with no responsibilities any longer. At least I'm not. I would definitely love to go away, just somewhere different.'

'I understand that, I really do,' Belle said while focusing on the flickering light from the candle playing across her friends' faces. 'It's just there's another reason we should have a holiday in Ibiza, something I've been waiting to tell you all week. Two things actually.' She took a deep breath. 'Last month I handed my notice in at work, then at the beginning of this week I accepted a job out in Ibiza. I'm moving there next week, only for the summer season, but—'

'Are you shitting me?' Gem shook her head.

Belle froze, hyper aware of the other guests, Gem's outburst out of kilter with the genteel English setting of the courtyard with the soft tinkle of water from the fountain and the pink and white roses climbing the stone walls.

'I know you keep your personal life off social media, but how could you not tell us about news this big!' Gem looked at Belle incredulously, then at Laurie. 'You didn't know about this either?'

'Not a clue.' Laurie turned to Belle. 'Why didn't you tell us?'

'I literally only found out about the position in Ibiza a few days ago, and as for quitting my job, I didn't want you to talk me out of it.'

'Because you know it's a risk?' Gem shook her head again. 'I don't understand. You're absolutely killing it at work. Why throw it all away?'

'I'm not throwing it away. I'm moving on to a slightly different role with new opportunities.'

Laurie frowned. 'But you said it's for the summer so only a temporary position?'

'It is, but it allows me to focus on what *I* want to do. I couldn't do that at Tockbeth Hall.' Belle hated having to defend her decision, particularly when she'd already questioned it enough herself. 'The truth is, I don't want to work with Isaac any longer and life had just become so... vanilla.'

Gem snorted and her face darkened. She placed her glass on the table with a thump. '*Your* life is vanilla? Try being me. All I have is the same bloody routine day in, day out and it's utterly soul destroying.'

'I get it,' Belle said gently while attempting to bury her dismay at Gem's reaction.

'No, you don't.' Gem's face was stony, her lips pursed tight.

'Fine, maybe it was the wrong choice of words. We're all in different places in our lives, dealing with different things. What I'm doing is what I think is right for me right now. Obviously it's hard to explain without sounding as if I'm moaning about my lot—'

'You're not moaning,' Laurie said firmly. 'This is exciting news, you absolutely should be free to share it and not have to justify yourself.'

'Hmm,' Gem huffed.

'Well, I'm thrilled for you.' Laurie shot Gem a warning look and turned back to Belle. 'Perhaps it'll be a chance to reconnect with a certain Spanish someone.'

A rush of sadness enveloped Belle. She really had nothing to complain about and yet she couldn't shake the feeling of discontentment, disappointment and failure that had slowly grown over the years. She continuously felt as if she was chasing something, never satisfied or completely happy, even when life seemed good.

Suddenly on the verge of tears and desperate to be on her own, she stood up. Not wanting them to see her cry, she paced away from the table, heading down the steps that led from the courtyard and into the Tudor knot garden with its neat box hedges and sculpted yew trees.

Laurie had hit a nerve with her 'a certain Spanish someone' comment. Ten years on, Belle was still holding on to an impossible dream, afraid of commitment and failing to move on from the perfect image she had of her ideal man – as unattainable as it was unrealistic. Maybe returning to the place where her last carefree memories were before the accident happened would be a mistake, but not facing up to things or reconciling her feelings about that intensely passionate week in Ibiza followed by a disastrous start in London had definitely been one.

The shadowed herbaceous border was packed with perennials and dotted with occasional solar lights that guided the way. The scent wasn't as sweet as it had been during the day when a purple and cream carpet of flowers had attracted bees and butterflies in the sunshine – a joyful reminder of summer, which redirected her thoughts to their Ibiza holiday. Laurie's words swirled in her head. Of course attempting to reconnect with Diego had been on her mind when she'd accepted the job. No man had lived up to him, and she was torn by the idea of revisiting a summer fling when she'd fantasised about it being so much more. It wasn't the job in Ibiza she was worried about but the thought of going back somewhere and it not living up to expectations. Gem had been right about that.

Belle reached the stone steps that led to the lake. The blanket of darkness stopped her from going any further. The wedding photos had been taken here earlier in the day, but now the lake looked vast and dark with only the moonlight pooling on the glassy surface. Belle shivered and couldn't help but think that swapping London for a summer in Ibiza would only be a good thing despite her reasons for escaping not being as straightforward as she was admitting.

Footsteps made her turn. Gem and Laurie were silhouetted by the inviting glow from the courtyard beyond the garden.

'I'm sorry.' Gem hugged her. 'I am happy for you, it's just my own shit I'm dealing with. I don't think you realise how lucky you are and how good your life is. I was surprised, that's all.'

'Everything's imploded since splitting up with Isaac and I've felt this desperate need to shake up my life and do something different. Like there's this spotlight highlighting all the negatives. I imagine it's similar to how you feel about being a mum and juggling that side of things with your plans—'

'The plans I once had, you mean.'

Laurie stepped closer, positioning herself between Belle and Gem. 'Belle was right before about us all feeling the stress of life in different ways. Even if we think each of us is doing okay, we don't really know what's going on beneath the surface, particularly if we're not honest with each other. I'm guilty of that by keeping my own struggles to myself. And Gem, just because you have children and exactly what I want doesn't give me the right to shut you down when you're complaining about your kids being a burden—'

'They're not a burden,' Gem cut in, 'I love my kids, it's just...'

Laurie hooked her arm in Gem's. 'I know, life's not perfect, for any of us. That's my point.' She slid her other arm into Belle's. 'So I think we should have our reunion holiday and go back to Ibiza as we promised.'

Gem sighed. 'It's hardly a reunion holiday when Belle will be flipping living there.'

'It can be. It will be.' Belle took Gem's hand and closed the circle. 'We don't want weddings to be the only time we see each other. I'm going to be on Ibiza anyway, working my socks off proving myself in a new job and not knowing anyone. It would be lovely to have you two coming out to look forward to.'

'As I said before, you can always look up Diego.' Laurie's eyes sparkled in the moonlight as she squeezed Belle's arm. Gem's hand momentarily tightened in Belle's too.

'The thought hadn't crossed my mind,' she said smoothly, while absolutely knowing it had consumed her for a lot longer than she cared to admit. 'But it's the job I'm moving for and the opportunity to focus on what I want to do. Spending a few months in Ibiza is the bonus. So what do you say?' She looked between them. 'We did make a promise. All you need to do is sort out flights; I'll organise the accommodation.'

'Someone *is* doing well.' Gem's smile didn't completely hide the underlying animosity. 'But yeah, I'm in if you are too, Laurie?'

'If this IVF cycle works and I get pregnant then no, if it doesn't...' She shrugged.

'Then it will be something good to take your mind off things,' Gem said matter-of-factly.

Belle squeezed Laurie's arm. 'There's every chance it will work because it's bound to mess up our plans, and my God, will we be happy for you if that happens.'

With Laurie in the middle and their arms still hooked in each other's, they strolled back towards the lights and music filling the fresh May evening. Unspoken tensions remained, and Belle was certain that all of them were still holding back on their true worries, stresses, desires and dreams, because it was certainly what she was doing. But a week away together in the summer, revisiting happier more carefree times, would allow them the chance to delve deeper and rebuild the friendship that had taken a battering due to distance, commitments, family, work and the ups and downs of everyday life.

Belle squeezed her friends' arms tighter and thought, *Ibiza, here we come!*

7

Instead of quaffing gin and tonic on the plane to Ibiza like she'd done ten years before, Belle opted for a black coffee and a bottle of water when the trolley came by. She wanted to keep her head clear, yet the flight filled her with nostalgia. She'd loved everything about Ibiza and had left the island believing her future would be bright and beautiful.

At twenty-one, Belle had taken little notice of the surroundings during the twenty-five-minute transfer from the airport to their hotel in San Antonio. It was different now in the taxi to Santa Eulalia and once they'd bypassed Ibiza Town with buildings, warehouses and occasional building sites cluttering the sides of the dual carriageway, rugged shrubland then great swathes of pine trees eventually took over along the roadside and she began to feel as excited as a child on Christmas morning.

Spirit was located right by the sea with its own stretch of beach in Santa Eulalia, a short walk away from the swanky marina with its lines of gleaming white boats and yachts. Belle's first impression was how different it seemed to her memory of pulsating and often gaudy San Antonio. There was still a plethora of hotels, restaurants and bars, but its more laidback vibe and the fact it was considered to be the cultural and gastronomical centre of the island greatly appealed. Even though Spirit was an adults-only hotel, the town itself was more family orientated and sophisticated than San Antonio. It was certainly a more chilled out and classier destination than she'd previously experienced.

Caleb greeted her in the cool of Spirit's lobby, which was all white walls and pale wood with splashes of green in the leafy palms housed in large rust-coloured pots. He was immediately recognisable from their Zoom calls but more arresting in real life and taller than she'd imagined, ruggedly attractive in jeans and a cream T-shirt. His handshake was warm and welcoming, and there was an energy about him that made her like him immediately.

'It's wonderful to finally have you here, Belle.' Caleb released her hand, organised for one of the staff to take her luggage to her accommodation, then chatted about the hotel as he took her on a tour.

Belle had done her research on Spirit, but the reality was even better. They strolled around, poking their heads into one of the sea-view rooms with crisp white walls offset by warming tones of burnt amber and natural wood. He showed her the shared office and introduced her to Giada and Miguel, a couple of the events and marketing team members. The restaurant and outdoor bars were the beating heart of the place and where Belle's energy would be focused. The spacious terraces were divided into different areas with plenty of greenery breaking up the predominantly white, wood and stone décor. There was a sunken area with cushioned seating and space to dance, with a DJ booth at the end of the bar.

'We mainly host weddings and private parties as well as dance nights for the hotel guests,' Caleb said as they reached the pool, which was located at the centre of the seafront grounds. 'It's as much an income for us as the hotel side of things, which is why this role is so important, particularly with our new restaurant Serenity down the coast.'

They crossed the pool deck with its beanbag loungers, white umbrellas and swaying palms. Billowing white curtains around double sunbeds were occupied with couples making the most of the pleasant temperature of a fine June day. Elegance and romance oozed in every direction and the beach beyond a treeline of palms and a shady juniper was lined with uniform white umbrellas.

The final stop was the bar where Caleb had interviewed Belle from less than two weeks ago. While he ordered them a drink, she settled herself on a cushioned seat in the sunshine and breathed in the heady scent of the sea.

Caleb returned with sparkling grapefruit and rosemary syrup cocktails and sat opposite her. 'In an ideal world I would have had you shadow Cara and have a proper hand over but she's had to drop everything to go back to Australia to help look after her dad – he's, um, not been given long to live.'

'Oh my goodness, I'm so sorry to hear that.'

'Cara's been with me through the good and bad times. I don't want to leave her in the lurch, so she has the job to come back to when she's ready.'

'Which, like I said, suits me just fine,' Belle said before taking a sip of the sweet yet refreshing drink. 'This is the perfect job to bridge the gap and it's a relief to get away from things in London. Plus Ibiza made quite an impression on me ten years ago.' *Both Ibiza and Diego*, Belle thought.

'You weren't tempted to stay?' Caleb raised his eyebrows and sipped his drink.

'There was definitely temptation, but I had a job lined up in London. Big plans, you know. It felt too risky to give that up on a whim back then.'

Caleb smiled. 'I did exactly that, gave up my life in London for the lure of Ibiza, and you're right, it was risky with no guarantees of it working out.'

'But it did for you.' Belle wafted her hand around the bar.

'It's been a long road to get here. A lot of hard work and sacrifices. Sometimes you have to take a chance, but there are also times when being sensible can be the best choice.'

'I definitely went the sensible route.'

'But now?'

'It feels a little riskier, but a risk I was willing to take.' For the first time in her life she was listening to her heart rather than her head.

'Something pushed you away, right? People don't tend to move countries, jobs and take on a lesser role for no reason.'

'Firstly, I don't consider this to be a lesser role, a sideways step perhaps, but you're right about there being a reason.' She stopped, covering her uncertainty over how to explain with a glug of her drink.

'One that you don't have to share with me,' Caleb said smoothly. 'I get it. I've had many moments in my life like that. I'm just glad this job was a risk you were willing to take, because I've been lost without Cara.' His cheeks were tanned but she noticed the slight flush, as if he'd said more than he'd meant to. 'I'm about to head over to Serenity. I'd like to show it to you before you get settled back here, if that's okay?'

'Yes, of course, I'd love to see it.'

Many of the guests said hello to Caleb as they walked back through the hotel's grounds and Belle was struck by how involved he seemed. The staff looked the part, slick and professional in off-white shirts, the Spirit logo on the fabric, smart in fitted black trousers or shorts. His ease with them and their genuine smiles confirmed her thought that he was hands on and very much involved in the day-to-day running of the hotel.

Outside, Caleb strode over to a black convertible Jeep with white dust splattered up the sides, which made it look like it was actually used off road. He opened the passenger door for her and scooted round to the driver's side. Of course he'd have a convertible. He lived on Ibiza and owned a luxury hotel.

With salty air buffeting her face and dance tunes playing on the stereo, the ten-minute journey to Serenity certainly beat her London commute on the Tube. It was a different life and she'd have a taste of it for a few months, which would hopefully pave the way to a newfound freedom.

Down the coast from Santa Eulalia, and nestled in a dip of a headland overlooking the sea not far from the small resort of Cala Llonga, Serenity was aptly named.

Belle realised she was holding her breath as she strolled through the bar with Caleb to where the restaurant tables were spaced out in front of floor-to-ceiling windows that overlooked the bay. The whole design, from the shades of white and sand to the natural materials of wood and stone, drew her eye to the large windows framing the sea and sky. She followed Caleb outside to a wraparound terrace filled with diners on one side and a bar area of comfy seating on the other, with steps leading to another spacious terrace below.

'It's magical at this time of day,' Caleb said.

Belle nodded in reply, having no words to describe the view in front of her. The sea rippled with the burnished red of the setting sun. San Antonio was famed for its breathtaking sunsets, while this side of the island got to enjoy the peace of sunrise. The people snuggled together on the padded wooden sofas had front-row seats to the very magic Caleb was talking about. Conversation was hushed between couples with their hands entwined as they gazed beyond the rocky border planted with cacti, herbs and agave plants to the sea dancing in the fading light.

This was a side to Ibiza she'd completely missed out on the first time: sophisticated and enchanting. The smell of booze and cheap perfume had been replaced by the fresh scent of the ocean and the mouth-watering aroma of seafood paella.

Enclosed by rocky cliffs that formed a private horseshoe bay, it was far removed from the vibrancy and nightlife of Ibiza Town which was a twenty-minute drive away. Belle's mind was already firing off ideas. The possibilities of how to utilise the space and the events she'd be able to arrange were thrilling. She was used to creating magic in a historic location, whereas here the natural surroundings were the stars; the palm trees edging the sandy terrace and steps that wound down to the pebble beach; and the endless blue reaching towards the hazy island of Formentera just a thirty-minute ferry journey away. Even the restaurant had been designed and built with nature and its surroundings in mind. There were no flashing lights or thumping beats. Inside, the lighting was honey-toned, bringing out the natural colours of the stone and wood, and the music enhanced rather than detracted, while outside, once darkness had descended, candlelight would flicker on the tables, adding to the romanticism of the location.

Caleb stood next to her. 'We had a soft launch in April so have just focused on the restaurant and nailing excellent food in an awe-inspiring location. We want it to be a destination that people make the effort to come to. There's the potential to use the space for more than just dining. Cara's already put plans in motion for an outdoor movie night, and I'm open to ideas. Come, you must be hungry. Let's get something to eat and you can tell me what you think.'

After a waiter had wafted by with seafood paella, Belle opted for a bowl of her own for dinner. They were joined by Raphael, Serenity's manager, a Spanish guy in his forties, slight and not much taller than her, calm and friendly, someone Belle could tell was in control and still had an eye on everything while he sat and chatted to them.

Caleb was friendly but reserved, an older and calmer version of the party-animal impression she'd had of someone who'd lived on Ibiza since their late teens. But then she'd changed in the decade since she was last here; she'd much rather enjoy dinner at a place like Serenity than party into the early hours every night.

The paella was one of the best things she'd ever eaten with juicy shrimps, jewelled red pepper, and the delights of cuttlefish and mussels hidden among the tasty rice. Every mouthful was pure joy and the setting only added to the experience as they talked, the number of ideas they discussed leaving her buzzing by the time Caleb drove her back to Spirit and showed her to Cara's apartment.

'We've put her personal belongings in storage,' Caleb said. 'It made more sense for you to be on-site. I'm sure it's been a long day so I'll leave you to get settled and we'll catch up again in the morning.'

They said goodbye and Belle entered the ground-floor apartment. It had been a long day but an optimistic one and she felt relief that it was ending on a positive note. Cara's apartment was compact but had everything she needed: a double bedroom, bathroom and a living area with a kitchenette and sliding doors that opened onto an enclosed and private courtyard garden. Belle stood on the threshold and soaked up the atmosphere of the distant voices and the gentle clatter from the hotel's restaurant, a soft doom doom doom from the bar and, if she listened hard, the swoosh of the sea just a short walk away through Spirit's grounds. The bright whitewashed walls of the courtyard were offset by the magenta flowers of a rock rose, and a palm tree shaded the beanbag chair below.

At the sound of her phone pinging, she retreated inside to retrieve it.

> Been thinking about you all day. Are you there and settled in? Send pics! I need to dream and have something positive to focus on – something else other than having to stick a needle into my stomach on a daily basis! Catch up with you properly in a couple of days? xx

Laurie's fertility struggles and her tearfulness at the wedding worried Belle, even if she was trying to be upbeat in her message. Belle was well aware how easy it was to put on a brave face and hide your true emotions when inside it felt like you were falling apart. She tried to bury the stab of annoyance that Gem hadn't messaged at all. She wasn't someone who forgot things, even if she complained her life was hectic and she had her hands full with the kids. Belle knew it was a conscious choice to not send a message. She sighed, equally annoyed with herself that she felt the need for validation, that she wanted Gem's approval. She certainly didn't want to be that needy friend, but she also didn't want to feel she had to hide her good news because Gem was jealous.

Yet despite those feelings of jealousy, she was still coming. Gem and Laurie's flights to Ibiza in July were booked. As well as having arranged with Caleb a week off for herself, Belle had reserved a room at Spirit even with the uncertainty of whether Laurie would be able to come. Maybe them all returning and dredging up the past would be a mistake. Belle had written the predictions they'd made for each other in her diary, determined to make Gem and Laurie's prediction for her 'having it all' come true. She had an awful lot, but she didn't have everything. And as for Gem and Laurie...

It would be fine. After less than twenty-four hours in Ibiza, she'd seen a whole different side that actually had outshone her memory of packed pool parties, semi-naked twenty-somethings drinking to excess and dancing till their feet ached – or bled in some cases. Twenty-one-year-old Belle would have scoffed at the idea of one day preferring chatting with friends over a quiet meal to clubbing, but she did – not that she'd say no to a night out at a super club, but time had passed and she'd changed. Ibiza might just be the perfect place for her to figure out where life would take her next.

8

'Hey, you surviving without me?' Cara's freckled face filled Caleb's phone screen and he acknowledged the sense of calm at seeing his best friend, even from afar. 'How's things working out with Belle?'

'You were right,' Caleb said as he slid open the large glass door of his living room and stepped onto the expansive L-shaped terrace. 'She is perfect for the job.'

'Of course I was right.'

'It definitely helps with her being on-site, so thank you for letting her bunk at yours.'

'Well, the place is technically yours, not mine, and it makes complete sense for her to stay there while I'm not. Just please remind her to water my plants.'

Caleb chuffed a laugh. 'How are you doing?'

Cara sighed. 'I'm—' A noise in the background made her turn. 'Hold on, be back in a minute.' There was fumbling and Cara disappeared, leaving the phone facing up to a white ceiling.

Caleb placed his coffee on the paving and sat on one of the double sun loungers. The terrace wrapped around two sides of the villa with uninterrupted sea views over Talamanca Bay all the way to the island of Formentera, with the glimpse of Ibiza Town to the right, its white buildings decorating green-clad bays. The pool was like a sheet of reflective glass jutting out of the hillside, and the island on either side curved in and out in a hazy line of green, white and stone.

This was his favourite time of the day when he could sit with a coffee in the morning sun to think and reflect. Paloma used to call it the magic hour. He used to love night time and although he could still be described as a night owl, his days of living for going out were well and truly over. Yet the fact that this time of day was when he was almost always alone wasn't lost on him.

'I'm back.' Cara's face filled the screen again.

'Everything okay?'

'I'm not really sure how Mum was coping on her own most of the time, because she sure as hell doesn't seem to be now. I know I've not been here long but I have zero time without being called to do something.' She breathed in deeply. 'I don't mean to sound selfish or quite so much like a shitty daughter – I'm just tired. Don't think I've got over the jetlag.'

'Maybe your mum's coping less because she doesn't have to constantly hold it together now you're back.'

'The whole situation sucks.'

'It was always going to.'

'Yeah, doesn't make it any easier.' She glanced away from the screen. 'Bloody winter here too. Missing summer on Ibiza sucks so much.'

'There's always next year. Summer is what Ibiza does best.'

'Says the person sitting on his epic terrace *on Ibiza* getting to enjoy all of that. Sorry, I really shouldn't moan. My sister's been doing a six-hour round trip every couple of weeks to help Mum and Dad as much as she can. Me being here is the least I can do after not being back for years. Plus I'm going to meet my niece for the first time next week. Silver lining and all.'

'Exactly, find the positives; that's what you've always told me to do. I'm a far more positive person since knowing you.'

Cara adjusted her nose-ring and shook her head. 'To be fair, when we first met it was hard for you to be any less positive.' She gave him a knowing look and blew a kiss. 'But things really are going okay with Belle?'

'It's only been a few days.' He scooped up his coffee mug and leaned his elbows on his knees. 'But yes, she knows what she's doing, is confident and independent – at least professionally she is; personally I think she has her struggles. She's been keeping herself to herself, which is absolutely fine, and she's working damn hard. She's already up and running with your open-air cinema. She's a go-getter like you.'

'Talking of go getting, I need to help Mum with Dad's meds before he goes to sleep. Talk soon, yeah?'

'Of course. Love you, C.'

'Love you too, knucklehead.'

Caleb leaned back on the sun lounger, his eyes sweeping across the terrace. The location of the villa had been the reason he'd bought the place, although the house itself had been neglected. The potential, though, had been incredible and they'd ended up rebuilding it into their dream house and renaming it Solace. He downed the rest of his coffee as his heart battered his ribs. It should never have been a bachelor pad, and yet that was what it had turned into. The rust-coloured pots on the terrace were filled with spiky cacti and weathered palm trees; Paloma would have added colour with flowers and cushions instead of the neutral grey, cream and white of the lounge area. He'd considered selling it, but with the rebuild of the villa near completion, Paloma had made him promise he wouldn't give up on his dream, even if it meant living here without her.

Caleb dumped his mug on the terrace and stripped down to his pants. He strolled to the edge of the pool, rolling his shoulders in an attempt to dispel the tension winding through him. The trouble with time in the morning to think was the way in which his thoughts negatively spiralled. He dived into the pool, breaking the still, glasslike surface with barely a splash. The cool water enveloped him. A refreshing swim was an effective way to temper his sorrow, to regain a semblance of control, to not only face the day but to run with it. Somewhere along the way, making joyful memories for his guests had become his only reason for getting up in the morning.

9

After a week living and working on Ibiza, Belle had eased into a routine. Her days started much like they had at home in London, with yoga followed by coffee and breakfast. Instead of eating toast perched at the kitchen island scrolling through emails, now she got to enjoy a bowl of yogurt, granola, honey and blueberries in the patch of sun that snuck into Cara's courtyard garden. Not only was the Spanish way of life more chilled out, but also she was on an island and working for a place where the slow start was encouraged.

She'd been meaning to phone Hannah all week but had been too busy, so she made time that evening after making a simple dinner for herself back at Cara's apartment. Although Cara's personal items had been stored away, there was still an imprint of her in the colourful cushions, the artwork on the wall and the leafy green plants.

Belle curled up on the beanbag in the courtyard garden with a glass of chilled lemonade while they chatted about work and how they were both getting on.

'I can't even begin to explain the absolute relief of not having to share a space with Jake and be civil all the bloody time,' Hannah said with a relieved sigh.

'Ditto. Not having to see Isaac at work has been good for me – freeing. I hadn't realised quite how wound up and stressed I was about everything.'

'We've both escaped the hell of failed relationships, although I think you may have lucked out in Ibiza. Is it everything you hoped for?'

'It's only been a week so it almost feels like I'm on holiday – a working holiday, mind. But sandals and bare legs and getting to feel sand between my toes every day is pretty special.'

'I'm trying not to be insanely jealous right now. It's raining here and I'm snuggled up on your sofa in my PJs and a jumper – you'd think it was March rather than June.'

Belle smiled and gazed up at candyfloss-pink streaking the darkening sky after a perfect sunny day. 'I won't torture you by describing what I'm looking at then.'

'Please don't.' Belle heard the smile in Hannah's voice. 'I adore your place, although the downside is being on my own. I'm not used to it.'

'It's a massive adjustment, even more so after a breakup even if you were desperate to have your own space. But you'll gain so much from the freedom of being able to focus on just you for a while.'

'I just wish you were here, house sharing again like when we first moved to London. Life back then was so much easier. Stress-free and happy.'

'Maybe for you.' Belle's stomach clenched, her reply more cutting than she'd intended.

'Oh God, I really didn't mean to remind you about what

happened,' Hannah said softly. 'I'm just talking about the good things when we lived together – the late-night chats and brunch at Mulligans; being lucky to find such a good friend when I was scared shitless about moving to London by myself and starting my first proper publishing job.'

'I felt the same way too, it's just everything back then was over-shadowed by the accident.'

'Which is why I'm selfishly wishing we were living together now. A chance to relive the good times without all the crappy stuff. Although I for one have a hell of a lot more emotional baggage.'

Unlike Hannah, she'd never become so invested in a relationship she couldn't easily get out of when things went wrong or got too serious.

'Anyway,' Hannah continued, 'it's probably a good thing living by myself and getting used to my own company because jumping into another relationship is the last thing I need. And however much I miss you, I'm sure Ibiza is doing you good.'

Hannah was right about that, Belle reflected once they'd said goodbye. She was right about not jumping into another relationship too. The change of country called for a change of attitude, and concentrating on herself without overcomplicating things with romance was definitely the way forward.

* * *

The weather heated up during the first couple of weeks in June and Belle settled into a new rhythm of living and working on Ibiza. The events and marketing team was small but worked like a finely oiled machine. Giada and Miguel were both efficient and capable, plus she had the use of Spirit's and Serenity's staff for the events as well.

The summer events were fixed in the diary, with three weddings at Serenity alongside numerous private parties at both locations. Those were the sort of events she could do with her eyes closed, and they were on a far smaller scale than the banquets and award ceremonies she'd managed back in London. So it was actually the one-off events and day trips for Spirit's guests that Belle initially loved the most because she went along to get a greater understanding of the island, which would enable her to promote the experiences to future guests. With a food tour in Ibiza Town, the option of a day spa retreat or horse riding in San Carlos, and wine tasting at Ibizkus winery not far from Santa Eulalia, Belle ended up playing as hard as she worked.

It was the contrasting sides of Ibiza she found fascinating. In the little time she had off, she didn't return to San Antonio or head to bustling Ibiza Town, but with the use of Cara's car she escaped to places like Cala Salada. Although it was just north of San Antonio, it seemed like another world with the sand lapped by emerald water, the rugged cliffs hugged by shady trees.

When it came to work and her new role, she appreciated Caleb's hands-off approach which allowed her time to get settled. He was always available to answer any questions and point her in the right direction, but without feeling the need to hover over her. They got into the habit of checking in with each other every couple of days and she found herself looking forward to having a quick drink with him while they debriefed. It was a chance to share ideas and explore new ones. Her work colleagues were friendly but they went home at the end of the day to their families. Not knowing anyone else, she began to realise her day brightened when she saw Caleb; she wanted to prove herself and make him proud.

As her time on Ibiza rolled into her third week, apart from a few messages in their WhatsApp group chat about organising their holiday in July, Gem's lack of communication was noticeable. And the next time she spoke to Laurie after an evening stroll along Santa Eulalia's seafront promenade, Belle had to ask the question that had been bugging her.

'Have you heard from Gem or is it just me she's ignoring?'

'I wouldn't take it personally.' Laurie sighed. 'Apart from a good luck message before my embryo collection, I haven't heard from her. But then completely out of the blue, this morning a gorgeous bunch of flowers arrived with a lovely note from her saying "thinking about you". I'm not sure she knows how to actually talk to me at the moment.'

'Or is worried about saying the wrong thing again, so is showing she cares in another way.' Belle's annoyance that she hadn't heard from Gem dissipated, knowing she'd at least been thinking about Laurie. 'So, how did yesterday go?'

'They put one embryo back.' Laurie took a long deep breath. 'So there's hope, but I hate this bit. I'm just emotionally exhausted. I'm done with the injections, the procedures, the discomfort, and apart from these horrible pessaries it's just a two-week waiting game now. That's the most terrifying bit of it all.'

'You've got this, Laurie. You've come so far and done so well.'

'I've taken a few days off work and Ade is taking me out for a meal and to the theatre this weekend. He only told me this morning.'

'Oh bless, he's a keeper.'

'Yeah, I know.' Although tiredness wound through Laurie's words, Belle could hear the love too. 'Enough about me. How are you doing?'

'I miss you.' Belle snuggled back on the sofa, tucking in her feet. 'I miss Hannah as well and my work colleagues – well, not all of them,' she said wryly. 'I underestimated how strange it would be being here on my own not knowing anyone. I like my new colleagues and I couldn't ask for a better, more chilled-out boss in Caleb, but it's not the same without friends. And, because I *really* want you to get good news in two weeks, it'll mean I won't get to see you next month either, but that will be a small price to pay for your happiness.'

10

'Sunday is my chill-out time.' Caleb gave Belle a shy smile as one of the bar staff handed them their drinks. 'You'd like to join me?' He gestured towards a cushioned love seat on the edge of Serenity's terrace.

Belle picked up her gin, strawberry and passionfruit cocktail and followed him over. They sat in silence for a moment, taking in the dusk-streaked sky. Belle inhaled the salty breeze and the mouth-watering waft of grilled seafood, still not quite believing after more than three weeks that this was her current reality. The vibe at Serenity was different than at Spirit and both places were aptly named. While she wasn't yet sure which she preferred, there was something incredibly special about Serenity's location.

'This is my go-to place for a Sunday evening nightcap,' Caleb said, raising his bottle of beer. 'It used to be the bar at Spirit where Cara and I would sit on the wall overlooking the sea, but here there's, well, this.' He gestured in front of them.

'Peace,' Belle said quietly. Even the chatter from the restaurant and the terrace packed with guests enjoying dinner and the view was muted, accompanied by a gentle beat, music that soothed rather than got the heart pumping. 'You really miss Cara?'

'Yeah, she's my sounding board as much as a friend. Actually more like a sister really, with both of us living far from family. We just clicked. She's damn good at her job too; helped me to succeed with Spirit far beyond what I hoped for.'

Belle pointed to herself. 'Big shoes to fill.'

'You're doing just fine.'

'Good to know, 'cos I'm loving it. And the way Cara's been running things has made it easy to pick up the reins.'

'Our social media followers have increased in the time you've been here – you understand how to showcase our places in the best possible way.'

'It's not exactly hard.' Belle swept her hand around and gave Caleb a knowing look.

A smile flickered over his face. 'I mean this as a compliment despite it probably not sounding like one, but my worry was your lack of experience with social media, because it's a big part of the job as well as running the events. You were honest that it wasn't a part of your previous job and that you don't personally use it.'

'For me, social media is fine when it comes to the aesthetics, showcasing and selling an idea or experience. It's creative and inspiring when you have something beautiful to work with. What I don't like is the intrusion into people's lives even if it's a personal choice. So just don't ask me to tackle TikTok.'

'No worries there.' Caleb laughed. 'We're selling a dream, a luxury lifestyle, even if most people only get to experience it for a week or two. Slick, sophisticated and sexy is the vibe I'm after.' He swigged his drink and clasped his hands round the bottle. 'I also don't mean to offend you by implying you're unusual staying off social media.'

'I don't avoid it completely; personally it's not for me, but it has its place and for events and marketing it's necessary.'

'A necessary evil I'm guessing...' Caleb looked at her pointedly.

Belle shrugged. 'When I was researching you and Spirit I noticed that you don't exactly plaster your life over social media either. Slick and professional accounts for Spirit and Serenity, but not for yourself.'

'Touché,' he said smoothly.

Worried she'd overstepped the mark, she blustered on. 'I find social media can be toxic. At least the way some people behave isn't healthy. Even if you don't intend to, it's hard not to compare yourself to other people.'

'You do understand that what most people post is a lie a lot of the time?' Caleb shifted in the seat and rested his foot on his knee.

'Oh, I get that but it's hard to separate reality from fantasy, at least I found it was, particularly if you're feeling low or vulnerable. In my first job I used it a lot, but I didn't want it spilling over into my personal life. You know how people share everything. I didn't want friends, or to be honest people I barely knew, to have a window into my life, even a false one.'

'A refreshing attitude to have.'

'I've seen it with my friend Gem in particular. She's a social media queen and is big into interior design and the aesthetics of everything. But she showcases a false reality, taking photos from an angle that doesn't include the clutter on the other side of the room.'

'Everyone does that.'

'Of course, but being constantly shown what's perceived as perfection isn't helpful.' Belle was acutely aware of what a snapshot of this moment would look like, her and Caleb looking snug together, with a backdrop of the golden-red light of sunset and the unrealistic impression it would give. 'If you only knew Gem through what she posts on Instagram you would see a glamorous mum of two, in control with perfectly behaved kids, a house to die for; you'd think her life was perfect.'

'When I'm guessing it's not.'

'Not that she'd ever admit it, but it's impossible for her to hide the reality from her friends who know her well. Although as time goes by I feel like I understand her less and less.'

'And you don't want to post on social media because your life isn't perfect either?' Caleb asked slowly.

'Is anyone's? Honestly, who can hold their hands up and say they wouldn't want to change something?'

Caleb nodded knowingly and glanced away. 'I would in a heartbeat despite having all of this.'

Sadness coated his words so Belle decided not to probe any further. Business and pleasure muddied the waters; she'd had first-hand experience with Isaac and she'd vowed never to do that again – not that she thought anything romantic would happen, she just didn't want to cross a line with her boss and become overly personal. She told herself it wasn't unusual for him to have a drink with his staff, so it wasn't as if he'd singled her out, plus she'd taken Cara's place who he was obviously close to.

They lapsed into silence. Whispered conversations spiralled into the night from couples snuggled together further along the terrace. She was acutely aware of Caleb's jean-clad thigh just millimetres away from hers. Serenity was all about love and romance and her own ideas for utilising the outside spaces leaned towards that vibe.

'I love how I've seen such a different side to the island,' she said, needing to fill the silence. 'It's not just about clubbing and having a good time.'

'No, it's not,' Caleb said, 'but that's what drove me here.'

'It's the reason why we came to Ibiza too.'

'I went on a club 18–30 holiday to Magaluf in the late nineties.' He winced and shook his head. 'I'm surprised I remember anything. I was eighteen, went with a couple of mates, you know the freedom of the first holiday away from your folks. My mum travelled a lot for work so I lived with my gran who was loving but pretty strict.' A smile crept across his face, crinkling the corners of his eyes and forming dimples on his stubbled cheeks.

'What did you get up to?'

He laughed and shook his head again. 'What didn't I get up to? Let's just say I had a damn good time. The club reps were only a year or two older than me, but they were bolder, funnier, sexier. They just swooped in and pulled girls I fancied like they were superheroes. I remembered thinking *I want some of that*. So before the end of the holiday I signed up for a holiday rep training session back in the UK. My gran wanted me to go to university so we compromised and I said I'd take a gap year, go travelling first then work as a holiday rep through the summer season in Ibiza, but you know.' He shrugged.

'You never left. Your gran was okay with that?'

'Not at first. But as well as playing hard I worked hard too, proved myself out here, earned shitloads of commission, got bigger and better gigs working for the super clubs. I managed to convince her that university was unnecessary when I was already learning everything I needed. I'm just mighty relieved that it was back in the day when there was no social media or smart phones to document everything. There's zero evidence of my hedonistic days beyond a handful of blurry photos.'

'Unlike me having every bloody thing documented.'

'The one advantage to being forty-two,' he said with a glint in his eyes. 'I started working in Ibiza in the late nineties right at the end of the really crazy period. Things are different now, back then anything and everything happened.'

'It seemed pretty insane when I was here in July 2013.'

'The summer of 2013,' Caleb said slowly, his eyes drifting off towards the sea. The sunset had faded leaving moonlit darkness and a fresh clear night. 'That was a year to remember. Lots of changes and a slightly weird vibe.'

'Really? All I remember was having the best time.'

'You were an Ibiza virgin, right?' He glanced back at her with a sly smile. 'You would have had the best time and been none the wiser. That was the year shedloads of new parties cropped up. Pacha celebrated forty years but they mixed things up too. Most people had an epic time but on the ground, the people working behind the scenes felt the strain – lots of new places competing for clubbers meant not everyone did well.'

'It was ten years ago; how do you remember something like that? I imagine all the summers would roll into one.'

'Generally they do, but that summer was special because I got married.' He suddenly had that lost look about him again, pain folding across his face. He breathed deeply and met her eyes. 'But as it was your first time in Ibiza you'd have noticed none of that and had the time of your life.'

'Yeah, I was drunk most of the time and didn't see much of Ibiza beyond pool parties and the inside of a few bars and clubs.' Belle gazed at the flickering light from the candle in the glass holder on the table. A wave of nostalgia washed over her. 'I think we only made it to a beach once or twice. The focus was on drinking, partying and having a good time. It felt so simple at twenty-one. I'm not sure I thought of Ibiza as anything beyond having a pool and club scene and being filled with young, beautiful people. I take it that's what made you want to stay?' She picked up her drink and took a sip of the smooth, fruity gin.

'Yeah, to begin with it was the lifestyle. There's a real joy to earning money while socialising and I proved to be rather adept at it.' He paused and glanced away for a moment, looking wistful. 'My mum is a well-known and respected foreign correspondent – I took her work ethic even if the career I followed was vastly different. My dad was never a part of our lives. I felt guilty being far from my gran, but once she realised I was onto a good thing here, she selflessly encouraged me to stay. I'd got used to hot days and sultry nights, not waking before midday and working till the early hours. There was no job that appealed to me back home. I was good at what I did, savvy and entrepreneurial – something else I took from my mum – and invested in projects which brought in more money and success, plus I became friends with this incredibly successful guy, Eddie Rosen, who'd established himself as a big player in San Antonio. I also fell in love.'

Caleb's phone ringing took them both by surprise and stopped the question Belle was about to ask.

'Sorry, I need to take this.' Caleb scrambled off the seat and paced away as he answered the phone.

The question 'is the woman you fell in love with the one you married?' never made it past Belle's lips. She wondered if he'd said more than he'd meant to. She was also left wondering what had happened with his wife. He'd fallen in love and got married, and he wore a wedding ring, but there was no evidence of a wife around – it was all a bit of a mystery.

This was the first time their conversation had become personal. She'd vowed to keep a professional distance with her work colleagues, her boss in particular, yet it felt easy talking to him. And that was all they'd been doing, talking. There was nothing wrong in having a professional yet friendly relationship.

Deciding to head back to Spirit, Belle left the comfortable depths of the love seat, yet she was unable to rid herself of the worry that she was attracted to Caleb. *Because he's a good-looking man*, she reasoned. He was older than the men she usually went for, not that age necessarily mattered. It was fine to appreciate him for his good looks and easy-going nature, but that was all it was – an appreciation from afar, because she was certainly not going to go down that road again.

* * *

Belle didn't see Caleb again until the following afternoon, when he found her in the office at Spirit.

'Sorry to have left abruptly last night. Cara phoned. She was starting her day while I was ending mine. She'd been working on something but it's madness when she's across the other side of the world and has enough to be dealing with. I suggested I pass it on to you.' He placed a couple of printed sheets and flyers on the desk in front of her. 'She was in talks with Ushuaïa working out a VIP deal for an outdoor club experience for our guests. I'll put you in touch with Diego to iron out the details.'

Belle's heart momentarily stilled as the name Diego evoked emotions and memories.

Caleb scribbled a name and number on a piece of paper and handed it to her. 'He'll be expecting your call, but any questions just check with me. Hopefully it should all be straightforward.'

Belle gazed at the name Diego Torres Corchado, only vaguely aware of Caleb leaving. She'd never known the surname of the Diego who'd rocked her world in the summer of 2013. Of course a summer fling had been all it was, yet the strength of the feelings that had followed her ever since…

Although Belle wasn't active on social media, she did have a Facebook profile even if she never used it. If this Diego Torres Corchado was on Facebook then she could look him up to see if he was her Diego. She felt absurd thinking of him like that when their time together had been fleeting if passionate. She scooped up her phone, clicked on Facebook and typed in his name. There were reams of people with a similar name but only one Diego Torres Corchado from Ibiza. With shaky hands, she clicked on him. The profile picture jumped out at her, a slightly older version of the young man she'd fallen for staring back at her. Heat rushed to her face. Belle glanced up. Miguel and Giada were oblivious, busy at work on their laptops.

Belle returned her attention to her phone. She had a few photos that she'd taken of Diego, but as time passed and she'd grown older, her memory of him had blurred. She scrolled through his profile. He was still living on Ibiza and worked as a marketing manager at Ushuaïa, so he was definitely Caleb's contact. Relationship status: single. His Facebook feed was sprinkled with photos with friends, at the beach, in a bar, partying. A couple of photos she assumed were of him and his family. Frowning, she clicked on one and zoomed in. Caleb. A younger Caleb with a huge grin lighting up his face, one arm laid across Diego's shoulders, his other around a young woman with dark curly hair, olive skin and rosebud lips.

Her heart stalled. Diego and Caleb knew each other socially? What were the chances? And now she needed to phone Diego knowing full well who he was when he'd be unaware of who she was. Unless of course they met in person... And would he even remember her? The way things had ended, she already knew she hadn't meant as much to him as he did to her. Yet seeing him again was something she'd dreamed about, and now there was a real possibility of that happening.

11

JULY 2013, TEN YEARS AGO

Belle locked eyes with Diego, the sexily confident guy who'd spoken to them earlier that day when he'd sold them tickets to Ministry of Sound at Eden. It was quite the existence trawling the beaches and bars drumming up business for the club, when chatting up girls and socialising seemed to be a huge part of the job. Lots of the people doing PR for the clubs were Brits, all young, but this guy had caught her eye for his Spanish good looks and ridiculously sexy accent. He was smooth as hell and she'd needed little persuading when he'd handed her a flyer, his fingers brushing hers. He'd flirted outrageously with all three of them, but when Laurie had put her arm across Gem's shoulders and told him 'us two are taken', he'd focused his attention on Belle, giving her *all the feels.*

Belle lost sight of him across the crowded beachfront bar and her attention was stolen away by Gem and Laurie. They were living the dream, the freedom as intoxicating as the plentiful alcohol.

An arm slid around her waist. She rolled her eyes at her friends, knowing that yet another bloke would try to chat her up the second she turned round, but Laurie's wide eyes and massive grin made her look instead of wriggle away.

Deep brown eyes and chiselled cheekbones danced in front of her eyes. So he had come over. Or perhaps he'd made his way across the bar trying it on with every girl before deciding to try his luck with her...

He leaned close, his breath hot against her ear as he shouted to be heard over the thumping music. 'I'm Diego.'

'I know, you told me earlier.'

'I wasn't sure you'd remember.' His arm remained on her waist, his fingers brushing the patch of bare skin between her skirt and crop top.

'Because you don't remember mine?' she challenged.

'I meet many people every day.' He tugged her tight to his chest. 'It is much harder for me to remember your name...' His grin widened. '*Belle.*'

Her heart dipped with an unexpected thrill. Perhaps she had made an impact and wasn't a last resort after all.

'You've finished working?' Belle tried to sound nonchalant despite a dizzying excitement ricocheting through her body.

'For tonight, *sí.*'

Belle caught Gem's raised eyebrow as Diego led her away from where she'd been dancing with her friends and ordered them a drink at the bar. She liked the assured confidence he exuded. The bartender finished making their drinks and Diego handed Belle a pornstar martini. She'd been on those all evening.

She looked at him in surprise. 'Now that is smooth.'

'I've been watching you.' He shrugged. 'I take notice.'

It could have sounded creepy, yet it was anything but. Actually, it was hot as hell. *He'd noticed her.* Belle tempered the heat rushing through her with a sip of the sweet yet tangy cocktail.

Diego found them seats at a free table at the edge of the bar where it was a little quieter. The view went past the palm trees to the bay, but she could still see Laurie and Gem dancing. They were fine and together, their drunken smiles suggesting they were having *the* best time, exactly as she was. She turned her full focus to Diego and the conversation flowed about his job and the places he suggested they should go on Ibiza. Belle talked about university and studying Business Management and Marketing, about how she, Gem and Laurie had been friends since they were little, and about the marketing job at an events company in London she'd be starting in September.

Diego swigged from his bottle of San Miguel. 'You have big dreams.'

'It's good to have something to work towards.' He was as easy on the eye as he was to talk to, not to mention focused and interested in her. Or at least he portrayed himself that way; perhaps this was all a ruse and he was biding his time before he went in for the kill – the bit of the night she was actually longing for. She turned her thoughts from Diego seducing her to the conversation. 'The truth is I feel utterly trapped in a small town where nothing happens and I know if I stay there my life will be boring and miserable. I went to university in Sheffield because I wanted to escape. Getting a job in London is the natural next step up. It's everything I want; the excitement and opportunities of a big city coupled with a dream career in events.'

'I went to London once with my family. We had a summer holiday in England when it rained every day. Our one and only holiday away from the Mediterranean.' The dimples in his stubbled cheeks deepened as he grinned. 'I was eleven or twelve, a difficult age to know the history of museums and old buildings, if you understand what I mean?'

'You mean you didn't appreciate those things.'

'Not one bit.' He laughed. 'I wanted beaches and to swim in the sea.'

'I imagine living on Ibiza is like a permanent holiday, apart from having to work.'

'Ah, but work is fun.' He winked.

'You like living here then?'

Diego shrugged. 'It is what I know.' He drifted a hand towards the bar filled with happy sun-kissed people, hands in the air as they danced, Gem and Laurie among them. 'And it is a good life.'

'I bet it is.' Belle sighed.

'My family have a restaurant in a village inland. Traditional with a very good reputation. Home cooked food made with love. Maybe one day I work there but I like this life. I like having fun while I'm young. I work hard but it is very different to being a waiter.'

'You mean you can flirt outrageously with every woman you meet.'

'I can do that working in a restaurant as well.' He flashed a sly grin. 'But I don't have my papa watching over me here.'

Belle matched his grin, her thoughts drifting to the kind of fun he was insinuating. 'You don't live with your parents then?'

'No, not in the summer season. I share with a few others. It's easier to be close to the bars and beaches to work these hours.'

'How do your parents manage running their restaurant without you?'

Diego tapped his chest, making Belle's eyes drop to his open shirt and the glimpse of his smooth, tanned pecs. 'I'm the youngest of six. They have much help.'

'Wow, that's a big family.'

'And always getting bigger,' he said. 'Two brothers are already married with children and my sister is getting married later this week.'

'She is? So a big celebration for your family.'

'She's my only sister so it is special.'

Belle whistled. 'Five boys and one girl. Your parents had their hands full.'

'Your family is not big?'

Belle shook her head. 'Nope, I'm an only child.'

'So you get all the attention.'

'Trust me, it can be suffocating – at least it is as an adult. They were too busy to pay much attention to me when I was growing up.'

'I had to fight for attention.'

'But I bet you had a lot more freedom than I did.'

'Maybe, but we grow up in different countries; it is probably different for different reasons.'

Belle snorted. 'How many times do you want to say different?'

'I like the word.' He laughed. 'I learn lots of English talking to women like you...'

Flirting with women like me, Belle thought. *No doubt seducing them too...*

'I like being the youngest. The baby of the family looked after and spoiled by my older brothers and sister.'

'Sounds like it has its perks.'

'Until my nieces and nephews came along, *sí*.' He slid his arm along the back of her chair, the brush of his fingers against her bare skin turning her stomach over in the nicest way possible. 'I'm no longer the youngest or, how you say in English... cute?'

'The cutest.' Belle's focus drifted across his face to the dimples half-hidden by dark stubble and his heartbeat pulsing in the hollow of his neck. She met his eyes. 'You're pretty damn cute to me.'

'You think so?' Diego said smoothly as he shifted closer. 'Because you are very beautiful.'

Their lips were tantalisingly close, the heat of his body just inches from hers. Then he closed the distance and kissed her. Everything else melted away until she was only vaguely aware of the people sitting at the tables next to them, of Laurie and Gem still dancing. Her whole being was consumed by Diego: the taste, the feel, the sensation of him, and the desire as their tongues clashed and their hands explored as far as they could in public.

God is he hot, Belle thought. And when he eventually said, 'Want to come back with me?' she didn't hesitate to reply, 'Yes.'

Belle briefly returned to her friends to let them know she was leaving and where she was going. Laurie hugged her tight and firmly said, 'Make sure you use protection.' She was always the sensible one, which made Belle smile. Gem made a crude gesture with her fingers and waved her away with a booming, 'Go get fucking laid!'

The easy conversation that had flowed at the bar ground to a halt during the short taxi ride to Diego's. It felt exciting and a little bit reckless to be going home with him even if her friends knew. With their hands entwined, heat pulsed through Belle. She was unable to even look at him without wanting to rip his clothes off.

They'd chosen Ibiza for its nightlife and hedonism, a place where they could forget about reality and soak up the sunshine, the beach vibes, the club nights, while making the most of being young and, in Belle's case, single. Real life would start soon enough with work, bills and worries, but there would be excitement and new opportunities too, even if there was no longer the safety net of living at home or with her university friends, plus she'd be a long way from Laurie and Gem. Next month everything would change, but right now there was nothing she needed to think about besides being with Diego and having a good time.

The taxi driver dropped them off outside a non-descript white building somewhere towards the outskirts of San Antonio. Chatter drifted into the night along with the beat of dance music. With his hand in hers, Diego led her inside and along a brightly lit corridor that made her squint. He unlocked a door that led into another hallway with rooms off it. Belle had completely lost her bearings by the time Diego pushed open a door to a small stuffy bedroom.

Her skin prickled with heat. Diego switched on the air-conditioning unit above the bed.

'We will die otherwise,' he said, dropping the control on the bedside table and moving towards her.

Diego wasted little time; conversation and flirting was officially over. She hadn't been wearing much to begin with, but it was a relief to get rid of her clothes and a thrill to see Diego without his. Sex with him was hot and urgent, yet he was as attentive and focused as he'd been when they'd talked, leaving Belle breathless for all the right reasons.

* * *

Belle stirred in the darkness and oppressive heat. At some point the air-con must have switched off. Sweat slicked her skin and the air was heavy with perfume, sweat and sex. A brief stab of guilt that she wasn't waking up in the hotel room with Gem and Laurie was quickly replaced by joy when she turned her head and took in Diego asleep next to her. The sight of his broad shoulders and muscled back made her want to smooth her hands over his skin.

The room was private but compact, just a place to sleep or bring a girl back to... The box of condoms was still lying on the bedside table. A pack of twelve that had already been opened when Diego had reached for them last night. Belle tried to push away the thought about how many other women he'd brought back here. He was twenty-four and an incredibly good-looking promoter on Ibiza; sleeping with a different woman every week probably came with the territory.

Diego yawned, shuffled and rolled over. As he stretched, his stomach muscles tightened and the sheet slipped further down his body.

'*Buen dia*,' he said groggily, his eyes only half open.

'Morning,' Belle whispered, half afraid to disturb the magic of the night before. She didn't want a hangover and the reality of the morning after to erase their ease with each other or the intimacy that had felt so natural.

Diego reached for the air-con control and switched it on. 'See, I say we die with heat.'

Belle's whole body felt on fire, but that might have had more to do with feasting on the sight of a naked Diego than the sweat-inducing stuffiness of the room.

He stretched again and tucked his hands behind his head. 'What are you doing today?' he asked.

Keeping the sheet covering herself, Belle shifted on her side to look at him. 'You don't remember selling us tickets for a beach cruise to Cala Bass something?'

'Cala Bassa.' He grinned. 'I'm good at my job.'

'You made commission out of the three of us then slept with me,' Belle said with laughter in her voice. 'I'd call you a bloody genius.'

Diego shrugged. 'As I said, I'm good at what I do.'

'That's not the only thing you're good at.'

Diego's eyes widened in surprise. 'I can show you again how good I am...'

'Ooh, I'm not sure there's time before the boat trip,' she teased.

'I can be quick.' He scooted his hand beneath the sheet and teased his fingers up the inside of her thigh. 'Unless of course you need to get back to your friends right now?' His teasing fingers stopped. His lips were ridiculously close, his body hovering ready to slide onto hers.

'Well maybe that'll depend if I get to see you again tonight?' She hoped she was asking in a way that didn't sound utterly desperate because, God, did she want to see him again. It would be torture to only have one night with him. Plus one morning, depending on how the next few minutes played out.

'I work first, but later yes, I'll be somewhere along The Strip.' His fingers continued up the inside of her thigh. 'I'll give you my number.'

Belle's heart flipped and skipped as she pulled him down on top of her. 'Then yes, I have time now.'

12

_____

JUNE 2023, PRESENT DAY

Belle decided that phoning Diego straight away would be for the best, like ripping off a plaster. She knew if she left making contact for another day she'd start overthinking it, become more and more worried and work herself into a state. All it really should be was a professional conversation with a contact of Caleb's about a business deal with Ushuaïa to benefit Spirit's guests. *That's all it is,* she told herself firmly as she plumbed in his number. She held her breath as it rang.

The last time she'd seen him he'd been naked in bed. It had been the second night she'd spent with him, and the last one – not that she'd known it at the time. She'd promised Gem and Laurie that she would be back in time to join them for a day at Ocean Beach with its poolside parties, so she'd left Diego sleeping with a quick kiss rather than what she'd really wanted to do to him... Her cheeks flushed as she remembered her intentions.

Part of her hoped he wouldn't answer and she could leave a message; the other half knew it would be so much easier to get this over and done with.

'*Hola.*'

The heat in her cheeks rushed *everywhere*. 'Hi, is that Diego?'

'Yes.'

'I've been given your number by Caleb at Spirit and I believe Cara has been speaking to you?' She took a deep breath. 'I'm Belle, the new events manager.'

'Cara said you're taking over from her.'

Diego's voice was smooth and deep, the edges of his accent softened by the years of speaking English. Belle had imagined she'd immediately recognise his voice, but despite his tone being smooth and sexy it could have been any Spanish man on the end of the phone as he ran through what he'd been discussing with Cara. If her name had jogged his memory, he didn't let it show.

'The best thing is to come and visit and I can show you the VIP area and what we have to offer,' Diego said after catching her up on the plans. 'Are you free tomorrow?'

His suggestion took her by surprise. How many times over the years had she dreamed of seeing him again? Yet the reality left her heart thumping and palms sweating.

'Yes,' she heard herself say. 'That's a great idea.'

'Good, I'll see you at three tomorrow.'

* * *

Belle woke many times that night with fragmented dreams that faded the second she opened her eyes. She wasn't sure if she'd been dreaming about Diego or if they were a twisted take on her recurring nightmare. There'd been plenty of times when she had dreamed about him before; plenty of times when she'd fantasised about him, even an odd occasion or two when she'd fantasised about him while being with someone else. She dragged herself from bed feeling tired, flustered and confused.

Belle had never been to Ushuaïa, the famous outdoor high-end club and hotel in Playa d'en Bossa, but she'd heard plenty about it. She'd never been to Pacha either and had been desperately jealous when she'd found out that Gem had gone there after they'd become separated on their last night in Ibiza. While Belle had taken a rather worse for wear Laurie back to their hotel, Gem had managed to hook up with a guy who'd worked at Pacha and from her sketchy account had had the time of her life. Belle had been well aware of what she'd missed out on: one last night with Diego. She'd unintentionally lost Gem but had been there for Laurie. However much she'd wanted to see Diego, there was no way in hell she would have dumped her seriously drunk best friend for the chance of having sex with him again. Friendship came first. Always. The trade-off had been not getting the chance to say goodbye to him.

By the time she got there the open-air party at Ushuaïa had already kicked off with the opening DJ playing under the blazing sun as people started to arrive before Tiësto headlined later. Belle felt the magic in the air and the sense of just how awesome the space was as she was greeted and escorted to the VIP area. The dance floor on three sides of the pool was expansive and guests were already milling about. She could imagine the crush of people later in the day dancing in front of the huge iconic stage with Ushuaïa emblazoned in red above it. Belle's heart was in her mouth as she was led past a bar towards the raised VIP area with sections of pale-gold seating that faced the stage.

Belle forced herself to keep walking when she spotted Diego chatting on the phone with his foot casually resting on his knee. A torrent of confused feelings enveloped her as she took him in. His curls were cut short and his hairline had receded a little, but he was still hellishly handsome. His broad shoulders were encased in a snug T-shirt, and Belle was transported back to being twenty-one, young, carefree and passionate.

She reached him and his eyes met hers. He said goodbye to whoever he was talking to and put the phone down.

She thrust out her hand and gave her best I'm-not-really-bricking-it smile. 'Belle,' she said confidently.

Diego stood up, grasped her hand and shook it. His tall, muscular frame was still imposing and the smile he beamed at her was the same as the one that had first made her melt. As his eyes traced her face, his smile faltered. 'You look familiar. Have we met before?'

Belle's cheeks flushed and her heart skipped. Any lingering romantic notion of them locking eyes, remembering their passionate time together then running into each other's arms was instantly quashed.

'Um, yes, we have.' She breathed deeply, wondering if it was the cologne he was wearing or just the general smell of alcohol, chlorine and her own sunscreen that was making her feel woozy. 'I was on holiday here in 2013. You were promoting a club in San Antonio and sold us tickets, then I saw you again later that night...' She looked at him intently, willing him to remember. She really didn't want to have to spell it out. 'We, er, kinda hooked up at Ibiza Rocks; I was with my two friends... It was July, the week your sister got married if I remember correctly.'

Diego caught his breath and his eyes widened. 'I remember. Belle.' He repeated her name, the sound of it rolling smoothly over his tongue. His eyes slid from hers to her lips, zoning in as if remembering. He nodded and returned her gaze. 'We, er, had fun.'

'Yes, we did.' Belle's cheeks exploded with heat as the memory of a stark-naked Diego doing all kinds of delicious things to her came crashing into her head.

Diego frowned. 'But you're here now because you work for Caleb?'

'Yes, exactly. It's a complete coincidence.' *Despite me wishing for this very moment for years*, she thought wryly. 'I'm on the island because I took this job covering for Cara for the summer. This is the first time I've been back in ten years.'

'And you're here alone?' Diego asked smoothly. 'No, um, husband?'

Was he asking because he was interested in the possibility of rekindling something?

'There's no one else, just me, which is why I took the job out here. No ties.' She shrugged nonchalantly. At least she hoped it came across that way.

Diego sat back down and patted the space next to him. 'Let's have a drink and talk then.'

He took two bottles of Sprite from the ice bucket on the table and cracked them open. Sitting this close to him, Belle was a bundle of nerves, glad of the chilled drink which went some way to temper her internal heat. The sun beat down. A plane coming in to land added to the background noise of people chatting and the beat of dance music. At least their initial conversation was focused on the safe topic of how Diego had come to work at Ushuaïa and the deal that Cara had been working on. Yet Belle's focus kept shifting to the past and the stark differences between then and now: sober instead of drunk; fully clothed instead of naked; in their thirties instead of twenties; strangers instead of lovers.

Belle felt suddenly conscious about having a drink with him, their history and intimacy as yet un-talked about. She had no clue what he was thinking or how much he even remembered. Was she only vaguely recognisable, just one of the many women he'd slept with? The Ibiza holiday had made a hell of an impact on her, most of it to do with him. He'd been a huge flirt then and she wondered if he'd changed at all.

When the conversation stalled, she decided to ask. 'What about you then?' She clutched the bottle and crossed her legs, conscious of what little space there was between them. Was her choice of skirt that only reached the middle of her thighs a good idea or not? 'Are you married?' she asked, even though she already knew the answer.

She caught his glimmering smile, a reminder of the way he'd once flirted with her. 'No wife. No one permanent.' *Some things obviously haven't changed*, Belle thought. 'I still work unsociable hours; it's a lifestyle that's never worked well with a relationship.'

She'd held a sensible mainly nine-to-five job with a few evening and weekend events thrown in, yet she hadn't managed to hold onto a permanent relationship either. Although she sensed he was perfectly content with his bachelorhood. She swigged her drink and avoided meeting his eyes. A strong sense that she was looking at the one who'd got away washed over her.

'I imagine it's not an easy way of life to share with someone.' Or was it more to do with his desire for freedom to flit from one woman to another...

'I like what I do; I always have done,' he said with an honest shrug. 'You've always wanted to do this kind of events work?'

And there it was, the confirmation that he didn't remember her, at least not what they'd talked about. But then, just because she remembered everything about their time together, why would he ten years on? They were strangers making small talk yet Belle felt as if she knew him. She remembered he had a faded scar on his knee from tumbling from a wall when he was a boy; she knew he had a small tattoo of a bird on his ribcage because she'd run her fingers along it and had kissed it on her way down to—

She stopped that train of thought right there. Their conversation had stalled again and she was wondering if she'd outstayed her welcome when Diego spoke.

'So,' he said, filling the silence. 'Are you still friends with Gem and er...'

'Laurie.' Belle nodded, relieved that he'd found something for them to chat about. 'We're still friends although we all live miles away from each other now. So, um, what about you? Do you just know Caleb through work?' She nearly said she'd seen the two of them in a photo together but stopped herself in time; she wasn't going to admit she'd been trawling through his Facebook profile.

'I do sometimes work with Caleb, but I've known him for years. He's my brother-in-law.' His eyes shifted from hers, glassing over as he stared towards the pool. The party atmosphere was in full swing with driving beats drifting into the sun-tinged air, and skimpily clad dancers on the podiums. 'I mean, he was, sort of still is, depending how you look at it. My sister died.'

13

'Your sister was Caleb's wife?'

Belle was bewildered by the connection. The sister of the man she'd fallen for all those years ago had been married to the man she was now working for. She didn't know what to say or think until she clocked the sorrow in Diego's eyes. 'I'm so sorry you lost her.'

'Thank you. But you didn't know?' He folded his arms across his chest. 'Of course you didn't; he rarely talks about her with anyone apart from Cara or Mama.'

'He's my boss so it's not really surprising that he hasn't.' Although when Belle thought back to Sunday and his comment about changing his life in a heartbeat if he could, it now made perfect and heart-breaking sense.

'So the wedding you went to when I was here, that was your sister and Caleb's?'

Diego nodded, pain washing across his face.

She remembered he was from a big family but he'd only had one sister; she couldn't even begin to comprehend how devastating that would be. Their second and last night together had been the day before the wedding. She remembered snatches of what he'd told her about how he'd been avoiding going home because his mum was in full mother-of-the-bride mode.

'Do you talk about her?' Belle asked softly, aware of the serious tone of their conversation as electronic beats dipped and spiralled.

'I do now but it took me a long time to even be able to look at a picture of her without breaking down.' Diego was staring ahead, focusing on the stage as if needing to distract himself, his tension and upset noticeable. 'She was the heart of our family and losing her broke us all.' He downed the remainder of his drink and stood up. 'If you have everything to get started your end, I should get on.'

His tone and demeanour had changed but she understood it was from grief. Also, she'd reappeared unexpectedly so there was every chance he was feeling uncomfortable too.

'Just call me if you need anything, and when things are in place with your guests let me know.'

Diego walked her out. The uplifting beat and the sun shimmering on the surface of the pool were at odds with what they'd just talked about as more and more people streamed in ready to party throughout the afternoon and into the evening. As they shook hands goodbye, all the what-ifs she'd dreamed about collided with a cold hard reality.

Belle didn't drive off straight away. The steering wheel was hot as she rested her hands against it and stared at the oversized flowers decorating the side of Ushuaïa Tower with its red hummingbird emblem. The job in Ibiza had come along at just the right time, her decision to apply impulsive, and she hadn't really known what she was hoping to get out of it beyond escaping an awkward situation back home. Seeing Diego had been unexpected because she hadn't intended to seek him out. But now she had seen him, she felt strangely empty. He was familiar yet a stranger. Her memories were clouded by drunkenness and the passing of time, yet moments of clarity broke through like rays of sunlight through a storm cloud: that adorably cheeky smile, the intensity of his dark brooding eyes and the way he still sat with one leg resting on the other.

What had she hoped for? A fairy-tale ending? For them to lock eyes and all those feelings that had been rumbling for a decade to come crashing back, his matching hers as he'd swept her into his arms? Real life was no fairy tale. As easily as you could grasp happiness, it could be snatched away again. What upset her most was that there'd been no instantaneous spark, and she was no longer sure about her own feelings.

Belle started the engine and drove away from Ushuaïa along the palm-tree-lined road. The other thing bothering her was she now knew something about Caleb that he'd obviously not been ready or willing to talk about. But that wasn't all she'd taken from talking to Diego. He'd remembered Gem's name. Belle frowned; he'd met her, what, once or twice? She didn't remember them even talking. But then as a confident, self-assured twenty-one-year-old, Gem had always been the one to capture people's attention; her outgoing personality was matched by a killer figure and outfits that accentuated her curves. But back then Belle had been the only single one, even if Gem had strayed a fair bit; Belle had flirted and Diego had reciprocated. And yet despite Belle having to remind him who she was, he'd clearly remembered Gem.

14

JULY 2013, TEN YEARS AGO

Laurie looked as if she'd been spun in a washing machine on a fast spin then spat back out. Her cheeks had lost all colour and her face was wet from Belle's attempt to wash the vomit from around her mouth, chin and off her clothes. She thought it highly unlikely that Laurie's sparkly sequinned top could be saved.

Belle had hoped that Laurie would feel a little better after being sick, but by the time she'd managed to haul her out of the toilets, she was still ashen and wobbly on her feet. With no idea of the time or how long they'd been gone for, all Belle was focused on was being responsible for Laurie. And finding Gem.

Leaving Laurie propped against the wall outside the toilets, Belle cursed as she made her way through the club to where she'd left Gem and her phone. The pounding beat thrummed to her core, the heat, the noise and the crush of bodies making her disorientated.

Other people were standing around the table, her phone was missing and Gem was nowhere to be seen.

Belle's heart hammered as she surveyed the writhing mass of clubbers on the main dance floor. Strobe lighting made their movements jagged; flashes of bare skin, hands in the air, a euphoric slow-motion wave of dancers that Belle felt detached from. Her own senses were compromised, as if she wasn't quite present. Without her phone and with Laurie's out of battery, she felt helpless and had no way of contacting Gem. Or Diego. God, Diego. Belle wanted to scream at Laurie for over-dosing on vodka and at Gem for being stupid enough to disappear.

The chances of stumbling across Diego between here and the exit were slim, but proved to be zero by the time Belle made it outside with Laurie and into a taxi. If she was in Gem's shoes and had found herself on her own, she reasoned she'd have gone back to the hotel to wait for them.

No such luck. Their room was as empty as they'd left it, with clothes scattered across the beds and used wine glasses cluttering the coffee table.

Shit.

Belle manoeuvred Laurie onto her bed and tugged various tops and dresses out from under her and dumped them on the chair. She plugged Laurie's phone in to charge and somehow managed to wiggle the vomit-stained sequinned top off her so she was just in her bra and skirt.

'If you need to be sick again, try to be sick on the floor,' Belle said with a sigh.

Laurie murmured something incoherent. She raised her hand as if to protest, then let it crash back down on the bed with a thump. Her eyes were barely open, dribble stained her chin and she looked ashen. Belle put her in the recovery position just in case.

Between the club and the hotel, Belle had sobered up, yet all that did was bring a mixture of worry about where the hell Gem had got to and annoyance that her night had ended like this. With her head in her hands, she sat on the end of her bed and took deep breaths, trying to force down the rising tears, but all she managed to do was breathe in the sickly combination of cheap wine and the smell of sick that had remained lodged in her nose.

Laurie was passed out and Gem was missing, yet all Belle could think about was Diego and what *she* was missing out on with him. Without her phone she couldn't even message him to explain why she hadn't met up with him. And when Laurie's phone was charged she didn't even know his surname to be able to look him up or to message him on Facebook. What the hell would he think? That she didn't want to see him? It was their last night in Ibiza, her last chance to spend time with him, to feel his hands on her, to kiss him, to do all the delicious things they'd done to each other the two nights they'd spent together so far. Bloody Laurie. What the hell had she been thinking snorting vodka? And although she was safe now, and would hopefully sleep it off before having to deal with the worst hangover of her life while travelling home, Belle couldn't leave her alone, not even for one last night with Diego. She'd never forgive herself if something happened.

She swapped the stale air inside their room for the balcony. It wasn't the greatest of views, just a few straggly palm trees, the road and another hotel opposite, but it was summer in Ibiza, the sea air was sultry and she felt better for it as she sat on one of the white plastic chairs and rested her bare feet on the balcony railings.

It was gone three in the morning, but with San Antonio's Strip within walking distance, the air was still alive with the beat of dance music, and lights shone from the surrounding hotels. During the two days since she'd last seen him, Belle's head had been filled with thoughts of Diego. She wondered how his sister's wedding had gone and how ridiculously handsome he must have looked in his suit. She'd so wanted to see a picture of him in it. He was the proud younger brother and the way he'd talked about his sister had left Belle with a pang of jealousy that they had such a close relationship. His obvious love for his sister and his excitement for her getting married had also made her sad to have missed out on all of that; sibling rivalry, a companion growing up, the chance of becoming an aunt. Diego may have made a quip about no longer being the youngest, but his love for his family shone through when he'd talked about his parents, his siblings and his nieces and nephews. Unless she was home, it was unusual for Belle to speak to her parents more than once a month, and get togethers were usually reserved for Christmas when she couldn't wait to get back to university.

Diego had talked about his sister marrying the love of her life and Belle hadn't been able to tell if he was simply happy for her or if there was a note of jealousy too, that she had something he had yet to find. Belle sighed, lifted her feet off the railing and breathed in the summer heat, wanting to commit to memory the intoxicating feeling of freedom and love she'd experienced this week. Marriage and kids were something that felt way in the future, and yet her brief time with Diego had meant everything.

Belle returned inside to check on Laurie and her phone. One bar of juice. And a missed call from Gem. She unplugged it and called her back. It rang and rang then went to answerphone.

'Yo! This is Gem. Leave a message – you know the drill!'

Beep.

'Hey, Gem. Are you okay? Where are you? We're back at the hotel; Laurie's been majorly sick. I went back to find you and you weren't there. I didn't know what to do but I had to look after Laurie. Call me back, yeah?'

* * *

At some point Belle must have fallen asleep, exhausted. She woke with a start, squinting at the sunshine sliding through the gap in the blinds. It felt as if someone was drumming against the inside of her head. She groaned and rolled over, wanting nothing more than to go back to sleep, but her eyes fell on Laurie in the next bed, one arm lolling off the side and something that looked suspiciously like sick on her chin.

Belle launched herself out of bed, immediately regretting it as her head protested and her stomach lurched.

'Laurie? Are you okay?' Belle put a hand on Laurie's back and breathed easy once she felt the rise and fall of her chest. She still looked deathly pale and had been sick again on the tiled floor. Belle retched then remembered the second problem from the night before. She spun round, once again regretting the too-fast movement; apart from an assortment of clothes piled on top, Gem's bed was still empty.

Belle scooped up Laurie's phone. Still nothing from Gem. She clicked on her name, her heart hammering her chest as it rang and rang then went to answerphone. With fear coursing through her, she left a message: 'Where the hell are you, Gem? Please tell me you've hooked up with some guy. I've been worried sick. If I don't hear from you in the next ten minutes I'm going to ask reception to contact the police.'

By the time she'd got a handful of toilet paper to clean the sick off the tiled floor, Laurie's phone pinged.

> Just listened to your messages, so sorry, I'm fine.
> Will be back soon xx

Finally, Gem. Belle's thumping heart eased as she sent a reply.

> Oh my God I can't even begin to tell you how
> relieved I am! X

After cleaning the floor as best she could, Belle attempted to wash away the smell and revive herself with a shower. She'd only just wrapped a towel around her middle when Laurie's phone rang.

Gem.

Belle snatched it up.

'Oh my God Gem, are you okay?'

'Yeah, I'm fine, don't worry,' she said wearily. 'Sorry for not messaging you before this morning.'

'Where the hell did you get to last night?'

'I could say the same about you.'

'I left my phone on the table, Laurie's battery had died; I couldn't get hold of you. I'm sorry.'

'It's okay, shit happens. And I have your phone.' A heartbeat of a pause. 'I'm on my way back.'

'From where? Where have you been all night?'

There was another pause followed by a muffled sound as if Gem was covering the phone. 'Long story, but I sort of hooked up with someone who worked at Pacha and I ended up back at his.'

'Well, I'm glad you're okay. A lot better than Laurie will be when she eventually wakes up. I'll start packing. See you when you get back.'

Belle should have felt relieved that Gem had got laid rather than injured, abducted or worse, yet jealousy consumed her. While Gem had been having a good time, she'd missed out on her last chance with Diego.

15

JUNE 2023, PRESENT DAY

On the way back from meeting Diego at Ushuaïa, Belle stopped at Serenity to ensure everything was ready for the first outdoor movie night before she returned to Spirit. She felt as troubled by what Diego had said as by how she felt seeing him ten years on. And, knowing that Caleb would be at Spirit, she was trying her best to avoid him, confused by all the things she'd learned that morning.

The sandy terrace above the path to the beach had been cleared of tables and chairs and the beanbag loungers had been brought out, spaced out in pairs with low wooden tables dividing the rows. It would be utterly romantic later with the bulb lights strung between the trees glowing, candles flickering in the frosted glass holders on the tables and *La La Land* playing on a big screen, but right that minute Belle felt completely alone, a feeling that would often rear its head when she was feeling low or worthless. When anything became emotionally tricky, her default setting was to run away.

She found a quiet corner in Serenity's bar to work. With the summer season starting in earnest there was lots to do. There were one or two private events a week at Spirit and three weddings at

Serenity over the summer, the first one taking place in just under two weeks' time. Plus there were the general marketing and promotional opportunities Cara had been working on. Ushuaïa could now be added to the list, and with Diego as the contact perhaps this morning wouldn't be the last she saw of him. She still didn't understand how that made her feel. She'd expected fireworks to go off in her stomach at seeing him again – that would have been clearcut. Coming face to face with him had knocked her sideways and instead of feeling euphoric she was left confused and uncertain. She'd had enough of second guessing everything to do with her heart.

Even with her uncertainty, being on Ibiza had allowed her the headspace to focus on what mattered and to make time for things that she was always too busy for or didn't have the option of back home: a leisurely breakfast, daily yoga, a stroll on the beach, a swim in the sea or even escaping somewhere further afield. Work had taken over in London, while here the work/life balance was encouraged because Caleb had made it a priority. The lifestyle was a dream. It made her wonder how she would feel about returning to normal life at the end of October.

After liaising with and co-ordinating the staff, then taking photos of the set-up to use on Serenity's socials, Belle relocated to the stone wall that ran along the side of the restaurant and overlooked the terrace set up for the movie night. It was the perfect spot to keep an eye on things.

She was just posting a photo on Serenity's Instagram feed when a shadow fell across her.

'This looks wonderful.'

Belle looked up at Caleb, his tanned face catching the golden light of dusk. He climbed over the wall and sat next to her, looking effortlessly cool and relaxed in snug jeans and a short-sleeved cream shirt. The top couple of buttons were undone, revealing a smooth tanned chest and the edge of a dragon tattoo that snaked up to his neck.

Belle shifted her attention back to the terrace where the honeyed light from dozens of lanterns flickered on the tables between the empty beanbag loungers. This was Belle's favourite time of the day, the sun a warm caress on her skin as the sea danced with pearly pink, iridescent mauve and a touch of glittering gold.

Accompanied by the sound of diners and the swoosh of the sea, the soft light was magical, the air tangy with zesty lemon and grilling seafood – and Caleb's cologne which was zingier and fresher than Diego's.

Belle's unease had abated over the course of the day but it returned with Caleb's presence.

'I've been taking photos,' she said to cover her discomfort. 'I'll take some more once it's dark and the guests start arriving.'

'See, the social media queen.' He moved closer as if he was going to knock his shoulder against hers, but stopped short, a breath of space between them. 'I'll send them to Cara; she'll be thrilled with what you've done here. I heard you met with Diego. Did you sort everything out?'

It took a moment for her to understand that he was talking about the Ushuaïa deal for Serenity's guests and not the state of her and Diego's non-existent relationship.

'Yes, everything's in hand,' she said, knowing this was the conversation she'd been trying to avoid because she was unsure how much to share. 'For such a big club it's a great deal for our guests. I just didn't realise the connection you had with Diego being your, um...' She couldn't bring herself to say brother-in-law, not after what she'd learned. She sensed him tense next to her. 'I'm so sorry about your wife.'

Caleb clasped his hands in his lap and ran his thumb over his wedding ring. 'I should have said something before, but I still find it hard to talk about her.'

'There's no reason you should have shared anything personal with me,' Belle said softly. 'I never expected you to and I didn't bring up what Diego said for you to talk about it. I just wanted you to know that I know.'

'How did it come up in conversation?' Caleb frowned. 'He's not usually that talkative, particularly about personal stuff.'

'Oh, really?' That certainly wasn't Belle's memory of him; he'd been chatty and easy to talk to, happily sharing his innermost thoughts, but it wasn't surprising considering the changes in his life since she'd last seen him. 'He didn't go into detail; I can't even remember how we got onto the topic.'

There was no reason to say anything to Caleb about her relationship with Diego and yet it felt wrong to withhold the truth, but not as uncomfortable as blurting out, 'Oh by the way, I had two incredible nights with your brother-in-law and have been fantasising about him ever since.' That would be a ridiculous thing to admit, not to mention inappropriate and unprofessional. When she said it to herself like that she saw the truth in it. Her fantasies about Diego were akin to dreaming about having sex with a celebrity. They were a fantasy, and she was only now beginning to realise the depth of her fixation.

With darkness, the first guests arrived and were shown to their seats. While more people drifted in, a couple of waiters delivered popcorn and glasses of Cava. Only a smudge of blush remained low on the horizon and the screen at the far end of the terrace was shrouded in darkness. Anticipation prickled up Belle's arms.

'A movie night was Cara's idea,' Caleb said as the beanbag loungers began to fill up, 'but having an outdoor cinema of my own has been my dream since I was a kid. As well as football, going to the cinema was my favourite thing to do. I loved the escapism and could forget about real life for a while. My gran gave me pocket money and I'd save up to buy a ticket. My older cousin worked at a cinema and used to sneak me into films I was too young for, because I was into sci-fi and fantasy, anything with things blowing up, dragons, zombies or horror that got my adrenalin pumping.'

'So nothing quite as romantic as we're showing tonight.'

'No, but this' – he opened his arms wide – 'is perfect. I don't think *Alien* would go down quite so well.' He gave her a wry smile.

'Definitely not. Blood and guts and being scared shitless isn't conducive to romance.'

'Not for tonight but actually I would argue it is. As a teen I took complete advantage of watching a scary movie with a girl and then, ahem, "comforting" her when she got scared. But here at Serenity, we're all about romance, dreams and making memories.'

'You're certainly doing that tonight.'

'*We're* doing that.'

It was generous of him to include her when all the hard work had already been done; she'd simply put what Cara had organised in place.

'I think Cara should take most of the credit,' she said.

The majority of the beanbags were filled now and glasses of Cava glinted in the candlelight. The smell of freshly made buttery popcorn sweetened the air.

'Cara should take credit for a lot of things.' Caleb leaned forward and rested his elbows on his knees. 'She came into my life a couple of years before I lost Paloma, and we may not have been friends for long but she knew what to say – or more importantly what not to say. When you suffer a loss like that you discover who your real friends are. Cara was right up there, supportive, selfless, someone I could lean on and talk to. She was my rock. Paloma's family as well, but they were going through hell too and dealing with their own grief.'

'It sounds like she turned up at exactly the right time.'

'It worked both ways.' Caleb turned to look at her. 'She'd just got out of an abusive relationship and had fled Australia, intending to bum her way round Europe. She started on Ibiza, working for me for the summer season and never left. Although I was close to Paloma's family and still am, the little there is of my own family is back in the UK. Cara's folks are all the way in Oz. We found each other.'

The breeze rolling off the sea was fresh, rustling through the palms and pine trees lining the sides of the terrace. Belle hoped the guests snuggled in their beanbag loungers would be warm enough, but she made a mental note to source throws for the cooler evenings.

'Did you always think of Cara like a sister?'

'We both like women so there was never any attraction to confuse our friendship; plus she's a little younger than me and had been through hell with a manipulative partner. While she helped me navigate my grief, I did my best to help her heal. I'm an only child but I imagine the love I felt and the way I wanted to protect her would have been much the same as if we were family.' Caleb sat upright and shifted on the stone wall so he was facing her, a glimmer of a smile gracing his lips. 'Did you think Cara and I were together?'

'I had wondered but only because you talk about her with love. Now I understand.'

'Friendship is all I've wanted since Paloma died.' Caleb looked thoughtful for a moment. 'I put my bachelor days behind me when I met her and even after I lost her I didn't want to go back to who I was. She changed me for the better and that's something I can hold onto always.'

His openness floored her. His outlook was refreshing. To have loved someone so deeply and yet be able to hold on to the good parts of their relationship and not the anger or bitterness he must have felt at losing her so young was moving and admirable.

'There's been no one since?' Belle asked quietly.

'I had my heart broken in the cruellest way; I never want to risk that kind of pain again.'

'Even if it means you'll always be alone?'

'Being on your own isn't the worst thing in the world, not if it's your choice.'

But it wasn't your choice, Belle thought. The untimely death of his wife had instigated him being alone. Maybe it was self-preservation, or like her, the fear of committing to someone without being consumed by love. Or how she imagined being truly in love would feel.

'Looks like we have a full house.' Caleb stood and gestured to where the last group of four friends were being led to their seats. 'Are you staying to watch?'

'Yes, I want to make sure everything runs smoothly.' Belle looked up at him. 'Are you? Staying, I mean.'

'Next time. I have a few things to do back at Spirit. I'll see you tomorrow.'

Belle watched Caleb walk away with his hands stuffed in his pockets until he was out of sight. In so many ways he led a wonderful life that people would envy, yet it was laced with sorrow. Her eyes drifted back to the terrace. She picked out the couples snuggled together on their beanbag loungers, their hands entwined, some whispering together, others toasting each other with their glasses of Cava. The emptiness Belle felt was acute. The scene before her was the epitome of romance yet it seemed unattainable. Was she jealous of the happy couples below? Absolutely. Did she want them to have the most incredible and memorable evening? Without a doubt. Perhaps she shared some similarities with Caleb, not willing to give her heart to someone for fear of it being broken, just for a different reason. She was definitely scared of something going wrong and of no one ever living up to her idea of the perfect man she'd concocted for herself.

As darkness and stars took over and *La La Land* started playing, Belle considered if it was actually self-preservation that had stopped Caleb from staying, because of course not facing painful emotions was the easier option, but it was a path she was no longer willing to take.

16

Belle sensed something had changed between her and Caleb since they'd chatted together before the outdoor movie; there was a new openness, certainly on his part. He'd always been relaxed and friendly, but he'd been surprisingly honest and had revealed a vulnerability that had moved her and also made her regret that she was withholding something from him when she knew of his relationship with Diego and he knew nothing about hers.

Friday came round, a late night in Ibiza with a DJ playing at Spirit, but 30 June was a date that was ringed in her diary with Laurie and a heart written next to it. After weeks of fertility treatment with injections, blood tests and scans, today was what Laurie had described as hell, the end of the two-week wait when she would find out if all the money, emotion, hope and worry they'd poured into the treatment would be successful or not. The wondering and torment of waiting to pee on a stick and discover if the future they envisaged would come true or not was happening today. It would also be the deciding factor as to whether she'd be coming out to Ibiza next month, and that left Belle torn, desperately wanting a positive outcome for her friend while selfishly thinking how disappointed she'd be if their holiday together didn't happen when flights had already been booked and their accommodation sorted.

Belle had been thinking about Laurie all day, frequently checking her phone to see if she'd left a message. When her phone did eventually ring and Laurie's name appeared, Belle's heart slammed into her ribs. Maybe she was phoning late because she'd gone out with Ade to celebrate, or perhaps she'd put off phoning because the result hadn't been what they'd wanted.

'Hi, Laurie.' Belle tried to sound natural but her voice was tight and her insides were twisted with anxiety as she curled up on the sofa in Cara's apartment.

'It was negative.' Laurie's tone was flat and neutral as if she'd already cried out all her disappointment and sadness.

'Oh Laurie, I'm so sorry.' What else could she say? Nothing would make the situation better. 'I wish I was there to give you a hug.'

'I wish you were here too. More than ever.'

A lump caught in Belle's throat. While Belle's move to London had got off to a traumatic start and Gem had ended up stuck and frustrated in Norfolk, it had been Laurie who'd silently struggled after her move to Manchester with Ade for his job. Belle loved city living and Gem would have moved to Manchester or London in a heartbeat, but Laurie was not a big-city type of person. The cracks showed when Laurie talked about Ade's friends rather than hers, as if she hadn't managed to make any of her own. They needed two incomes to pay rent and bills so she'd been forced to take a fill-in data-entry job at a recruitment company while she continued to look for her ideal job in a bookshop or theatre or arts-based environment. The trouble was, jobs like that didn't pay well, so eventually Laurie had given up looking. Gem always made snide remarks about how lucky Laurie was but she never saw how dissatisfied she was or how much she'd given up to support Ade. But then Gem made out that her life was far happier and more perfect than it actually was, so why would she see past someone else's veneer? They were all guilty of misleading each other by hiding their true emotions and feelings.

'I knew our first IVF cycle hadn't worked,' Laurie said, bringing Belle back to the present, 'but this time I was certain it had. I felt different and yet still nothing. It's like my body's playing tricks with me. Maybe getting my hopes up was a mistake. I didn't believe we'd get lucky on the first go and that proved to be right. I don't know why I went into this one with a more positive attitude, but I did. I'm massively regretting that now.'

'Don't let go of that positivity. I remember you telling me about a couple of women who didn't even manage to have an egg fertilised. So getting this far twice is something. Just think how long it takes for some women who don't have any fertility issues to get pregnant—'

'Unless of course you're Gem,' Laurie said bitterly.

'What I'm trying to say – badly – is this outcome doesn't mean there's no chance.' Belle paused. 'Will you try again?'

'I think we'll manage one more round, yes.'

Belle stopped herself from saying 'third time lucky' because that was far from helpful when she knew there were no guarantees, and what element of luck there was didn't mean it would go their way however many times they tried.

'We're going to take a break for a bit; we've done two cycles practically back-to-back and that's been tough. Honestly, the hormones have played havoc with me and I just need some normality. A bit of time when I'm not continuously holding out hope for something.'

'What you need is a holiday.'

'Lucky I've got one lined up then,' Laurie said with a hint of a smile in her voice. 'Some time away is definitely needed; the stress we've put ourselves under...'

Did they need time away from each other? Belle was trying to read between the lines, sensing that Laurie was holding something back.

'Ade could do with getting away too but he's thrown himself into work, which always tends to be his coping mechanism. I don't have that option with my job because it's the last place I want to be.'

Yes, there was definitely underlying tension, although Belle would have been more surprised if they weren't struggling in some way. Yet Laurie and Ade were the strongest couple she knew, happily together since they were nineteen. If they didn't make it, what hope did anyone else have? What hope did she have of being in a relationship as perfect as theirs? On the outside. That's what it always came down to; however perfect things appeared, no one really knew what anyone else was going through.

'Well,' Laurie said with a sigh. 'There's nothing to stop me coming to Ibiza any longer. If there's a silver lining to any of this then it's getting to see you.'

Laurie's words filled Belle with joy, the flip side being yet more disappointment for her friend. She missed Laurie. Spending time together would help rekindle their friendship and bring them closer.

'Have you told Gem yet?' Belle asked.

'No.' Belle imagined her scrunching her button nose. 'I'm not sure she'll say the right thing and I don't want to get upset. I'm already upset but I don't want to be upset *at her*. I'll message her tomorrow.'

That was the friendship that really needed fixing. All three of them had drifted away from each other and Belle missed the close-ness they once had. She didn't know if time together in Ibiza would help but at least it would be a start. And she needed to be a better friend, one who wasn't so tied up in her own worries that she failed to see what was going on in her friends' lives. Or worse, saw their troubles but chose to ignore them because it was easier. She needed to ask the difficult questions and give her support unconditionally.

'I can talk to Gem first if you'd like?' Belle suggested. 'It's about time I gave her a call.'

'Really? Would you mind?'

'Of course not.'

Laurie's relief at not having to break her sad news to Gem was palpable as they said goodbye. Having children wasn't something that Belle had spent much time thinking about; she needed to find love and be in a steady committed relationship before even thinking along those lines, but having a family was something Laurie had wanted for years.

Belle pocketed her keys, grabbed her phone and headed out to call Gem. She liked the vibe of the beach at night with the sound of the surf rushing onto the sand mixing with the chatter and upbeat music drifting from Spirit's beachside restaurant and bars. The tables were packed and people were still by the pool which glowed aqua amid the warm lamplight and flickering candles.

How hard was it to phone someone she'd been friends with since they were children? She strolled away from Spirit down the beach towards where the Río de Santa Eulalia met the sea and clicked on Gem's name before she could change her mind. She should have got the kids to bed by now; if she wanted to chat, she'd answer.

'Hey, stranger.'

Belle bit back a retort that Gem was just as guilty for letting weeks go by since they'd last talked. 'Hey, I've just spoken to Laurie; she did a pregnancy test earlier today.'

'Ah shit,' Gem said. 'What was the outcome?'

'It was negative; she's understandably gutted.'

'I bet she is. I'd totally forgotten it'd be round about now.'

'She didn't expect you to remember.' Belle kicked off her shoes and enjoyed the feel of the sand between her toes as she wandered back towards Spirit.

'But of course you did.'

'Yes, I did,' Belle said through gritted teeth. 'But perhaps it's better that I was the one she spoke to – less potential for conflict when that's the last thing she needs at the moment.'

'Yeah, because my life's so perfect. She's not the only one going through shit.'

'She doesn't think she is.' Belle sat down on the sand on the quiet stretch between Spirit and the beach bar by the river. 'But unless you talk to us and actually tell us what's going on, how are we ever going to know any different?'

'Dan's left me.'

Belle's heart dropped into her stomach. She wasn't expecting that. 'Oh shit, Gem. When did this happen?'

'Weeks ago.'

Belle shook her head. 'That's why he wasn't at the wedding? Why the hell didn't you tell us then?'

'It was my one night to myself; I didn't want to ruin it with tears, although we managed plenty of that without me unloading my sob story as well.' There was a hint of humour in her tone, the Gem of old filtering through. 'We're still figuring stuff out with the house, the kids. It was supposed to be a trial separation but considering he's moved in with the woman he was cheating with, it seems pretty fucking over to me.'

'Oh my goodness Gem, I'm so sorry.'

'I really don't need your pity.'

'Me being concerned that you're going through something like this is not pity.'

'Yeah, well, it's not like this will surprise you when it's been a long time coming.'

Belle faltered, not knowing how to reply, because wasn't that the truth? Gem and Dan should have split up years ago. It had been Gem's intention to after their Ibiza holiday when she'd behaved like she was single, which would have been fine if she actually had been. Her heart hadn't been in the relationship, and the only reason she'd stayed with him was because she'd found out she was pregnant. They'd remained together because their circumstances had changed with a baby neither of them had planned.

'What a state, eh?' Gem broke through Belle's silence. 'I'm home alone with a nine- and four-year-old because I've been dumped by their dad; Laurie's crying her eyes out because she can't get pregnant even with bloody help, and you're off in Ibiza chasing fuck knows what.'

Belle sucked in a sharp breath of salt-tinged air. 'I suggest you don't answer if Laurie calls you tomorrow. If you need to scream and vent and blame everyone else for your problems, give me an earful, not Laurie.'

'Yeah, yeah, I get it, Laurie's fragile while I'm ballsy and can take all the shit thrown at me.'

'That's not what I'm saying at all, Gem.' Belle's eyes blurred as she watched the tips of the waves break, foam and bubble. 'I hate that you're so sad. I hate that every time I've spoken to you recently you've been angry and scared. I just wish you had some of Laurie's vulnerability so you could open up and share your feelings instead of bottling everything up, putting on a brave face and blustering through by attacking everyone else.'

'Yeah well, I'm definitely not like Laurie. And do me a favour when you next speak to her, please don't say anything about me and Dan.'

'Oh for goodness' sake, Gem. Why the hell not?'

'Because I'm a fucking failure and she has the perfect relationship.'

'And you don't want to tell her because, what? You think she'll judge you? Look down on you? She is the kindest and most supportive friend – she'll 100 per cent be in your corner, Gem.'

'Maybe, but I'll tell her in my own good time. Please promise me you won't say anything.'

'Fine, I won't.'

Gem let out a long, shuddery breath. 'Everything's got to me today.' The anger that had been coating her words dispersed. 'I noticed this morning that Dan had updated his Facebook profile to "in a relationship" with *her*. It's nothing, a meaningless status when we've been broken up for weeks. But it just upset me. It suddenly feels very real.'

'Oh Gem, you need to go easy on yourself. You have two kids together. It's bound to be hard and confusing. But I'm glad you felt like you could confide in me.' Belle scraped her fingers through the cool grains of sand. 'By the way, the flowers you sent Laurie the other week after her embryo transfer was a really thoughtful gesture. You don't have to speak to her to show you care.'

'I know.' Gem sighed. 'I'm sorry. Thank you for phoning. I don't mean to snap and rage all the flipping time. And I'm gutted for Laurie, I really am. I'll message her now.'

After saying goodbye to Gem, Belle remained on the beach for a while. Both of her friends' upset had got to her, their disappointments out of kilter with how happy she should be sitting on a beach in Ibiza. The salty breeze dried her tears and left her cheeks feeling tight. She wrapped her arms around her legs and watched the moonlight dance on the inky sea where it rippled all the way to the horizon. Two different beats mingled from the beach bars on either side of her, a reminder of the past and the good times she'd shared with her friends.

The three of them had always worked and their differing personalities complemented each other. Yet Laurie was worried about talking to Gem and while Gem had confided in Belle, she didn't want Laurie to know the truth about her and Dan. The three of them being together on Ibiza again was probably a bad idea, yet they all needed to face up to the reality of their lives and somehow attempt to mend their friendship.

17

Talking to Belle before the outdoor movie at Serenity had felt as easy as if Caleb had been talking to Cara, although Belle was less acerbic and didn't tease the hell out of him like Cara did, but then they didn't know each other well and he had to remind himself that their relationship was different.

He hadn't seen much of Belle for the rest of the week until the Friday evening when he'd been in the restaurant chatting to a couple in their fifties. He'd spotted her pacing on the beach while talking on her phone, her white dress bright in the moonlight. She'd remained sitting on the beach long after she'd finished the call, hugging her knees like she needed a friend.

On the way to his car, Caleb had considered going over to see if she was okay, but she'd stood up and brushed the sand off the back of her dress and the moment had passed. He'd walked away, not wanting her to think he'd been watching, and headed home instead, but the image of Belle on her own looking sad and vulnerable stayed with him.

He'd woken late the following morning remembering fragments of a dream, a woman in white whose face he couldn't see clearly.

A message buzzed on his phone.

> I'm going to cook bullit de peix later. Come eat with us.

Somehow his mother-in-law Maria always knew when he needed comforting and a reason to not be on his own. Maria and Juan warmly embracing him into their lives because of his love for their daughter had meant so much and he'd clung on to the big happy family he'd gained as an adult but had missed out on growing up.

Caleb stretched out in the king-size bed. Cara had commented more than once that Solace was like a show home. The kitchen was barely used because he tended to eat at Spirit – or at his former mother-in-law's most weekends – but he did love to cook. It just felt pointless only cooking for himself now. The same way his bedroom was neat and functional, unfinished without pictures on the wall or cushions scattered on the bed because it was just him. One wardrobe was full of his clothes, the other, which should have been Paloma's, had remained empty. The only personal items were on his bedside table: a lamp, a small stack of books and a framed photo of Paloma. He had other ones in the drawer, photos from their wedding day and their brief few years together before their lives had been flipped upside down, but he still found it too painful to look at them.

Maria understood how the mornings were the worst for him, waking up without Paloma. The few times he'd woken up with someone else next to him the guilt had been all-consuming.

He thumbed a reply to Maria to say he'd see her later, threw off the bed covers, showered then made the first espresso of the day. He drank it on the balcony that overlooked the terrace, the midmorning sun making the white of Ibiza Town further along the coast sparkle.

* * *

Paloma's parents' house was further up the coast towards the village of Cala Llenya. The drive always made Caleb think about how different his life would have been if Paloma had lived. He would probably have worked just as much but she'd have been by his side, running the restaurant at Serenity. A place that embodied the romantic and peaceful side of the White Isle, that had been her dream. His love for Ibiza had been born from the partying side of the island, so his focus had always been on giving the guests a good time rather than a quiet time. He'd loved how she was the ying to his yang. She'd changed him, some friends had argued tamed him, but he'd been fine with that, happy to put his lothario ways behind him because rather than spending occasional nights with random women, he wanted to spend his whole life with the woman he loved.

Children had been part of their long-term plans, but following chemotherapy, Paloma had gone through an early menopause. She'd been an incredible auntie to her eldest niece and nephew for three all-too-brief years. There were four more little ones now, the nieces and nephews Paloma had missed out on getting to know, but she lived on in their hearts. Maria, Juan and her brothers made sure of that. Caleb struggled with the memories, and talking about her made him relive his loss, reopening wounds he wanted to stay patched up. But he'd never had the chance to heal. The Torres Corchado family had embraced him when Paloma had brought him into her life and they'd clung on to him when they'd lost her.

Caleb swiped angrily at his tears and tried to concentrate on the road. The island had lost its charm without her. Yet with the roof down and the sun shining, the buffeting wind made him feel alive and guilty, always guilty for being the one still experiencing life, although he knew Paloma would chastise him for thinking like that, for being so focused on work that he was missing out on the things that had once made life so good. She'd have said watching a film with Cara or playing an online game with friends who lived thousands of miles away wasn't really socialising. They'd planned a life of working hard but playing harder, but it didn't feel the same without her.

Caleb parked outside Maria and Juan's house. From the road it was unassuming, a single-storey building with white-washed walls and blue shutters shaded by trees. Their house felt lived in, homely and filled with love, somewhere he was drawn to yet was a constant reminder of the future he'd lost.

A narrow path filled with pots of flowers, herbs and cacti ran along the side of the house and the front door was open, as always. What was unusual was how quiet it was, no voices drifting through or kids careening about outside.

'Maria?' Caleb called from the dusky hallway.

'*Estic a la cuina!*' she shouted back, and Caleb followed the mouth-watering smell of onions and garlic frying into the rustic kitchen, the heart of the home and Maria's pride and joy.

Conversation with Maria and her family was usually a mix of Catalan and English and after twenty-four years on the island, Caleb effortlessly switched between the two. He kissed Maria on each cheek and looked around. 'Where is everyone?'

'They will be here soon.'

'Do you need any help?'

'You can chop the potatoes.' Maria gestured to the work surface as she stirred the onions and green pepper she was sautéing in a heavy casserole dish. She swept in chopped tomatoes. 'How are you managing without Cara?'

Caleb took one of the peeled potatoes, started chopping it into chunks and shrugged. 'We message each other every day.'

'It is different though without your friend here. You lean on her as much as she leans on you.' Maria tapped her fingers to her heart. 'It's not just about work.'

'No, it's not, but I'm doing okay, Maria.'

'Good, I'm glad.' Her tight grey curls bounced as she nodded. 'Once you finish the potatoes you can chop the almonds.'

She gave the vegetables in the pan a stir then started chopping the parsley on another board. Juan, with their eldest son Lluís, was the chef at their family-run restaurant in San Carlos, but at home the kitchen had always been Maria's domain. Caleb would argue that the same meal made in Maria's kitchen always beat the restaurant equivalent. Not that he'd ever admit it out loud to Juan – he'd risk being lynched. Maria cooked with love for her family, long lazy lunches that lasted well into the evening.

Maria swept the parsley into a bowl and glanced sideways at him. 'You are still coming over next weekend as well?'

'Of course.' Caleb finished with the potatoes and started on the toasted almonds. Maria would get them done twice as fast but she liked having the company of someone who didn't try and take over. 'But about that, you know how I sometimes bring Cara...' He cleared his throat. 'How would you feel about me bringing a new friend?'

Maria's eyes narrowed, her olive skin crinkling. 'What are you really asking me, Caleb?'

'I'm asking exactly that: if you're happy to have an extra person to feed?'

Maria's neat eyebrows raised as she added the potatoes to the pan with a splash of water. 'You know the answer to that: of course

I am!' On another board there were two different types of rock fish already skinned and boned which she set about cutting up into pieces. She wiped her brow with the back of her hand and looked at him intently, her dark eyes hawklike. 'You understand we will all be happy for you to find someone special.'

'It's not like that,' Caleb stressed as he added the chopped almonds to a bowl of saffron, garlic and the parsley Maria had prepared. 'She's just a friend – the person who's taken over from Cara – but a stranger to you.'

'Like Cara was a stranger at first – although Cara will never be special in the way I'm suggesting, huh?' Maria said with a gleam in her eye. 'Or is it the same with this new woman who has taken over from her? What's her name?'

'Belle.'

'A beautiful name.'

'It is.'

'Also a Spanish name like Isabella. Does she like women?'

Caleb forced himself to not roll his eyes and shook his head. 'No, I don't get that impression.'

'Mmm.' Maria stirred the potatoes frying in the pan. 'Do you get the impression she likes you?'

'Maria!' he scolded, his reaction coming out harsher than he'd meant it to.

'I'm sorry. I worry about you. We all do.' She wiped her hands on a cloth. 'Paloma would,' she said softly.

Caleb breathed deeply as a tightness across his chest threatened to consume him. 'I should never have asked about inviting her over. The simple truth is, she's away from home and here on her own after having a difficult time from the little she's said. She reminds me of Cara in that respect, so yes, I'm befriending her, that's all. But it'll just be me next Saturday.'

'No, it won't; it will be the two of you.' Maria gave him a firm nod. 'She is very welcome. You bring her.'

There was no arguing with Maria. Even if she hadn't been his former mother-in-law, he would have done as she wished. He'd always respected her and had been happy to marry into the family, but his love for her had grown after losing Paloma. The strength she'd had in the face of tragic loss had floored him; she was the beating heart of the family and the one who held everyone together supporting them through their own individual trials and staying strong in the face of their greatest sadness. And she'd always been there for him, a shoulder to cry on even when she was struggling with her own grief.

Later that evening, when Caleb was sitting by himself on the wall at the end of the terraced garden, Maria joined him. The sound of Diego and Àngel, one of his older brothers, arguing good naturedly drifted into the night. Life hummed around them: the scritch scritch of nighttime insects and other voices from the surrounding houses. A dog barked, which set another one off. Up at the house, Àngel's wife Gabriela was shouting at the children to get their shoes on, telling them it was late and they had church in the morning. Everyday family life was happening around him yet he was always on the periphery.

'You are very thoughtful tonight.' Maria stretched out her legs and grimaced. 'And I've been on my feet too long today.'

'The food was delicious as always, Maria. The company too. Thank you.'

'And thank you for your help.' Maria placed her hand on his where he was leaning on the wall and patted it. 'You are thinking about Paloma, *sí*?'

'Always.'

'It's hard for you to be here, I understand. It's hard for me when I see you too. You remind me of Paloma and how happy she was. You make me wonder what would have been if she'd lived.'

Caleb caught his breath. The view down the hillside of silhouetted trees and the other houses glowing golden in the darkness became blurred with tears. Nothing good came of wondering about a different life, one filled with children, laughter and happiness, yet he couldn't help it, particularly when spending time with Paloma's family was wrapped up in that loss.

'I can also see you are conflicted,' Maria continued. 'The way you talked earlier, as if needing my permission to invite someone else into your life whether as a friend or more. You have been part of our family for twelve years, Caleb. Nearly five of them without Paloma.' Maria curled her fingers between his, her plain gold wedding band glinting in the moonlight. 'I miss her with my heart and soul, my whole being, but I have the rest of my family to think about, to be strong for. I'm fortunate to be surrounded by family and love every day. No one will ever replace my daughter, but I have my sons to focus my love on, their wives and partners and more than anything my grandchildren to help me heal. I'm sad for you, Caleb, that you haven't found anyone to fill the hole Paloma left. Please don't believe any of us would think any less of you for wanting to find love again.' She leaned close and held his cheeks in her hands. Her face was soft and hopeful, filled with understanding as she looked at him intently. She released him and stood. 'Now I must go and help find shoes and say goodbye to my grandchildren before their poor mother explodes with frustration.'

* * *

After spending the evening wrapped up in a bubble of love with Maria and her family, Caleb's loneliness was acute when he returned to Solace. The villa should have been somewhere he found comfort, but it was with Cara and Paloma's family, and when surrounded by his guests and colleagues, that he felt most at peace. Solace was beautiful but empty, and yet he couldn't give it up.

His thoughts turned to his conversation with Maria about Belle. Over the last couple of weeks he'd found himself noticing her more and more. He'd tried to convince himself he was just keeping an eye on how she was getting on with the job, but he'd found it hard to shift his attention elsewhere, because there was something about her that... what? Captivated him, was that it? He had told Maria the truth about Belle reminding him of Cara. There was the same vulnerability and history of them needing to escape: Cara from an abusive relationship in Australia, and Belle... well, he was still trying to figure her out. She was running away from something, or perhaps it was more to do with her trying to find something.

There was a stark difference between Belle and Cara though, in the way he looked at her, his attention zoning in on the curve of her hip in that white dress or her full lips as she talked or laughed. Fuck, that joyful sound that made him want to make her laugh. These unexpected feelings left him puzzled and confused, because it was more than her being an attractive woman. It was the way she made him feel when he was around her, the pull that could be passed off as friendship, the way her company was easy, like Cara's, except that he didn't fancy Cara.

Maria was right about the hole Paloma had left; it had been patched up on occasion but it always reopened like an old wound. In his line of work it was impossible not to meet women; he was friends with Paloma's younger brothers Tomàs and Diego and they'd often been the instigators. And it wasn't as if he'd never been tempted, but it had just been sex, nothing more. He'd also learned that the guilt and sorrow he felt the morning after took weeks to get over, trying to relearn again and again how to let go of Paloma. He couldn't see how he ever could.

18

The first wedding of the summer took place on the first weekend in July, and it had been a hectic week leading up to it. With the wedding party staying at Spirit but the wedding ceremony and reception taking place at Serenity, there had been lots for Belle to organise and co-ordinate. Cara, with a freelance wedding planner, had planned everything meticulously and as Belle had managed much larger-scale events in London, she found there was little to stress about.

Caleb spent most of his time at Spirit or out and about liaising with suppliers and partners, but he was around for Serenity's first ever wedding. Even on a regular day, with couples having dinner and drinks on the terrace that overlooked the sea, it oozed romance.

The wedding ceremony itself was magical. The natural canvas of the sandy terrace was laid out with rows of wooden chairs. The aisle led to a thatched pergola simply decorated with pink and white roses nestled among fronds of greenery. With the ever-changing blue of the sea just metres below on one side and the rocky cliff and palm trees as the backdrop on the other two sides, nothing more was needed. The bride wore a white lace dress, the groom a powder-blue suit and the bridesmaids were in pink floaty dresses, while the guests wore the colours of summer.

After the photos were taken on the terrace with family and friends, the photographer took the bride and groom down to the beach, while drinks and canapés were served on the restaurant terrace, allowing time for Serenity's team to set up for the sit-down meal.

Satisfied that all was in hand, Belle wandered down to the beach to take her own photos, managing to get into shot both the bride and groom strolling hand in hand along the pebbles, as well as some of the wedding guests on the jutting terrace above. After posing in front of the vivid blue sea, they headed back up the beach and strolled below the restaurant terrace which was perched on an outcrop of rock.

Belle saw what happened next as if in slow motion. A child up on the terrace leaned over the wooden railing to wave at the bride and groom below just as the glass in his other hand slipped.

Belle's heart thundered in her chest. 'Watch out!'

The groom tugged his new wife out of the way. Narrowly missing her head, the glass smashed on the stones, splashing liquid and sending glass flying. The bride, still holding onto the groom, lost her footing as she tumbled backwards, landing with a thump and pulling her new husband down with her.

Swearing under her breath, Belle rushed over and reached them just before the shocked photographer did.

'God that hurts!' The bride grimaced with pain as she clutched at her ankle.

'Don't move,' Belle said to the bride as she offered her hand to the groom to haul him back to his feet. She spoke into the radio clipped to the pocket of her dress. 'Raphael, can you get someone to bring an icepack, first-aid kit and a damp cloth down to the beach ASAP, please.' She turned back to the bride, whose already delicately pale face was now linen-white, her brow creased like she was on the verge of tears. 'It's all going to be okay,' Belle said with a calmness that she really wasn't feeling. 'And your husband made an epic save.'

There was a flicker of a smile at that.

'You warned us just in time,' the groom said. 'It could have been so much worse.'

'Yes, a concussed bride would not have been ideal,' Belle said, crouching down to inspect the bride's ankle. 'An injured ankle isn't great either but hopefully it's just a sprain and this will end up being a memorable moment from an incredibly memorable day.'

From up above Belle could hear the hushed but stern conversation the mum was having with the little boy who'd dropped the glass.

The bride gestured upwards. 'That's my cheeky nephew getting the telling off.'

'And luckily he was only drinking lemonade and it hasn't stained your dress.'

Caleb arrived armed with the first-aid kit and icepack, the fear in his wide eyes mirroring how she'd felt just moments before.

'And now we have Serenity's very own CEO at our beck and call.' She gave him a nod and slight smile as she took the items from him. Their fingers brushed. She wrapped the icepack and handed it to the groom to hold against his wife's ankle.

'It doesn't look swollen,' Belle said, 'and we'll see if you can stand in a moment.' She gave the bride a reassuring smile and caught Caleb's relieved look as he started to clear away the smashed glass. Belle got back on the radio. 'Can someone bring two glasses of champagne and a couple of cushions to the beach, please.'

Within a couple of minutes, one of the waiters had brought

them down. Belle made the bride comfortable with a cushion to sit on and another to support her ankle. Caleb handed them the champagne.

Belle stood back a touch. 'Do you know what, if you're happy to sit here for a bit and rest your ankle, this will make a lovely photo.'

With the glasses of champagne placed on a rock next to them and the icepack hidden beneath the lacy, fanned out skirt of the wedding dress, the bride rested back against the groom, his arms encircling her as they gazed into each other's eyes. The photographer crouched down to take photos. The backdrop was the pebble beach and the palm trees edging the terrace.

After twenty minutes of rest and with their champagne drained and romantically intimate photos taken, Belle strapped the bride's ankle with a compression bandage. With help from her husband, they made their way back up to the terrace to be greeted by friends and family and a tearful apology and cuddle from the bride's nephew.

Long palm tree shadows provided patches of shade across the tables covered in white tablecloths with plumes of oyster and mushroom-coloured pampas grass as the centrepieces. The guests enjoyed the sit-down meal of roasted seabass with pumpkin purée and pickled vegetables. The heat of the afternoon turned into a balmy evening, the retreating sun making the sea glitter pink then gold. As darkness took over, lanterns were lit and a jazz band started playing. The sound of a sultry saxophone and a double bass filled the sheltered bay, the music entwining with laughter while conversations flowed and couples danced.

Belle stood on the periphery, watching the waiters seamlessly deliver drinks and clear away empty glasses, while the bride and groom danced together. Their loving smiles erased any lingering worry that the earlier mishap had spoiled their day.

It was only Caleb handing her a champagne cocktail that made her tear her eyes away.

'Cheers.' Caleb knocked his glass against hers. 'To a hell of a day. You were super calm under pressure earlier and dealt with the situation beautifully.'

'It's rare for an event to go without a hitch; I mean, a bride injuring herself is a seriously big hitch and incredibly unfortunate, but these things happen.'

'The way you turned it around and found the positive was incredible, thank you.'

Belle raised her glass and took a sip of the bubbly champagne cocktail with the added tartness of passionfruit, sweetness of strawberry and kick of vodka. 'I think we should be thankful for an understanding couple and a pretty chilled-out bride.'

Belle followed Caleb to the stone wall that edged the top terrace where they'd sat and talked before the movie night. A couple of the wedding guests were perched further along chatting. Belle and Caleb sat down too, gazing over the terrace that twinkled with lights and swirls of colour as the guests danced.

Belle sighed. 'You're in the business of making dreams come true.'

'I guess I am,' he said softly.

'You don't think of it like that?'

'Ensuring guests have the best time is what I've been striving for ever since I came to Ibiza, even more so since I started Spirit. It doesn't matter who they are or why they're here: getting married, celebrating a birthday, someone travelling alone or with friends and family. It is mostly loved-up couples though.' Caleb looked thoughtful as he watched the scene below filled with life and love.

'Do you find it hard watching people on the happiest day of their life?' Belle asked. 'The reminder of your own wedding must be hard?'

There was a pause and Belle found herself holding her breath, unsure if Caleb would even answer, worry coursing through her that she'd overstepped.

'We got married at Spirit, although if we'd had Serenity back then I'm certain we'd have chosen to get married here.' Caleb folded his hands in his lap, his thumb and middle finger turning his wedding band, something she'd noticed him do before. 'Paloma wasn't one for being the centre of attention and she wanted a quiet wedding, but her family is big so it was hard for them to not take over. I made up for it with just my mum and gran and only a handful of close friends and extended family from the UK. There are reminders all the time about what I missed out on, but I want my guests to be happy, to have the time of their lives and to want to return. Just because I'm sad doesn't make me wish for other people to suffer the same way.'

'Oh goodness, no, of course not. I never meant that.'

'I know you didn't, but I also understand how people think I'm torturing myself with Spirit and Serenity by hosting weddings and anniversary parties, but this is my business. It's my life. It was what I was working towards before I met Paloma. Despite everything, I still can't think of a better job.' He gently knocked his arm against her shoulder and smiled. 'Making people's dreams come true.'

She swept her hand around. 'This is actually my dream job.'

'You mean that?'

Belle nodded. 'It's making me re-evaluate what I want from my own events business, what I want to focus on and where. I have lots of experience, but I need to hone it in on a particular area. Plus, there's a freedom here that's missing in London. I'm sure it's probably because I have more responsibilities back there. Here it feels as if I'm on an extended holiday, but perhaps it's the slower pace of life, the party atmosphere, being surrounded by people celebrating the good things in life. It's wonderfully refreshing.'

'Obviously I moved here for the party lifestyle, but the spirit of the island – both sides of it – and its people won me over.' Caleb folded his hands together, his shoulders bunching forwards as he glanced sideways at her. 'Talking of a slower pace of life, I'm having lunch with my former in-laws tomorrow and they've invited you. Well, I, er, invited you. Cara often came. I thought you might like the company.'

Was he blushing? Or was he just blustering through an invitation because he was trying to make it sound casual?

'Most of the family will be there. It's joyful and communal – a lazy lunch that will go on well into the evening, and Maria and Juan are the most incredible cooks.'

Belle considered it for a moment. Diego would probably be there. Was this really a situation she wanted to put herself in? Yet the idea of being enveloped by a loving family, eating delicious food and spending time with Caleb away from work was tempting.

'Yes,' she said. 'I'd love to come, thank you.' Because she realised she would, but it was more about Caleb and not saying no to him rather than the opportunity of reconnecting with Diego.

'Thank you again for everything you did today.' He swung his legs back over the wall, stood up and surveyed the terrace before turning back to Belle. 'Cara would be proud as punch.'

'It's been a good day.'

'If you've got this, I have paperwork to do so I'm going to head home.'

'Yes, of course.' Belle stood up too and walked with him to the corner of the restaurant. 'They look happy dancing the night away.'

'I'll pick you up from Spirit at two tomorrow.' He leaned close and kissed her on each cheek. His hands on her arms, firm and comforting and wanted all at the same time, made her tingle and flooded her core with warmth. His lips left her cheek but he kept hold of her and he was still so close that if he leaned down slightly their lips would touch. A dusting of dark stubble flecked with grey framed full lips, and the way they were slightly open, sent her heart fluttering. She shifted her gaze upwards and their eyes locked momentarily before his gaze dropped to her lips. He shifted closer and she felt the caress of his breath and then... Something changed. His focus flicked back to her eyes and he dropped his hands from her arms as he stepped back. 'Tomorrow,' he mumbled as he strode off, leaving her as confused as she was aroused.

Belle turned back to the wedding party below, the terrace a swirl of summer colour after a day full of love and hope. Yet all she could think about beyond the imprint of Caleb's lips on her skin was that after making someone else's day the happiest of their lives, he was heading home alone and not to the woman he still loved.

19

When Caleb said goodnight to Belle it hadn't been the first time he'd kissed her cheeks, but it had been the first time it meant something and the first time he'd considered doing more. His insides somersaulted at the feel of her smooth skin and the way she sank into him when he held on to her a touch too long as he focused on her lips, pink and plump and so insanely kissable. She smelled of a mandarin-fresh perfume and sunscreen and summer. Perhaps he was reading into things that weren't there. It had been a euphoric end to a day that could have gone so horribly wrong were it not for Belle's quick thinking and calm, efficient, confident management of the situation. Perhaps that was what made kissing her goodnight feel different. Except, on his way home he played the moment over and over in his head, from the way she'd looked at him to the way he'd wished her lips were on his, biting, teasing, kissing.

He phoned Cara the minute he got back to Solace. It was early in the morning in Australia and she was up and about while he was heading to bed alone. He told her what had happened, and it was good to talk to the only person who would understand his confused feelings and wouldn't judge, who wouldn't try and push him too hard about not doing something with Belle or about actually doing something... Because his thoughts were spiralling that way and his body was certainly betraying his head. Cara was his sounding board and his best mate, who told him the truth and allowed him to feel everything he needed to: grief, confusion, desire, hope, possibility, a crazy mess of difficult emotions that constantly fought each other.

Even after talking to Cara and hearing her pragmatic 'you're a hot-blooded man attracted to a beautiful woman who you're drawn to so there's nothing wrong with fantasising even if you don't act on it' talk, it didn't make him feel any less anxious about taking Belle to Maria and Juan's the next day. When they arrived there together, no one said anything about Belle being there in place of Cara, but he could tell they were wondering what his relationship with Belle was exactly. He didn't have to try and see it through their eyes to know what they were thinking when he was trying to figure out if his attraction to Belle was about more than just the way her hair fell around her shoulders or the way the necklace she wore drew his eyes to her smooth skin and down to the curve of her breasts...

The second Maria caught Caleb's eye and gave him a slight nod, he knew she'd caught him looking at Belle. There was a sadness in Maria's eyes that was always there, but a warmth shone through in her gentle smile that was enough to calm his racing heart. Why did looking at another woman still feel as if he was cheating? It wasn't as if he'd never been with another woman since Paloma... But of course it was the way Belle made him feel that was different. Was that why he'd asked if she could come? To test the water? To see the family's reaction to another woman, someone who wasn't a comfortably safe and platonic friend like Cara?

Belle was quiet but friendly. He'd sensed how overwhelmed

she'd been when they'd first arrived to a cacophony of people and a barrage of names. A drink had been handed to her and food offered straight away, yet she'd taken it in her stride, politely accepting one of Maria's homemade ham croquettes and rolling her eyes at its deliciousness – Caleb knew because it was one of his favourite things – and he loved how she'd immediately told Maria just how good it was.

She was unsurprisingly reserved but she happily chatted to Maria and Gabriela who both made sure she was included. Caleb watched her take everything in, trying to get to grips with the names and relationships of what was a sizeable family for someone who was an only child. Of course she'd already met Diego at Ushuaïa, and the other three brothers, Lluís, Àngel and Tomàs, who all still lived on the island, were as friendly and easy going as Paloma had been. The fifth brother, Javier, lived in Barcelona. Even though he wasn't there, it was still rare to have everyone else together, but Maria insisted that they did this once a month, although it wasn't easy to fit it in alongside running the family restaurant. Since Juan had semi-retired, his two eldest sons were running it, Lluís in the kitchen and Àngel at the front of house. It was the perfect balance because Caleb knew how relieved Maria and Juan were to not have the two of them fighting for dominance in the kitchen.

It was well past three by the time they sat down to eat. A huge paella was placed in the centre of the table with extras like bread and aioli, marinated olives and various salads. Caleb joined in with the conversations that bounced around, but he found himself keeping an eye on Belle most of all, loving the way she eagerly accepted piles of food and seemed genuinely happy to be there. When she caught him looking at her and smiled, it sent his heart racing.

20

Caleb's presence at Maria and Juan's was comforting, because apart from her parents' thirtieth wedding anniversary, Belle had never experienced a family get-together quite like it. Weddings and funerals were the only time she was ever around lots of relatives. This was just a normal weekend for the Torres Corchado family.

When Belle was growing up it had only been her mum, dad and her, and with the rest of their family spread all over the place, the only thing that had come close to this kind of joyfully loud gathering had been spending time with Laurie's family. Gem's too. Before she'd had children, Gem's mum had been a massive clubber, and her love of eighties' and nineties' pop and dance music lived on with after-school kitchen discos dancing to Soul II Soul, Madonna and Neneh Cherry. Belle's own parents had more of a comfy slippers and Radio 3 vibe about them. From what Caleb had said, he'd missed out on all of this too. It was no wonder he'd embraced Paloma's family just as they'd taken him to their hearts.

She'd expected the food to be good but it was sensational. Perhaps it was the combination of the company and warmth of a loving family along with the location and the delicious food that made it special. She remembered bits about what Diego had told her about his parents running a restaurant, yet she was in this strange situation where no one else knew their real connection, not even Caleb, and it was far too awkward to reveal it now, particularly when he was the person who kept stealing her attention. Diego was as good-looking as he'd been when she'd first met him but it was Caleb who she found herself drawn to. Although older, he was equally handsome, but in a way that had grown on her rather than the in-her-face immediacy of Diego's bulging biceps and smooth ridged chest. The short-sleeved shirt Caleb was wearing was open at the neck, the linen thin and pale so she could make out the imprint of his tattoo across one side of his chest. The scaled face of a dragon reached all the way to his neck. The laughter lines around his eyes showed that despite everything he'd been through, there'd still been happiness. Because happiness was here in abundance, even though she was with a family who had all lost someone special: a sister, an aunt, a wife, a daughter. It was an unfathomable loss but one they dealt with collectively while still managing to find the good in life. What she loved most was how Caleb was still very much part of the family, which said an awful lot about him and left her feeling honoured to have been brought into their fold.

With four of the brothers there, plus two wives and a partner, six grandchildren of varying ages, Caleb and her, they squeezed on to two long bench tables on the covered terrace at the back of the house. The children argued about who was sitting where until Maria made an executive decision and arranged them all at one end of the table. Everyone else sat where they liked and Belle found herself squeezed between Maria and Àngel's wife Gabriela with Caleb opposite next to Diego. Drinks were poured and the last of the dishes were brought out. Maria encouraged everyone to help themselves.

'You came to Ibiza before, *sí*?' Maria asked Belle once she made sure the food was being dished onto plates.

Belle didn't dare meet Diego's eyes.

'Only for a week on holiday when I was young.'

'You are still young!' Maria dolloped two large spoonfuls of paella onto her and Belle's plates. 'You like our island enough to come back to live though.'

'Yes, it was always my intention to come back, but the job at Spirit came along at exactly the right time.'

'We are glad. With Cara gone, Caleb struggles. It is good to know he has you.'

Maria's words were as warm as a hug. To know she was doing him some good pleased her no end, yet she was uncertain if there was more meaning to Maria saying 'he has you'.

Overthinking things had long been a problem, particularly when it came to relationships. Dissecting things had ultimately destroyed every one. She didn't want to settle when it came to love; she wanted to fearlessly and passionately love and to be with someone who felt right in every way, who she could connect to in heart, body and soul. No one so far came close and that included Diego, of that she was now sure.

Caleb had been right about lunch turning into dinner. Eating was a blissfully long and leisurely pastime for Diego's family. While the youngest grandchild had a nap, everyone else ate, chatted and ate some more. It was wonderful to be pulled into such a big loving family even for a short while. She'd made good friends in London, but since living on her own, there were plenty of moments of loneliness. She could only wish for something as wonderful as this in her life.

After they'd finished eating and had cleared away all the empty bowls and plates from the table, Belle didn't avoid Diego on purpose, but she certainly didn't go out of her way to speak to him.

He took her by surprise when she was on her own for a couple of minutes and came over.

'You've made an impression on him.' Diego nodded to where Caleb was deep in conversation with Lluís. 'Only Cara's ever had an invite over here.'

Belle pursed her lips. 'I think he's just being nice.'

'Caleb is nice but he tends to do things for a reason. You being here is meaningful.'

'Are *you* okay with me being here?'

The awkwardness she felt was more from embarrassment that they'd had sex than wishing they could rekindle and repeat.

'I'm okay with it.' He shrugged and lowered his voice. 'It was only sex.'

Wasn't that the truth, yet at the time it had felt like so much more – *he'd* seemed like so much more: a perfect, utterly gorgeous man who had stolen her heart.

'I get that you must have had a different woman in your bed every week, but when I introduced myself at Ushuaïa, you didn't remember me, did you?'

'Is that a fair question when you assume how many women I've been with?'

'I think it is.' Belle held his gaze. 'Particularly when you remembered Gem without me even saying her name.'

Something like surprise or shock or maybe even guilt flickered across his face.

Belle sighed. 'But we really don't need to talk about this, certainly not here. It happened, it was a long time ago and it's not relevant any longer. I don't want either of us to feel uncomfortable about something we did ten years ago, because like you said, it was nothing more than sex.'

'Had you wanted to see me on your last night?'

A flicker of uncertainty flared inside her. Was it possible that he regretted missing out on their last night together as much as she had? If the abrupt text message he'd sent the next morning after she'd apologised for not meeting up with him was anything to go by, then no, he hadn't regretted it. Yet despite him probably not feeling the same way, she wanted to be honest with him.

'Oh my God, I wanted to see you so much.' It was her turn to keep her voice hushed, aware of his family around them, Caleb most of all. 'That whole night was a disaster and I had no way of contacting you until I got my phone back.'

'Because Gem had it,' Diego said with a shrug. 'And you had to look after your friend.'

'Yeah, I couldn't leave her, and after I lost Gem and had no way of contacting her or you...' Her voice trailed off.

The cologne he wore wasn't as overpowering as it used to be, a more subtle vanilla and oak scent that she was only picking up on because they were leaning close. Ten years ago it had been strong and zesty and in-her-face, as bold as he'd been. And it was only talking to him now, remembering, that she was connecting things. There had been a zesty cologne on Gem too when she'd got back to their hotel after being out all night.

Belle sat up straighter on the bench as thoughts chased round her head. 'You remembered Gem's name,' she repeated, 'but only have vague memories of me...'

'I did remember you.'

'Only once I jogged your memory about who I was.' Her thoughts spiralled tighter and tighter. 'You just said Gem had my phone, but there's no way you could know that, because I never told you. Unless...' Suddenly her muddled thoughts were replaced by absolute clarity. 'Unless you were with Gem that night. You were, weren't you?'

Diego glanced around at his family, opened his mouth then

shut it as he turned back to Belle. 'It's difficult to explain what happened and how we ended up together—'

'Oh my God, you really were! How the hell did you two...' She held up her hand and lowered her voice. 'Actually, I don't want to hear any more.' Her heart pounded and her skin crawled with a sudden uncomfortable heat. She scrambled off the bench and paced away from him. Feeling utterly foolish, she retreated inside to find the bathroom. The last thing she wanted to do was have a conversation about what he'd got up to with one of her best friends while surrounded by his family. While Caleb was here.

Everything she'd believed about Diego, about their time together, what he'd meant to her and what she'd possibly meant to him, had been destroyed by a well-hidden truth that she hadn't had a clue about. Until now.

21

JULY 2013, TEN YEARS AGO

The ease Gem had felt the night before with Diego disappeared as quickly as the sun behind a cloud the instant she opened her eyes. Disorientated by being in a strange room, it took her a moment to realise her phone was ringing, the light too bright for her tender head. Before she could grab it, the caller rang off.

Diego stirred and rolled over, all tousled bed hair and unfamiliar features. They met each other's eyes, groggy from lack of sleep and massively hungover. Immediate regret clamped around Gem's heart. Diego's eyes shifted from hers. He moved onto his back, ran his hands over his face and up through his dark curls. The shame she was feeling wasn't because she'd cheated on Dan but because she'd cheated with Diego. He may have only been a summer fling for Belle but Gem was acutely aware she'd crossed a line that should never be crossed with friends. Yet the night had been epic, not just because it had ended with her having the best sex she'd ever had, regardless of being drunk, but because of all that had come before it: partying at Pacha with Diego, baring their souls and talking to each other about everything, connecting as much emotionally as they had physically. None of that could erase the sickening feeling of regret...

'Last night was...' Diego's voice was raspy, as if his throat was dry.

'A mistake,' Gem said firmly. 'You don't have to say it, I know.'

He turned to look at her. His cheeks tightened and there was something in his expression that made her falter. 'A mistake' was what he was going to say, wasn't it? Because however fucking good last night had been, it should never have happened.

And yet the way he was looking at her made her want to repeat it over and over again. She tore her eyes from his and grabbed her phone from the bedside table. Her heart dropped at the sight of the missed calls from Laurie's phone. Nausea wound its way through her and her stomach constricted. The vice around her heart tightened, and her pulse raced like she'd overdosed on caffeine. She clicked on the voicemail Belle had just left.

'Where the hell are you, Gem? Please tell me you've hooked up with some guy. I've been worried sick. If I don't hear from you in the next ten minutes I'm going to ask reception to contact the police.'

'Is everything okay?' The care in Diego's deep voice sent her insides swirling, because of course nothing was okay.

'My friend's worried.' She deleted the message. 'Wants to make sure I'm all right.'

Their eyes met, and she imagined both of them picturing Belle; she couldn't bring herself to say her name out loud, not when she was lying naked next to Diego.

There was no way she could return her call and speak to her, not like this. It would be hard enough to lie to Belle when she was back at the hotel, impossible while she was still in bed with Diego.

Gem breathed deeply and thumbed a reply as the pounding in her head intensified.

> Just listened to your messages, so sorry, I'm fine. Will be back soon xx

Belle replied within seconds.

> Oh my God I can't even begin to tell you how relieved I am! X

Gem desperately wanted to escape but the need to have a shower, to wash away the scent of *him* before she went back to the hotel, was far more pressing than escaping the awkwardness of the morning after the night before.

She locked herself in the tiny ensuite. The events of the last few hours played over and over as she showered. The best night of her life had been tarnished by the reality of the cold light of day, her mistake still imprinted on the sweat-soaked sheets.

Diego called her a taxi and thoughtfully checked she had enough money before walking her out of the apartment block maze to the entrance. He looked as if he was going to say something but then thought better of it. His dreamy eyes were filled with what she assumed was regret and his forehead was creased with worry. He kissed her on each cheek then wrapped his arms round her. Gem rested her head against his chest and breathed in his intoxicating citrusy sweaty scent. She hugged him tight, not wanting to let him go, a million thoughts fighting with each other. He wasn't going to see either her or Belle again, but that didn't help erase her guilt. With a sigh, Gem extracted herself from his arms, but before she could walk away, he grabbed her and pressed a piece of paper into her hand. Without faltering, she shoved open the glass door of the apartment building and stepped into the sunshine.

'Gem!' She turned back at Diego's shout. 'I had the best time with you.'

Gem opened her mouth to reply, but the door shut closed with a thump, Diego already retreating.

Tears lodged in her throat as she unfolded the piece of paper. All that was written on it was his name, 'Diego Torres Corchado', and his number. Gem stared at it so hard the pen marks danced and her eyes blurred. She crumpled it up, went to drop it in a nearby bin but hesitated and stuffed it into the bottom of the bag slung across her chest.

It was early still but the sun was already too bright, reflecting off the white buildings and making her wish she had sunglasses to help ease her hangover. The thought of having to lie to Belle made her nausea intensify; it would be far easier to speak to her over the phone than lie to her face. It was cowardly, but it was all she could cope with.

She breathed deeply and rang her.

Belle's voice was filled with relief as she answered, and the lie Gem spun about spending the night with someone who worked at Pacha slipped easily from her mouth. She told herself she was simply bending the truth to protect Belle.

The moment Gem entered their hotel room, Belle enveloped her in a tight hug.

Belle's breath was hot against her neck. 'I've been so worried about you.'

She pulled away and Gem could see her taking in her damp hair and her clothes stale with smoke, drink and sweat. Oh God, clothes that had been pressed up against Diego, then removed by him.

Gem pulled Belle's phone from her bag and handed it to her, desperately wanting to focus her attention on something other than her. 'Not being able to contact you is where it all went wrong, otherwise I would have let you know that I wasn't coming back till the morning.'

'Well, at least one of us had a good last night,' Belle said jokingly, her smile blatantly forced. The underlying disappointment was impossible to miss. 'Mine was memorable, just in a completely different way.'

'You didn't, um...?' Just as she hadn't been able to say Belle's name earlier, she found it impossible to say Diego's name now. Feigning innocence was purely to protect Belle because what good would come of admitting the truth when they'd be heading home in a few hours?

'See Diego? Nope, had to look after Laurie.' Belle shrugged. 'It's not like I'm ever going to see him again.'

Belle echoed Gem's earlier thought. Gem's stomach twisted with nausea, anxiety and worry. She turned her attention to Laurie spreadeagled on the bed, a snore fluttering with every breath. 'She's really okay?'

'She's going to feel like shit for probably a week and might never drink again, but she'll survive. We'll need to wake her in a bit.' Belle's face crumpled with disappointment. 'It's time to go home.'

* * *

Unlike the journey to Ibiza, which had been noisy and boisterous with excitement, when Gem had actually felt sorry for the cabin crew trying to manage pissed-up twenty-somethings alongside a handful of families, the flight home was noticeably subdued. Laurie was squished in the window seat, her head lolling against the side. When they'd finally managed to drag her out of bed earlier that day, she'd been sick again and looked like death. Not that she seemed much better now, clutching a sick bag like it was a comfort blanket. Gem was rapidly wishing she wasn't trapped in the middle seat between an ill Laurie and a melancholy Belle. At least Belle didn't seem keen on talking. Gem didn't think she could cope lying to her any more than she already had. Belle kept looking at a message on her phone. Gem assumed it was from Diego but didn't dare ask. Not long after she'd returned to their hotel and had given Belle back her phone, Belle had messaged him. If Belle's mood was anything to go by, his reply had not been what she'd hoped for – if he'd replied at all.

Gem swallowed. Her heart felt as if it was being squeezed. Her stomach churned with anxiety. She still had Diego's number on the piece of paper he'd given her which was hidden safely away in an inside pocket of her bag. She couldn't even look at Belle without feeling shame and regret, her friend's obvious sadness and disappointment written all over her face.

As well as Belle being unusually quiet, Laurie had barely spoken either apart from shortly after take-off when she'd breathed heavily into the sick bag then muttered, 'I am never snorting anything ever again.'

If Gem had been as ill, she might have considered never touching alcohol again either, but her night with Diego was a far bigger regret than Laurie having drunk too much.

From towards the back of the plane a baby started crying, earpiercingly loud in the hungover quiet. Laurie groaned and shifted closer to the window. Belle clicked off her messages, shoved in earphones and closed her eyes.

As they flew towards the UK and back to real life, Gem tried to focus on the positives. She had the rest of the summer to enjoy before she'd be escaping overseas again, yet she couldn't shake off the feeling that a little piece of her heart had been left behind on Ibiza.

22

___

JULY 2023, PRESENT DAY

'You're quiet,' Caleb said on the drive back to Spirit after lunch at Maria and Juan's.

On the horizon, the sky was awash with dusky pink and fiery red. Caleb had been right about a long lazy lunch lasting into the evening.

'I'm just thinking,' Belle said as they sped along the tree-lined road back towards Santa Eulalia.

'About what?'

Gem and Diego was what she was thinking about. She turned the depth of her friend's deceit over and over in her head. Her shock at Diego's confession had made her want to phone Gem and yell at her, but she certainly hadn't been prepared to do that at Maria's.

'I was thinking how lovely it was to have a proper family meal like that,' she said instead.

Caleb made an appreciative huff. 'It's one of the things I love the most too.'

'I think that's why friendship has been so important to me,

because I'm not close to my parents and I have so few memories of joyful family times, which I'm guessing Maria and family have often.' Belle turned her head to the open window and relished the breeze massaging her face. 'I assume it's similar with your friend-ship with Cara. I'm closer to my friend Hannah in London than I am to my own family and it's the same with childhood friends like Laurie...' She couldn't bring herself to say Gem's name, not without the fear of her true feelings tumbling out.

'It'll be good to have your friends coming out then and to take time off. You must miss them.'

'Uh huh.' *One of them at least*, she thought.

'By the way,' Caleb said, clearing his throat, 'there was a cancel-lation so I swapped your friends from a standard room to a pool-side suite, so there'll be space for all three of you.'

'Oh my goodness, you didn't have to do that.'

'It's my pleasure.' His expression was unreadable in the dusky light, his attention firmly fixed on the road.

By the time Caleb had dropped her back at Spirit, she'd calmed down. Chatting to him about something unrelated had helped; the last thing she now wanted to do was talk to Gem. She felt foolish for not seeing through the lie Gem had spun and for being so ridiculously hung up on a man who'd thought so little of her that he'd slept with one of her best friends when the opportunity arose. Because what was there to be mad about when actually, in hind-sight, Gem had done her a favour? Any lingering rose-tinted longing for Diego had evaporated with the truth.

She kept her emotions in check, something she'd got good at doing since the accident. Decompartmentalising and convincing herself she was fine had been easier than actually dealing with feelings, although often that would backfire when underlying worries would slip out as a recurring nightmare. But as for the Diego situation, she'd have the opportunity to confront Gem when she came out to Ibiza the following weekend. There'd be no escaping her and her lies then.

The week flew by in a whirl of organisation and celebration with a private party at both Spirit and Serenity, and Belle was grateful to have work to focus on.

The first club night at Ushuaïa for Spirit's guests was scheduled for the week when Laurie and Gem would be staying, which focused her mind on her friends and cemented the thought that her dream about the 'what could have been' with Diego was well and truly over.

When Gem and Laurie arrived a week later, everything was fine. At least, it was on the surface. Belle was acutely aware of the underlying tension with Gem, and just how heartbroken Laurie was following a second failed IVF. The three of them hugged and Belle showed them to the poolside suite, yet she was chock-full of mixed feelings. The last time she'd seen Gem had been at their friend's wedding in Norfolk. The last time they'd properly spoken, Gem had entrusted her with the news about her and Dan having split up, something Laurie still didn't know about. Now Belle knew the truth about what had really happened in Ibiza ten years ago, it would only be a matter of time before it all came tumbling out.

'Wow, this must have cost a fortune.' Laurie gazed round open-mouthed at the spacious suite with touches of wood and stone alongside pops of burnt orange and zig-zag patterned cushions. 'You seriously have to let us pay our share.'

Belle shook her head. 'I got a staff discount, plus Caleb upgraded us to this room when there was a cancellation. And honestly, it's my treat. It's only one room, not three.'

Laurie ran her hand along the crisp white bedspread. 'It's certainly better than the San Antonio hotel we stayed in.'

'We were twenty-one and skint,' Belle reminded her.

'I'm still bloody skint,' Gem grumbled, 'and being thirty-one doesn't make a blind bit of difference apart from it being even more depressing.' She turned to Belle. 'But I'm grateful for your generosity. Sort of figured you wouldn't have offered unless you wanted to and could afford it. So thanks.'

Although it was said with a begrudging tone, Belle let it slide. The minute they arrived was not the time to let rip with Gem about everything she'd been bottling up over the last week. There would be opportunity for a serious talk later.

Laurie opened the doors to the pool and stepped on to the sun-drenched deck. Belle followed her out to where the wooden steps disappeared into the azure water. The pool wasn't private but it was only shared with four other luxury suites, each with their own swim-up terrace. Belle couldn't think of anything better than waking in the morning, slipping into a bikini and diving straight into the pool.

Laurie turned back to Belle. 'I can't even begin to explain how much I need this.'

'I think we all do, in our own way.'

Gem joined them on the wooden deck. 'You've been out here for weeks.'

She already looked effortlessly cool with her hair swept up into a messy bun and sunglasses shading her eyes. Her lips were glossy, and a white maxi dress with pink flowers accentuated her tan. Belle wanted to hate her. She should hate her, but what good would that do when all she really wanted was to forget about everything?

They changed into swimsuits and bikinis, lathered on sunscreen and spent the rest of the afternoon switching between sunbathing and taking a dip in the pool. They chatted, read, listened to music and snoozed. Belle had a week off and it was a chance to be a tourist for a short time. She was determined to make the most of it.

Gem was doing laps of the long curved pool when Laurie put her book down, shuffled onto her side and leaned close to Belle who was lying on the beanbag lounger next to her.

'Does Caleb like you by any chance?' Laurie wedged her sunglasses in her dark hair and gave Belle a knowing look.

'Where on earth did that come from?'

'It's just a thought.' She shrugged. 'There's something in the way you talk about him.'

'He's a friend, but more importantly, my boss.'

'I'm only saying it's incredibly generous of him to give us a swim-up room. Maybe he thinks of you as more than just an employee.'

'He only upgraded us because of the cancellation.'

Laurie raised an eyebrow. 'Even so, he didn't give it to anyone else now, did he…'

Belle bristled. This line of questioning from Laurie was unexpected, and frustrating because it had truth in it. Even the idea that Caleb might like her more than just a friend thrilled her. And maybe it was obvious that she liked him; the attraction she'd felt the other evening had been undeniable, but it was probably down to the setting and the euphoria of a successful wedding. What troubled her was that Laurie's comments were something Gem would have said. Something Gem would have noticed, not Laurie. Belle wanted to brush away the implication that Caleb liked her in that way, because her attraction to him left her feeling vulnerable and worried about making a mistake again with someone she worked with.

'He does think of me as more than just an employee because

we're a team. That's why he's so successful, because he treats people right and values them whether they clean the rooms or organise the events. But as I said before, he's my boss.'

'So? It's not as if you've never been in a relationship with someone you work with.'

Belle shook her head. 'Don't even go there.'

'What?' She held up her hands. 'I was only making an observation.'

'Caleb is... lovely. The perfect boss, so no way do I want to risk anything there. But he's also all kinds of complicated.' *And all kinds of wonderful too*, she thought, her heart overriding her head because the more she got to know him, the more she was drawn to him. 'He lost his wife to cancer a few years ago too. But the main thing is I don't want to be with anyone. I shouldn't be with anyone. I need time to figure me out for once and not jump headfirst into another relationship that could be doomed from the start.'

'Are you trying to convince me or yourself you don't like him in that way?' Laurie said pointedly.

'No one needs convincing of anything,' Belle said matter-of-factly. 'I'm just stating the truth.'

'Or are you still dreaming of Diego?'

Belle sighed and swung her legs off the lounger so she could sit closer to Laurie. Gem was down the other end of the pool, floating on her back, gazing up at the cloud-free sky. 'I've seen him. A couple of times.'

'You've what!' Laurie sat bolt upright on her lounger.

Belle shook her head. 'Calm down, nothing happened. You're reacting like I slept with him or something. We just talked.'

'How did you track him down?'

'Caleb knows him. He's sort of a business partner, so as events manager I've had dealings with him.'

'You certainly have had dealings with him.' Laurie raised an eyebrow. She settled back on the lounger and looked intently at Belle. 'So? How was it seeing him again?'

There was nothing more Belle could say about the connection with Caleb without Laurie being even more convinced about there being a potential romance, and the full truth... Well, she didn't want to go there, not without confronting Gem first. Everything about being back on Ibiza was different, from where they were staying to how she'd changed, grown up and moved on. 'There was no spark, no desire. Just memories that should remain firmly in the past.'

'Oh Belle, I'm sorry.'

'No, don't be; it's a good thing. I think I had an unhealthy obsession.'

The crease between Laurie's eyebrows deepened. 'I knew you liked him, but I didn't realise you felt quite that strongly about him.'

'Because I never shared my feelings. It seemed a ridiculous notion to have believed I'd fallen in love. No way was I going to admit that to you and Gem.' After everything she'd found out, she was relieved she hadn't.

'You could have confided in me, Belle. I don't think it's ridiculous to know instantly that you love someone; it's how I felt about Ade.'

'Yeah, well, it seemed crazy at the time. Then, when we got back, I was straight into my new life moving to London, starting a new job and then... Well, you know what happened.'

Laurie took Belle's hand and squeezed it. 'It's a big year for lots of reasons, isn't it? The ten-year anniversary of the accident will be a difficult day to get through.'

'It is, so let's enjoy ourselves and celebrate life and being together.' Belle pulled off her beach cover-up and dropped it on the sun lounger. 'Fancy another swim?'

The water was cool to begin with but with the sunshine dancing on the surface it soon felt warm. She swam to the opposite side and rested on the underwater seat with Laurie, enjoying the sense of weightlessness. Behind her were palm trees and the edge of the outdoor terrace of Spirit's bar. Beyond, the beach was hidden from view behind a white wall.

Gem swam over and bobbed up next to them. 'What have you two been gossiping about?'

Belle flashed Laurie an imploring look not to say anything.

'About Belle having seen Diego again.' Laurie caught Belle's strained face too late.

'You have?' Gem's eyes widened a touch but if she was surprised or felt any guilt, she was hiding it well.

'Only because Caleb works with him,' Belle said coolly.

'Yes, and we also talked about Caleb,' Laurie swiftly cut in, 'and how generous of him it was to put us in a swim-up room.'

Gem snorted. 'You mean how much he fancies Belle.'

Belle opened her mouth to protest then closed it. There'd been little point in arguing with Laurie so there would be no point in arguing with Gem, plus she didn't want an argument to turn into *that* argument. There was also an undercurrent of something in her tone... A harshness that she was probably noticing now because she knew exactly what Gem had got up to in Ibiza. Was Diego the reason she'd been reluctant to return? Because she feared dredging up the past and the truth being revealed?

Belle decided not to say anything. She just dipped her head beneath the water, slicked her hand through her wet hair and floated on her back so her line of sight shifted away from Gem because she didn't understand the look she was giving her – one of jealousy? Annoyance?

The tepid water was going some way to tempering the heat building inside at Laurie's certainty that Caleb liked her. The idea turned her insides to mush. She floated away from her friends and considered how she could even contemplate anything happening with Caleb when he was dealing with his own emotional torments.

23

For the first couple of days, Belle's fears about them being back on Ibiza together were unfounded. She kept what she'd discovered about Gem and Diego to herself. Belle noticed how tightly wound Gem was, as if constantly keeping her emotions in check. The same way Gem presented only the good side of her life on Instagram, she projected that perfection in the way she looked too. She'd also made it clear she wanted to completely switch off from everything back home, conveniently taking talking about Dan off the table. The only mention of her home life was when she'd disappear for ten minutes each evening to phone her kids.

Perhaps the first day or two together was easy because it felt like a proper holiday. But instead of drunken pool parties and dancing till the early hours, they went up the coast to Cara Nova beach which was nestled in a pine-forest-hugged bay. They spent the day flitting between lazing on the sand and having a cooling drink in one of the beach bars and eating octopus timbal and summer cannelloni on the decked terrace of Aiyanna, shaded by sweeping palms and large colourful parasols. Belle noticed they skirted around emotional or revealing topics and kept the focus on where they were, what they were going to do, see and eat, subjects with little risk of conflict.

Early in the evening on their second day, they found a table on the terrace of Spirit's bar and ordered a selection of tapas dishes including Padron peppers, leek croquettes and crispy coated calamari.

Gem dipped her bread into the aioli and took a bite. 'God that's powerful. No kissing anyone tonight.'

'But delicious,' Laurie said, scooping a liberal helping of the aioli onto a chunk of bread.

They were in mid-conversation about whether they should order a jug of sangria as a nod to their first Ibiza holiday or stick to a more sophisticated bottle of Cava when Belle glimpsed Caleb across the other side of the bar slowly making his way towards them.

Annoyance rushed through her because Gem had noticed him too. The slight pursing of her lips and the way her eyes traced him from head to toe showed she found him attractive. As Caleb reached them, Gem sat upright, her ample boobs front and centre. Belle was never sure if she did it on purpose or if it was an involuntary reaction to a good-looking man, because she'd always been a massive flirt. This time, it got Belle's back up.

Caleb smiled and his eyes rested on Belle.

She cleared her throat. 'These are my friends Laurie and Gem. This is Caleb, my boss and owner of this incredible place.'

Caleb shook their hands. 'Finally I get to meet Belle's friends. It's good for her to have your company. I know what it's like to work a long way from home. You've got everything you need?'

'It's generous of you to have put us in such a beautiful room.' Gem's voice was like honey.

'My pleasure. It's the least I can do. Belle taking over as events manager so quickly got me out of a real difficulty. I like the connection she has to the island and her desire to come back – Ibiza is my home and a place I fell in love with when I first came here, so I get that you three wanted a reunion holiday.'

'Ah, you know about our ten-year pact to return.' Gem ran a finger around the rim of her glass. 'Or maybe it was more about her connection to Diego Torres that drew her back.'

'Gem,' Belle said, sudden panic rushing through her. She didn't know what to say to take the conversation in a different direction. Laurie tensed next to her.

Caleb frowned. 'Diego Torres Corchado?'

Gem looked at him quizzically. 'You know him?'

'He's my brother-in-law.'

Belle's chest tightened.

Gem sat forward, her mouth open as she looked up at Caleb. 'Are you freaking kidding me? Diego's your brother-in-law? *The* Diego? Belle massively had the hots for him. Probably still does.' Gem snorted and turned to her. 'Have you ended up in his bed again yet?'

Belle wanted the ground to swallow her up. She shot Gem a warning look. She may be teasing but there was defiance in her stance and her squared jaw, a hardness about her that hadn't been there when she was younger. She'd been mouthy and confident, but never purposefully mean. Knowing now what she did about Gem having spent the night with Diego, she knew it was coming from an unhealthy place. Not understanding why Gem was trying to provoke her, Belle shook her head and bit her tongue. Caleb had obviously heard enough too, because he muttered something and walked away.

Belle watched his retreating back as dismay mixed with rage tore through her. She whipped back round to Gem. 'You really don't know when to shut up.'

'What?' Gem's nostrils flared as she glared at her. 'We all know Diego's the real reason you came back.'

'How can you sit there and say that when you know what really happened?'

Gem momentarily faltered. 'What the hell are you talking about?'

Even with music playing and many conversations happening around them, Belle was conscious of their tone, tense and cutting. She breathed deeply, trying to temper the hot anger bubbling up.

'There's a lot we need to talk about,' she said as calmly as possible.

Gem folded her arms, her whole demeanour defiant and ready for an argument. 'You want to talk about the past and the ridiculous bloody predictions we made? Then let's talk about it and share how fucking far off the mark we were!'

'Yes, I want to talk about stuff. And yes, we made some silly predictions when we were idiotic, self-centred, naive-as-hell twenty-one-year-olds who had no idea about how utterly crap life can be. This holiday wasn't supposed to be about rehashing ten years ago and the life goals we had; I intended it to be about spending time together, the sort of quality time we used to have. Maybe coming back to Ibiza was a mistake but maybe it also gives us the chance to share what's going on in our lives and support each other.'

'You really want me to share what's going on in my life right now?' Gem glared at Belle. 'Because I'm up for talking about the predictions you two made for me and highlighting my failures.'

'What failures?' Laurie dropped a half-eaten piece of calamari on her plate and shook her head. 'You have a beautiful family, two gorgeous kids, a man who—'

'Don't.' Gem shook her head. 'Don't say it. You know nothing. Understand nothing.'

'Why the hell would she, Gem, when you won't talk to her?' Belle choked on her own words because wasn't that exactly what she'd been doing with Gem? But this was different. 'How about actually being honest with *both* of us.'

Gem's nostrils flared. 'You really want me to tell the truth?'

'Yes,' Belle challenged.

Gem turned to Laurie. 'Me and Dan have split up.'

'You've what?' Laurie reached across the table and touched Gem's arm. 'Oh my goodness, Gem! When did this happen?'

'A while ago.'

Laurie frowned. 'Why did you break up?'

'Oh, take your pick. I could give you a long list of reasons – because we don't love each other, because we drive each other crazy and not in a good way, because we're both fucking miserable and it was only the kids keeping us together, but the main reason is Dan walked out because he'd met someone else.'

'Oh Gem,' Laurie said softly. 'I'm so sorry.'

'Don't be.' She flashed them both a look of defiance. 'Us breaking up was inevitable. I don't really care about him being with someone else and I know it's not the first time he's been unfaithful, it's just the first time it's meant something. It's not like I haven't cheated on him.'

'No, it's not.' Belle let out a long breath. The sophisticated bar with its natural wood, shady palms and white- and stone-coloured cushions was at odds with their conversation and the unsettled and confusing feelings swirling in her stomach. 'You realise you said Diego's full name to Caleb before. *I* didn't even know his surname.' She shook her head. 'Because it wasn't just anyone you cheated on Dan with when we were here last, was it?'

Gem stared at her across the table, her blue eyes wide. 'He told you.'

Laurie put her drink down and frowned. 'Who told her what?'

'Do you want to tell her or shall I?'

Gem's jaw clenched. 'I didn't think either of us would ever see him again. There was no point in upsetting you for no reason.'

Belle leaned across the table and kept her voice low and steady. 'You have no idea how long I've held on to an impossible dream about Diego, thinking my feelings for him were more than just lust, wondering if I'd made a mistake not being brave enough to tell him how I felt. I held on to this idea that he was the perfect man for me, that we were perfect together, when in reality he was just hellishly good in bed – but of course you know that. I was young, naive and infatuated and have compared him to every single man since, when he wasn't worth it.'

'Wait. What?' Laurie looked between them before focusing on Gem. '*You* slept with Diego as well?' Her voice was incredulous. 'How could you? You know how Belle felt about him. Of all the things you've done, that just... I don't even know what to say.' She shook her head and shot Gem a look of loathing. 'How on earth did it even happen?'

Belle drained the rest of her Cava. 'The last night when you were out-of-it drunk and I was taking care of you, Gem hooked up with him.'

'I was left on my own.' Gem visibly bristled. 'And I'm well aware it was no one's fault – I'm the last person to berate Laurie for getting so shit-faced she could barely stand or you going off to make sure she was okay – but I ended up in a scary as hell situation with a group of horny drunk guys and Diego was there. He saw what was happening, swooped in and saved me.'

'So you thanked him by having sex with him.' Belle shrugged.

'It wasn't like that.' Gem rubbed her fingers against the side of her forehead, her bangles clinking together with the movement. 'Yes, there were opportunities when I could have come back to the hotel and I chose not to... I honestly can't explain how euphoric that night was, confusing too and surprising. So many things. You have no idea either how much regret I felt, but also how much I've thought about him too, wondered if things had been different, if I'd been brave enough to tell him that I think...' A shuddery breath cut her words short. Her eyes were damp, her cheeks flushed. She grabbed her phone and stood up. 'I'm sorry Belle, for everything.'

24

'I don't know what to say,' Laurie said after Gem had disappeared from sight. 'I am beyond shocked.' She put her hand on Belle's arm. Her nails were neatly trimmed with just clear polish, her black hair sleek and pulled away from her face in a low ponytail. If she was wearing any make-up it was subtle. It was strange how unlike each other they were; Laurie and Gem, the two extremes. Perhaps Belle fitted in somewhere in the middle and that was what united them, all three individuals with differing personalities but a friendship that had bound them tight since they were children, weathered all the ups and downs. Could it continue to do so?

Belle felt hemmed in, sitting in a public bar surrounded mostly by couples, although there were a few groups of friends scattered about. She was acutely aware that even though she worked in a background capacity running the events, the bar and waiting staff were familiar. Even with lowered voices, she and Gem must have made a bit of a scene if anyone had paid them much attention.

'Do you mind if we take a walk?'

The sun loungers still had a few people camped out on them, but Belle and Laurie walked down the beach away from the busier stretch, the buttery yellow sand soft beneath Belle's feet. She carried her flip-flops in her hand and relished the salt breeze blowing away the heat and the aftermath of that conversation.

'Why didn't you say anything to Gem before now?' Laurie asked as they left their footprints in the damp sand along the shoreline and cut past a couple smooching on a lilo.

'Because it was easier not to and I didn't know how to broach it. I guess I was hoping for her to come clean, but then why would she when she's held on to this secret for ten years? Diego only told me the weekend before last.'

'He just admitted it?'

'I suspected because of something he said.'

'But Caleb didn't know about the two of you?'

'Nope.'

'And you do like Caleb,' Laurie said tentatively. 'I saw your face crumple when Gem asked if you'd slept with Diego again.' They stopped and sat down on the sand. It was far enough away from Spirit for the sounds of the hotel to merge into the background while the lap of the waves folding onto the beach took over. 'And also by his reaction, he really likes you too.'

'He said nothing.'

'Exactly. He seemed shocked and hurt. That speaks volumes about the way he feels, Belle. Trust me, from someone who's found my soulmate.'

'Although you and Ade aren't having an easy time of it at the moment, are you?'

'No, we're not. Going through IVF has put a pressure on our relationship that I hope won't prove to be too much. But what else do we have if we don't try again for a family?'

'Each other. You have each other, Laurie. And even if you don't want to think about it right now, there are other ways of having a family. Through a surrogate. Or adoption.' Belle let out a long, frustrated sigh. 'It's always the bloody Gem show or some drama surrounding me. We should talk about you too you know.'

'What, and continue Gem's great idea to revisit the predictions we made for each other?'

Belle gave a hollow laugh. 'That was my bad idea.'

'But it seemed like a good one at the time.'

'Because we were all young enough to hope that we'd ace at life. We weren't grown up enough to understand all the trials that were in store for us.'

'Do you know what our holiday gave me? Clarity. That I didn't want to be with anyone but Ade. He didn't try and talk me out of going on holiday with the two of you to Ibiza of all places. If he was worried I'd cheat on him, he never said, and when I got back he must have trusted me enough to think that I hadn't and loved me enough to propose.'

'He trusted you because he knew you would never do anything. You're not Gem.'

'I did think about it though.'

Belle turned and frowned at her friend. 'What? Cheating on Ade?'

'Briefly. I don't mean cheating cheating. I considered kissing someone on our last night – before I got completely wasted.'

'Well there's no harm done in thinking about doing something. We'd have all been better off if Gem had only considered sleeping with Diego rather than actually having had sex with him.'

The sun-blasted sand was warm against the soles of Belle's feet. She dug her toes deeper until she felt the cooler, damper grains. Laurie had always been the easy friend, the antidote to Gem's fieriness, and Belle had never been more grateful for her ability to listen and comfort, as well as share her own truths.

'Perhaps you should have gone after Gem.' Belle clutched her bare legs and rested her chin on her knees. She stared out, mesmerised by the rhythmic lap and retreat of the waves.

'Gem needs to calm down. I think some time to mull over things might be a good thing.' She squeezed Belle's hand. 'I still can't believe about her and Diego, though.'

'I can. I mean, it doesn't really surprise me if the opportunity arose – and it did. It's absolutely something Gem would do. You saw what she was like flirting up a storm with every good-looking man. It was inevitable she'd cheat on Dan, it was just a case of who with. What I really don't understand is how she and Dan managed to stay together so long when she was thinking about dumping him *before* Ibiza.'

'She got pregnant, that's why.'

'No wonder she's so blinking angry about everything if she's been living a lie all this time.'

'And I mouthed off to her about how lucky she was to have children.' Laurie picked up a stone and rolled it between her fingers. 'I've always been envious of her with two beautiful kids to love. I understand not everyone wants to be a mother and what a stressful struggle motherhood can be *even* if it's what you want, but it doesn't stop me dreaming of that or being jealous. Life is just unfair at times.'

'It's the same way she looks at our freedom and envies us that. We all want what the other has instead of making the best of what we've got.'

'That's just human nature.'

'Yep. But even though Gem wishes she had more freedom, she loves her kids, but her relationship with Dan has never been like yours and Ade's. I'm not sure she's ever been truly happy.'

'Every time I've taken a pregnancy test and it's been negative, it's like a little part of me dies. The hope I started out with gets chipped away each time and that excitement and anticipation about whether it'll be this month we get good news turns to anxiety and the fear that it'll never happen. And you're right about there being other ways to start a family, but we're not there yet. I'd do anything to have children, that's why it hurts so bad when Gem complains and wishes she had her freedom or her pre-kids body back when I'd do anything to be in her position.'

'Except you wouldn't, Laurie. I know how important starting a family is to you, but do you understand how incredible it is to have found your soulmate? You have each other. You'll get through this whatever the outcome.'

'Maybe.' Laurie chucked the stone back on the sand. 'But I'm struggling to understand what our life would look like without children in the future.'

'Families come in all different guises,' Belle said softly. 'And a family can just be two people as well. I know it's not what you dreamt for yourselves but you and Ade are a family. And think of all the people who have extended families through godchildren or friendships that feel closer than blood relatives.' Belle unclasped her hands and shifted on the sand to sit cross-legged facing Laurie. 'Or there're people like Caleb who have lost their soulmate completely, who are still grieving their loss nearly five years on; but his in-laws are still family. His best friend is like a surrogate sister. It's not a traditional family by any means and I know it's an example without children. I'm just hoping you can see that the connection you and Ade have is what most people crave. I'm certain Gem does and I know I do.'

'So then, tell me the truth about Caleb.' Laurie took Belle's hands and held them in her lap. 'Is there something between you?'

'Honestly, I don't know how I feel about him, apart from confused because my emotions are fighting each other. It all went wrong with Isaac to the extent I didn't want to be around him. It was stressful at work, and I don't want to go down that road again.'

'Does he treat you like an employee or a friend? Because from the way you've talked about him I'm guessing option two. And from his reaction about you and Diego, I doubt very much he would have reacted that way if he didn't have feelings for you and wanted to be more than just friends.' Laurie stood, brushed off the sand and held out her hand to pull Belle up. 'And that's coming from someone who knows what it's like to have found my soulmate. Exactly as you pointed out.'

25

JULY 2013, TEN YEARS AGO

Laurie had been waiting at the bar to be served for what felt like an eternity. She'd been passed over and elbowed by a pushy group of women, fellow Brits who looked and sounded as if they were on a hen do, if their shrieks and matching pink T-shirts were anything to go by. They'd already been served despite her having been waiting longer. Gem wouldn't have stood for it and would have mouthed off at them; perhaps Belle would have too, although she was sure, like Gem, Belle would have caught the bartender's attention because she oozed confidence and looked like a goddess in a sparkly gold playsuit with her hair falling in beach-tousled waves.

Someone elbowed her again and she sighed at the thought of yet another person to fight with for the bartender's attention.

'Sorry, didn't mean to jab you then.' A deep voice with a gentle Irish lilt made her turn.

She looked into the smiling freckled face of a man around the same age as her and shrugged. 'That's okay.'

'What can I get you?'

Laurie swung back round so fast she almost gave herself whiplash. The bartender was looking directly at the blond freckled guy next to her. Of course he was. She was shit at this. Or invisible, perhaps that was the truth of it. Maybe that was worse, not being noticed, something that was always so obvious when she was with Belle and Gem. She was petite, dark-haired and easy to overlook next to voluptuous Gem and classy Belle.

The Irish guy pointed at her. 'She was here first.'

The barman turned his attention to her and Laurie gave the freckled guy a grateful smile and ordered a bottle of water.

'You've been waiting here a while,' Irish guy shouted over the pulsing beat of the music.

So he at least had noticed her.

'I seem to be a pro at getting ignored!'

'Well, I'm not ignoring you.' He moved closer and flashed her a winning smile. 'Can I buy you a drink?'

Laurie leaned back a little to look at him, her vision wobbling as she did. His cheeky charm and good looks reminded her of a slightly older Niall Horan. 'I should buy you one as a thank you for being honest about me being here first.'

'We might be waiting a while in that case.' He laughed. 'But how about one drink. It's shameful to drink just water all night!' He gestured at the bottle the barman placed in front of her.

Laurie faltered, then thought, what harm would a drink do? 'Okay, thank you. One drink.'

Flashing her an extra big smile, he caught the barman's attention and ordered two vodka shots.

He turned back and shouted close to her ear. 'I'm Fionn.'

'Laurie.'

'Let me guess, you're on a hen do?'

'No, a holiday with friends.' She leaned into him. He smelled of a woody Lynx deodorant. 'We've just graduated so celebrating together. How about you?'

'A lads' holiday which we've done every year since we were seventeen, like.'

'Always to Ibiza?'

'Anywhere hot and we can get cheap tickets. Although my pale-ass Irish complexion doesn't react well to summer in Ibiza.' He pulled down the neckline of his T-shirt to reveal the sunburn on his shoulder.

'Ouch.'

'Tell me about it. Serves me right for drinking too much and falling asleep in the sun. Got shitty friends who found it funny and left me sleeping. I was just lucky they didn't draw a cock and balls in sunscreen on my stomach.'

'I'm not sure lucky is the right word…'

He grinned and gestured at her black hair. 'You look like you fare better than I do.'

'Probably, yes. I have friends who'd wake me up if I fell asleep in the sun! Also my mum's Japanese and my dad's Italian. I inherited his complexion and my mum's preference to stay out of the sun. And I always lather my skin in factor 50.'

'I inherited my parents' "let's not give a shit and deal with the consequences after" attitude.'

'I'm definitely a think-first kind of person.'

'You're sensible. Probably keeps you out of a shitload of trouble.'

Or makes life rather boring and predictable, Laurie thought. 'What sticky situations have you got yourself into?'

They knocked their shots of vodka together and downed them. Then she listened, quietly enraptured as Fionn rested his hand on her waist and got up close and personal as he shouted to be heard while telling her about his cousin's country wedding when someone left the gate to the neighbouring field open and they were joined in the marquee by a couple of goats and a donkey. Then there was the time on last year's lads' holiday when he'd gone skinny-dipping with a girl and his mates nicked his clothes – he stressed how neither friends nor farm animals could be trusted. With his effortless gift of the gab, his storytelling was amusing and endearing.

Fionn was... nice and funny. Like Ade. He was also exceedingly attractive. So someone she'd go for if she *wasn't* with Ade. Her heart faltered. How easy would it be to kiss him? What happened on holiday stayed on holiday, wasn't that Gem's mantra? Gem would have no hesitation kissing him if she was in her shoes; she'd snogged plenty of blokes over the last few days even if she hadn't taken it further than a bit of fondling. But Laurie wasn't Gem and she loved Ade, whereas Gem... Who knew what on earth she was doing with Dan besides stringing him along and wanting the best of everything: uncensored fun on holiday and a boyfriend to go back to. Laurie was doubtful about how long they would last.

She made up her mind and shifted so close to Fionn she could feel his hot breath on her skin. 'By the way, I, um, have a boyfriend. Back home.'

'That's cool. You probably won't be surprised to learn that I don't have a girlfriend – you know, lads' holiday and all, but don't worry, I won't try and jump you.'

She grinned. 'Well that's a relief!'

'To be honest, sexy time at the moment will hurt like hell.' He pointed to his sunburnt shoulders.

'I'm sure you wouldn't turn someone down given the chance.' Laurie raised an eyebrow.

'Aye, that I wouldn't.' He pointed to the empty shot glasses. 'You want another or do you need to get back to your friends?'

'They're taking time out from dancing. I can stay for another.'

Fionn caught the barman's attention again and ordered not two but four shots of vodka.

The barman lined them up in front of them.

Laurie turned to Fionn. 'You mean business.'

'Do you want to know a trick for spending less but getting drunk quicker?' He pushed one of the vodka shots towards her. 'You snort it.'

'You are utterly mental!' Laurie laughed, yet she still found herself following his lead, tipping a bit of the vodka onto the bottom of an empty glass. Three, two, one... On his countdown she snorted it. Her nose ignited as if it was on fire. They turned to each other with tears of pain and laughter streaming down their cheeks.

It was going to be a night she probably wouldn't remember.

26

JULY 2023, PRESENT DAY

Belle and Diego. Belle and fucking Diego. As Caleb paced across the bar away from Belle and her friends, the idea of Belle and Diego together was wedged firmly in his head. He should have stayed, because storming off without saying a word had definitely made it a thing, but he just hadn't been able to. What the hell was he supposed to say to Belle after her friend had dropped that bombshell?

Belle's horrified face had perfectly captured how he'd felt. And now he was more confused than ever over his feelings for Belle and even less certain how she felt about him.

Her and Diego. What were the chances? Had anything happened between them since she'd been here? He remembered them talking together at Maria's but he assumed they were talking business. Fuck! He reached his car and fired off a quick message to Diego.

Any chance you have time to stop by the house this evening. We need to talk.

By the time Caleb had driven to Solace and Diego had replied with a thumbs up, he felt calmer, but the revelation that Belle and Diego had once been intimate had sucker punched him in the gut.

He still had work to do but he could do it just as easily at home as at Spirit and he was glad of the headspace. He sat up at the kitchen island with his laptop and immersed himself in emails until his stomach rumbled.

He'd just taken a pizza out of the oven and was cutting it up on a board when Diego appeared at the open patio doors.

'Front gate was open,' he said, sidling in. 'Everything okay?'

Caleb cracked open two bottles of beer and handed one to him. 'There's pizza if you're hungry.'

'I ate earlier.' He raised the bottle. 'Beer's good though.'

Caleb grabbed a slice of pizza, sat at the table by the open doors and waited for Diego to join him.

'Why didn't you tell me you knew Belle?'

Diego frowned then shrugged. 'I don't know her.'

'You slept with her.'

'Ten years ago.' He returned Caleb's gaze. 'Does it bother you that I did?'

'No, it's just, um...' And now he was floundering for an answer because yes it did bother him when he felt it really shouldn't. 'I was surprised by the connection, that's all.'

'I slept with a lot of women back then.'

'Yeah, I get it. She wasn't actually the one who told me—'

'Because it's none of your business and you're her boss,' Diego commented.

'Exactly. But you usually tell me everything.'

'I really didn't think it was relevant.' Diego swigged his beer. 'It was a long time ago.'

With an eight-year age gap between them, Caleb had known

Diego since he was in his early twenties and was fully aware how he'd behaved back then. It hadn't been much different to his own behaviour at that age.

'Maybe I should have said something.' Diego scrunched his lips and tucked his free hand in his armpit. 'Mama said you like her—'

'Maria is making more of our relationship than there is.'

Diego leaned forward and placed his bottle on the table. 'Is she? Then why are we having this conversation?'

Caleb inwardly grimaced. He had him there. Why the hell bring this up with Diego if it wasn't because it bothered him?

'The whole conversation and the way I found out was strange, as if Belle's friend was having a dig at her.'

Diego's eyes narrowed. 'Which friend?'

'The one with the sharp tongue and killer curves.'

'Gem,' Diego said with an intake of breath. 'She's here on Ibiza?'

'They're here for a week staying at Spirit.'

Diego rubbed his hand across his stubble. 'I didn't remember Belle. I mean I did, but only when she reminded me. It was Gem I remember.'

'Wait.' Caleb frowned. 'You slept with them both?'

'Don't look at me like that. I don't feel good about it but I was twenty-four and having the fucking time of my life. You remember being that age. You made Paloma perfectly aware of what you were like.'

'What I was *once* like.'

'*Sí*, I have grown up a little since then but I can't change how I behaved. I was single, they were willing. I didn't intend to sleep with them both, but I did nothing wrong.'

'Does Belle know about you and Gem?'

'She didn't, but I sort of told her about it when she came for lunch the other weekend because she realised I knew something I shouldn't. She worked it out for herself.'

'How did it even happen?' Caleb shook his head. 'Don't answer that.' He definitely didn't want to hear the sordid details, but he felt guilty now for unwittingly leaving Belle on her own to deal with a messy situation.

Caleb took a bite of the now-cold pizza and dropped it on his plate.

Diego swigged his beer and gazed out through the open patio doors. 'I remembered Gem because there was something special about her.'

Like there's something special about Belle, Caleb thought.

'I watched my sister marry you, the love of her life, and I was supposed to see Belle again the night after—'

'Hold on, you hooked up with Belle the week we got married?'

'Yes, and I was supposed to see her the last night of their holiday and somehow I ended up with Gem.' He shrugged.

'*Somehow?*' Caleb shook his head. 'Somehow you slept with two best friends on the same holiday without either of them knowing?'

'No, Gem knew I'd already been with Belle.'

'Bloody hell, Diego. No wonder the two of them seem pissed at each other.' Caleb was fuming on Belle's behalf; some friend Gem was.

Diego clasped his hands around the bottle of beer. 'I never expected to see either of them ever again. But I remember Gem because I've thought about her since.' Diego shrugged. 'You know I've never made a relationship work, I still prefer a good time with zero commitments. But that night with Gem, we just connected. I talked to Belle plenty, but I *really* talked to Gem, opened up to her in a way that I never do. She told me all kinds of stuff too; it wasn't just about sex.'

'If it was Gem you connected with, why the hell did you go for Belle in the first place?'

'I was working, selling club tickets, got chatting and was flirting with all three of them. It was Gem who I'd noticed first, it's just their other friend made it clear that she and Gem weren't single.'

'So you decided to try your luck with Belle instead?' Caleb clenched his fists.

'I did fancy her, but Gem caught my eye.' He rubbed his hand across his stubble and took a swig of beer. 'I had every intention of seeing Belle again on their last night and never expected what happened with Gem to happen. I gave Gem my number but never heard from her.' He folded his arms across his chest as if he was trying to close himself off. He didn't meet Caleb's eyes. 'I thought about getting in touch with Gem, but never got further than thinking about it.' He shrugged. 'It was one night that shouldn't have happened, but I was glad it did.'

Caleb's jaw tightened. 'They're going to the Ushuaïa club night so you'll have every chance to see her. You slept with them both, Diego. You've talked to Belle; at least do the decent thing and talk to Gem, particularly if you have feelings for her.'

'I said we connected with each other ten years ago. I didn't fall for her,' he said brashly, but there was something about his sudden brusqueness that suggested Gem had got to him more than he was willing to admit.

'But you liked her enough to have remembered her, and I get the feeling you still do, so don't ignore her or let the situation with her and Belle get worse.'

'Maybe take your own advice then and talk to Belle. What have you got to lose?' Diego drained the rest of his beer and stood up. 'Are you coming with them to Ushuaïa?'

'Nah, going to give it a miss. Not sure I'll be particularly good company that day.'

Diego frowned before realisation crossed his face. 'The twenty-first of July.'

'It would have been our tenth wedding anniversary.'

Diego gripped Caleb's hand and kissed him on each cheek. 'If you change your mind and need company, you know where I'll be.'

27

Gem was lying on the bed with the curtains drawn when Belle and Laurie returned to their room after their chat on the beach. Belle was unsure if she was actually asleep or pretending, but either way she obviously didn't want to talk. She was playing the victim, which should have annoyed the hell out of Belle, but she actually felt sorry for her having been burdened by a secret that must have been tearing her apart. Unless of course Gem hadn't considered it to be a big deal to keep the secret at all?

Belle and Laurie tiptoed past her bed, grabbed towels and sunscreen and spent an hour in the pool making the most of the gentle heat of the evening. They showered, dressed, then strolled through Santa Eulalia and along the palm-fringed promenade to the marina which was packed with yachts and bustling with people eating and drinking in the bars and restaurants lining the waterfront.

Breakfast the next morning was a sullen affair with Gem finally joining them after having slept for fourteen hours straight. Belle noticed how puffy her eyes were behind her sunglasses as if she'd been crying. Never one for conflict, Laurie looked decidedly uncomfortable, while Gem, with deep frown lines and tight lips, was broadcasting 'don't you dare mess with me' vibes.

Belle had never been so glad for the distraction of food, a breakfast of poached eggs and avocado on toast. Laurie tucked into her pancakes with wild Ibizan strawberries as eagerly as Belle did with hers, while Gem sipped her orange juice and picked at a morsel on her plate.

Eventually Belle put her knife and fork down and turned her focus to Gem. 'Are we just going to pretend that yesterday never happened?'

Gem shrugged. 'Works for me.'

'Well, for me it doesn't. We actually started to open up to each other so don't go closing yourself off again.'

'I opened up and now feel like shit. Not something I want to repeat today or any other day, quite frankly.'

They were at a table with a view towards the pool, blue and inviting in the morning sun. A whisper of a breeze wafted the white chiffon curtains around the closest double day bed. Guests were already radiating to the beanbag loungers to laze by the pool all morning. Belle would much rather be doing that than instigating this conversation.

'The truth's out in the open now about Dan, about Diego,' she said. 'So let's talk; let's figure stuff out.'

'You want to compare notes about what Diego was like in the sack, huh?'

Belle sat back in her chair, Laurie's wide-eyed look of shock echoing her own. 'That is not what I meant and you know it. Why would you even suggest that? And why the hell are *you* so angry with *me*?'

'I'm not angry with you.' Gem pushed her poached egg and smoked salmon around the plate with her fork. She'd barely had a mouthful, while Laurie had quickly resumed eating. 'I'm jealous of you and angry with myself.'

'Why on earth would you—'

'Be jealous of you? A million reasons, Belle. I'm jealous of your effortless beauty and how you manage to look just as beautiful the minute you get out of bed as well as when you're made up to the nines; I'm jealous of how you've aced your career and worked hard to get where you are, particularly after such a shitty start in London. I'm jealous of that too, that you have this glamorous London life, which I so desperately wanted but ended up stuck in the backend of nowhere.'

'My life in London has not always been glamorous.'

Gem reached out her hand but didn't quite touch Belle. Her face softened as she looked at her. 'I know it hasn't been. You went through an awful time but you got through it and made something of yourself. That's what I'm jealous of, and what I admire about you too. It's not all negative feelings, I promise. It's how I feel about myself that's the real problem; constantly comparing myself to other people is torturous but I can't help it. I have so many regrets for the many times I've messed up – they're always in the background tormenting me.' She wedged her sunglasses in her hair and turned to Laurie. 'And to not leave you out, there's a hell of a lot about your life I'm jealous of too. The perfect relationship that I would love to have. To have *ever* had. I've never been truly happy with someone. Yes, I'm sorry, but the honest truth is it makes me sad and bitter. That's what my problem is and why I'm so flipping angry all the time.'

Gem shoved her sunglasses back on and folded her arms.

'Do you feel better for that?' Belle asked.

Gem gave a tepid smile. 'I do actually, thanks for listening.' She tied her hair into a messy bun and sighed. 'Most of all I'm sorry for being a shitty friend. For not being honest with either of you. And for what I did to you, Belle.'

Belle placed her knife and fork neatly on her plate. 'You need to stop blaming other people for your mistakes. Being jealous of us or anyone will only make you more miserable. Start looking at what you do have and how you can change things. Being open and saying sorry is a start.'

'You're right. I need to own my mistakes, particularly drunken ones of the past.' Gem wiped her eyes beneath her sunglasses. 'I'm just fed up and don't want to think about anything. Can we please get away from here today, go somewhere peaceful. Somewhere that doesn't remind me of ten years ago and that side of Ibiza.'

It was so unlike Gem to suggest the need for peace and quiet that Belle and Laurie immediately agreed.

After breakfast they packed a bag for the day and Belle drove them across the island to Port de Sant Miquel, a small resort on the quieter north coast. Although there were still plenty of people about, there was a different vibe than at Spirit, with more families than couples camped out beneath the cream umbrellas on the beach. It was a world away from their experience of San Antonio. Two large hotels were built into the cliffs to the right, the surrounding pine trees encroaching and softening the boxy lines, but it was the sheltered bay with its sloping beach and clear and shallow water that stole the show.

Gem seemed keen to get going, so they took the dirt path beyond a rustic-looking beach bar that led away from the resort and up into the trees towards the Torre des Molar, an eighteenth-century stone watchtower with views over the privately owned S'Illa des Bosc and the surrounding coastline.

They walked along the dusty stone path between the trees, the fresh pops of green in every direction a world away from the vibrant beach resorts. Gem led the way at quite a pace, making

Belle wonder if she was attempting to pound away her worries. Belle hoped this was what Gem needed, because the sun on her shoulders along the sun-dappled path with only birdsong and the chatter of insects for company was soothing and beautiful.

It wasn't far until they descended to Caló des Moltons, a small picturesque bay that could only be reached on foot. The sea, dappled turquoise and dark blue, was so inviting that they peeled off their trainers and socks by the shore and cooled their hot feet in the crystalline water. Laurie hooked her arm in Belle's and Gem's. They gazed out together, the water lapping their feet, united as they breathed in the summer air. Gem's mood in particular had been uplifted by the fresh air, walk, sweeping views and peace of the quieter north. A day out somewhere that didn't remind them of a holiday fuelled by alcohol, partying and men was exactly what they'd needed. Just the three of them, pretending to be the best friends they once were. Belle had hoped this time together would bring them closer. So far all it had done was reveal secrets and lies, and highlight disappointment and frustration. Whether they could rebuild their friendship, particularly hers and Gem's, was a worry for another day.

28

The Ushuaïa VIP Experience was for the guests staying at Spirit. It was an event that would start in the afternoon when a fleet of blacked-out Mercedes people carriers would taxi guests to the huge outdoor clubbing venue in Playa d'en Bossa for an evening of dancing to the best dance and house music on Ibiza. At least, that was how Diego had pitched it. And, with Calvin Harris headlining, the evening promised exactly that. With three more Ushuaïa VIP Experiences lined up over the summer, Belle was keen to experience it for herself, plus she hoped it would be a chance for her, Laurie and Gem to continue enjoying themselves and forget about the stresses of real life for a few hours.

'I'm not sure I should go with you to Ushuaïa,' Gem said as they were having pre-club drinks on their sunny pool terrace. 'You know who will be there and you're pissed at me. You'll have a much better time without me.'

Belle swigged her glass of rosé Cava and shook her head. 'I am pissed at you but not because you slept with Diego. I've already told you I'm pissed because you didn't talk to me. You're still not really talking to us.' She motioned between her and Laurie. 'So come to the club, have a good time, see Diego and stop shutting us out.'

Belle left them getting ready in the suite while she went back to her apartment to find something to wear. After an intense couple of days of revelations and heightened emotions, it was good to be on her own for a short while. She flicked through her wardrobe, uncertain what to wear for an evening at an iconic super club where she might bump into Diego and Caleb. It wasn't unusual to go a day or two without seeing Caleb, but after what Gem had blurted out, it had crossed Belle's mind that he was actively avoiding her.

On the bed she laid out an emerald and gold leopard-print maxi dress with a plunging neckline, with a shorter floaty blue one, and mulled over the look she was going for while she did her make-up in the bathroom.

When her phone pinged she expected it to be Laurie urging her to hurry up, but she was surprised to see a message from Cara.

> Hey, Belle. Hope you're getting on okay and sorry to disturb you on your week off. Just wondered if you'd seen or heard from Caleb today? Today being the 21st for you and not the 22nd as it now is here – it's confusing being in a completely different time zone!

Belle reread the message and considered how best to reply.

> No, I haven't, but I think he may be avoiding me… Bit of a long and rather embarrassing story on my part and things feel rather complicated but I'm sure he'll fill you in at some point. Anything I can do to help?

It didn't take long for a reply to flash up.

No, ta. Just wanted to check he's okay.

Belle slicked on a deep pink lipstick and wondered why Cara was concerned. She stared in the mirror and pressed her lips together with a satisfying smack. Her phone pinged with another message.

But in case you're not aware, today would have been his and Paloma's tenth wedding anniversary. That's why I'm worried about him.

Belle's heart dropped as she thumbed a quick reply.

Oh God I didn't realise.

And here she was getting dolled up for a night out wondering if she looked good enough and stressing over what Caleb had thought about her and Diego, when he was dealing with something monumentally more emotional and challenging.

Another message from Cara appeared in answer to Belle's first reply.

Oh, and if by complicated you mean the almost kiss that happened between you two at the Serenity wedding, I kinda know about it and think it's a bloody good thing and probably should have been an actual kiss. Just saying. x

Belle pressed her palms against the edge of the sink and stared at the screen, taking in Cara's words, particularly the 'probably should have been an actual kiss' bit. How on earth should she reply to that? How to explain the mess and confusion and the conflicting emotional messages Caleb must be receiving when they'd had *that* moment the night of the Serenity wedding, then, less than two weeks later, he had the image of her having been with Diego thrust in his face, while today he was dealing with an incomprehensible loss.

She thumbed a reply and sent it.

> If today would have been his anniversary it's probably for the best nothing really happened. His emotions must be all over the place. But if I see or hear from him of course I'll let you know x

Within moments Cara replied.

> I should be with him and I'm not. He could really do with a friend. Feeling kinda helpless so thanks for being there x

Cara was his best friend and was worrying about him thousands of miles away. Belle wasn't sure what she could do to help if he wanted to be on his own. There was probably little anyone could do when such a sad milestone was reached.

Belle opted for the emerald maxi dress, deciding it was classier to show either cleavage or legs and not both like she'd done when she was twenty-one. Gem had gone short, her long tanned legs smooth and gleaming, the high neck of the dress jewelled and sparkling, the snug fit accentuating her curves. Belle wondered if it was all for Diego. Laurie was as classy as ever in a simple black dress, her hair straightened and shiny where it grazed her shoulders.

Ushuaïa pulsated with people and music, the hypnotic beat of the crowd-pleasing DJ MK getting the evening started in style. Spirit's guests had two tables reserved in the second VIP area next to the pool with an unspoilt view across to the stage. With a host bringing them ice buckets filled with drinks, all they had to do was sit back and soak up the party vibe. Belle considered partying from

5 to 11 p.m. was far more civilised than dancing till the early hours, particularly when Spirit's guests had a luxurious hotel to return to.

The atmosphere kicked up a notch as the sun began to go down. The dance floor surrounded three sides of the pool and was packed with partygoers, the energy magically euphoric. From the VIP area they were able to dip in and out. They experienced the thrill of being in the midst of everyone on the dance floor, then escaped back to the comfort of their tables where they could look out across the sea of dancers to the stage.

The DJ was backlit and the lights were beginning to pierce the dusk. A wave of hands reached up, phones in the air and heads back as people gazed up at the sunset-streaked sky with cotton-candy clouds and the white underbelly of a plane as it came into land at the nearby airport.

Diego was no longer trawling the beaches and pool bars promoting events at the clubs; he was now one of the people organising them. Although it was still a serious amount of money to spend on drinks to secure the table, with mates rates – or brother-in-law rates – it was a ridiculously good arrangement.

Laurie was on her feet dancing next to a couple of Spirit's guests and Gem was sitting on her own nursing a glass of champagne.

'You doing okay?' Belle curled her arm around Gem's shoulders and leaned close. 'You seem to be avoiding Diego.'

'It's quite easy to avoid someone when they're doing their best to avoid you too,' Gem said cuttingly.

'He's busy working, so not technically avoiding you.' Belle sighed and removed her arm from Gem's shoulders. Why the hell should she care if Gem wasn't having a good time when she'd brought the situation on herself? 'Maybe talking to him will help clear your conscience. He was single, I was single, you weren't, but from what you said he meant something and I know how that feels. So maybe seeing him again will help you to figure out what he means to you now, if anything.'

The guests from Spirit were having the time of their lives, Laurie too, and Belle eventually gave up on Gem when nothing she said would shift her from the depressed slump she was in. She didn't need to be worrying about Gem when she was already concerned enough about Caleb, who hadn't yet shown up.

The blue sky had darkened to indigo when the atmosphere switched again. The darkness was spliced by lights flashing across the Ushuaïa stage, and a voiceover boomed out over an electronic beat. Practically every phone in the place was raised in anticipation. The strobe lighting flickered faster and faster, and the silhouette of Calvin Harris behind the decks sharpened into focus. The lights dimmed, then 'Blame' started up, blue and pink lights flickering across the stage, the vocals of John Newman matched by the screams from the dance floor. Even Gem was finally on her feet and Belle's worries subsided.

A few minutes into the set Diego pushed through the people in the VIP area and came over.

'Cara messaged me!' His hand was warm on her bare shoulder as he shouted in her ear. She could smell his cologne and tried her hardest to block out the memory of what that reminded her of. 'She can't sleep for worrying about Caleb. He's not answering his phone either. I think someone should go check on him. I'd ask Mama but it's a long way for her to drive and I don't want to upset her, so...'

'I'll go, of course I'll go.' Belle glanced around their section of the VIP area. 'The guests though...'

'I'm here; I've got it. I'll make sure everyone gets back to Spirit. I'll call you a taxi.' He grabbed her hand. 'Just one other thing. Me and Gem, are you...?' He glanced in Gem's direction where she and

Laurie had their backs to them, their arms around each other by the pool.

'It's fine, Diego.'

'And you and Gem?'

'We're working through a lot of shit. You are an added layer of complexity.' She grinned at how sheepish he looked. 'You should really talk to her though.'

Belle should have felt gutted leaving in the middle of Calvin Harris's set, 'We Found Love' swooping out over the crowd, the stage lit up ruby-red and smoke billowing up in shafts of light as hundreds of phones were raised in the air showing multiple images of the stage on screens. But she realised she wanted to make sure Caleb was okay not just for Cara's and Diego's sakes but to ease her worry too.

After letting Laurie and Gem know what she was doing, Belle took a taxi from Playa d'en Bossa. Her feet and fingers still felt as if they were thrumming from the dance beat. Instead of continuing in the direction of Serenity, they turned off and drove through Cap Martinet, one of the most exclusive areas on the island. The taxi climbed a narrow road up a tree-carpeted hillside, its tyres churning up white dust, the rocks edging the side of the road glowing in the taxi headlights. To the right where the trees thinned out, the hill dropped away with Cap Martinet lit up below and the moonlight reflected in the dark sea.

The taxi driver waited while Belle pressed the buzzer next to the gated entrance to Solace. The villa itself was hidden from view and apart from the taxi's rumbling engine, there was only the sound of cicadas making a racket in the surrounding trees. Her heart raced as she waited, wondering what to say if he answered.

'Belle?' Caleb's voice crackled to life in the darkness, making her jump. 'What are you doing here?'

He could see her. She flushed. 'I, er, Cara was concerned she'd not heard from you, not that she expects you to talk or anything like that, she just wanted to make sure you were okay. Diego too.'

'They sent you out here to check up on me?'

'I offered because they're worried about you. I am too. And they're your friends.' Belle found herself holding her breath when he didn't reply straight away.

'I'll message her now.' Caleb's voice filled the night and the gate buzzed open. 'And don't just stand there, come on in.'

29

A solar-lit driveway led to a landscaped parking area with only Caleb's Jeep in it. He met her at the wooden double doors set in a white wall. He looked relaxed in dark grey joggers and a white T-shirt which made her feel too dressed up in her green leopard-print maxi dress. His feet were bare and his hair tousled as if he hadn't properly got up, which, given the significance of the day and the fact that he'd hidden himself away, was probably right on the mark. She'd anticipated being turned away with a gruff 'leave me alone', and certainly not invited in. Perhaps he needed company even if he hadn't realised.

Belle marvelled at the clean lines of the villa. The white walls continued inside but were complemented by touches of dark wood panelling and a beige-grey tiled floor, sleek and masculine. The open-plan living area with its floor-to-ceiling windows and sliding doors onto a terrace took her breath away. To be wealthy enough to live somewhere like this was insane, but her overriding feeling was how empty it felt, as she looked past the large sofa to a dining table that could seat ten in front of an industrial-style kitchen. She could imagine him knocking about here, a bit of a lost soul on his own in a home that should be filled with laughter and love. Perhaps she was making assumptions; perhaps he held parties with the place heaving with people, but from everything she'd learned about him she thought not.

An overwhelming sense of having invaded his privacy came over her. 'I'm really sorry if you wanted to be alone, but Cara was worried enough to message—'

'I've been completely unsociable, I know,' Caleb cut in. 'I'm sorry.'

'You have nothing to apologise for.'

He gestured to the sofa that faced the open terrace doors. 'Make yourself comfortable. Would you like a drink?'

'Oh, only if you're having one.'

While Caleb headed to the kitchen, Belle went and stood on the threshold of the terrace. The gentle sea breeze and peaceful night was a tonic after the heat and thumping beat at Ushuaïa. She'd never been more mindful or appreciative of how special the two extremes of the White Isle were than tonight. The velvety black sky mirrored the sea except it was scattered with stars. Her eyes drifted across the terrace, taking in the different areas for lounging and dining, plus a breath-taking infinity pool.

She returned inside and sank onto the deep sofa. Caleb's lifestyle was luxurious and enviable but also lonely, the place sparsely furnished, the only hint of him in the books that filled the shelves behind her and a couple of framed photos.

Caleb placed two steaming mugs of peppermint tea on the coffee table and joined her on the sofa. His face was pale, while his broad shoulders hunched inwards. Belle didn't know what to say because there was an unspoken tension, either because it was an emotional day for him or due to Gem's awkward revelation.

She decided to try and clear the air. 'I know we've not seen each other since that evening in the bar when Gem, well... said a bit too much. Are you angry with me?'

Caleb frowned. 'Why would I be angry?'

'Because you seemed to storm off.'

'I'm not angry.'

'Disappointed, annoyed then? Pick an adjective.'

Caleb glanced away and let out a sigh. 'Confused.'

'Because you were surprised?'

'Not that Diego slept with two friends on the same holiday, no.'

'Oh, you know about that as well.' Her heart fluttered. 'So you've talked to him.'

'Yeah, I talked to him. He's always been like a younger brother and we usually talk about everything—'

'Oh God.'

'But he didn't say a thing about knowing you till I asked.' He leaned forward and lit the candle on the coffee table. There were soft touches here and there: board games stacked beneath the coffee table, geometric-patterned cushions on the sofa and candles softening the hard edges and neutral colours. He blew out the match. 'I like you, Belle, and I didn't know what to think. The way Gem talked about you and Diego. There was a bitterness there that I didn't understand until he told me he'd slept with her too, but I was upset because I could see you were upset.' He breathed deeply. 'To be honest I wasn't keen on the idea of you and Diego together like that.'

Belle tensed, her breath hitching as she tried to decipher what that really meant. That he liked her as a friend and didn't want to see her get hurt? Or that he liked her enough to be jealous of her and Diego together? Confused was the perfect word to describe her swirling feelings; he wasn't the only one feeling that way.

'I should have told you that I knew Diego, it's just...' Belle wrinkled her nose.

'It wasn't the easiest conversation to have with your boss, that ten years ago you'd slept with his brother-in-law?'

Her cheeks burnt hot. 'Exactly that.' She picked up the tea and blew on it, needing something else to focus on.

'I didn't think I'd be good company today.' Dimples formed in his stubble. 'But there you go, you made me smile. I didn't even want to speak to Cara. I didn't want to get upset and I knew I'd start thinking too hard and getting angry at how fucking unfair life can be.'

'I take it being on your own didn't help?'

'Nope, not one bit.' He slid his arm along the back of the sofa. 'All I've done is felt sad and bitter, moping about being unsociable and miserable when I should have been channelling my efforts into remembering Paloma for all the good she brought into my life. How blessed I was to have had her love for seven years. It ultimately made me a better person. But in reality all I've done is be angry at the world.'

'I sometimes get angry at the world as well, but you have reason. Something shitty happens to me and I think I'm being punished when actually bad shit happens to everyone. That's life. Sometimes you just have to deal with things and not place blame. It's not life conspiring against me even if it feels that way.'

'It's hard not to think like that though.'

'Yes, when you're young you believe you're invincible and the world revolves around you.'

Caleb grunted in agreement.

'I used to think like that after having the best time at university, acing my degree while playing a lot harder than I worked.' Belle took a sip of the peppermint tea and put the mug back on the table. 'After graduating I had an incredible summer with our holiday to Ibiza, then I split my time between Sheffield where I went to uni and back home with friends before moving to London.

I had the best time followed by the worst. It was out of my control, but I felt my decisions and not being brave enough to take a chance on something contributed to it, because part of me wanted to stay here on Ibiza.' Her cheeks flushed hot again, undecided if she should explain her feelings. But not being open about things in the past had always led to heartache. 'I was pretty infatuated by Diego.'

Caleb shook his head but his smile eased her worry about talking so openly. 'He has that way with women. It's nothing to be ashamed of or embarrassed about.'

'Even though I had this exciting new start in London to look forward to, I was gutted to leave Ibiza. And London did get off to a good start. I made new friends and although the job itself wasn't quite what I'd hoped for, it was my foot on the career ladder and I was earning decent money. Life was pretty good. Then shit hit the fan.'

Caleb rested his forearms on his knees, leaned closer and looked at her with concern. 'What happened?'

30

SEPTEMBER 2013, TEN YEARS AGO

In the six weeks since Belle had moved to London, she'd started her first job in marketing, made new friends and had kissed one guy. As things went, her new life post-uni and away from her parents in Norfolk had got off to a good start, even though the long commute from her shared house was the worst part of the working week and the job wasn't exactly what she'd been hoping for.

The thought of sharing a house with three strangers had been nerve-wracking but also the perfect way to not feel quite so alone in a big city. They were all professionals. Two were in their mid-twenties, and the third, Hannah, was new to London as well and had just spent a gap year in Australia. She was also working in marketing, although for a publisher rather than a corporate events company. They'd hit it off immediately.

Ibiza felt like a distant dream, yet Belle frequently woke up thinking about Diego and often fell asleep fantasising about him too. She and Hannah had been on a couple of nights out, one when they'd got chatting to a couple of men. While Hannah had gone home with one, Belle had felt nothing when the bloke flirting with her had kissed her. Admittedly, he didn't have Diego's Spanish good looks, his charm or utter deliciousness, nor were they basking under the Mediterranean sun on the White Isle either... She certainly had post-holiday blues and the thought of jacking it all in and heading back to Ibiza was massively appealing, particularly when the job proved to be little more than grunt work. What marketing she did get to do was uninspiring, which wasn't helped by her tetchy line manager.

Belle's fifth week in her new job started off as normal. She'd got into a routine of grabbing breakfast in the shared kitchen, saying a quick hello to any housemates who were around, then walking to the bus stop. She'd been late two days in a row in her first week due to roadworks and snarled up traffic, which hadn't gone down well with her easily irritated boss. Belle had now switched to an earlier bus which meant getting up at silly o'clock, but at least she wasn't pissing anyone off by being late. The commute sucked, but she was able to listen to music or read. She was beginning to see the same people on the journey, a couple who even returned her smile.

Monday morning was her least favourite time of the week, not helped by it being a drizzly day at the end of September, but at least she managed to get a seat downstairs by the window. Summer seemed a long time ago. Her one regret about Ibiza was not suggesting to Diego that they kept in touch, but not having the chance to see him one last time had been out of her hands.

She opened up her text messages and clicked on Diego's name, re-reading for what felt like the millionth time the one she'd sent him after Gem had finally got back to their hotel.

> I'm so sorry I didn't get to see you last night. Laurie was sick so I had to help her and I didn't have my phone so couldn't contact you – it was a nightmare, the worst bit not seeing you x

She scrolled down to the reply he'd sent.

No problem. Things happen.

That had been it and her heart had sunk. Even two months later it made her tearful. She'd wanted to suggest they met briefly before they headed to the airport but there was no hint from that text that he'd want to, no sense that he'd missed spending one last night with her. Not knowing how to respond, she hadn't replied at all.

With a sigh, she clicked off the messages. Even with the bus lanes, the journey was slow, all stop and start. She glanced out of the grimy window to see where they were then scrolled through the photos on her phone, stopping when she found one of her and Diego in Ibiza, a selfie she'd taken on the second evening they'd spent together. His arms were draped over her and their beaming smiles matched. She remembered the thrill of being with him, buzzing with the love or lust coursing through her. It highlighted how emotionally lost she felt now.

She could still message him and see if he wanted to connect on social media, but each time she thought about it she stopped herself. What would she gain beyond torturing herself, glimpsing his carefree Ibiza life, wondering who he was hooking up with while mulling over the 'what ifs'? There was no point. And as the days, then weeks, went by since the holiday, the idea of reconnecting with him seemed less and less likely.

Belle sighed again, clicked off the photo, popped her earphones in and listened to a dance hits playlist. The bus was finally going faster so they must have been out of the worst of the traffic.

A man in a seat across the aisle stood up, a frown creasing his forehead.

The bus was still moving and a couple more people were on their feet. Belle peered through the window. With the rain streaking the glass, she couldn't see much but she didn't think they were near a stop.

She pulled her earphones out and Avicii's 'Wake Me Up' was replaced by raised voices.

'You've gone the wrong way!' A woman in her forties wearing white trainers and a smart trouser suit was working her way down the bus.

The road ahead didn't seem familiar to Belle. She had only been in the job a few weeks but she'd already done this bus journey countless times. They'd never gone this way.

The woman had nearly reached the driver. Through the front windscreen, Belle could see a stone bridge with a height restriction warning in the middle of it. It certainly didn't look tall enough for a double decker bus. The driver didn't seem to be slowing down either. If anything, the bus was going faster and veering to the right.

Cold fear inched through her. Belle reached out her hands, ready to brace.

She was thrown forward with the impact, the bang as loud as if a bomb had gone off, followed by the screech and crunch of metal tearing. Her wrists smashed into the seat in front, followed by her forehead. Waves of pain ricocheted the length of her arms all the way to her shoulders.

Didn't people say that accidents often happened in slow motion? Perhaps that was the case if you were watching from afar, but being involved in one was a whole different matter. The impact was over in seconds, allowing no time to process anything, but the aftermath was fragmented. Vague images twisted around moments of vivid clarity: a young woman across the aisle, her glasses smashed and blood pouring down her cheek; the sound of moaning from somewhere on the top deck, more upsetting than a blood-curdling scream. There was screaming too, lots of it. And shouting, a tense conversation behind her, someone asking someone else if they were all right.

The pain in her wrists was unbearable when she tried to move. Her head throbbed as nausea and dizziness duelled with each other. She remained slumped in her seat, her body achy and tense as she tried to make sense of what was happening around her.

Another scream, commotion outside, sirens. Someone sobbing. The smell of smoke. Her heart raced in panic. The metallic taste of blood. Was she bleeding? Perhaps she'd bitten her tongue. Her vision was blurry as if she'd woken up after a heavy night out. An intense pressure in her head. Every movement painful.

More voices surrounded her, then someone was talking close by. Talking to her.

'Let me take a look.'

Belle squinted as a light was shone in her eyes, replaced by someone in a dark green uniform. A paramedic. 'Can you tell me your name?' he asked.

She opened her mouth but even that was an effort. 'Belle.'

'I'm here to help, Belle. Just keep your eyes open and focused on me, okay.'

Everything hurt, everything ached, everything was fuzzy as if she was wading through a distorted dream. Snatches of clarity, yet nothing made sense.

As she was guided into the back of an ambulance, the thought that her London life had got off to a good start vanished. How many lives had been changed? She wanted to rewind time to never get on the bus. No, scratch that, she wanted to rewind time to July and Ibiza, to Diego's arms around her waist and his lips on hers. One moment in time that had been perfect.

31

Caleb had been quiet as Belle told her story. The words tumbled from her because she rarely talked about the crash, and when she did it felt as if she was reliving it, noticing all the details, remembering the smells, the sounds and the emotion. Her heart raced, palms sweated and a tightness crawled across her chest.

'I still have flashbacks of the driver crumpled in front of the smashed windscreen. A lone white trainer covered in blood. I won't have a nightmare for months, then something triggers it and I can get the same nightmare a few days in a row.' She shook her head and sipped her lukewarm peppermint tea. 'It'll be ten years ago this September, not that I'm comparing it to your loss in the slightest.'

'I didn't think you were. But there's all kinds of trauma. Mine's loss and working through grief, but your trauma is physical and psychological. It's a loss too because it sounds as if it changed your outlook and made you grow up quickly. You're still healing and it takes time to regain confidence.'

'I sometimes work through the memories to see if I missed anything. Like, did the driver look unwell when I got on the bus?

What if I'd asked him if he was okay? What if I'd taken more notice of what was going on around me? Just everything. Would it have been possible to have saved anyone? The driver had a heart attack, which was what caused the crash. He died in hospital. A young man sitting at the front of the top deck died instantly on impact with the bridge. The woman who walked past me to check on the driver had life-changing injuries.' Belle sucked in a ragged breath. It was awful to say out loud the destruction and loss that had been caused.

Caleb lifted her chin with his fingers so she was looking at him. 'It's hard when you play over and over what you could have done differently, when nothing you did would have changed the outcome.'

'Except for not getting on the bus.'

'People would still have died,' he said gently.

'I know, but at least I wouldn't have had to witness it, however selfish that makes me sound.'

'Self-preservation isn't selfish, at least not in this case. You're not wishing for anyone to have been there or to have got hurt; you're just wishing that you weren't. Traumatic events change us forever, both good and bad. They make us who we are, negatively in many cases but sometimes even a little stronger.'

'I didn't feel stronger; I still don't. The aftermath was shocking. The next few weeks were a struggle and the following few months just difficult, frustrating and disappointing. It made me realise how quickly life can be turned upside down and how fragile it is.' Belle watched the candle flicker in the light breeze that drifted through the open doors. 'I'd been in a bubble of naivety, living a sheltered life and wasn't equipped for such big, confusing emotions or to suddenly have no support network. Most of my friends were far away and I didn't want to admit defeat and go back home to my parents. I had a boss who couldn't give a shit about a new employee who needed time off for hospital appointments while recovering from two broken wrists and concussion. After a blissful summer it was a rude wake-up call.'

Caleb drained the rest of his tea and placed the cup on the coffee table. 'Paloma's cancer diagnosis was my wake-up call about how short life can be. Because we knew how long she had left, we tried to make the most of it, make memories together. I can't begin to comprehend the shock and pain of losing someone suddenly and not having a chance to say goodbye or tell them how much you love them.' He looked thoughtful as he gazed out towards the expanse of moonlit sea. 'Every morning I told Paloma I loved her, but after her diagnosis I told her every time I left her even for a short while, just in case. I lived in fear of every I love you, every kiss, every hug being our last.'

'That is a heartbreakingly beautiful way of looking at an awful situation.'

Had they moved a little closer to each other as they'd been talking? Caleb's arm was still resting along the back of the sofa but not quite close enough to touch her shoulder. The space between them seemed smaller. He didn't look quite as sad or washed out, just contemplative. His voice had softened as he'd shared his love for Paloma with her, and it seemed a perfect way to mark a sad anniversary of the happiest day of his life.

'There'd be no grief without love and that would be a miserable world to live in, to never experience the joy of finding that person who makes you happy, makes you feel safe, who loves you unconditionally. Even after going through all that pain, it wouldn't stop me from doing it all over again.'

'Do you think there is someone else out there you can love as much?' The words left her mouth before she considered them.

'I know there is.' He met her gaze and held it. 'Of course it would be different, but falling in love and finding that one person to share your life with emotionally, mentally and physically is human nature.'

'You said "*one* person".'

'Because there wouldn't be more than one person at a time not unless you're into breaking hearts.'

He was a romantic who'd had his fairy tale but never got his happy ever after. Yet he believed there was a chance of finding that kind of love again. To find it once would be enough for Belle.

'I've never experienced true love, not like you.' She sighed. 'I envy you that even if it came with the pain of loss, the same way I envy the relationship Laurie has with her husband. To have found that one special person.'

'You've been in love though?'

'I'm not sure I have, which I guess answers your question. I had this unrealistic idea of love and what I thought the perfect man should be like, which has sabotaged every relationship I've had.' The breeze curling through the open doors was going some way to help cool her hot cheeks. 'I've blamed my own confused feelings and my uncertainty on partners, comparing them to what I thought love should feel like. So no relationship has ever lasted. I'm the problem, but I've always found fault in them, always compared them to—' She stopped herself from saying Diego's name, because she realised how pathetic it sounded and what a mistake it had been comparing every romantic relationship she'd had to an unrealistic idea of love. She hadn't fallen in love; she'd been swept up in the euphoria of him and Ibiza and the freedom it offered. They'd never even had a relationship, just sex and one-sided feelings. Her life spiralling into months of pain, tests and procedures had shone a light on Ibiza for what a good, carefree and memorable time it had been. Of course nothing would match that, but she'd been looking at it through the disappointment of the job and the pain and aftermath of the accident.

'I've compared past partners to an impossible dream,' she finally said instead, because that was the truth. 'A lot happened in those few months after Ibiza. I had the accident, Gem discovered she was pregnant and Laurie's boyfriend proposed. Our lives changed. And I couldn't shift the feeling that as soon as I was in a good place, something bad would follow. I constantly set myself up for failure. It's like a self-fulfilling prophecy.' She shook her head and tucked her legs beneath her, smoothing her hands over the folds in her silk dress. 'I'm so sorry, I've dumped all my emotional shit on you when you're dealing with enough of your own today.'

'Honestly, it's been helpful to not focus on just my own shit. I didn't want to talk to or see anyone today but I'm glad you came over. I'm glad I'm not dealing with this alone.' His jaw tightened and the way his eyes glinted damp in the soft candlelight made Belle want to hug him.

'You know you never have to deal with things alone. You have so many people who care for you and love you.'

'I know. I've just conditioned myself to getting through the pain and on with things. To not bother friends and family with my sadness, although I confide in Cara loads. But I've loved talking to you and I like spending time with you.' He dropped his hand from the back of the sofa, his fingers gravitating to his wedding ring. 'I want to let go, and I don't. It makes no sense. I want to move on yet I can't. At least not on days like today where everything reminds me of her.'

Belle couldn't bear his sadness any longer. She closed the distance and put her arms around him. His whole body was rigid as she pulled him close, encircling him, desperately wanting to show him he didn't have to deal with his hurt by himself. She rested her head in the crook of his neck. He sucked in a sob, his chest reverberating against hers before he finally let go, wrapping his arms tight around her too as his tears fell, damp on her shoulder, his hands warm against her bare back. She held him and let him cry, aware of his muscles slowly relaxing until he sank completely into her and sobbed.

They stayed cocooned together until his tears eased, his breathing regulated and her foot lost feeling beneath her, but she wanted him to hold on for as long as he needed, so she didn't pull away. When he did release her to wipe away his tears with the back of his hand, the other remained on her hip.

'You left your friends at Ushuaïa?' he said, breaking their silence.

Belle nodded and glanced at her watch. 'They'll be back at Spirit by now. I should really call a taxi and go.'

'You don't need to. It's late.' The way his eyes grazed her face made her heart jump. 'I have a guest room. Made up ready for all the guests I never have.' He smiled sadly. 'You're welcome to sleep here.'

Belle faltered. The desire to stay was overwhelmingly strong but it was more about the way he was looking at her, imploring her to stay as if he couldn't face being on his own even if they weren't going to be together. The thrill at that thought was extinguished as quickly as it had flared, the reminder of what this day meant to him overriding everything else.

Cara's words 'be a friend to him' came back to her. 'Thank you. I don't suppose you've got a spare toothbrush?'

'I'll find some toiletries.'

While Caleb disappeared, Belle sent a message to Laurie, not wanting them to worry or speculate about where she was.

> I'm staying over at Caleb's in the guest room.
> Hope the rest of your night was fab! I'll see you in the morning. Xx

Laurie replied with just a heart emoji.

Caleb gave her a quick tour of the rest of the house, the snug and his office downstairs, then upstairs he pointed out his room, a bathroom, another bedroom and then the guest room. He'd already laid out towels, a toothbrush, toothpaste and what she presumed was one of his T-shirts for her to wear. The room was elegantly furnished with picture windows on two sides allowing an unparalleled view of silhouetted trees before the hillside dropped away to reveal the dark curve of the island and the sea glittering like black opal.

Belle tore her eyes from the midnight view and turned back to him. 'This is perfect, Caleb, thank you.'

She wanted to go over and kiss him, and not just an almost kiss this time. The desire in the pit of her stomach was hot and bubbly, making her unable to think straight. Actually, all she was thinking of was how much she'd like to take his hand and pull him towards the bed. She cut her thoughts short because she absolutely couldn't go there, not with him, not tonight. Perhaps never.

As if sensing her internal struggle, he gave her a weak smile and took a step back. 'I'll see you in the morning. *Bona nit.*'

* * *

After getting Belle settled in the guest room, Caleb retreated to his own bedroom. He closed the door and leaned his forehead against it, breathing hard, trying to calm his thundering heart. He'd never been more conflicted in his life. His body ached for the woman who would soon be lying in bed across the other side of the house, while his head was filled with the memories of the woman in the photo on his bedside table. Tonight was not the time to act on impulse, to give in to what his body was urging him to do or what his heart was telling him.

With his breathing calmer, he stripped off his T-shirt and

joggers, climbed into bed and pulled the sheet up tight around him. He hugged the pillow and gazed at Paloma, a photo taken on their honeymoon, the joy on her face infectious as she stood in the turquoise shallows of Mnemba, an island off the coast of Zanzibar, a dhow floating in the background. He kept this photo on his bedside table because it took him right back to that moment when life had been perfect. Perfect and short-lived. Paloma would forever be as she was in that photo, frozen in time aged thirty-six when she'd died. He had countless photos and videos of her, but his memories were like an old film reel, faded and distorted. Was he remembering the event, or just an impression because a photo had prompted it? Five years was a long time to miss someone, to know that they'd never make you laugh again, or cook you eggs in the morning exactly the way you liked, or come to bed with you after a difficult day.

He traced his fingers across the picture. 'I'll always love you and you'll always have a place in my heart.'

There was a but to that sentence even if he wasn't able to say it out loud. He switched off the bedside light and rolled onto his back. Through the floor-to-ceiling windows, Ibiza Town glowed in the bay further along the coast, a view he'd fallen asleep to countless times. Yet he couldn't sleep and he was afraid to close his eyes because when he did, it wasn't Paloma on that Zanzibar beach who entered his thoughts but Belle in that dress with her dreamy eyes and uncertain smile. Belle who was lying in bed in a room close by. The distance might as well have been a million miles.

32

JULY 2013, TEN YEARS AGO

After marrying the woman he loved, being enveloped by Paloma's family was what filled Caleb with the greatest joy on his wedding day. Being embraced by Paloma's brothers as one of them and being part of that camaraderie and teasing meant everything. He'd never experienced anything quite like it, even with close friends.

The wedding party was getting ready at Maria and Juan's with the bride and groom separated on either side of the house. Maria flitted between them all, organising everyone and delivering snacks and drinks, being the ultimate host as she made sure everyone had everything they needed. Her excitement at her only daughter getting married was infectious. They'd be joining Caleb's mum and gran and a handful of his friends at Spirit for the wedding in a couple of hours' time, but he was more comfortable with the noise and abundant love of his adopted Spanish family. With a hands-off mother busy with her career, he'd resigned himself a long time ago to a functioning albeit distant relationship with her, and although he was incredibly close to his gran he was far happier to be with the Torres Corchado family.

The women were with Paloma in her old bedroom helping her

to get ready. Caleb was unconvinced about how much help they'd be, imagining the stress Paloma might be feeling with her aunts taking over, her sisters-in-law weighing in, her mama fussing around. But, as the only girl with five brothers, no doubt she'd accept the fuss in good spirit.

Caleb was having an easier time of it with just his best man Ross from home and Paloma's brothers to contend with, although Diego hadn't yet turned up. Calls had been made and Maria was on the war path. The time was ticking by before they'd all be making their way across the island to Santa Eulalia.

'Perhaps he's going to meet us there,' Lluís suggested to his mama when she came in tutting for at least the third time that morning.

'Perhaps he is still in bed drunk and will miss his sister's wedding altogether!' Maria snapped back at her eldest.

Caleb and Lluís gave each other a knowing look. Caleb knew exactly what Diego was like and why he was probably late. His love of the ladies and partying till the early hours had been his main reason for moving out of the family home into a staff apartment in San Antonio, although he'd told Maria it was more for convenience rather than to make his healthy love life more manageable.

And so when Diego did rock up with just minutes to spare, Maria wasn't reserved about showing her annoyance even though he looked impeccable and enviably fresh in his suit and tie.

'You're late,' Maria growled.

'Sorry, Mama.' He kissed her on each cheek. 'I was working late and slept in.'

Lluís waited until their mother was out of earshot. 'Working late, huh? Not kept up all night between some woman's legs?'

Caleb secured his cufflink and shook his head. 'Seriously, Lluís, it's my wedding day to your sister. Do we have to talk about this?'

'Sorry, just happy that my young and single brother is getting some action.' He grinned at Caleb. 'You'll understand once you've been married long enough.'

'Again, we're talking about your sister.'

'I had a good night.' Diego shrugged. 'That will hopefully be repeated tomorrow,' he said under his breath to his brother.

Caleb smirked and turned back to the mirror to adjust his tie. Diego was practically a carbon copy of Caleb at the same age: ridiculously confident, assured in his good looks with an eye for the ladies, so he couldn't really blame him for being late or for the conversation going in that direction. As for Lluís, he'd married young, had two children, a lovely but formidable Spanish wife, supported his parents at their restaurant and worked harder than anyone. He couldn't be blamed for wanting to live vicariously through Diego and his frequent conquests.

'Well, I'm glad you got here in time,' Caleb said, slapping Diego on his back as they made their way to the waiting taxis.

Diego draped his arm across Caleb's shoulders. 'I wouldn't have missed it for the world.'

Somehow they managed to get out of the house and into the taxis without Caleb laying eyes on Paloma, and the groom and the rest of the men set off across the island ahead of the bride and her entourage.

'Are you nervous?' Lluís asked as they drove along the main road through Santa Eulalia.

'No. Why would I be? I want to spend my life with Paloma.' He glanced at Lluís. 'Were you nervous marrying Ana?'

'Yes, but only because I was anxious about being the best possible husband and living up to the expectations of being the eldest son. Of having a marriage as solid as my parents'.'

'No pressure then.' Caleb laughed. 'Maybe I am nervous now.'

It seemed fitting to marry Paloma at Spirit. Since arriving on Ibiza he'd taken chances and made a huge leap of faith leaving everything he knew back in the UK. He'd made money, driven himself, partied hard, had an entrepreneurial spirit – hence the name of his hotel – and was perfectly matched by Paloma with her contrasting gentleness, unassuming beauty and family values. They had met when Caleb and Àngel had worked together and had become friends. She'd tamed his wild ways and had made him think about other people rather than just himself.

Ibiza was the island he'd returned to for a good time, a place where he'd made his fortune. His first few years had been a whirl of parties, women, late nights, hard work, making money, learning, networking and investing, but now his life was shifting into a different gear, one of a work/life balance of love and support, of building a home and future together. All that would come after marrying the woman he loved.

* * *

October 2018, Five Years Later

Caleb had watched Paloma sleeping many times, always a peaceful and joyful experience, but not any longer. Each laboured breath made him fear it was her last. The more he focused on her breathing, the more blurred her features became with tears. The honey-tone of her skin had bleached to alabaster. She looked frail and too delicate to touch. All Caleb wanted to do was scoop her up into his arms and never let go, but he was afraid of hurting her.

Seven years together wasn't enough; five years was cruelly too short a time to be married. They'd made memories together but that wouldn't be enough either. It would never be enough. The idea of having to face life without Paloma was incomprehensible.

Over the last few days her lucid moments had become sporadic.

Caleb hadn't left her side, and a tiredness crawled through him that he'd never experienced before. He was fearful of falling asleep in case he woke up to discover he'd lost her. Maria kept him company, although neither of them said much, but they comforted each other as best they could. Maria cared for Caleb as much as her daughter, forcing him to eat and drink, to get a shower while she sat with her daughter and wiped her brow with a cool damp cloth.

Caleb refused to leave Paloma's side at night, choosing to drift off in the armchair next to her, while Maria and Juan slept in the next room. It was a particularly cool, clear October night, the blanket covering him not enough to keep the chill at bay. Caleb remembered focusing on the moonlight sliding through the gap in the curtains and watching the dust motes swirl together like lovers dancing before he'd drifted off.

'Caleb?' Paloma's voice was little more than a whisper but enough to stir him from his tortured semi-asleep state.

'I'm here.' He shot up from the armchair and sat next to her on the bed. He brushed the loose strands of dark hair from the side of her clammy face.

Wide-eyed, she looked up. 'I thought you'd gone.'

'No,' he said, sorrow choking him as he took her cool hand in his. 'I'm here, I'm not going anywhere.'

Her eyelids fluttered closed and his heart sank. Had she fallen asleep again?

'Thirsty,' she said, forcing her eyes open.

He held the cup to her cracked lips and she sipped the water. The shadows circling her eyes were even more prominent than they'd been when he'd kissed her goodnight. He'd slept fitfully, jumping awake numerous times to lean forward and look at her, holding his breath until he'd been able to make out the shallow rise and fall of her chest.

Paloma nodded her thanks and he placed the cup on the bedside table.

She slipped her fingers between his. 'Promise me you'll be happy again.'

Caleb's breath caught in his throat. 'I'll never be happy without you.'

A tear slid down her cheek and he wiped it away.

'Don't say that,' she said softly. 'You have the whole of your life ahead of you. I want you to be happy, to finish our house, to do all the things we talked about. To find someone to love again, the way you've loved me.'

Caleb shook his head, unable to bear the thought of life without her, even less so the idea of someone replacing Paloma. Their time together had been too brief. Their hopes and dreams shattered. The family he'd imagined would never exist.

'How am I supposed to live without you?' Caleb pressed his head gently into the crook of her neck, which was cool against his own hot skin. His tears dampened the pillow.

'One day at a time,' Paloma whispered. 'I'll be with you always, wishing you all the happiness you deserve.'

33

JULY 2023, PRESENT DAY

Belle woke to the sunrise which cast an amber glow on the horizon. It wasn't the sort of place where you wanted to draw the curtains and shut out the view. With the trees screening the window to the side and just open sea through the one in front, there was plenty of privacy. The view stretched endlessly, breathtaking in its beauty as the sun's rays waltzed on the surface of the sea.

It was the peace that captivated her the most, so different to waking up in London. Even on Ibiza in the apartment tucked away at the rear of Spirit, there were always the sounds of the hotel, people chatting, the beat of music and an occasional car from the road. With its large windows and modern lines, Belle imagined this house was soundproofed and with only her and Caleb at the other end of the corridor, there was utter peace. She could imagine the joy of waking up to this each morning or sipping a coffee while basking in the sunshine on the terrace, yet once again it accentuated how lonely Caleb must be. The uninterrupted quiet was already giving her too much time to think. She'd fallen asleep playing over everything they'd talked about and had woken to thoughts of Caleb and the way he made her feel. She was drawn to him and wanted to be with him in all senses of the word.

She threw off the sheet, connected her phone to the Bluetooth speaker and chose a dance hits playlist on Spotify. The uplifting beat of Becky Hill and Chase & Status's 'Disconnect' filled the room as she stepped into the ensuite to shower and brush her teeth.

The silky maxi dress felt too dressy to change into early in the morning, yet she felt underdressed in Caleb's T-shirt. It had an unexpectedly fresh floral scent and was soft against her skin as she padded barefoot past the closed door of his room and downstairs.

Wandering through the expansive living area on her own felt strange, like the morning after spending the night with someone, except they hadn't. Hopefully that would mean there'd be none of the awkwardness.

The view from the ground floor was just as impressive as from the guest bedroom. In the daylight, she could see the pool jutting out of the hillside, enticing in its sleek coolness. What a place to live, and yet what good was having all of this if he wasn't happy? That was the crux of everything. Because at the heart of every failed relationship she'd had was the reality that she hadn't been happy with them or herself.

The industrial-style kitchen was spotless with a polished concrete worktop and dark wood cupboards. She made a coffee and found oat milk in the fridge which was well stocked with food: lots of leafy greens and fruit, cheese and chorizo. His kitchen was obviously not just for show.

Taking the coffee with her, she stood by the floor-to-ceiling window in the living area and enjoyed her chilled-out start to the day as she soaked up the view. She considered how long she should stay and if it would be rude to call a taxi and leave before

Caleb got up. Not that she was in a rush; Laurie and Gem would be sleeping in.

She slid open one of the doors and stepped barefoot onto the terrace, the stones not yet warmed by the morning sun. She had an overwhelming desire to stay. Caleb might wake up alone but she didn't want to be gone without having said goodbye. She wasn't replacing anyone, she was simply being a friend, exactly as Cara had suggested.

Belle sat on the end of a padded day bed that faced the pool. She could see along the coast towards Ibiza Town, the bay studded with gleaming white buildings. She sipped the creamy coffee and basked in the stillness. A leisurely morning was one of life's little luxuries; she didn't even have her phone with her. It was refreshing to just sit and think – or not think. To just be.

The sun was higher in the sky and she'd finished her coffee by the time the sound of a door sliding open made her turn. Caleb was barefoot in shorts and a T-shirt, clasping a mug as he strolled towards her.

'It's like you've read my mind.' He sat next to her with his coffee. 'This is where I start every day, gazing at that view and contemplating things.'

'It's the perfect spot.'

'You slept okay?'

'Really well, thanks.' They stared out together. 'Is this your routine then, a coffee out here looking at all of this?'

'Most days, yes, followed by a swim then a run listening to music. It helps to focus my mind before the day begins.'

'I popped on a dance hits playlist when I woke up and nearly started my day with a bop about my room.'

'What stopped you?'

'Being sober.'

Caleb laughed. 'It is first thing in the morning.'

'Yeah, but I don't tend to dance unless I've had a few.'

'Even if you're on your own?'

'Even on my own.' She sighed.

'I bet you did when you were younger.' There was a resigned tone to Caleb's words as if it was the case for him too. He placed his half-finished mug of coffee on the terrace. 'How about a swim? Would you be up for that?'

'I would be but I'm not about to go skinny dipping.' She refrained from pointing out the fact that she was only wearing a T-shirt and knickers and he did a very good job of maintaining eye contact.

'You can always keep the T-shirt on.' His smile was adorably persuasive. 'I promise you the view from the end of the pool is worth it.'

Without waiting for her to reply he stood, peeled off his T-shirt and dropped it next to her. He paced away a couple of steps then turned back, an enticing smile lighting up his face, but her eyes were drawn to the black dragon tattoo that covered almost one side of his chest. The tail started beneath his arm and the body curved up across his left pec, to where the head finished on his neck, eye-catching in its dominance. He seemed less stressed and emotional than he'd been the night before, when the significance of the day had laid heavy on his heart. It filled Belle with joy to see the change in him.

Sod it, she thought as she stood up and watched him dive into the pool with barely a splash, swimming half the length before breaking the surface.

The sun had climbed high enough to heat the morning air, but Belle gasped at the cool shock of the water as she slid into the pool. Her T-shirt ballooned and she tugged it back down. The combination of the refreshing water and the gentle caress of the sun was magical as she swam towards Caleb at the end of the pool. His arms were resting on the stone edge. She joined him, letting her legs float out behind her. The way the pool jutted out of the hillside gave her the feeling of being on the edge of the world with nothing in front of them except the shimmering sea and sunkissed sky.

'It's magical.' Belle was unable to tear her eyes away from the view, but she was aware of Caleb watching her.

'Told you it was worth it.'

Her T-shirt was now see-through and clingy. It wouldn't have made much difference if she'd taken it off. Every part of her was conscious of an unspoken desire and magnetic pull, yet she was uncertain if he sensed it too.

She felt hidden beneath the water but she had no idea how she was supposed to maintain her dignity once she got out. Perhaps she shouldn't worry; she was sure Caleb had been privy to plenty of wet T-shirt competitions when he was a young holiday rep, and as a club promoter he would have had semi-clad women thrusting themselves in his face on a daily basis, and yet...

They were walking a tightrope when it came to friendship and maintaining some kind of professionalism. One slip and there was the potential to mess everything up, yet it could be completely and utterly wonderful.

34

With Belle so focused on the view, it allowed Caleb to soak her up. Stare – that was actually what he was doing because he was mesmerised by the dusting of freckles across her cheeks and the way her eyes were wide with wonder. Her lips were slightly parted and the tendrils of hair that had escaped from a messy bun framed her face. His attraction was undeniable and confusing.

As if sensing the intensity of his look, Belle pushed back away from the end of the pool. For a split-second, Caleb caught sight of her out of the water. The image of the now see-through T-shirt moulded to her breasts snatched his breath away. He averted his eyes and powered across the pool to widen the distance between them, although the cool water did little to dampen the blood rushing to a certain part of his body. He climbed out and left a trail of water across the cream-coloured stones. Grabbing a couple of towels, he shook one open and held it in front of himself as he headed back to Belle who was still submerged in the water.

'I'm going to make breakfast,' he said, leaving the other towel on the side next to the pool. 'Do you like eggs?'

Belle nodded, although her confusion at his abruptness was obvious, but he didn't dare hang about or try to explain, because to do so would mean admitting how he felt. He wasn't ready for that. He dried himself and retreated to the kitchen where he kept busy cooking Spanish-style scrambled eggs, although his thoughts continued to torment him.

Belle joined him when he was dishing up, back in her dress from the night before with her damp hair loose around her shoulders and a make-up free face, her natural beauty somehow even more enticing.

He took the plates over to the table in front of the windows where he'd laid out cutlery, orange juice and a cafetière of coffee.

She was quiet and he couldn't read her, although that probably had a lot to do with them not having really talked this morning along with his reaction in the pool. There was something between them though, an energy, a connection that he'd felt before, but last night it had manifested into so much more.

Belle swallowed a mouthful of the eggs with chorizo, cooked potato and piquillo peppers. 'This is delicious.'

'One of my favourite breakfast dishes.'

'I wasn't sure you cooked.'

'I do sometimes but it's much nicer cooking for someone else.' Aware of how flustered he felt around her, he poured the coffee into mugs and concentrated on his own plate of food.

'Thank you for suggesting I stayed last night.' Belle looked at him thoughtfully. 'I'm glad you weren't on your own all day yesterday. I can only imagine how challenging it was.'

Caleb took a mouthful of the eggs and considered how much he should share. The smoky paprika and the silky texture of the eggs combined with the sweetness of the peppers helped to ground him. Breakfast with Belle. Recently that had crossed his mind on more than one occasion, but he was glad they were eating together after only having spent the night talking.

'Paloma's always with me in some form or another,' Caleb said slowly, picking up his coffee. 'There are reminders everywhere and of course on days like yesterday the feelings are acute. But as time goes on, she's not at the forefront of my mind like she was in those first couple of years. When I'm busy, so many other things take over and I get to the end of the day and realise I haven't had the time to think about her. Perhaps it's my head playing tricks making me think if I don't focus on her I can believe that she's still here waiting for me to get home. My subconscious torturing me.'

'Do you dream about her?' Belle asked.

'I have two recurring dreams that often happen at times when I'm stressed or have a decision to make, when I'm worried about something. Or simply when I'm missing her. I dream about our wedding day but I always wake up just as I catch my first glimpse of her walking down the aisle. The dream never gets any further than that.'

'And the other one?'

Caleb dug his fork into the scrambled eggs and stalled while he chewed. 'The other dream is the last conversation we had and her last words to me. Words I've played over and over, committing them to memory and beating myself up about because she wanted me to promise something I wasn't sure I'd be able to keep.' Buttery light slanted through the windows and across the end of the table where Belle was sitting, making the golden strands of her hair glow. Caleb cleared his throat. 'How about you? Do you have the nightmare about the accident often?'

'Only occasionally, thankfully. They've lessened over the years but like you, it often comes back at times of stress or when I feel particularly emotional – and not necessarily in a bad way. They've just become a part of life and a way of processing things I guess.'

Caleb grunted. 'You find a way to keep going else you'd simply give up. That's not helpful for anyone. Over time the trauma lessens whether it's the grief of losing someone you love or the shock of being involved in something traumatic.' He sat forward, cupped his hands round his mug and stared out through the windows to the terrace, where the edge of the pool glistened in the sunshine. 'It's the emptiness that I've struggled with the most. The finality of loss. How incomprehensible it is that I'm never going to see her again, laugh with her or grow old together. Our story was cut short and it makes me wonder about what could have been.'

Belle slipped her hand over his and pulled him back. His gaze switched from the terrace to her blue eyes which were so open, warm and loving. She managed to convey so much without having to say a word. In that moment, her gentle compassionate touch meant everything.

* * *

It was late morning by the time Caleb drove Belle back to Spirit. When they said goodbye, he didn't kiss her cheeks but held her tight, breathing in her freshly washed hair and the scent of cherry on her skin. He could feel her warmth and the rise and fall of her chest through the thin material of her dress, and it took all of his resolve to let go.

'Thank you for coming over and for just being there.' He'd thought he had to get through yesterday on his own when actually talking about Paloma and sharing his heartache with Belle had been helpful and meaningful. Her company was needed and wanted even if he hadn't considered he could have it.

Belle nodded, her cheeks tightening a touch as she squeezed his hand.

Caleb watched her walk away and it wasn't confusion he felt

any longer. It wasn't relief or sadness either. What he felt was something he'd only had brief snatches of over the last few years. Happy.

35

Back in her apartment, Belle swapped her dress for shorts and a top thrown over a bikini. If her head and heart had been twisted with conflicting emotions the evening before, then everything had been turned upside down this morning. She hadn't trusted herself to say anything when Caleb had dropped her off. The idea that she was even entertaining the possibility of her and Caleb was tricky. Wasn't getting involved with someone she worked with exactly what she'd sworn herself off?

But the way she felt when around him, she'd never felt anything like it, and that scared and thrilled her because it was more than just wanting to be with him physically. She'd seen the desire in his eyes in the pool and wondered if he'd been thinking about sleeping with her. And the way he'd shot out of there as if he'd been stung. She hadn't intended to be provocative, but she'd been well aware of the impact that getting into the pool dressed in a white T-shirt would have. Although he was the one who'd suggested it. They were toying with each other, neither of them ready or willing to make a move for fear of what? It wasn't rejection. Deep down she knew it was through fear of where it would lead, what it would mean and the feelings that would be stirred.

Belle hadn't heard from either Laurie or Gem since she'd messaged Laurie the night before. Their room was empty but the doors were open and she could hear them talking on the poolside deck.

She took a deep breath and joined them.

Gem glanced over her shoulder and lowered her sunglasses. 'Ah, you're back. Laurie said you spent the night with Caleb.'

Laurie, lying on the next beanbag lounger, shook her head. 'That's not what I said, Gem.'

Belle sat on the end of the third lounger. 'I stayed in Caleb's guest room and we talked a lot, that's all. If his wife had lived, yesterday would have been his tenth wedding anniversary, so for you to insinuate that anything else happened...' Belle shook her head at Gem.

There was no way she could put into words the emotions of the night before and the events of this morning without it sounding more than it was.

'Poor bloke,' Laurie said. 'I can't even begin to imagine what he must have gone through.'

'He needed a friend and someone to talk to, that was all. I'm sure the end of my night was less eventful than yours,' Belle said somewhat truthfully, eager to move the conversation away from Caleb. 'How was the rest of the Ushuaïa party?'

'We missed you,' Laurie said, 'but we danced till our feet ached and, unlike clubbing in Ibiza ten years ago, I can actually remember everything about the night, which is rather refreshing.'

Belle looked at Gem. 'And did you speak to Diego?'

'He was too busy working.' Gem wedged her sunglasses into her hair, her nostrils flaring. 'Have you eaten?'

'I had breakfast at Caleb's.'

'Well, I'm flipping starving.' She scooped up her phone and stood up. 'I'll go get us a table at the restaurant; join me when you're ready.'

As soon as she closed the sliding door to the room behind her, Belle turned to Laurie. 'Someone doesn't want to talk about him,' she said under her breath.

'She avoided him all evening.' Laurie shrugged. 'And it wasn't that he was too busy, because a couple of times he attempted to come over. I don't know if she's feeling ashamed or just guilty, or what it is, but she was having none of it.'

'She's too pig-headed and stubborn for her own good.'

'Or still feeling guilty about sleeping with him behind your back.'

'I've forgiven her; I don't want her to feel guilty for my sake. I'm over it. I'm over him.'

'But don't you see that's part of the problem, the way you've risen above any pettiness or holding what she did against her. She's jealous of not just how you look and the life you've built but because you're a good, kind person. She's always been envious of you.'

'That's not true, at least not when we were younger. I was the one who envied her, for her absolute confidence, how stunning she always looked, how effortlessly she could talk to anyone. We both did.'

'And I still do,' Laurie said sadly, 'but for different reasons now, whereas you honestly have nothing to be jealous of any longer.'

Belle took Laurie's hand. 'All we seem to be doing is talking about me or bloody Gem. How are you coping?'

'I'm doing okay. Being here is helping and it's good to have something else to talk about with Ade. But I'm sad.' Her fingers tightened in Belle's. 'I haven't physically lost someone but it's still a grieving process.'

'You've lost what you hoped to have in your future; that's a big thing to get over. It'll take time. Just don't give up.'

'I won't.' Laurie paused and gazed towards the pool before turning back to Belle. 'What really happened last night with Caleb?'

Belle had bottled up so many of her feelings before; was she really going to do it again? How could she expect Laurie or even Gem to share their innermost thoughts when she couldn't reciprocate?

So, much like she had with Caleb the evening before, Belle opened up to Laurie about her last few weeks on Ibiza culminating in the morning with Caleb. She shared her confusion and uncertainty about whether she should entertain the idea of something happening with him.

Laurie listened intently, and when Belle finished she just smiled. 'I knew straight away there was something between you. And I'm certain he has feelings for you as well.'

'You don't know him, Laurie.'

'No, but I know you and he'd be mad to not fall for you.'

'I didn't say anything about him falling for me or vice versa.'

A soft smile graced her lips. 'I've never seen you like this.'

Belle rubbed her fingers across her forehead and grimaced. 'What, stressed?'

'No, glowing.' Laurie sat upright and took Belle's hands. 'You've never been afraid to be bold and do things even if they scare you – moving to London, coping on your own after the accident instead of running back home, building your career by taking risks and saying yes. Don't let a chance at happiness pass you by because you're scared to take a leap of faith and let someone into your heart. There's always the potential for a relationship to go wrong, for your dreams to not work out, but that shouldn't mean you give up on love or hope. Isn't it better to take the chance and fail than fear the unknown and risk missing out on happiness?' She scrambled up and pulled Belle to her feet. 'Come on, we'd better go and join Gem so she doesn't complain that we stood her up.'

* * *

It was lunchtime and Spirit's restaurant was beginning to fill up. The place was alive with conversation and the bustle of the waiting staff bringing tapas to the tables. Gem was nowhere to be seen.

'Where on earth has she gone?' Laurie glanced around, then at her phone and frowned. 'Let's get a table and message her. I'm starving.'

'She did seem off.' Belle wandered to the edge of the terrace with Laurie. 'Maybe she wanted to be alone?'

It was unlike Gem to go off without saying a word; if she was upset about something she'd let it show, as in-your-face with her negative feelings as her happiness was boisterous. Closing herself off concerned Belle, particularly when the recent revelations meant she'd been dealing with so much on her own. She had some mum friends and a couple of other old school friends in Norfolk, but did Gem actually talk to them? Belle was doubtful.

'Over there, on the beach.' Laurie pointed. 'Is that her?'

Belle lifted her sunglasses and squinted, shading her eyes with her hand. Wearing a hot pink dress and with blonde hair tied up in a loose ponytail, it certainly looked like Gem, a hunched figure hugging her legs as she stared out to sea.

Belle sighed, knowing another emotional conversation was imminent. 'I think so; why don't you wait here and I'll go talk to her.'

Laurie readily agreed. Belle didn't blame her for being keen to escape any further drama. Gem was hard work at times and Laurie's emotions were heightened, none of which was helped by the mess of hormones she was experiencing post-fertility treatment. Belle knew there was only so much Laurie could take of Gem moaning about her life, particularly her kids, even if she loved them more than anything in the world.

Belle reached Gem and sat in the sand next to her. Gem dropped her sunglasses over her eyes but not before Belle noticed she'd been crying.

'Hey,' Belle said softly. 'You weren't at the restaurant. We were worried about you. You okay?'

Gem glanced round. 'Where's Laurie?'

'Getting us a table.' Belle sat cross-legged, wishing she had a hat on in the unforgiving midday sun. 'Do you want to talk?'

Gem's arms tightened a fraction around her knees. Her pink dress was eye-catching and suited her perfectly, her manicured nails a paler bubble-gum pink. Her legs were smooth and tanned in a natural way though Belle knew it was from a bottle. On the outside she was the picture of perfection, but hidden truths were beginning to bubble over as if the cork was about to pop.

'It was obvious you were upset when I got back, and I promise we don't have to talk about Diego or Dan or anything else if you don't want to. We can just sit and watch the—'

'I'm so fucking miserable, Belle.' Gem's words cut her off. 'With everything. There's nothing good in my life and the things that should be good, like the boys, just cause me stress through no fault of their own. It's my own shit I need to deal with, but I don't know what to do. Even here it's like there's a constant storm cloud over my head. I have this desperate need to enjoy myself, to make the most of time away from the kids, but it's nothing like how it was ten years ago because *everything* has changed. My life is nothing remotely like it was.'

Belle gently touched Gem's arm. 'But you just said yourself there are good things, like your boys.'

'I love them but I didn't plan to be a mum. It feels like life's passing me by and I have nothing to show for it beyond Jack and Oscar.' She glanced sideways at Belle. 'But stuff that I've actually done. There's nada.'

'But Oscar will be going to school in September, so you'll have a bit more time to focus on yourself and what you want to do.'

'Do you know how hard it is to find a decent job that fits around school hours?' She scrambled to her feet and wiped her glowing forehead with the back of her hand. 'And with Dan gone I'll have even less support.'

'What about your parents?' Belle got to her feet too and scurried after Gem as she strode off down the beach away from Spirit.

'They already help enough as it is. I was beginning to focus on how I could go about getting my interior design business up and running, fitting it in around the kids and part-time work, when Dan walked out.'

'It's only been a few months, Gem. Your life's been turned upside down and you've been dealing with this all by yourself. I presume your parents know?'

'Oh yes, they're as disappointed in me as I expected.'

Belle frowned. 'Your parents are the most supportive parents ever. There's no way they feel like that about you. Sad because your relationship with Dan has broken down but not disappointed. Do you not think you're projecting your own disappointment onto them?'

'Yeah well, I feel utterly shit about myself so I wouldn't be surprised.' They reached the end of the beach where the mouth of the river met the sea. The bar on the corner was packed with people eating and drinking, the tables and chairs spilling out onto the sand. Gem paced past and onto the path that ran alongside the river, her fists clenched tightly, her knuckles white. 'I had a plan and put pressure on myself to start working towards my dream then Dan goes and has an affair. He not only ended our relationship, but he also destroyed my ability to get myself out of the godawful situation I'm in.'

'But you weren't happy with Dan.' Belle had to up her pace to catch up with Gem. 'I know the timing sucks and maybe it's not what you thought you wanted, at least while Oscar is still so young, but it's done now and there's a freedom that comes with that. A chance to start afresh however hard it is. You deserve to be happy, Gem.'

'Being a single mum, trying to start a business, trying to keep the kids alive while focusing on myself – it's utterly overwhelming.'

'Okay, so forget about the big picture; why don't we just focus on here and now. This week. We've got two days left together. What do you want to do? How can we make you feel better?'

'I don't know, that's part of the problem. I'm wound up tight in here.' She shoved her fist into the centre of her chest.

Belle didn't know if it was a good idea or not to suggest it, but the worst that would happen would be for Gem to shoot her down. 'You could always have a fling; help you move on from Dan. Make you feel better about yourself.'

Gem snorted and picked up the pace. The Río de Santa Eulalia to their left glinted in the sunlight. 'That used to be my go-to fix but I'm older and wiser now and believe it or not, sex with some random stranger is not going to make me feel any better even for one night.'

'What if it doesn't have to be a stranger? What if it's with someone you already know... Why don't you talk to Diego?'

'Stop.' Gem ground to a halt next to the bridge that curved across the river. The shade of the trees in the park on the other side looked cool and enticing. 'I honestly never expected to see Diego ever again and it's brought back all these feelings and worries that I thought I'd laid to rest.'

Belle opened her mouth to say something but Gem cut her short.

'I know you're not angry about what happened and you're a flipping saint for it even though I'm truly sorry and mortified. It's actually seeing him again that's got me in a state.'

'Because you still like him?' Belle said slowly.

'Yes, but it's more than just liking him.' Gem breathed deeply and looked around as if gaining strength from the picturesque, sun-kissed surroundings. 'It's wishing I'd done things differently when I found out I was pregnant with Jack.'

'I don't understand. What's any of that got to do with how you feel about Diego...?' The second the words were out of her mouth, Belle knew, confirmed by the tearful look of sorrow on Gem's face as she wedged her sunglasses in her hair.

'It's got everything to do with it because I don't think Jack is Dan's. I'm pretty certain Diego is actually his father.'

36

SEPTEMBER 2013, TEN YEARS AGO

Gem knew what the outcome would be without needing to do a pregnancy test, but she did one anyway.

Two lines that changed her future.

The nausea wasn't because of food poisoning, her tender breasts weren't because her period was due, last month's spotting wasn't just an abnormally light period. She was pregnant. She was fucking pregnant. And of all the places in the world to find out, she was in a dimly lit hole of a skanky bathroom in Thailand.

After returning from Ibiza, Gem had just a couple of weeks back home before she was off again with summer clothes, flip-flops, mozzie spray and sunscreen squeezed into a backpack. She'd met Cerys, her best friend from uni, at Gatwick airport, their excitement bubbling over as they'd embraced each other.

During their first two weeks island hopping in Greece, Gem had had a niggling worry and had bought a pregnancy test on the last day before they flew to Thailand. And then, swept up in everything, she'd kept putting off taking the test, reasoning the way she felt was down to the food, the heat, the mosquito bites. She'd tried to behave normally, drinking, partying, sunbathing, sleeping in late, but the thought of alcohol made her nauseous, and she constantly felt tired and irritated by the attention of too many drunk blokes. Lounging on the beach was fine but at night she was restless and would lie awake in the morning worrying while Cerys continued to sleep like a baby in the bed next to her.

Like a baby.

This could not be happening.

Still holding the test in her clammy hands, Gem shut the door on the rank bathroom and sat down with a thump on the end of her bed in their compact and basic beach bungalow.

She tried to work out the dates and kept coming back to the same conclusion. There was a chance that it could be Dan's, but it was unlikely. That night in Ibiza with Diego, she'd been crazy drunk by the time they'd wound up in bed together; he'd been far from sober too. She'd felt invincible and impassioned and so wrapped up in him that it had been hard to think straight. That night had been everything; he'd saved her, delighted and consumed her, and had given her the best night of her life before they'd even got back to his room. She hadn't asked him to wear a condom and she sure as hell couldn't remember him mentioning it either or pausing to put one on. They'd been foolish and reckless. But she'd never had a night with Dan like she'd had with Diego; she'd never felt that free and passionate or so goddam wonderful. One fucking euphoric night that would haunt her for the rest of her life.

Maybe she'd miscarry. The moment the thought entered her head she regretted it. That was an awful thing to hope for, and yet this was so far from what she wanted. One night was all it had taken because she was always so careful with Dan, while with Diego... Gem rested her elbows on her bare knees and stared at the pregnancy test clutched in her hand. The beach bungalow was stifling, the fan in the centre of the ceiling barely moving, and there wasn't a breath of wind filtering in through the open door. Sweat trickled down the side of her face. The dark wood walls were oppressive and gave the feeling of being trapped, accentuating the tightening fear in her chest that being pregnant was effectively a prison sentence.

Gem stuffed the positive test into the front pocket of her backpack and headed to the door. The bungalow was cheap and functional, just a place to sleep with a much-to-be-desired bathroom, but at least she and Cerys weren't having to share it with anyone else. Cerys had booked their accommodation in Greece and Thailand, while Gem had sorted out the Australian leg. Gem had suggested they stayed near Patong Beach and had hoped that they'd be somewhere where they could lounge on the beach during the day and party at night, but Cerys had opted for much cheaper accommodation further up the coast. Gem had not been impressed by the distance to get anywhere, let alone where they had to sleep. Cerys had exceeded herself with the location though, because once Gem stepped outside the depressing bungalow onto silky, caramel-coloured sand, it was enough to soothe away her annoyance, worries and fear, even if temporarily. Backed by rainforest, the beach was studded with boulders that made perfect spots for sitting with a drink to watch the sun go down. Depending on the time of day, the sea changed from emerald-green to turquoise, the shallows clear and warm – a true backpacker's dream.

Cerys was lying further down the beach sunning herself. They'd been friends since the start of university, hitting it off straight away, and their six-month backpacking trip had long been in the making; they'd been saving for the last eighteen months. Gem should tell her, but she didn't want to, not yet. This was her time, her chance for the last bit of fun before real life and focusing on her career would begin, although that was now suddenly and scarily in question. Maybe she should cut her travelling short, go home and get a termination. She gulped back a sob. This wasn't a decision she could rush. Although scared, she was determined to push the reality of her situation to the back of her mind. She stretched, reaching her hands towards the sultry blue sky, and relished the heat of the sun on her bare shoulders. She could pretend that her life hadn't just turned to shit for a little while longer, plus she needed time... Time to decide what to do and who to tell. Dan or Diego. Her easy carefree life had just got complicated.

37

'What would you do?' Gem looked imploringly at Belle, the whites of her eyes bloodshot from tears.

'I'm not sure I'm the best person to ask.' People walked by on the path next to them, relaxed in shorts and summer dresses, many stopping to take selfies on the bridge. Belle was still trying to take in everything Gem had said. 'I've been constantly running away from things – relationships, difficult situations and not dealing with my emotions. I've tended to bury stuff in the hope that it will go away, but that's not a smart strategy because it just festers and makes things worse.'

'Yeah, well, I've managed to let things fester for ten years,' Gem said bluntly. 'I had a similar attitude when I found out I was pregnant and carried on travelling as if ignoring the truth would simply make it disappear. And I can't exactly ignore the fact that I have a son who doesn't know who his real father is.'

'How certain are you?'

'Certain.'

'Did you suspect at the time?'

'I had a pretty good idea; we weren't exactly careful.' Gem's cheeks flushed crimson. 'Oh God, I should so not be talking about this with you.'

The future Belle could have had flashed through her mind. What if it had been her who'd not been careful with Diego? How would she have felt about being pregnant? Would she have tried to contact him then? How different would her life have been? She might not have moved to London, wouldn't have had the accident. But then everything would have been different. The thought of being stuck in Norfolk relying on her parents filled her with horror; even the accident hadn't forced her back. Dealing with the aftermath on her own in London had been preferable. Nope, she didn't want Gem's life, because after a challenging start, hers had worked out all right. She never gave herself credit for all she'd achieved. Plus she was back here, doing what she wanted, taking chances and moving on. And she'd met Caleb. Even thinking of him now filled her with hope and excitement and longing.

'Gem, it's fine to talk about this. Diego is ancient history, just a notch on my bedpost like I was for him, but for you he means something monumental and that's a whole different thing. You obviously exchanged more details with him than I did, so why didn't you tell him when you found out you were pregnant?'

'I did contemplate telling him, but what the hell was he going to do from Ibiza? I knew exactly what his lifestyle was like; why would he have cared?' Gem took a shuddery breath and started walking back the way they'd come towards where the river merged with the sea, its dependable rhythm soothing as it lapped the sand. 'Would he even have believed me? I went for the easy, safe option and let Dan assume it was his. I might have even convinced myself it was his.' She shrugged. 'What happened in Ibiza stayed in Ibiza, right? I was pregnant, scared shitless, forced to cut my backpacking trip short. I honestly didn't know what the hell to do, but Dan was there. He stepped up when he didn't have to.'

'You were a couple, Gem, and if you gave him no indication Jack wasn't his...' Belle trailed off, a lump in her throat. 'Do you think he suspects?'

'Jack and Oscar look nothing like each other.'

'But Jack looks like you.' Could Belle see any of Diego in Gem's eldest? He definitely had Gem's features, but with olive-toned skin and darker hair, so maybe.

'One of the main problems was we didn't talk to each other,' Gem continued as they reached the beach again and strolled onto the sand. 'At least not about important stuff, so if he had a suspicion he kept it to himself. We only stayed together because of Jack. Remember, after Ibiza I had every intention of finishing with him. I should have done that before I went travelling with Cerys, but I didn't want the hassle of a breakup while life was so fucking good.'

'But there must have been something more between you two because you had Oscar as well. I assume he's—'

'Yes, 100 per cent he's Dan's.' Gem's eyes flashed with defiance as she kicked at the sand. 'I did love Dan in my own way. He stuck by me after Jack was born and that was admirable, and I was so overwhelmed that I wanted to make things work with him. I'd compromised so much by then and honestly life wasn't awful, it just wasn't what I'd hoped for. Naively I thought completing our family would help, I don't know, bring us closer together, but he obviously had other ideas. I mean, we were so bloody young. I didn't want to settle down and have kids and neither did he, it was just as we got older it was a hell of a lot easier for him to have an affair than for me to have one – not that I was contemplating that in the slightest.' Coming to a stop, she sighed and planted her feet in the sand with her hands on her hips. Spirit was in view, its white walls gleaming, the restaurant tables and the sun loungers on the beach filled with guests. 'But none of this is helping me right now because I didn't expect to be in this situation here on Ibiza with the chance of seeing Diego again. So, what should I do? Should I tell him or not?' She looked imploringly at Belle.

'I guess my question is what's your reason for wanting to tell him? For financial support?'

'No, nothing like that,' Gem said vehemently. 'I keep thinking if I was in his shoes, I would want to know. I also wish I'd had the guts to say something ten years ago, but I can't change that.'

'But you can make up for it now.'

Gem pursed her lips. 'You moving to Ibiza and the connection you have to Caleb putting you back in contact with Diego, it feels like a second chance to make things right.'

'Then why didn't you talk to him at Ushuaïa? Laurie said you were avoiding him.'

'Because I didn't know what to say and I was scared of blurting out something I'd regret.'

'But what do you have to lose by telling him? He has a right to know, and isn't there a chance that he might be open to doing a DNA test?'

'He doesn't need to for me to know. I got a paternity test done and Dan's not Jack's biological father. That's why I'm so sure.'

'Oh my God, Gem.' Belle put her arms around her then pulled back. 'Wait, so how on earth does Dan not know?'

'I managed to swab the inside of his cheek when he'd fallen asleep after being out drinking one night, so I did it without him knowing.'

'Surely that's—'

'Illegal. Yep.' Gem ran her fingers across her forehead. 'I shouldn't have done it; and I definitely should have been honest with him, but the not knowing... My God, it's eaten away at me for years.'

'And there was no one else?'

'No, no one, just Dan and Diego, so that means...' She

shrugged and Belle felt her shudder. 'I got the DNA test done not long after Oscar was born when Jack was young enough for me to pass off swabbing his cheek for a different reason. I've sat on the truth for four years because why say anything when I was never going to see Diego again? Until now. You're the only person I've told. The truth would turn Jack's world upside down when he's already struggling with the breakup.'

'And unless you come clean with Dan there's not a lot you can do.' Belle gazed out at the perfect view of blue sea and sky. 'You need to put this right for everyone's sake, Gem. For your sanity.'

'I'm worried about putting Jack through more emotional upheaval and what everyone will think. Dan especially. I'm worried it'll change how he feels about Jack.'

'Even if you weren't right for each other, Dan's a decent guy. Do you honestly think he wouldn't love Jack just as much? He might feel betrayed, but he's still Jack's dad and will always be part of his life. Keeping this to yourself will eat away at you more than it already is and being here now is an opportunity you shouldn't ignore.' Belle hooked her arm in Gem's and they started walking up the beach towards Spirit. 'Don't beat yourself up about what's done. We've all made mistakes. I'm beginning to learn it's best to talk and get things out in the open even if it's hard. You've talked to me, now all you need to do is the same with Diego.' Her earlier thought about leading the way by being open and truthful with Laurie and Gem returned. 'Also, the reason I'm no longer hung up on Diego is because there's someone else I like a hell of a lot more.'

'Caleb,' Gem said with a glimmer of a smile as they reached the wooden steps that led from the beach to Spirit's restaurant terrace. 'Like that wasn't obvious.'

'So, how about I have a chat with Caleb and see how we can sort out this messy situation with Diego.'

* * *

That evening after Gem had caught Laurie up on the news about Diego actually being Jack's dad, Belle took them for a meal at Serenity, firstly because she wanted to show off the place and secondly because she knew Caleb would be there so she'd have the chance to talk to him.

If having a heart-to-heart with Caleb the evening before hadn't blurred the line between him being her boss or a friend, then broaching the subject about her best friend's son being his former brother-in-law's would do the trick.

Confiding in Caleb felt risky particularly when there was every chance Gem would chicken out of telling Diego altogether, but it was a risk she felt was worth it. So while Gem and Laurie ate pistachio cheesecake with tangerine sorbet and took in the view of the peaceful bay in the ethereal evening light, Belle headed inside to where Caleb was sitting at the end of the bar scrolling on his phone.

His smile when she slid onto the stool next to him sent her insides spinning, and despite their physical distance she felt closer to him than before, yet there was an awareness that every look, every touch, could mean so much.

'Hey, I'm glad you brought your friends here for a meal.'

'It's my favourite place.'

'Mine too.' He gestured towards the outside terrace. 'They're still here?'

'Yes,' Belle said, taking a deep breath. 'But I wanted to talk to you before we went back, something about Gem and Diego...' And so she told him everything she'd learned, her chest tightening as the lines on Caleb's forehead deepened.

'Sheesh,' Caleb breathed out through his teeth. 'And you're okay with this?'

'I'm fine with it,' Belle said firmly, wanting to press upon him that she had absolutely no feelings for Diego any longer. 'I'm just glad that Gem's finally shared what's going on because she's been dealing with it on her own for a long time. She needs to have a chance to talk to Diego, and whether he wants to hear it or not, he deserves to. Gem sure as hell needs to get this weight off her chest. I don't know how to make that happen and I was wondering if you could? I'm really sorry for asking.'

'Why are you sorry? I'm glad you trust me enough to tell me.' She was acutely aware that his hand was resting on the bar just inches from her elbow.

'I have an idea.' Caleb smiled. 'It's Gem and Laurie's last night tomorrow, right?' At Belle's nod he continued. 'Then we'll have dinner at mine; Lluís will be working, but I'll invite Diego, Àngel, Tomàs and their wives. Gem and Diego will have the chance to talk. No pressure, I promise.'

38

Caleb was an Englishman in Spain making Italian pizza, but it was something he was good at and enjoyed doing, plus it was an easy way to feed a few people. The nerves were still pinging about in the pit of his stomach at the idea of entertaining at Solace, of having more than just a couple of people over at a time. Entertaining friends and family with dinner parties, barbecues and pool parties had been Caleb and Paloma's dream and he'd shied away from it since her death, afraid of the feelings it would conjure while resolutely refusing to embrace that side of life without her. Belle had instigated this. The idea had popped into his head and he had no good reason to not suggest it.

He cracked open a bottle of beer and took a long swig. Leaning his phone against a utensil pot, he Skyped Cara while stretching out the pizza dough on the kitchen island.

Cara's beaming face appeared on the screen.

'You look happy,' he said, 'for first thing in the morning.'

'Yesterday was a good one. Dad was feeling a bit like his old self, so I'm hoping today will be more of the same.'

'Sorry I didn't call the other day, it was just...' He shrugged.

'Hey.' Cara leaned right into the screen. 'Don't apologise. You had every right to deal with the anniversary how best you could. I'm just glad you let me know you were okay. So Belle came over?'

'Uh huh.'

'Anything you want to share?' Cara's blue eyes bore into him through the screen. 'You know you can tell me anything, right?'

'Yeah, I know.'

'How about I go first.'

Caleb stopped stretching out the dough and frowned at her.

Cara's grin was the biggest he'd ever seen. 'I kinda hooked up with my friend Naomi, you know the one I've fancied since I was like nineteen. We went out with mutual friends the other night and just clicked.'

'And when you say hooked up, you mean...'

'We kissed. A lot.' Cara grinned again. 'And talked so much about everything. Sharing our shitty experiences with our exes, the stress of illness in our families. Just talked and offloaded and it was so good.'

'So you're not missing me too much then?'

'Oh, I still miss you like crazy, knucklehead, but you're not exactly a friend with benefits, are you?' She winked.

That put a smile on his face.

'Now, your turn.'

Caleb focused on kneading the next ball of dough rather than Cara's intense look. 'I didn't kiss Belle if that's what you're fishing for, but I wanted to. Oh fuck it, Cara, I wanted to do a whole lot more than kiss her, but shit... My head and my heart were so damn twisted.'

'It's okay to feel like that and okay to be conflicted. Obviously the timing was so not right.' Cara stopped talking and sucked in a breath. 'It wasn't so much the idea of being with her, was it, but the feelings you have for her, right? You do have feelings?'

Caleb slapped the dough onto the surface and leaned his hands against the edge of the worktop. He stared towards the picture windows and the darkening sky. The remnants of the sun cast a golden-red glow on the sea.

He sighed. 'I wish you were here to help me figure this out.'

'Hey, only you can figure out the way you really feel. Go with your gut, it's what you've always done when it comes to business and it usually pays off. Also, don't be afraid of taking a chance with Belle.'

That feeling he'd had yesterday morning when he'd hugged Belle goodbye returned, an all-consuming warmth reignited.

'What are you doing by the way?' Cara asked.

'Making pizza. I've, um, got a few people coming over tonight.'

'You have?'

'Yeah, there's a whole thing going on with Belle's friend Gem – you know I told you all about Belle, Gem and Diego—'

'Yep, the threesome.'

'It wasn't a threesome, Cara.'

'In my head it was...'

Caleb shook his head and stretched the dough out on a pizza tray. 'Well, there's a chance that Gem's nine-year-old son is actually Diego's.'

'Are you freaking kidding me?' Cara's eyes widened as her nose nearly hit the screen. 'I'm missing out on all the gossip *and* a party at yours.'

'It's not a party; it's a small gathering. Just dinner. A chance for Gem and Diego to talk.'

Cara pursed her lips and looked at him sternly. 'You so rarely have people over. This is special, Caleb.' She paused. 'Wow, you're really doing this for her. Belle's properly got under your skin, hasn't she?'

Caleb didn't know how to reply to that so he didn't. When the front gate buzzer went with the arrival of Àngel and his wife Gabriela, he said goodbye and prepared himself for everyone's arrival.

* * *

Caleb had forgotten what Solace must look like through other people's eyes. He knew how lucky he was to call it home, but he'd worked hard for it and had got used to living in a place where he could wake to the view of Ibiza Town bathed in sunshine, dive into the pool whenever he wanted, and sit with a beer watching the sunset from his terrace.

Laurie definitely couldn't hide her awe as she wandered through the house open-mouthed. She was the quietest of the three friends with a gentle personality that was overshadowed by Gem's voluptuous in-your-face confidence and Belle's unfettered magnetism. It didn't surprise him one bit that Diego had wound up with Belle and Gem, both blonde, both his type, but he was mighty relieved it was Gem who was about to have a difficult conversation with him and not Belle. Things could have been very different.

It felt strange, yet not unwelcome, to see Solace coming alive as people started to arrive. Apart from Belle and her friends and Diego and his brothers, he'd only invited a couple of other friends and their partners. Solace was made for entertaining, the sliding doors giving an effortless transition between inside and out, although everyone radiated to the terrace, which was bathed in the gold-tinged dusk. The candles in the lanterns were lit and the outdoor lights cast palm-tree shadows across the cream walls.

Gabriela helped him finish the pizzas and they took them out to where everyone was sitting around the huge table that dominated the side of the terrace with its view towards a glittering

Ibiza Town. With plenty of wine, beer and food, the chatter flowed and happy voices rose into the night. It felt good to have his home filled with friends and laughter, a joy long absent. Caleb dipped in and out, flitting between the kitchen and the terrace, catching snatches of conversation as everyone relaxed and chatted together. His eyes were constantly drawn to Belle, who was sitting with her friends looking radiant in a metallic black playsuit.

What he also noticed was the distance between Gem and Diego at opposite ends of the table, so when he spotted Gem taking her glass of wine over to the outdoor lounge area while Tomàs, Gabriela and Belle were clearing the plates away, he went over to Diego.

'Hey.' Caleb clutched Diego's shoulder and leaned over, keeping his voice low. 'Why don't you go have a chat with Gem; there's something she wants to tell you.' If Belle's fears about Gem clamming up proved to be true then this was a risky move, but as Gem didn't seem keen on veering towards Diego, he decided to instigate it.

Maybe it was something in his tone that made Diego take notice, or perhaps he didn't need much persuading, but with a nod he grabbed a bottle of Ibizkus White and sauntered over to her.

Laurie, still sitting at the table, caught Caleb's eye and gave him a smile. She shifted her chair to face the seating area and Gem as Caleb joined her.

'Hey, they're talking.' Belle slid onto the seat between Caleb and Laurie and topped up her wine.

Caleb caught her eye. 'I gave him a nudge.'

The three of them chatted about Solace and its transformation, and how different it was on the island over winter without the hordes of tourists, although Caleb was well aware they were all trying to subtly keep an eye on Gem and Diego.

'I think she's telling him,' Laurie whispered as she leaned closer to Belle and Caleb.

It certainly looked that way to Caleb too, even though Diego had his back to them. Gem was doing all the talking, her elbows resting on her knees as she leaned forward. Diego's shoulders were hunched. Gem's face was flushed and impassioned as she talked. Diego suddenly stood up, shook his head then paced across the terrace.

Belle flinched and Caleb's stomach muscles tightened. He didn't know Gem at all but she looked like she was trying her hardest to hold it together. Then Diego turned on his heel and marched back to Gem. He took her hand and led her across the terrace and into the house.

Caleb, Belle and Laurie looked at each other.

'Do you think one of us should follow, make sure they're okay?' Laurie looked between Belle and Caleb.

Belle shook her head. 'They need to figure things out. Let them.'

Whatever lingering feelings Belle may have had for Diego, she'd certainly put them behind her. Caleb admired her openness and how important friendship was to her – a good person to have on your side or in your life. He surreptitiously watched her as she and Laurie carried on talking, the concern for their friend obvious. Caleb loved her for it.

He froze. The thought had slipped into his head effortlessly. He loved lots of things about her, the things that made her a good friend, a brilliant employee, a generally wonderful person; that must be it.

Oh God.

He downed his beer and glanced to where everyone else was still chatting, empty beer and wine bottles cluttering the table. Replenishing the drinks seemed the perfect excuse to put some distance between himself and Belle. He left them talking and escaped to the kitchen, raiding the fridge for drinks and putting together a plate of *ensaïmades*, spiral-shaped sweet pastries. The only sound was the chatter and music drifting in from outside, so wherever Gem and Diego had disappeared to, at least they weren't having an argument.

When Caleb returned outside, Belle and Laurie were still deep in conversation, so he placed the drinks and pastries on the table and joined his friends. It was good to talk and laugh together. Belle and Laurie eventually joined them, he assumed once they realised that Gem and Diego had lots to talk about and would probably be gone a while.

It was a couple of hours later when Gem emerged from the villa and made a beeline for the seating area away from everyone. Belle caught his eye, worry for her friend written all over her face. She and Laurie took their drinks and went and joined Gem.

A few minutes later Diego appeared, his face set in a frown as he headed the opposite way. He took off his shoes, sat by the pool and submerged his feet in the water.

Caleb grabbed two beers and joined him. Kicking off his sneakers, he sat on the stone and dunked his feet in the cool water too. To their left, the vast sea glittered ebony in the moonlight. Across the pool, his friends' faces were lit by the flickering light from the lanterns.

Caleb handed Diego one of the beers. 'You doing okay?'

Keeping his eyes fixed ahead, Diego swigged from the bottle. 'Did you know what Gem was going to tell me?'

'Yeah, Belle told me.'

'And that's why you invited us all here?'

'Mostly, yes. So are you okay?'

Diego nodded. '*Sí.*'

Caleb was finding it hard to work out how Diego was feeling;

he looked thoughtful – which wasn't really surprising – but also strangely calm.

'What happened when you went inside?'

'I thanked her for being honest with me, took her in my arms and kissed her.' He turned to Caleb and shrugged his shoulders. 'I didn't want to risk my brothers wolf whistling or saying something crude. It was not the right moment to make fun. Then we talked. A lot. I got angry that she hadn't told me sooner, but she had her reasons. I also realised I wouldn't have changed my life even if she had said something. I was too selfish. I wouldn't have been ready or responsible back then. I'm glad she's told me now.' He took another sip of beer. 'His name's Jack.'

Caleb leaned back on his hands and studied Diego, an immense sense of pride sweeping through him. He'd witnessed his mistakes, had listened to his frustrations and heard all about his conquests over the years. He worked as hard as he played, yet Caleb still thought of him as a lad, single and up for a good time, the younger, carefree, cheeky brother he'd never had but one who'd come into his life when he'd met Paloma. He couldn't be prouder of the way he'd handled the bombshell Gem had dropped. He was a father of a nine-year-old boy he'd never met and at the age of thirty-four he was acting his age rather than in the way Caleb had feared.

Caleb gripped his shoulder. 'You have a kid, Diego.'

'It's a lot to process. But yes, I have a son.' Diego's grin said it all. 'With Gem.'

The way Diego said her name, Caleb just knew there was something still there. Although the news had come out of the blue, it had brought Gem back into his life. Who knew how they were going to navigate everything, but the spark obviously still flamed.

'Have you ever wondered if you've got a child anywhere?' Diego asked.

Caleb shot him a look that he hoped conveyed something along the lines of 'what the hell are you talking about'.

'Oh come on,' Diego stressed. 'You must have considered it. I'm talking years ago when you had a different woman every night.'

'Not every night and no, because I was always careful.'

Diego grunted.

Caleb clasped his beer on the stone between his thighs and stared down at his toes wiggling in the water. In the darkness, the pool shimmered a midnight blue. He often sat here, his place of contemplation, before diving in for a night-time swim.

'I always hoped to have children. It was what we'd planned, me and your sister. She'd have made a great mum, the same as you're going to be a brilliant father.' He knocked his bottle against Diego's.

'This is going to blow Mama's mind,' Diego said with a grin.

'Maria is going to explode – the questions, oh my fucking God Diego, can you imagine the amount of questions she's going to have!' Caleb shook his head at the thought of Diego's wonderful but formidable mother finding out that she had another grand-child. 'Please let me be there when you tell her.'

The evening couldn't have gone any better; the bravery Gem had shown in being honest with Diego had been matched by his maturity in how he'd dealt with the news. But as everyone started to leave and a taxi was called to take Belle, Gem and Laurie back to Spirit, he began to realise there was only one way that the night would be absolutely perfect.

He watched Diego say goodbye to Gem and the easy way he slipped his arm round her waist and pulled her to him. His kisses to her cheeks lingered while his hands on her waist drifted slightly lower. He was confident and in full control of his emotions, seem-ingly knowing what he wanted and on the surface unfazed by all that he'd learned. As Diego let Gem go, her expression spoke volumes – that hard edge Caleb had so far witnessed was softened by a real smile that reached her eyes. There was something else in the way her eyes remained fixed on Diego, her confidence matching his, confirming Caleb's earlier thought that whatever had been ignited ten years ago was still very much alive.

Caleb sighed, turning away to find Belle also watching Gem with Diego. It was a bizarre situation for her to be in the middle of, her friend and her holiday fling forever tied by the child they'd unintentionally made. Belle's focus flicked from them to him and he melted, desperately wishing he had the same ease and confidence with Belle that Diego had with Gem.

Belle walked towards him, her short playsuit showing off long tanned legs that made him go giddy with desire.

'Thank you so much for tonight.' She took his hand, and he tried not to tense or to worry if anyone was watching them. 'It went better than I dared hope.'

'You're going back in the taxi with Gem and Laurie?' Caleb knew she was but he asked anyway because he was unable to verbalise 'please stay the night'.

'Yes,' Belle said, her eyes tracing his face in a way that made him wonder if she was thinking the same thing.

She reached up and kissed him on each cheek. Her breath tickled, her perfume was seductively sweet, her hand on his bare arm almost more than he could bear. And yet, once again, he watched her walk away, his head and heart twisted in a power battle that he wasn't going to come out of unscathed. The whole evening had been about openness and telling the truth, so taking a chance and opening up his heart to the possibility of happiness, wasn't that a risk worth taking?

39

'I am so going to miss this place,' Gem said with a sigh as she closed the door to their poolside room behind her. She dragged her suitcase into the hallway and turned to Belle. 'But I'm going to miss you more.' She pulled her into a tight hug. 'Thank you for everything, for being so understanding and for making me talk to him.'

The second Belle and Laurie had joined Gem at the seating area on Caleb's terrace after she'd talked to Diego, she'd burst into tears as if she'd been bottling everything up all evening – or more likely for the last few years – and she finally felt able to release it.

'He doesn't hate me,' she'd said, clutching a tissue. 'He was shocked but he didn't doubt me when I said Jack was his. He just held me and kissed me and told me it was all okay. I can't even begin to tell you how that made me feel. Even if I don't know what happens next or how we navigate our way, how I broach the subject with Dan, how I eventually tell Jack. Diego's going to do a DNA test before I say anything so we have proof, then who knows.' She'd shrugged. 'We exchanged numbers and are going to keep in touch.'

Even if the future was still uncertain, Gem's relief had been obvious. And now in the hallway at Spirit, happiness beamed from Gem as she let go of Belle.

'You're a good friend,' Gem said softly. 'And I'm going to try and be a better one.'

Laurie slid her arms around both of their waists. 'Do you know how happy it makes me to see you two smiling at each other? And honestly, Belle, I'm so glad you made us do this and I'm unbelievably grateful to you – and Caleb,' she said, squeezing Belle's waist, 'for putting us up somewhere so incredible. You've made me see things in a different way this week and to put things in perspective. I've realised the older I get the more disappointments there are, but there are plenty of good things too. I've been reading a book about the power of positivity. The defeatist attitude I had was not helpful. I'm trying to adjust my mindset. You and Gem were right about me living a little and not being so focused on fertility treatment. This week has gone a long way to doing that.'

Gem laughed. 'Not that we were in any sort of position to give you advice about a positive mindset, let alone how you should tackle IVF.'

Laurie shook her head. 'You absolutely were, because you were able to look at the situation with fresh eyes. I'm way too involved and invested. I've read far too many conflicting things about trying to get pregnant and I was in a complete muddle. I've been wound so tight, I could barely breathe let alone relax. A Spirit house cocktail with a salty breeze through my hair, dancing the night away at Ushuaïa and eating pizza with my best friends on a terrace overlooking the Med, made all my worries seem insignificant. I'm going to hold on to that feeling when I get home, have a glass of wine when I feel like it and just try and enjoy life with Ade. Make the most of what we've got.'

'A pretty successful week all round then,' Gem said with a grin. 'Now all that's left is for Belle to take a chance with Caleb.'

Easier said than done, Belle thought but, as she hugged Gem and Laurie goodbye, she resolved to be brave and honest like Gem and positive and hopeful like Laurie. Who knew where that mindset would lead.

* * *

Returning to Ibiza had been the right decision: eye-opening, eventful and impactful. Each of them had needed to hear hard truths and learn to embrace the ups and downs of life as well as accept that although things didn't necessarily work out the way they'd envisaged, it didn't mean they'd failed. Changing, adapting and navigating a trickier path had made each of them the people they were today. Belle couldn't have asked for more. She felt closer to Gem and Laurie than she had in ages, a reminder of a time when their friendship meant everything and they'd share their hopes, dreams, successes and disappointments without letting anything else get in the way: men, jealousy, their own insecurities or any sort of toxicity.

With the importance of their friendship brought back into focus, Belle phoned Hannah later that day.

'Did I ever tell you how grateful I was for the way you supported and looked after me following my accident?'

Hannah laughed. 'What on earth brought that up?'

'I've been talking about the past a lot this last week, reliving that time – the first holiday to Ibiza and the hell that happened after.'

'You were so unbelievably brave. Honestly, I would have left London and gone back home if it had been me. You stuck it out in pain, scared, worried about your job, how to pay the bills. The least I could do was be your friend.'

'You were more than just a friend, Hannah. You were there for me every step of the way, going with me to appointments and listening when I needed to mouth off about my shitty boss. You encouraged me to stick up for myself when all I wanted to do was quit. Honestly, without you being my rock back then, I wouldn't be where I am today.'

'Well, you've done the same for me now, being my saviour by letting me stay here. I feel better than I have done in months, and Jake and I are actually managing to talk civilly to each other.' There was a lightness to Hannah's voice that Belle hadn't heard in a long while.

'Having your own space has obviously done you both good.'

'Mmm, yes,' Hannah said, suddenly sounding cagey. 'Except he suggested I move back in on a trial basis...'

'Why would you even consider that...? Oh wait, he wants you to move back in as together together?'

'Yep, but there's no way I'm going there, Belle. No way. He's cheated once, how can I trust that he won't do it again? I did too much for him when we were living together and I think he's realising the grass isn't always greener. He's cheated, possibly regrets it now and wants his easy life with me back again.'

'You are worth so much more. He didn't deserve you back then, he certainly doesn't now.'

'No, I know. Because having space and time away from him has really made me see things clearly and I understand exactly what was wrong. It wasn't me. The strain in our relationship and the breakdown was all his doing, so thank you, I am so completely done with him.'

It warmed Belle's heart to hear her friend sound so positive and clear about what she wanted – or more to the point, what she didn't want any more. It was only after they'd said goodbye that Hannah's clarity made her consider her own wants and desires, not that they were quite so straightforward.

Over the following week, two private parties at Spirit and another outdoor movie night at Serenity kept Belle busy, so she didn't see much of Caleb, and when she did have free time he didn't seem to be around. Not that she was actively looking for him, and of course he was a busy guy, juggling a lot.

When the following weekend came and went, she did wonder if he'd gone to Maria's for a family dinner. The stab of envy she felt took her by surprise and it was impossible not to wonder if he hadn't thought to invite her, or worse – he hadn't wanted to. The pragmatic side of her reasoned it was probably best to maintain their professionalism as work colleagues but she missed talking to him, she missed his slightly crooked smile and the way being around him made her feel, and she thought about him more times than she dared to admit.

* * *

Caleb knew he was purposefully avoiding Belle so he didn't have to deal with his feelings, but that only led to guilt because his response to run away wasn't fair on her. Of course, being genuinely busy with investment plans and organising meetings gave him an excuse, but he could easily make time for her if he chose to. Perhaps he was being cowardly, or maybe it was self-preservation to bury his confusion and troubled feelings. It was definitely a bad idea because it was making him stressed and miserable when time spent with Belle had the opposite effect.

'Where is Belle?' was Maria's first question when he turned up for dinner that Sunday.

'Oh, I wasn't sure you'd want an extra person to feed this weekend,' he replied lamely.

'What are you talking about?' she scolded. 'Belle is always welcome.' She shook her head and tutted. 'Bring her next weekend, *sí*.' It wasn't a question.

Caleb escaped from beneath her glare into the garden and found a quiet spot on the wall away from the kids screeching around playing hide and seek.

'What the hell are you playing at, Caleb?' Diego perched next to him. 'Mama said Belle was welcome but you didn't invite her.'

Caleb grunted. 'It feels... complicated.'

Diego snorted. 'Yes, of course it is, most good things in life are. Doesn't mean you should ignore a tricky situation. Last weekend you literally told me to go and talk to Gem, knowing what she was about to tell me. Whatever has gone on between you and Belle—'

'Nothing has happened,' Caleb said vehemently.

'You don't have to have had sex for something to have happened. Anyone with eyes and half a brain can see there's something between you. The chemistry is obvious.'

Caleb stood up and paced to the edge of the garden, trying to disguise the sudden distress Diego's words had caused. Because he was absolutely right, their chemistry was electric, the feelings she stirred undeniable, and yet he was intent on denying himself even her friendship.

'You can't ignore her,' Diego continued. 'You're going to confuse and upset her. And end up hurting her too. She doesn't deserve that.' He sighed. 'I really don't know what we can do to make you see that it's okay to let go, but it is.' Diego squeezed Caleb's shoulder and walked away towards the light and laughter on the top terrace.

Caleb understood what he meant by 'let go' because it was

what he'd been battling against every time he was around Belle. Not being around her seemed the easier option; except it wasn't, because he was hurting and Diego was right, if he carried on like this he'd hurt Belle too. How could he be sure that he was ready when letting go had the potential to change everything?

40

The beginning of the week was a scorcher. Even at dawn, the air felt sultry and the usually cool apartment stuffy. Belle did her morning routine of twenty minutes of yoga before having a stroll along the beach and a swim in the sea. She returned to the apartment and sat outside in the courtyard garden to eat her breakfast while listening to the birds and gazing up at the cloudless blue sky, the promise of a hot Ibiza day in the air.

She'd just finished getting dressed in a white maxi skirt and crop top when a message from Cara popped onto her phone.

Love what you're doing on the socials, Belle, it's so good to know Spirit, Serenity and Caleb are in safe hands. I hope you don't mind me messaging you like this. I talk to Caleb all the time but he has a habit of soldiering on even when he's falling apart. So I thought I'd come directly to you and ask a favour. He has this investment opp to take a look at later today and I think you should go with him. Not that he needs hand holding, but he will need to talk it through, which of course he can do with me, but as I'm halfway round the world dealing with a whole load of shit and won't have seen the place, I think he'll need to debrief with someone who can actually cast a critical eye over it. Cheers, doll.

The message puzzled her with Cara's concern about Caleb worming into her heart, the words 'falling apart' jumping out. He'd certainly closed himself off, at least from her, which made it all the more concerning that Cara was confiding in her, suggesting she was really worried about him. She also had mixed feelings about going somewhere with him when they'd hardly spoken to each other over the last week.

Yeah I can go if you think it'll be helpful. He might not want me to though...

She considered whether she should tell her more, mention that Caleb was giving her the cold shoulder, but then the chances were if Cara spoke to him regularly that piece of information had the potential to get back to him, so she left it and sent the message.

As Belle was washing up her bowl and mug, she noticed that Cara was writing something in reply, then she stopped as if thinking it through. Belle was heading out of the door by the time the message did pop up.

You're his events manager and the perfect person to help him talk through a decision like this – professionally. And I kinda know about the time you've spent together recently. He's needed the support and if he's confused over anything then that's for him to figure out. So don't worry. I'll suggest it and I'm sure he'll agree. All will be good. x

Professionally. That was the word that now stuck out. Their relationship had strayed from that, and what good had it done? When she'd first arrived and they'd talked and spent time together there'd been a friendliness that had felt natural, yet over time a professional distance had slowly disintegrated. Ignoring her own advice about mixing business with pleasure had been foolish because her desire, longing and delight in spending time with Caleb had been tarnished by confusion, uncertainty and anxiety.

She decided to get on with her day and if Caleb agreed with Cara that he wanted her to go with him then she was sure he'd let her know. With a wedding happening at Serenity the following week, she worked on that in the shared office. The next Ushuaïa club night was happening on Friday evening so she dropped Diego an email, which was far easier than having to talk to him. Not that she minded any longer. A definite weight had been lifted there, but she wasn't ready to have a conversation about him, Gem and Jack. She'd seen him chatting to Caleb by the pool at Solace after Gem had told him the truth, but she hadn't spoken to Caleb beyond work-related matters since then. She definitely wasn't going to broach such an emotive subject with Diego.

As she stopped for lunch to have a sandwich on the stone wall that edged Spirit's grounds, it crossed her mind that she'd already reverted to her old habits of pushing her worries to the back of her mind to avoid dealing with them – a short-term fix, and not a great one either.

It was only a shadow falling across her that alerted her to Caleb. He sat on the wall next to her, facing towards Spirit's garden and the poolside suites rather than the beach. 'Cara said you're coming with me this afternoon.'

'Only if it'll be helpful and you want me to – it was her idea,' Belle said coolly, not wanting him to get the wrong end of the stick.

'It's a good idea.' He seemed distracted and didn't catch her eye. 'Pack a bag with swim things and evening wear. Knowing Eddie, he'll want us to experience all La Retirada has to offer. I'll meet you out front in an hour.'

Belle sighed as Caleb strode away and she was left staring out at the sea rhythmically folding onto the shore. A young couple who were staying at the hotel were strolling along the beach hand in hand. There was a heaviness in her heart, a foreboding sense that going with him was a mistake when things felt so uncertain. She desperately wished they could return to the easy way they'd had with each other when she'd first arrived.

* * *

By the time Belle met Caleb by his Jeep and they'd left the hotel grounds, the day was blisteringly hot. With the roof up and the air-conditioning on, the drive inland was actually pleasant.

'I've behaved badly,' Caleb said while keeping his eyes fixed on the road. 'By keeping out of your way...'

'So you have been intentionally avoiding me?'

Caleb's jaw tightened.

'It's okay.' Belle sighed. 'You're entitled to protect your mental health or whatever it is you've been doing.' Her words came out snappier than she'd intended.

'None of this is straightforward, you understand.' And now his voice was clipped.

The ball of tension that had formed the moment she'd read Cara's message intensified, but this time she wasn't going to allow her unsettled feelings to fester.

'Just see it from my point of view,' she said as Caleb shoved the Jeep into fifth gear and sped along the country road past rows of fruit trees and scorched ochre-red soil. 'You did something amazing for me so I could help my friend. I confided in you because I thought we'd progressed to that stage of our...' She was going to say 'relationship' but that sounded far too serious. 'Friendship,' she said instead. 'Perhaps I was wrong, because after a wonderful evening at yours with you hosting a party simply to enable Diego and Gem to talk, you ghosted me.'

Belle grimaced at her choice of words because it made it sound as if they were in a romantic relationship rather than just being friends and that he'd cut off all communication, which he hadn't – it had just felt as if he had. But then again, real friends didn't behave this way with each other, blowing hot and cold. She'd put a lot of focus on friendship over the past couple of weeks and Caleb's behaviour didn't feel friendly.

'I...' Caleb began to say then closed his mouth, his hands tightening on the steering wheel. 'It's been hard, you know.'

'No, I don't know because that's my point, you've shut me out rather than talked to me.' Her voice was rising, the ball of tension worsening.

'I've needed space. It was a mistake for us to—' He stopped short, cutting off whatever he was about to say, but Belle understood perfectly that getting close to her had been the mistake because they'd become this muddled nothingness which they now had to navigate their way out of while spending the rest of the day together. The lines between colleagues and whatever the hell they were now had been blurred.

Belle wanted nothing more than to ease their awkwardness,

but she was also furious with herself for allowing her heart to run away with her, to have even contemplated something more happening with him.

'Why don't I make it easy for both of us and suggest we stick to a strictly professional relationship. No further awkward intros to your friends and family; no more confused feelings or uncertainty. You're my boss and I'm your employee. End of.'

Anger had made her speak without thinking it through, but she didn't want to become fixated again on someone she couldn't be with. Caleb wasn't in the right place emotionally and he might never be; she didn't want to fall for someone who was never going to let her into his heart. She'd had plenty of one-sided relationships and they'd never worked out.

Caleb's grunted acknowledgement suggested he felt the same.

Edmund 'Eddie' Rosen was a British expat still living a carefree and single lifestyle in his sixties. He had a shock of white hair, a deep tan and laughter lines. He wore a short-sleeved shirt completely unbuttoned that revealed tufts of white chest hair and a belly that suggested he enjoyed food and booze. His booming voice reached them before he did. He greeted them with kisses to each cheek, his larger-than-life look matching his personality. Throwing an arm around each of their shoulders, he talked non-stop as he led them across the sun-baked courtyard.

Eddie was everything Belle had hoped Caleb wouldn't be – over-the-top, flashy, big and brash, but she was mightily relieved that his upbeat personality erased the unbearable tension that had built since Belle had suggested to Caleb that they be nothing more than colleagues. They hadn't said a word to each other since. If she'd been hoping that it would clear the air, she'd been mistaken.

As he took them on a tour, her impression of Eddie was at odds with the place itself. La Retirada was quite something. The finca, a restored 500-year-old traditional farmhouse, was as unflashy as it got. On the outside, its stone walls were painted white, while the courtyard tiles were a pink-tinged terracotta that brought colour to the predominately white, stone and leafy green surroundings. The pool was the centrepiece with double day beds shaded by thatched roofs and fig trees. There was a barbecue area with an outdoor kitchen, and the terracotta pots with tall cacti were bold against the bright walls. Inside, the thick stone walls were invitingly cool. The place may not have been ready for paying guests but it looked finished to Belle with simply furnished but charming rooms that flowed from one to another, a living area with a wood burner at the heart, everywhere luxuriously rustic with beamed ceilings, exposed stone and wooden lintels.

After Eddie had given them the full tour, he led them to an outdoor sofa and chairs beneath a large fig tree, its canopy of leaves encompassing them like a natural umbrella. He returned a few minutes later with a jug of cloudy lemonade clinking with ice cubes.

'Homemade from the lemons in the grove,' Eddie said as he poured them each a glass.

La Retirada was rustic and enchanting and Eddie was surprising, bold and memorable. His outgoing personality and confidence reminded Belle a little of Gem, which made her wonder if there were struggles beneath his confidently loud veneer.

Belle sat back and listened as Eddie and Caleb talked business, Eddie catching him up about his plans. The delays had meant the retreat hadn't been ready to open for this summer season but that hadn't stopped Eddie from already planning an on-site restaurant in one of two converted barns to sit alongside the finca which would serve as a yoga and art retreat. The restaurant was the part of the project that he was pitching to Caleb as a business proposal to partner up on.

Belle felt a little out of her depth as she listened and she hoped it didn't show. Perhaps her discomfort stemmed from feeling like the odd one out. Instead of it being Cara sitting with them, she was the new events manager. The obvious friendship Caleb and Eddie had made her realise how recently she'd entered Caleb's life, while the tone of their conversation on the drive over had left her stomach churning.

Belle took a sip of the lemonade, to ease the tension she was feeling. It was fresh, a perfect balance of sweet and sour, and the cool drink refreshed her senses, allowing her to refocus on the conversation. The ideas Caleb and Eddie were bouncing between them were exciting, including using the produce from the finca's almond, lemon, orange and fig trees in the restaurant kitchen. The vibe of La Retirada reminded her of Serenity but it was surrounded by olive groves with views to distant mountains rather than by the coast with its mesmerising sea views. It was very Caleb, the farmhouse a traditional take on Solace, so a place she knew would appeal to him. He'd bring fresh and suitable ideas to it. That was if he'd even want her opinion.

'You look thoughtful, Belle. What do you think?' Eddie switched his attention from Caleb to her. It took her by surprise and she realised she must have been in a daze, her mind racing away with a million possibilities.

She felt both of their eyes on her, Caleb's in particular, and she wanted more than anything to make things right between them, to not feel distraught by the thought that shutting down the possibility of anything happening between them had been a mistake. More than anything, she wanted to be able to look at him without her heart colliding with her ribs.

What she understood most of all was the need to be truthful

and not second-guess what Caleb would want to hear. It was his money, his investment, ultimately his decision, but Cara had wanted her here for her honest opinion.

'I think there's so much potential, not just with the setting but the focus on the ingredients grown here. There are opportunities galore: olive grove picnics, olive picking parties, communal feasts, cooking retreats. A restaurant could be at the heart of all that.'

'Oh, I like you, Belle,' Eddie said, sitting forward and clasping his hands together. 'Sparkling with ideas.'

'There's a lot to think on, Eddie, before we get carried away with the possibilities.'

Belle's cheeks flushed as Caleb's eyes grazed her face, the shafts of sunlight through the translucent leaves dappled on his.

'Yeah, yeah, I know you, Caleb. Keeping your cards close to your chest. How about we stop talking business and have a proper drink. How often do we get to do this and catch up?' Eddie slapped Caleb on the back. 'And you must stay! That way you can both get a real feel for the place. Sunset on the terrace is special, I promise, and sunrise in the olive grove before a swim is magical.' He sat back, spread his arms out along the cushioned back of the sofa and gave a satisfied smile. 'We'll fire up the barbecue; it'll be like old times. No need to drive back; I can put you up for the night.' He looked between them with a raised eyebrow. 'One room or two though?'

'Two,' they said in unison.

Eddie laughed. 'I wasn't sure. You seem, er... good together.'

41

Caleb couldn't help but say yes to Eddie. He always had been persuasive and he liked him a lot – it was just he could only manage him in small doses. A night away from Solace, relaxing with a beer somewhere other than Spirit or Serenity, was appealing. His only worry was how Belle felt about it.

He caught her eye and she shrugged an okay, a hint of a smile on her lips. They'd sat apart the whole time they'd been here and yet Eddie had sensed something – enough to question the sleeping arrangements.

Diego's warning about the risk of shutting out Belle and hurting her had come true on the drive over and he was furious with himself for not handling the situation better. At least here Eddie's upbeat personality had won her over and La Retirada had obviously charmed her. Serene in white, she looked far more relaxed than when they'd arrived flustered and pissed off with each other. The evening sun slanting through the leaves made her hair shine golden, her lightly tanned skin glow and her freckles more pronounced.

God, was she beautiful.

Caleb was glad of Eddie's boisterous company. With the sun going down, he showed them to their rooms in the finca before lighting the barbecue on the poolside terrace. What had taken him by surprise was Eddie being at La Retirada on his own when he was usually never short of company. He'd been married and divorced three times and had four grown-up kids. He had a life-style most people craved and his other hotel in San Antonio was vastly different, as glitzy and glamorous as La Retirada was tradi-tional and sophisticated. Caleb couldn't help but think that despite the multitude of women who hung out with him in San Antonio, the friends who visited, the guests he entertained and befriended and the party lifestyle he had, he was incredibly lonely, and this was accentuated by him being at La Retirada on his own. It shone a light on Caleb's own lifestyle, although his loneliness had been through death rather than divorce.

When they'd talked earlier, Eddie had said he was moving in a different direction with the retreat, focusing on health and wellbe-ing, a place where groups of friends could congregate to escape the hectic pace of life. Eddie was incredibly successful and had supported Caleb's own dreams over the years but his worry about partnering on the restaurant had been how different their tastes were. Then he'd set eyes on La Retirada with its sympathetic restoration, and restraint when it came to the colour and décor. Eddie meeting them alone instead of Eddie plus an entourage had been refreshing and made Caleb realise how much he must want the partnership.

He was still damn good company though, with many stories to tell that beggared belief and left Belle wide-eyed and occasionally blushing, as they feasted on homemade beef burgers and char-grilled aubergine. Having lived on Ibiza for decades, Eddie had seen and done it all. He entertained them with his effortless story-telling and charm, and the tension that had wound between Caleb and Belle on the journey over slowly unravelled over the course of the evening with wine and beer, good food and company.

It was Eddie who uncharacteristically instigated the end of the night with a gruff laugh. 'I need to take my blood pressure meds. Oh the joys of getting old, so you kids enjoy yourselves while you're still bloody young. If you need me, I'll be in the room across the other side of the courtyard. The house is yours so treat it like your own.'

Eddie's wink was just for Caleb, because Eddie had known him since well before he'd met Paloma and had been as much a mentor in women and partying as he'd been in business and building a life on the island.

Caleb's heart dropped when moments after Eddie had hugged them both good night, Belle stood up.

'Sleep sounds like a good idea.' The look she cast him was neutral although her tone was tinged with sadness, or perhaps he was projecting his own sorrow, imagining that was how she was feeling. He felt helpless about how to make things right between them.

They said goodnight without a hug or a kiss and the distance between them couldn't have been more apparent. Caleb remained out on the terrace for a little while longer, his loneliness acute in the stillness of the Ibizan countryside with only the sound of cicadas for company, the night time heat away from the coast as heavy as his thoughts. Eventually he headed to bed alone.

* * *

Belle woke with a start, her heart pounding, her palms sweaty, her legs tangled in the bedsheet. Fragments of a nightmare remained, distorted like an image in a broken mirror. She lay still, trying to regulate her breathing. The silence was somehow unnerving, no voices or traffic, not even the distant sound of the sea like at Spirit. Caleb's room was just on the other side of the living room, but the distance between them seemed to be widening.

Too many thoughts clashed. The night was oppressive, her skin slicked with sweat, her heart still racing. She threw off the sheet and paced from the room, needing to shake away the tormenting images. The stone tiles in the living room were wonderfully cool and there was enough moonlight slipping through the window to make out a shadowy figure...

'Holy shit!' Belle pressed her hand to her chest.

'It's only me.' Caleb stopped short. 'I thought I heard you scream.'

'I had a nightmare. Sorry if I woke you.'

In the silvery light she could make out a dark outline of ridged chest muscles and strong thighs.

'I wanted to check you were okay.'

'Yes, I don't fully remember it once I'm wake,' she said, her heart now racing for a completely different reason. 'It's just the feeling it leaves me with. Panicked.' Not that she was feeling like that any longer; coming face to face with Caleb in the middle of the night in just his pants had dispersed the nightmare like smoke on a breeze.

There was also zero chance of mistaking how she felt right now for anything other than desire and she was wholeheartedly regretting what she'd said to him on the drive over. Even if he had feelings for her, she imagined they would be torturous and confusing. It was no wonder he'd tried to distance himself. Instead of getting angry with him, she should have been tolerant and understanding and as forgiving as a friend. Right now, hot desire coursed through her, but this time she was going to be patient. If he wanted something more, he needed to make the first move.

* * *

Caleb knew he was lost. In the dim light he was able to make out Belle's golden hair loose around her shoulders, her slender curves encased in just knickers and a thin white vest top that showed off absolutely everything. Despite the lust he felt, he had an over-whelming desire to scoop her into his arms, take her to his bed and just hold her, to soothe her to sleep and fend off those nightmares.

It was the pool all over again, except he wasn't going to run away this time. Ignoring her and pretending he didn't have feelings would only hurt them both. The truth was, the more time he spent with her the surer in his heart he was of what he wanted. Just because he was scared to open up to someone again, emotionally, mentally and physically, didn't mean he shouldn't.

'Would it help if you weren't alone?'

She looked at him wide-eyed as if trying to make sense of his meaning, the distance between them out of kilter with his suggestion.

'We can just sleep.' He reached out his hand and held his breath as she studied him, her face a myriad of emotions. It felt as if an infinite amount of time passed before she closed the distance between them and took hold of it.

In a daze, he led her to his bedroom and pulled back the sheet. She paused before lying down with her hand tucked beneath a pillow, the curve of her hip silhouetted and her blonde hair pooling around her shoulders. Perhaps she understood that he needed her company as much as she needed his.

He slid onto the bed next to her, tentatively scooching closer so he could slide his arm around her waist. She smelt of honey and felt warm and wonderful.

There was no way Caleb could spoon her and there be zero attraction. He tried to subtly shift his groin away from the curve of her bottom, determined to get through the night without acting on his desire because his intention had purely been to help erase Belle's worries and fall asleep together.

The rise and fall of her chest synced with his, yet her breathing was short and sharp. Was she nervous? Unable to relax? Aroused? That thought was ridiculously appealing. His mind was spiralling from falling asleep together to what it would be like to press his lips against the curve of her neck, to really kiss her, or to explore her body the way he'd been fantasising... He reminded himself again that he'd invited her to bed for comfort and to sleep. That was all.

Caleb was just about winning the battle in his head when Belle took his hand and placed it on her breast. His breath stilled and his heart pounded.

'It's okay,' she whispered.

His hand cupped her perfectly, her nipple through the thin material hard. He buried his face in her hair and while his hand stroked, Belle responded by pushing back against him. She'd given him permission to touch and he couldn't stop, not now. And that soft moan when he dipped his hand beneath her top and felt the smooth warmth of her bare skin set his insides on fire.

She rolled over to face him and his heart flipped, the same as it had earlier beneath the fig tree when he'd noticed just how beautiful she was. There was vulnerability, but no uncertainty as he traced his fingers through her hair and down the side of her face to her lips. He kissed her deeply and passionately. They held each other and time became meaningless as they were lost in kisses. He revelled in the feel of her fingers gripping his shoulders, pulling him closer, as if she too couldn't get enough.

It was like a switch had flicked, with neither of them able to hold back any longer. In the night-time shadows, Belle's skin was pale, the curves and dips of her body deliciously enticing as he stripped away what little she was wearing, while her eager fingers made light work of his pants. Her lips were soft on his, the feathery caress of her fingers echoing his own as they touched and explored each other.

As he flipped her onto her back and manoeuvred between her legs, she caught his face in her hands and looked at him intently. 'This can be just sex if that's all you want.'

He circled his fingers up the inside of her smooth thigh and felt her back arch as he stopped short of where he knew she wanted him to be. 'This is about more than just sex. It's about me wanting to be *with you* in all senses of the word.'

Because at that moment she was everything: flesh and blood and all the good things in life. She was real and here and he was happy.

* * *

'But sex is a good place to start,' Belle whispered as he kissed her again deeply and sensually, his tongue toying with hers while his fingers travelled the short distance from where they'd been hovering to the place where she could no longer think straight.

Caleb laughed as he dipped his head, his hot breath teasing across her collarbone to her breasts.

The rational part of her brain that had been firing off all sorts of worries left the building as her body took over and a burning heat rushed everywhere as they finally got to enjoy each other in the best possible way.

Afterwards they lay together in the dark with Caleb's arms around her. Belle snuggled back, the warmth of him against her bare skin delicious in the cool of the air-conditioned bedroom. She slid her hands over his arms and pulled him even closer. She'd never felt this way with anyone, so comfortable yet turned on, so satisfied yet craving more, craving him. They'd taken a chance and had been open and honest with each other and that meant everything, because he made her heart sing.

And then a juddering thought steamrolled in.

'This wasn't the first time since...' Belle shuffled round and looked at him aghast. 'Was it?'

Caleb shook his head and brushed a kiss on her cheek. 'No. I've had sex a few times, but that was all it was. No emotional connection, only guilt.'

'Do you feel guilty now?' Belle asked tentatively.

Caleb shifted down so they were facing each other on the feather-soft pillows as he held her gaze. 'No, not guilty, just loved.'

42

Sunshine streamed through the bedroom window, casting a warm patch across Belle's stomach. Memories from the night danced through her mind as delicious and enticing as the sight of Caleb lying next to her. The sex had been satisfying and sensual, and everything she'd hoped for. They'd been open with each other too, talking about what they liked, and it had been different to anything she'd experienced before. Everything felt right and when he turned over and met her eyes it wasn't sorrow she detected but a gentle contentedness which matched her own. The way he tugged her close until she was lying against his chest, his arm resting along the curve of her hip, felt natural, as if they'd been doing this for many mornings.

'I should have talked to you rather than gone out of my way to avoid you.' Caleb's hushed voice sounded loud in the quiet of the morning.

'And I should have been more understanding about how hard this must be for you, when instead my insecurities came out in a negative way.'

Caleb shook his head and circled his fingers against the curve of her hip. 'Not that any of it matters now. Wishing we'd done things differently doesn't change a thing. And perhaps it wouldn't have made a bit of difference but I can't think of a better place to be than where we are right now.'

With the morning already heating up, they dragged themselves from the bed and made coffee. Caleb wedged the door to the finca's living room open so the sound of birdsong drifted in, while the sunlight cast a block of inviting warmth across the muted terra-cotta tiles. They sat together on the sofa facing the open door that framed the view across the courtyard to the converted barn that would one day host wedding receptions and yoga retreats. For the moment, though, the peace was magical, their focus on each other as they chatted.

A knock made them turn. Eddie was standing in the doorway of the finca in just swim shorts with a towel flung over his shoulder, his bronze skin gleaming in the morning sun. 'First a swim, then you kids want breakfast?'

Belle could see him quickly assess the situation, the two of them in just their underwear sipping coffee together on the sofa, as comfortable with each other as they'd been distant the previous evening. The wink he aimed at Caleb before he left them with the comment 'I'm sure you've both worked up an appetite' was as unsubtle as he was, but it made Belle smile.

She raised her coffee cup to her lips and slid her bare legs over Caleb's. 'I am rather peckish.'

'You and me both,' Caleb said with a grin.

He changed into swim shorts and she into a bikini and they joined Eddie in the pool, the cool water the perfect contrast to the heat of the morning sun.

Eddie got out first, telling them breakfast would be ready in twenty minutes, and they soon followed, dripping water across the stone-tiled courtyard as they made their way to the farmhouse.

When Belle started towards her room, Caleb grabbed her hand and with a grin tugged her in the opposite direction to the shower in his ensuite. If there'd been any lingering uncertainty about the night before being a good idea, it was extinguished as Caleb swiftly removed her bikini. The hot water pummelled her skin while Caleb's hands stroked. The sensation of kissing Caleb while being soaked set every nerve ending on fire.

'Remember Eddie's cooking breakfast for us,' Belle said as she came up for air, the torrent of water splashing off their bodies where they were pressed tight together.

'Eddie won't mind being kept waiting.' Caleb ran a soapy hand down Belle's back. 'Shower sex is something he will most definitely approve of.'

Belle approved of it too and she was as ravenous as Caleb was by the time they joined Eddie at the table in the courtyard, and they enjoyed a breakfast of Spanish omelette washed down with freshly squeezed orange juice.

Belle's first impression of Eddie had jarred with the place he'd created, but for all his crazy stories and the gaudy way he dressed, there was a man beneath it who obviously craved the sort of peace and understated beauty he'd created at La Retirada. It was the same with Caleb; his love for the partying side of Ibiza had morphed into something more refined and appealing with Spirit – even more so with Serenity. Belle knew in her heart that him partnering with Eddie would be a positive thing for them both. Her only reservation was the sobering thought that it would probably happen when Cara was back and after she'd left.

Not that she should be worrying about any of that now, on a hot Ibiza day in a place as stunning as this after a few hours with Caleb that had been utterly wonderful. She was sorry their time with Eddie had come to an end, although she could sense Eddie's delight at how effortlessly La Retirada had won them over.

He walked them to the Jeep and slapped Caleb on the back, grabbed his hand and hugged him tight.

Eddie opened the Jeep door for Belle, took her hand and kissed her on each cheek.

'You look after him.' His voice was gruff but it was lined with love as he clutched her hand tight and looked intently at her with his piercing blue eyes. 'He needs someone like you in his life.'

On the drive back to Spirit, all the tension, uncertainty and annoyance that Belle had felt on the drive over had well and truly gone. Their true feelings for each other had been shown through actions as much as words. Caleb was quiet but in a reflective sort of way, and it was a comfortable silence that allowed them both time to think.

Caleb gave her a long lingering kiss when he dropped her back at Spirit. Belle knew for certain that she'd never felt this free or wonderful or sure about anyone ever before. She just needed to be patient to allow him the time to figure out how they navigated this new relationship.

Before she opened the door, he reached across the gearstick and caught her hand. 'Last night was everything.' His eyes roved across her face. 'But we need to take things slowly.'

Belle cupped his face in her hands and nodded. 'One day at a time.'

* * *

Later that evening, Laurie had arranged a video call with Belle and Gem in the hope that it would become a regular thing where they'd have a chance to talk properly.

'This is the continuation of us being open with each other,' Laurie said as she tucked a strand of hair behind her ear. 'You know, instead of bottling things up the way we have been.'

Laurie was curled up in the armchair in the reading nook in the living room of her and Ade's flat in Manchester. Gem was sitting up at the breakfast bar in her kitchen with her back to the patio doors that looked out on to a dark garden, while Belle was in the beanbag lounger in Cara's courtyard garden with her laptop resting on her knee, the sweltering early August evening making her uncomfortably hot even in shorts and a sleeveless top.

'The kids are in bed?' Laurie asked.

'Only just.' Gem sighed, picked up a bottle of wine, waggled it in front of the screen then poured herself a large glass. 'I'm not sure how I managed late nights in Ibiza; I've been shattered since I got back.'

'Have you talked to Diego yet?' Belle stretched her legs out and picked up her glass of water.

A smile crossed Gem's lips. 'We've messaged each other a couple of times. Let's just say we're taking tentative steps. He's not told his family about Jack yet, but he will do once the test results come back. He's not talked to you?'

'I've not seen him.' At the fluttering in her chest, Belle took a big breath. 'I've barely seen Caleb either till last night...'

'What happened last night?' Gem frowned.

'What didn't happen.'

Gem popped her glass on the breakfast bar with a thud and leaned closer to the screen. 'Shut the front door. Are you saying what I think you're saying?'

'You slept with him?' Laurie's delicate voice had gone unnaturally high.

'That's exactly what I'm saying.' All the feelings from the night before and of waking up with Caleb tumbled back.

Acutely aware of her friends' exclamations, Belle scrambled from the beanbag and retreated inside to sit cross-legged on the sofa while she told them all about the last week, from Caleb avoiding her to their road trip to La Retirada that had culminated in the best night of her life.

'Oh Belle, I'm so pleased for you,' Laurie said with a sigh, the happiness on her face genuine.

'Me too.' Gem raised her glass and tipped it towards the screen. 'You absolutely deserve something this good in your life. And Caleb' – she whistled long and low – 'he's quite a catch. So what happens now? And when the job comes to an end in October?'

Belle held her hand up. 'I'm not thinking about that. We're going to take it slowly. There's a lot to navigate, particularly for him. We have no plans to see each other tonight.'

'But it'll happen again, right?' Gem looked at her aghast. 'Please tell me last night wasn't a one-time thing?'

'Oh, it's definitely going to happen again.' Belle smiled. 'It's strange though. I've been thinking about our first holiday and I realised that without me and Diego happening, I probably would never have met Caleb. Honestly, the reason I wanted to come back to Ibiza wasn't because of the pact we made but because I was chasing an impossible dream of what I thought my life should have been like.'

'Well, duh. I could have told you that.'

'Gem,' Laurie warned. 'I think it's wonderfully romantic that Belle's found her happy ever after. All these connections and experiences are intertwined in a weird way but they've brought the three of us closer together and, even better, brought good things into both of your lives.'

'It's true.' Gem nodded. 'I never believed I'd ever see Diego again and although I have to be careful how I go about moving forward, life feels hopeful. I honestly haven't felt this positive in years.'

'It's the same for me too. Plus I've got some news,' Laurie said with a smile. 'It's not what you think because a miracle has not happened and I'm not pregnant naturally—'

'Bet you're having fun trying though,' Gem cut in.

'Actually, yes we are.' Laurie's cheeks flushed. 'I've taken your advice about relaxing and not fixating on doing everything by the book. There's fun in our lives again and we're both happier. So we've decided to delay a third round of IVF until next year so we can just be a normal couple for a while. It's taken a toll on both of us emotionally, on me physically, not to mention financially, and honestly it's put a strain on our marriage that I didn't think was possible. To be so desperate for something while completely overlooking how happy we are together, it just wasn't healthy or sustainable. So we're taking a break and we're going to go away over Christmas. Just the two of us. No parents asking us unhelpful questions. No one to give us well-meaning but misplaced advice on how we can up our chances of getting pregnant – or worse, telling us how they managed it. Nope, we're not doing any of that. We're having Christmas on our own in a cosy cabin in the Lake District.'

'That sounds bloody perfect,' Gem said.

'I'm so happy for you both.' Belle curled her feet beneath her. 'You have each other and hope. That's kind of a perfect combo.'

'Yes,' Laurie said softly. 'Hope and positivity are hugely important. And Gem, it sounds like you have that in bucket loads again. You have your spark back.'

'I'm not the only one.' Gem jabbed a manicured nail at the screen. 'Your spark is firing on all cylinders, Belle. Hope for the future, and a man deserving of you, and your happiness.'

43

JANUARY 2019, FOUR YEARS AGO

Solace had only been finished a few months before Paloma had died and at that point she had already been ill. In her last few weeks she'd wanted to stay with her parents in her childhood home to allow her mama to look after her, and so Caleb wouldn't only have sad memories at Solace. She'd desperately wanted it to be a happy place for him, a home filled with laughter, love and people, but it had felt so empty when she'd left, he'd spent all his time with her at Maria and Juan's.

Now, three months after losing her, Solace was even emptier, its peace and beauty lost on him. He went through the motions of daily life, dragging himself out of bed, pummelling himself awake in a scalding hot shower because he wanted to feel something other than hurt or anger or sorrow or grief. Something other than totally and utterly bereft.

The winter months on Ibiza were hard with the hotel closed between November and March. Only the restaurant at Spirit remained open. It used to be a time he and Paloma loved, a time to reflect and recuperate, to travel and make plans. The first winter without her was even harder. He still had work, ideas brewing and things to do, but everything was an effort and nothing brought him joy any longer. Cara kept his spirits up as best she could. She seemed to understand when he needed a friend and wanted to talk, and she'd sometimes crash in one of the guest rooms so he wouldn't be alone in the morning.

One clear, cold night in January, when the ebony sky was scattered with silver stars, Caleb needed a friend more than ever. Cara brought out drinks and blankets to the terrace and he followed her lead, taking off his trainers and socks, rolling up his jeans and plunging his feet into the pool. Even though the water was heated, it still felt cool against his skin and refreshing.

Cara popped the cap off a bottle of beer and handed it to him. He'd had a particularly bad day when everything had felt like it was going wrong, although nothing really had. He'd taken his anger and frustration out on one of the waiting staff, which had made him feel even worse about everything.

'Thank you for not hating me.'

'Oh for fuck's sake, Caleb. You woke up feeling awful, had a shitty day and took it out on someone who didn't deserve it. Everyone understands why it happened and knows that's not who you are. No one's thinking badly of you, least of all me.' Cara pulled the blanket up to their waists. 'I understand you're upset; hell, I'd be mad at the world too if I was in your shoes, but you've got to think of the positives.' She draped her arm across his shoulder. 'You and Paloma had the best relationship. I saw that; everyone around you saw that and is heartbroken for her as much as for you. For the life you two should have had.'

'You're not helping, Cara.'

'I'm getting to the point, I promise.' She squeezed his shoulder and put her hand in her lap. 'Although you didn't have anywhere near as long as you were hoping for with Paloma, what time you had together was what some people can long for the whole of their lives and never find.'

'And that makes me lucky?'

'It makes you luckier than you'll ever know, but it also makes the hurt all the more awful.' She kicked her feet out and Caleb watched the ripples spread across the pool, dark and cool, so different to summer when the water sparkled enticingly.

Summer in Ibiza. He'd always loved that the most: the heat, the people, the parties, the atmosphere, the vibrancy, just everything, but it had been Paloma who'd opened his eyes to the chilled-out winter months where he could take stock and make the most of what he'd achieved.

'And none of this is fair,' Cara went on. 'You were with someone you loved with all your heart and Paloma was all that's good in this world, while I was in a relationship that I was desperate to get out of with someone who treated me and the world like their own private punchbag. My ex got a restraining order and got lucky winning fifty grand on the lottery, while Paloma got cancer. Life fucking sucks and can do one most of the time, but I'm a good person, you're a good person. I can continue hating my ex although it won't help anything and you can continue to love Paloma, but we will both heal and find a way to move on. Even learn to love again.'

Too choked up to say anything, he took her hand and held it on the blanket in his lap. He gazed out at the view he'd shared too few times with Paloma. He was grateful to be sharing it with Cara now, although he didn't understand how he'd ever find it in his heart to be happy to share it with someone else the way he had with his wife.

He had so much support, from friends both on the island and elsewhere. Paloma's family needed him as much as he did them, but it had been Cara who was his rock, who he knew he could talk to and lean on whatever time of day. She comforted him but also told him the truth and that was what he loved most about her. She wasn't afraid to kick him up the bum when he needed it. A month after losing Paloma and on the second day he hadn't made an appearance at Spirit, Cara had come round and found him in bed, the sheets wrapped round him, his pillow soaked with tears and sweat. She'd made him coffee, untangled the sheets and held him as he sobbed. Then, in no uncertain terms, she'd told him he stank and marched him into the shower. He couldn't remember getting undressed or how he even managed to wash. He had a vague recollection of Cara washing his hair and muttering something along the lines of 'you owe me big time for this'. And he did; she'd been the greatest friend, the person who told him hard truths and didn't shy away from an uncomfortable conversation or situation.

'Don't think too hard about the future,' Cara said uncharacteristically gently. 'Just take it day by day and be open to the possibility of happiness.'

'That's what Paloma said.'

'She was a wise woman.' Cara nudged him. 'Which kinda makes me wise too, don't you think?'

44

AUGUST 2023, PRESENT DAY

After dropping Belle off at Spirit, Caleb returned to Solace. He'd intended to work, but he found himself pacing up and down the sun-blasted terrace, unable to focus on anything apart from Belle and the image of her lying next to him, her hair golden on the pillow. He was desperate to tell someone, to talk through his feelings, to make sense of his emotions and to calm his racing heart. He didn't want to confide in Diego and he couldn't talk to Maria, not about something so intimate, however relieved she'd be that he'd found someone.

Shit. Had he found someone?

Cara was the only person he wanted to talk to.

Still pacing, he video called her.

Bleary eyed, Cara's face appeared on the screen. 'Hey, is everything okay?' She yawned.

'Oh shit, Cara,' Caleb said as he headed inside to see her more clearly. 'I totally forgot the time difference. I can call later once you're up.'

'No, it's okay. I'm awake now.' She flung a cover off. 'Just going to go into another room so I don't wake Naomi.'

Cara turned the phone towards the bed. Caleb could just make out long dark hair spilling over a pillow.

'Oh, I see,' Caleb said with a smile. 'You're not alone.'

'No, I'm not.' She closed the bedroom door and went downstairs into the snug off the living room. She turned on a light and sat in an armchair.

'And your parents are fine about her staying over?'

'You're seriously asking me that?' Cara shook her head. 'I'm thirty-seven years old.'

'Yeah, sorry, didn't mean it quite like that.'

'After the shit-show of my last relationship and me leaving the continent, I think they're just glad I'm home and happy. But my love life is obviously not what you were calling about, so what's up?'

Caleb sat on the edge of the sofa opposite the open doors where a light breeze drifted in. 'Do you remember that conversation we had a few months after Paloma died? We sat here with our feet in the pool in the middle of winter and talked and drank pretty much all night. You told me that one day I'd find the strength to move on, to even find love again.'

'Yeah, I remember. It was the day you were in absolute pieces.'

'One of many,' Caleb grunted. 'I was in a bad place that night. You helped, but I didn't truly believe what you said. I couldn't even begin to understand how my heart wouldn't constantly feel like it was breaking, let alone be in a good enough place to be able to love someone again, to find space for someone else in my heart as well as Paloma.'

'Wait, wait, slow down.' Cara rubbed her eyes and squinted at him. 'I feel like I've missed a chunk of information here.'

Caleb ran his hot hand down the leg of his shorts. 'I spent last night with Belle.'

'You mean you went to Eddie's together?' Cara suddenly sat

forward, her frown turning to open-mouthed surprise. 'Oh, you actually mean you *spent* the night with her.'

'It was late, Eddie invited us to stay over so we did in separate rooms, but Belle had a nightmare and I, um, suggested she might feel better if she wasn't alone.'

Cara snorted. 'Caleb Levine, that was a bold move.'

'I honestly only meant for us to cuddle.'

'But...'

'It was Belle who instigated things and there was no fucking way in the world I could ignore how I felt once I'd touched her.'

Cara wafted a hand in front of her face. 'You better go easy on the details or you're going to get me all hot and bothered.'

'I've only ever felt this way with one person before, Cara.'

'Oh Caleb,' she said gently.

'It's been so much to take in and process. I didn't want to say goodbye when I dropped her off this morning yet I knew I needed to be alone to figure stuff out.'

'You just need some time. It's new and exciting and scary to open yourself up like this again – that's the key thing, because you haven't before now. It's brave and fucking perfect, Caleb.' Cara grinned at him. 'So my advice from what, four years ago, was spot on then?'

'Yes it was, because I think I love her.' His heart dropped into his stomach at saying out loud what he'd realised that morning.

'Oh my God, Caleb. I wish I was there to give you an almighty hug.'

'You were right about me taking a chance and being open to the possibility of happiness again.'

'Of course I was right.' Cara grinned at him. 'I was also right about Belle being perfect.'

'You meant for the job though.'

'Oh I'm not sure about that, I meant *perfect*. Looks, personality, experience, job-wise. The whole damn package.'

'Oh, so you're taking credit for this now, are you?' He couldn't help but smile.

'Considering it was me who suggested that Belle went with you to Eddie's, then hell yes am I taking full credit for you and Belle winding up together last night.'

'And as Naomi's in your bed, I assume things are going well with you two?'

'Yeah, it's a big step, but it feels right, you know?'

'Cara?' A voice in the background made her turn.

'Oh bugger, think I woke Mum up.' Cara stood and paced to the door.

'Cara!' The same voice, high pitched and more insistent.

'I'm downstairs, Mum, what's up?'

'It's your dad.' Her mum's voice was panicked and breathless. 'He's not breathing.'

'Oh shit.' Cara's face reappeared on the screen. 'Caleb, I've got to go.'

45

The first moment Belle knew anything was wrong was late that evening when Caleb knocked on her apartment door.

She couldn't mask her surprise at seeing him standing there. Her heart beat faster and heat pooled in the pit of her stomach.

'Everything okay?' She noticed frown lines creasing his forehead and how washed-out he looked.

'It's Cara's dad, he died earlier today.'

'Oh my goodness, I'm so sorry.' Belle opened the door wider to let him in.

'I can't stay,' he said, making her heart drop. 'I'm going out to Australia to spend a few days with her. Help them out.' He reached for her hand. 'I'm flying first thing tomorrow. I just didn't want to leave without saying goodbye.'

Was he running away? Belle immediately dumped the thought, because of course he wasn't. A neediness and desperation was creeping into her head that she didn't like one bit. His best friend was grieving. He wasn't running away from potentially difficult emotions here but he was going to comfort a friend and support her when she needed him, exactly as Cara had done following Paloma's death.

Belle desperately wanted to be with him; she didn't want any distance between them, let alone for him to be on the other side of the world. Last night had meant everything, but it was more than that. He was someone she wanted to confide in as much as make love to, someone to bounce ideas off as well as talk late into the night with.

Belle closed the distance between them and put her arms around him. 'Have a safe flight and send my love to Cara. And don't worry about anything back here; it'll be in safe hands.'

'I know it will be.' He tugged her close and kissed her passionately.

* * *

Being with his best friend and her family while they grieved made Caleb look back on his own loss. This time he was the strong one comforting Cara.

The time away gave him clarity about his feelings for Belle because she was in his thoughts constantly, a companion to his memories of Paloma. But Belle was back at Spirit alive and beautiful, sexy and wonderful. The time apart was a good test because understanding his true feelings would have been harder if he'd been around her all the time. He longed for her and desperately missed spending time with her, chatting and laughing, sharing ideas and talking through challenges. He missed kissing and touching her, and more than anything he missed waking up with her. It had only happened once but he wanted it to happen again and again and again.

They messaged each other every day but he'd held off phoning or video calling her because the time apart was helpful, at least for him. He was worried how sleeping together then him taking off may have looked to her, but Cara reassured him that if Belle really had feelings for him then she'd understand. Most of all, he was glad to be able to support Cara and help her wade through the aftermath of losing her dad. He met her family for the first time: her mum, sister, niece and nephew. Her friends too, including Naomi, who was as perfect for Cara as he'd hoped she would be and was there for her as much as he was. What would happen to their relationship when Cara returned to Ibiza would be a worry for another time.

Ten days was too short a time to be with Cara and her family, but far too long to be away from Belle. Returning to Ibiza was filled with mixed emotions, particularly as he was heading home to decisions and a potential new start. Jetlag combined with his arrival back at Solace at an unsociable hour made night and day merge into one and he didn't wake until late in the afternoon when Maria phoned, inviting him and Belle over for Sunday lunch the next day.

After getting off the phone with Maria, he messaged Belle and invited her over.

Despite the lightness Caleb felt in his heart, the August evening was oppressively humid, and when Belle arrived they retreated to the terrace and plunged their feet into the cool water of the pool. She looked radiant in a white maxi skirt and sleeveless top with a bikini beneath, which conjured up memories of her in his T-shirt in the pool...

They caught up on their time apart and it felt good to be home. Even better to be with Belle.

'Being away from you was helpful.'

'You should explain yourself quickly, Caleb Levine!' Belle leaned back on her hands and gave him an appraising look, although she couldn't completely disguise her smile.

'I mean, the distance allowed me to work out my feelings. About you.' It was all coming out in a muddle, but then being back in her presence was having that effect. 'What I'm trying to say – badly – is that time apart made me certain about wanting to be with you. Here. Right now.' He tugged her close, planted a kiss on her forehead and breathed her in. She smelled of summer. 'I'm not worrying about the future, or what comes next.'

'I've never been someone who's looked too far into the future apart from where I want to be in my career,' Belle said, snuggling closer to him. 'Relationship-wise I've always focused on the past which hasn't been healthy. The things I've wanted to change and can't. You're right to not worry about what comes next. And I've actually found the time apart helpful too. It's given me space to think.'

Caleb raised an eyebrow, wondering if she was going to elaborate.

'Oh, you want to know what I've been thinking about?' She laughed. 'Our night at Eddie's – that's been on my mind a lot and how good it was and how much I've missed you. I don't want to change anything because it feels so right. I've come to the conclusion we should live in the moment.'

'Day by day, like you said.'

'Exactly.'

The way she smiled melted his heart and he knew without a doubt that slow was the way to go, to enjoy what they had right now without worrying about the future or picking apart the past.

Belle slid her hand into his and leaned her head in the crook of his shoulder. 'But ultimately I do want what Laurie and Gem predicted for me ten years ago.' Her voice was silken in the fading light, Ibiza Town like a beacon in the dusk. He focused on the movement of her feet beneath the water and the feel of her fingers between his. 'A dream career, dream man, dream life. A family of my own. I want it all, if that's not too greedy.'

'Not greedy, it's hopeful.'

'But one step at a time, right,' Belle said with laughter in her voice.

'Oh, we absolutely shouldn't get ahead of ourselves.' Caleb paused but then took strength from her openness. 'But I still want what I've always wanted – to love and be loved. To eventually have a family. To be happy.' He shrugged and buried his lips in her honey-scented hair. 'But I'm talking way in the future.'

'That doesn't stop you from being happy right now though,' Belle said gently.

'Oh, I am happy, more than you could ever know.'

Belle clasped his hand tighter then lifted her head away from his shoulder with a gasp. 'Where's your wedding ring?'

Caleb reached beneath his T-shirt and pulled out the ring on a chain around his neck. 'It's here, kept close to my heart.' He brought the ring to his lips and kissed it, then tucked it back against his chest. 'It felt like the right time.'

Removing his wedding ring but wearing it in a different way was a promise to himself to let go and start anew. It was also his way of showing Belle that whatever this was, it was something he wanted.

Belle rested her hand against his chest, leaned close and kissed him.

'Would you like to stay the night?' he asked when they eventually pulled away from each other.

'More than anything.'

* * *

Maria had spoken on many occasions to Caleb about him embracing the possibility of finding someone special in his life again, but he'd been uncertain how she'd actually feel if it ever happened. He could tell Belle was nervous when they arrived at Maria and Juan's the next day, more so than the first time she'd come over for lunch, but back then they'd just been friends. Caleb kept a tight hold of Belle's hand as they walked down the path at the side of the house, deciding that action rather than words was the best way to show the change in their relationship. He wasn't yet sure what she was. Girlfriend? Partner? Lover? None felt quite right. She was Belle, he was Caleb and they were together. That was enough for now.

Everyone was outside, and with most of the family there, the garden was filled with people, conversation and laughter. Gabriela, Ana and Àngel were bringing out bowls of food from the kitchen and the long table on the terrace was already filled with dishes. Delicious smells wafted into the heat of the afternoon from where Juan was grilling meat on the barbecue.

Maria's smile didn't waver as she caught sight of them. Her eyes dropped briefly to their entwined hands and back up again to Caleb. She paced over and greeted him with a kiss to each cheek and did the same to Belle, ushering them to the table. The greetings that were called out, and the way Diego clamped his hand firmly on his shoulder, leaned close and whispered in Catalan 'I am so happy for you, brother' left Caleb choked up. The love that flooded through him at Paloma's family's openness and acceptance blew him away.

He sensed Belle relax too as the children were herded to the table. With Maria's help, Juan brought over some of the barbecued food: smoked-paprika steaks and pork burgers with piquillo peppers and serrano ham.

Once everyone was settled, Maria stood and raised her glass.

Her soulful eyes took in each and every person round the table and lingered on Belle, then rested on Caleb.

'To family and friends, old and new.' She looked at Diego, dipped her head and smiled. 'To those we love and those we miss with all our hearts.' Her gaze returned to Caleb. 'To hope, happiness and love.'

Caleb knew the last part was aimed at him and Belle. He did everything in his power to hold it together, especially when Belle reached beneath the table and clasped his hand.

* * *

'Paloma must have been a wonderful woman, because she comes from a fabulous family,' Belle said a few hours later as she cast her eyes over the wondrous sight of the big and loud family scattered across the terrace. The food had been demolished, the children were playing and the grown-ups were sitting in various groups drinking and chatting. 'I understand how they embraced you as a son and held on to you for dear life after you all lost her, but to welcome me into their home, to be genuinely happy for you and open towards me, that takes a special kind of strength and a huge heart. You were all lucky to have Paloma in your lives even if it was for too short a time.' She turned back to Caleb and her stomach clenched at the sight of the tears streaking down his face and catching in his stubble. 'Oh God, I'm so sorry. I've said too much.'

He shook his head and wiped his face with the back of his hand. 'No, you haven't. What you said was beautiful and so true.'

The serious and reflective mood that had filtered round the table with Maria's touching toast had slowly dispersed over the delicious lunch. As the afternoon rolled into the evening, the wine and beer flowed. Both of them were grateful for Diego and his brothers entertaining everyone with stories before Diego and Tomàs got out their guitars and started to play.

'You and Diego,' Caleb said, shaking his head. 'I still can't believe it.'

'What?' Belle folded her arms and tried to look incredulous. 'That I managed to pull him?'

Caleb nearly choked on his Coke. 'No, unfortunately that I believe – can't get that image out of my head. What I couldn't believe was how ridiculously jealous I felt when Gem said that stuff about you two. I knew then how much I liked you.'

'What were you jealous of?' Belle batted her eyelashes, enjoying teasing him as much as she adored how open he was being with her. After years of shutting down her own emotions when things got serious or uncomfortable, it was refreshing to embrace this newfound freedom of not being frightened by her feelings.

'I was jealous that he knew you before I did and was confused by how betrayed I felt when Gem asked if you'd slept together again. There was absolutely no reason for me to feel that way when we weren't together. I had no right to you and yet...'

'You should know how horrified I was when Gem said that in front of you, not because it was inappropriate with you being my boss and Diego your brother-in-law but because I was ashamed of what you'd think of me when I was so ridiculously drawn to you.'

'There's nothing to be ashamed about.' He gave her a sly smile. 'I remember perfectly well being twenty-one and enjoying summer in Ibiza.' He lowered his voice. 'To be honest, I'd have been more surprised if you *hadn't* had sex with him.'

Belle manoeuvred even closer to him on the bench, laid her hands on his thighs and matched his tone. 'I really don't think we should be talking about me having had sex with your brother-in-law. It sounds wrong on so many levels.'

'It really does. Former brother-in-law sounds less problematic.' He pulled out his wedding ring on the chain round his neck, pressed it to his lips then slipped it back beneath his T-shirt. 'Because that's what he is.' He took her hand and pressed it to his chest. 'Neither of us has anything to feel ashamed or guilty about.' He rubbed his thumb up and down hers and leaned so close she could feel his heat and smell the spiced citrus and sandalwood notes of his Tom Ford fragrance. 'How about we say goodnight to everyone and head home.'

Those words, so meaningful and filled with emotion, were matched by a look that she could only describe as love. This was what it felt like to be loved and to be in love. Of that she was certain.

Maria's hug goodbye was heartfelt and the gentle nod she gave Belle as she clasped her hands spoke volumes. Diego's kiss to each cheek, which once would have sent her heart racing, was nothing more than friendly.

'Good things came out of our holiday ten years ago,' she said, smiling up at him. 'You and Gem for one, and now me and Caleb.'

'You're perfect for each other. And he's a lucky man.' His eyes grazed her face, the hint of the cheeky smile that had stolen her heart a decade ago appearing. 'He's also a good man and deserves to find happiness with you, Belle.'

* * *

In the heat of the August evening with the wind whipping past and Santa Eulalia glittering in the darkness, Belle and Caleb were both quietly reflective as they drove. The evening was just getting started with people beginning to head out for tapas or a cocktail by the beach. Later on, the night air would pulse with laughter, chatter and the best dance music, but for Belle and Caleb as they whizzed along the dark road there was simply freedom and peace, hope and anticipation.

Belle had expected Caleb to drive straight to Solace, but he turned off towards Cala Llonga as if heading to Serenity. Instead of driving down to the restaurant, he parked on the hill above. 'I want to show you something.'

Caleb took Belle's hand and led her along a well-hidden path through the forested hillside. The dense pine trees blocked out the moonlight, so Caleb used the torch on his phone to light the way. The track finished at a rocky outcrop overlooking the sea. Defying gravity, pine trees grew out of the cliff below them. In the curved centre of the horseshoe bay, Serenity's three terraces were cut into the hillside, their honeyed light contrasting with the white surf of the moonlit sea churning onto the pebbled beach.

'I've never brought anyone here,' Caleb said as they gazed out together. 'Before I took over Serenity, I came here on my own to get a better view. I made my decision the moment I laid eyes on it from this angle, and that was without it looking anywhere near as wonderful as it does now.'

Belle realised she was holding her breath. Buttery light pooled into the darkness and the only sound was the swoosh and suck of the sea, distant voices and a faint melody drifting out to the dark horizon.

He didn't need to say that Paloma had never seen Serenity. She understood that being here together now was special because it was a place that he was sharing with just her.

She breathed deeply and took his hand, wanting to commit this moment and feeling to memory, because it was perfect.

'I, um, don't know how to say this...' Caleb switched his focus from Serenity to her. 'Maybe I'm trying to attempt to show you my feelings, rather than explain. By bringing you here, by wanting you to stay the night again, by—'

'I love you, Caleb.'

His eyes widened and he drew her to his chest. For the first time in her life, Belle had known exactly how to put into words what she was feeling.

With his fingers in her hair and her arms wrapped around him, passion and longing threaded through them.

'I love you too.'

Caleb kissing her on the cliff overlooking Serenity was everything. Loving him was effortless. Their attraction pulled them together like two magnets, a perfect and satisfying connection. There was no need to think about the past or wonder about the future when gazing at each other with the sea rippling silver in the moonlight was just the beginning of their happy ever after.

EPILOGUE
DECEMBER, FOUR MONTHS LATER – LAURIE

Laurie wrapped a blanket around her shoulders and took her mug of coffee out onto the wooden deck. The trees directly in front of the cabin were bare, their branches frosted and sparkling in the weak December sun. With the hillside dropping away into a sweeping valley of patchwork fields broken up by the darker sections of trees and hedges, the view to the snow-covered Helvellyn mountain range was majestic. The biting wind whipped at her hair and chilled her cheeks, but it also made her feel incredibly alive. Surrounded by peace and nature, her worries and real life felt far away.

She heard the door to the cabin slide open. Ade wrapped his arms around her. 'Merry Christmas.'

Laurie nestled against him, his warmth welcome as their breath fogged together.

'Merry Christmas.' Absolute contentment swept over her. 'This was the best idea.'

'I know.' He squeezed her tighter. 'I'm full of them.'

A big Italian/Japanese-fusion Christmas, although always joyful, was not what either of them had wanted, nor had a hectic traditional Christmas with Ade's family appealed either. Neither of them felt able to cope with the reminders of what they were missing out on when this Christmas marked the fourth since trying to start a family of their own. The disappointment was wearing. Space, inspiring views and time to themselves was exactly what they needed.

They retreated to the flickering heat pumping from the wood burner and a breakfast of French toast with crispy smoked bacon. Things had been good between them since Laurie had returned from Ibiza. Although the questions and interest from their families had been unintentionally stressful, the support from Belle and Gem had been heartfelt and had brought her friends closer. Focusing on what she had rather than what she didn't had improved her mental health and her relationship with Ade. It had allowed her the headspace to switch from constantly thinking about having a baby to ways in which life could be improved right now, instead of putting things on hold because of an uncertain future. They had sex because they wanted to rather than because she was ovulating. They had conversations about things besides fertility treatment, switching their focus to other dreams and not putting off making plans because Laurie *might* be pregnant. Trapped in an exhausting cycle of constantly wishing for something had been unhealthy and detrimental to them as a couple.

Laurie watched Ade as he finished his French toast. His eyes were drawn outside, the morning light on the distant mountains softening the harsh winter lines and the cool colours of frosted green and brown on the lower slopes. He'd recently grown a beard, which suited him.

He pushed his glasses further up his nose and put his plate on the coffee table. 'I know you're watching me.' He turned to her with a grin.

'It's 'cos you're so handsome.' They'd been together since they were nineteen and, whatever life had in store for them, she couldn't imagine growing old with anyone else. 'I've been thinking about next year.' Laurie pulled the blanket up around them and took his hand. 'Not a New Year's resolution as such but I keep thinking about doing something drastic. Starting off as I mean to go on by, er, handing my notice in...'

'Yes.' His grip on her hand tightened as he nodded. 'You should absolutely do that, Laurie.'

She leaned back, completely taken aback by his serious expression and unquestioning support. 'I thought you'd suggest I wait and see how the third IVF goes before making such a big decision.'

'You're miserable at work and have been the whole time. I'm not sure sticking it out and hating it while going through treatment is beneficial.' He lifted her chin and kissed her. 'So yes, do it. First day back at work in January. Then start looking for something you love.'

'I've already dropped my CV off at a bookshop.' She shrugged. 'It was on a whim; saw the advert and thought, what do I have to lose.'

Outside, the wind swirled, whistling down into the wood burner and knocking the overhanging tree branches against the roof. Laurie shifted closer to Ade, so familiar and comforting, the smell of fried bacon mixing with his musky cologne.

'I've also got some news.' He put his arm around her. 'Now seems like the perfect time to share it. From March I'll have a choice of changing my contract to predominately homeworking. I'd only have to be in the office once a month or so, which means...'

'We could move out of Manchester,' Laurie said breathlessly.

'I know you constantly look at houses on Rightmove.' The knowing look he gave her was adorable. 'I've had a look too and there's a house in New Mills I think we should look at. The Peak

District on the doorstep, and still commuting distance from Manchester.'

Laurie threw her arms round him. If she'd felt content out on the deck earlier, the feeling was amplified now. She'd never loved him more than she did in that moment. He'd understood her struggles and seen the sacrifices she'd made to support him and now he was helping her with her own dreams, whether that was a new job somewhere she'd be happy or a move away from the city. There was still so much uncertainty but there was also the potential of an exciting new start that could be actively planned and not just hoped for.

Ade held her tight. 'I think we need to live for the here and now, not what may or may not happen in the future. All I care about is us being happy.'

With tears in her eyes, Laurie kissed him. 'I want us to be happy too. It's all that matters.'

* * *

July, One Year Later – Gem

Gem had never been more nervous than on the drive to Maria and Juan's house. Jack was going to meet Diego and his new extended family for the first time. She was so grateful that Belle and Caleb were coming with her and that she had their support. Jack and Diego had video called each other a couple of times and had bonded over football and Diego's promise that he'd teach Jack to play the guitar. Her nervousness was less about Jack and Diego but about how the rest of his family would react.

Belle had told Gem all about being witness to Diego telling Maria that he was a father and that she had a nine-year-old grandchild she hadn't yet met. After her initial shock had worn off, she'd berated him for having had unprotected sex – which left Diego red-faced and his brothers and Caleb sniggering like teenagers – then pulled him into a crushing hug. Gem liked the sound of Maria enormously and from everything Belle had said, she couldn't have hoped for a better family for Jack. This still didn't take away her nerves.

With Caleb and Belle leading the way, Jack took everything in his stride as they entered the terraced garden at the back of the house. They were greeted by adults chatting, music playing and children running around. The delicious smells of cooking food wafted into the summer air. There was no time to feel nervous as brothers and wives were introduced, drinks were placed in their hands and they were enveloped into the beating heart of the family.

Gem couldn't have been prouder of the way Jack had handled her and Dan's breakup and the news about his biological father. That initial conversation with Dan had been the most stressful of her life, but the one that had followed with Jack, with Dan by her side, had been a revelation.

'Two families means two lots of presents on birthdays and Christmas, right?' Jack had shrugged. 'I can live with that.' Trust him to have seen the silver lining of having two dads and a complicated family set-up. Of course it hadn't all been plain sailing. His true emotions and underlying confusion rose to the surface at times, particularly when he was tired or something else troubled him. But Gem had quickly realised that honesty was the best way forward. Burying truths and emotions had done no one any good, least of all her.

As Belle had predicted, Dan had led the way, once again stepping up like he had when Gem had first told him she'd been pregnant with Jack. His openness, acceptance and understanding made her question why on earth they hadn't worked out. But sitting on

Maria's terrace under the Ibizan summer sun, she knew the truth. She'd never loved Dan the way she loved Diego. She was still getting to know Diego, a process they were both navigating and trying to figure out. Their feelings weren't one sided, he'd said as much, but they weren't straightforward either.

Gem's fears during the drive over were unfounded because the Torres Corchado family were as wonderful as Belle had said. They were big-hearted, open and so incredibly loving. They'd kept Caleb close when they'd lost their daughter and had accepted Belle when she and Caleb had got together. Gem swallowed back tears but realised she was fighting a losing battle with her emotions because this was a hell of a wonderfully emotional day. The only thing that would have made it better was if Laurie could have been here too, but she was a day away from the end of her two-week wait and her third round of IVF. Although with Belle having made a permanent move to the White Isle, and with Gem's own connection to the island and Diego, there would be many more chances for them to all be here together again.

The mouth-watering smells from the meat roasting on the barbecue drifted into the air. Gem chose a spot away from everyone to sit and have a quiet moment. Jack was chatting and laughing with Diego's eldest niece and nephew. His cousins. The thought swooped in, battering her heart in the best possible way. He hadn't lost a family but had gained an extra one. Dan was still his dad but Diego was too, and he'd brought extra cousins, aunts, uncles, grandparents, a new culture and love into his life. Shit, it was only a matter of time before she completely lost a grip on her emotions.

Gem switched her attention to Belle and Caleb and the effort-less way they had with each other with gentle touches and the looks of love that would make even the most cynical heart melt. Although they were perfect together, her initial thought had been he was too good to be true. She'd been doubtful that they'd last the summer because while Caleb was navigating love after loss, the thought had crossed her mind that Caleb was purely Belle's replacement for Diego. She was glad to have been proved wrong. Their love ran deep and seeing them together highlighted what perfect partners they were, their love more than just physical. They worked closely together and supported each other unconditionally. It was the kind of relationship Gem could only dream of. Yet she felt lucky and actually happier on her own. Independent yet still supported by her family, her friends and by Dan who she had a renewed respect for. And Diego. Diego was the love of her life. But her life was in England, his on Ibiza. While the children were young, she couldn't disrupt their lives or take either of them away from Dan, but there was hope and possibility and freedom, and she was more than okay with that. When she was with Diego, everything made sense; the sex was incredible but also they had a solid friendship and understanding, plus a bond through Jack that would always pull them back together again.

Belle heading towards her holding out her phone turned Gem's attention away from her thoughts.

'It's Laurie.' Belle sat next to her on the stone wall and put her on speakerphone.

'I did the test a day early.' Laurie's gentle voice was overpowered by the chatter and commotion from the terrace so they had to concentrate to hear her. 'I couldn't bear the wait any longer.'

'And?' Gem prompted, leaning closer.

'I'm pregnant.'

It took a moment for her words to sink in before Gem and Belle turned to each other. Their squeals drowned out Laurie's own laughter.

'Honestly, this is *the* best day,' Gem said, trying desperately to hold it together because she was on the verge of sobbing happy tears. 'You're pregnant. Jack's cool about meeting Diego and the rest of his new family. I'm happy, you're happy, and Belle's unbelievably happy and loved up.'

For the first time, Gem's happiness for her friends was genuine, without a hint of jealousy.

'Next time I'm in the UK,' Belle said, 'we'll have to get together and celebrate.'

'We might be in our new house by then, with two spare rooms to put you both up in.'

'Two spare rooms till the baby comes along.' Belle grinned.

Laurie breathed deeply. 'It's still early days.'

'I know it is, but it's positive and hopeful and so exciting.' Belle put her arm round Gem and she felt the comment was as much for her as it was for Laurie.

A positive pregnancy test of her own that had once felt like a life sentence had actually been anything but. Gem was incredibly proud of the young man she was bringing up and of Oscar too, and how Dan and Diego were fitting in to all of their lives. She was proud of herself as well, for facing up to the mistakes she'd made and for being brave enough to be truthful and open. Life was never easy and would always throw curveballs. Although she wasn't exactly where she wanted to be, she had dreams, determination and a loving, gorgeous family. And Diego. He was sitting with Caleb at the table watching Jack with his cousins. Gem went over and curled her arms round him and when he pulled her onto his lap, beyond the love she had for her children, she'd never felt a love like it.

Whatever they were to each other, whether friends, lovers, partners or a messy combination of them all, they were parents and in each other's lives. That meant everything.

* * *

April, Three Years Later – Belle

In a white dress, Belle swirled across Serenity's sand-covered terrace, the euphoric house music competing with the voices and laughter that surrounded her.

'Here comes Daddy and Auntie Cara,' Belle said, hitching her eighteen-month-old son Arlo higher on her hip as Caleb and Cara danced towards them and swept them into their fold.

Cara looked radiant in a fitted white suit, while Caleb was effortlessly handsome in his, the jacket long removed and the top couple of buttons of his shirt casually undone. Arlo, matching his dad in his own white suit with the cutest waistcoat, had stolen the show. Belle knew she was biased, but it was hard not to be. At Cara and Naomi's request, everyone was wearing white, which was rather fitting for a wedding on the White Isle.

Enveloped in Caleb's and Cara's arms, her son was pressed tight to her chest as they danced together beneath a clear sky sprinkled with stars. Life didn't get much better.

Belle hadn't made the mistake of leaving Ibiza for the second time. After a memorable summer when her relationship with Caleb had blossomed from a tentative love to an overwhelming desire to be a permanent part of each other's lives, Belle hadn't wanted to leave. When Caleb had asked her to stay, she hadn't hesitated in saying yes.

Things had slotted into place when Cara had made the difficult decision to remain in Australia. Losing her father had highlighted how fragile life was and her relationship with Naomi had strengthened. By the time Caleb had started the conversation about how to navigate Cara's return, the decision had already been made. Belle had taken over as permanent events manager, while Cara stayed on the other side of the world with Naomi and her family where she got to be a part of her niece's and nephew's lives.

Belle understood how much Caleb missed his best friend, because it had been the same for her. However much staying on Ibiza and being with Caleb was right, it was a completely different life. She missed Hannah and her friends in London, she missed Laurie and Gem too, but the trade-off was worth it because she was so in love with Caleb. And it wasn't exactly hard to entice friends out to visit. Even Belle's parents made an occasional trip.

Continuing to work for Caleb at Spirit and Serenity had put her own business plans on hold. As she'd once said to Caleb, he was in the business of making people's dreams come true and she couldn't think of anything better to be doing with her life. Instead of focusing on developing her own plans, she helped Gem set up her interior design business and even commissioned her to consult on the design plans for the La Retirada barn restaurant once the partnership between Caleb and Eddie had been confirmed. Her decision to stay on Ibiza had also continued to help Hannah, giving her friend the time and space to get through her divorce while staying in Belle's flat.

Belle hadn't thought life could get any better until she discovered she was pregnant on a trip to the UK. With most things shut down in Ibiza over the winter months, February had been the perfect time for Belle and Caleb to visit Laurie and Ade in their new house in Derbyshire before their long-awaited baby arrived. Sharing her own pregnancy joy with Laurie had meant everything, the idea of becoming mums within a year of each other beyond perfect, but it had been Caleb's emotional response to the prospect of becoming a dad that had left Belle a teary hormonal mess. Their age difference had never bothered Belle, but for Caleb, entering his mid-forties after losing the hope of a family, a second chance had meant the world, so Belle delighted in telling him the happy news.

Now on Ibiza, celebrating Cara's wedding as a family with Caleb and Arlo meant everything. Her life had come full circle and was filled with happiness. Plus life was about to change once again. Cara was returning to Ibiza with Naomi to start a new life together and while Belle was going to focus on events at Serenity, Cara was taking over the reins again at Spirit. It hadn't been an easy decision and compromises and sacrifices had been made, but Belle knew how much Cara returning meant to Caleb.

While Naomi pulled Cara back onto the sandy dancefloor, Caleb put his arms around Belle and planted a kiss on Arlo's head. 'Maria's going to take him home.'

'So we'll get a night to ourselves,' Belle said with a smile, although her greatest joy was seeing her boys together. Arlo was a perfect mix of the two of them, with her blonde hair and the shape of Caleb's face, and he doted on him, his patience for a family worth the wait.

After lots of kisses and cuddles from Belle and Caleb, Maria managed to peel Arlo from Belle's arms, although his piercing cry echoed across Serenity as they left. Belle told herself he was in safe hands and his distress would be forgotten as soon as he was strapped into his car seat. She'd have been distraught too, being dragged away from such a wonderful night.

The music switched to chilled Ibiza vibes. Caleb kissed Belle and placed her favourite champagne cocktail in her hand. He led her to their spot on the wall that overlooked the terrace where dancing couples in white twirled.

They'd made a life together and started a family. They worked together, shared ideas, made time for each other and their friends and families both on Ibiza and in the UK, and they loved each other passionately. Paloma remained a part of Caleb's life because he still loved her and always would, but he had room in his heart for Belle too. He loved Arlo fiercely and they hoped they'd be blessed with a brother or sister for him. Paloma's family were their family too, Maria and Juan surrogate grandparents, and Diego was like a brother. They were entwined together through Paloma, Belle and Caleb, Gem, Jack and Diego. Belle understood that Paloma asking Caleb to promise that he'd be happy and find someone to love again had led them to this point. They'd both learned that loss, disappointment and challenges danced hand in hand with hope, love and happiness. That was what made the good times so special.

As fairy-tale endings went, Belle couldn't have asked for more.

ACKNOWLEDGEMENTS

I ended up writing *An Island Promise* over the winter months of 2023/24 and it proved to be pure escapism, immersing myself in Ibiza's stunning locations while I tried to weave together Belle's, Laurie's and Gem's stories.

As with many of my books, I've used some fictional places in real settings. I had great fun coming up with Spirit and Serenity and although both are fictional, I took inspiration from Hotel Riomar in Santa Eulalia and Amante Ibiza near Cala Llonga.

The 'sticky middle' is always the hardest part of writing the first draft of a novel, but with *An Island Promise,* I got to the point where the story just ground to a halt and I didn't know how to move it forward. Fortunately this coincided with a writing retreat in Devon where I had a few days of dedicated writing time, meals cooked for me, fabulous company and wine o'clock! So a big thank you to the wonderful Debbie Flint who runs Retreats for You and an extra big thank you to fellow writers and new friends Sarah, Nicolle, Charlotte and Glenys for the inspiration, support and encouragement. A good chunk of the novel was written while on the retreat and it was when Caleb's voice entered the mix which just worked. Plus, he was great fun to write!

As always, there are plenty of people to thank for helping to shape this book into something fit for publication, from my brilliant friend and beta reader Judith to my wonderful copy editor Candida and proof reader Jennifer. The whole team at Boldwood are superb and a joy to work with. Thank you to the wonderful and supportive writing community and to my fabulous readers.

An Island Promise is dedicated to Caroline Ridding, my editor at Boldwood who I've been lucky enough to work with over the last three years. Her encouragement and support have meant the world and her insightful editing always helps to make my books the best they can be.

I definitely needed my family's encouragement and support while writing this book, plus their patience when I ended up working weekends and through much of the Easter holidays to get it finished! Thank you Nik and Leo. And thank you Mum for your unwavering belief in saying 'You'll get there.' I certainly did!

ABOUT THE AUTHOR

Kate Frost is the author of several bestselling romantic escape novels including The Greek Heart, and The Love Island Bookshop. She lives in Bristol and is the Director of Storytale Festival, a book festival for children and teens she co-founded in 2019.

Sign up to Kate Frost's mailing list here for news, competitions and updates on future books.

Visit Kate's website: www.kate-frost.co.uk

Follow Kate on social media:

 facebook.com/katefrostauthor

 x.com/katefrostauthor

 instagram.com/katefrostauthor

 bookbub.com/authors/kate-frost

ALSO BY KATE FROST

One Greek Summer

An Italian Dream

An Island in the Sun

One Winter's Night

A Greek Island Escape

An Island Promise

LOVE NOTES
LOVE IN EVERY CHAPTER

WHERE ALL YOUR ROMANCE
DREAMS COME TRUE!

THE HOME OF BESTSELLING
ROMANCE AND WOMEN'S
FICTION

WARNING:
MAY CONTAIN SPICE

SIGN UP TO OUR
NEWSLETTER

https://bit.ly/Lovenotesnews

Boldwood

Boldwood Books is an award-winning fiction
publishing company seeking out the best
stories from around the world.

Find out more at www.boldwoodbooks.com

Join our reader community for brilliant books,
competitions and offers!

Follow us

@BoldwoodBooks

@TheBoldBookClub

Sign up to our weekly
deals newsletter

https://bit.ly/BoldwoodBNewsletter

Milton Keynes UK
Ingram Content Group UK Ltd.
UKHW042129030924
1487UKWH00007B/50

9 781802 804911